LINDSAY BUROKER

STAR KINGDOM

SHOCKWAVE

BOOK ONE

Shockwave

Star Kingdom, Book 1

by Lindsay Buroker

Copyright © Lindsay Buroker 2019

FOREWORD

EIGHT YEARS AGO, WHEN I FIRST STARTED PUBLISHING my writing, it was all fantasy all the time. As someone with a degree in Culture, Literature, and Arts, I was leery about venturing into science fiction and "getting it wrong." I still worry about that, to be honest, even though I've since written my Fallen Empire series and some shorter space-opera adventures.

But it's a genre I've always loved, especially as a kid devouring Star Trek reruns and watching the original Star Wars trilogy over and over and over. (This delighted my parents, since we only had one TV in the house at the time, and it was front-and-center in the living room.)

I'm delighted to be back in outer space with this new series, Star Kingdom. I've been jokingly calling it Big Bang Theory meets Star Wars. I'm not sure how accurate that is, but it is a chance for some smart, geeky heroes to shine. (Because, as we all know, Mr. Spock was way cooler than Captain Kirk in the original Trek.) I hope you have fun with the new crew and enjoy their adventures.

Before you jump in, please let me thank those who've helped me put this book together: my first readers, Rue Silver, Sarah Engelke, and Cindy Wilkinson, and my editor, Shelley Holloway. Also, thank you to Jeff Brown for illustrating the covers for this series.

Now, let the adventure begin…

PROLOGUE

"**W**HEN CAN I EAT NORMAL FOOD AGAIN?"

"Normal?" Dr. Yas Peshlakai looked toward the vat lamb and rice dish on the bedside table. It was bland, as he'd ordered, but ought to pass for normal on Tiamat Station.

"Yes." President Sophia Bakas smiled and folded her hands atop the blanket, the silver light of a faux moon streaming in the window and highlighting a surprisingly girlish expression on her timeworn face. "Deep-fried, ice-creamed, and alcohol-filled."

"Ah. *Normal* food. Well, I'm not your regular doctor, Madam President, but I recommend you give your liver time to recover from the poison before consuming more. You do have two years left to serve, and the station inhabitants are quite fond of you."

"Yes, and it is good to be liked. By *most* people." Her long fingers curled into the blanket, tendons standing out under her papery skin.

"Star Kingdom zealots aren't people."

"My charming young intelligence officers tell me the poisoners were loyal station citizens, irritated that the vote went against them. It seems they hoped to rush along my passing so the more Kingdom-friendly Vice President Martinez would be in charge." Bakas shuddered, her narrow shoulders hunching. "I don't understand why anyone would want to live under that backward rule again. Under their draconian laws, half the people here wouldn't be allowed to breathe the air there. They don't allow genetic engineering on human beings, not even to cure diseases. They don't even allow modifications to their plants or food. And their backward stances on marriage and relationships." Bakas shuddered again, perhaps thinking of her two wives.

"I gather it's the other half of the people who are a problem."

"I'm glad you're not one of those zealots. And that you were able to identify the poison." President Bakas grasped his hand. "Thank you, Doctor."

"It was a simple matter, as I knew it would be as soon as I heard the symptoms. During my years at the university, I took several toxicology classes, and for one, I wrote a paper on the ongoing alterations to the *archexia* family of plants to create potent hallucinogens as well as more deadly substances. It was published in *Galactic Plantae*, a prestigious peer-reviewed journal in the field. I understand professors at several universities throughout the system are now teaching from that article. It's shameful that so few doctors are familiar with the less well-known uses for the plants. Your personal physician should have…" Yas made himself close his mouth and shrug. It wasn't his place to denigrate others. Not everybody had been granted the educational opportunities he had, though it was difficult to fathom that anyone but the best would have been selected to work for the president.

"You're a touch arrogant for someone so young, aren't you?" Bakas smiled.

"I'm thirty-five, ma'am."

He had been a surgeon as well as a toxicology consultant for nearly ten years. The latter was an interest he kept up with, not his main profession, but it pleased him that the station hospitals often sought his advice on tough cases.

"That makes you a mere child, good doctor."

Since she was approaching a hundred and fifty, he couldn't argue with her perspective on age. But the rest?

"I merely state the facts, Madam President. I do not, as arrogance would imply, exaggerate my own worth or importance."

She arched her eyebrows.

"A former girlfriend called me lovably pompous," he conceded.

"Former? Perhaps your pomposity wasn't so lovable after all." Her smile turned into a yawn.

"You should rest, Madam President."

Yas drew her curtains, eyeing the bright full moon hanging in the starry sky, all of it a technological illusion to hide that the only thing above them was the other side of their habitat. If one hadn't been to a real planet, one might believe the station was a natural place, with parks and cities and lakes, birds and insects and animals. One might forget that it was a giant cylinder spinning inside a hollowed-out asteroid in System Hydra's Beta Belt, miles of stone protecting its inhabitants from the sun's radiation.

"I'll rest a bit," Bakas said with another yawn.

Yas made sure she had water, then dimmed the lights as he stepped out of her bedroom. Two presidential bodyguards were posted to either side of the door, and he nodded to them as he passed.

"She's fine," he said.

They nodded back.

They had no reason to question him. Yas's prominent family was known and trusted on the station, and his father had donated to the president's election campaign. Yas had grown up here, leaving only for a few volunteer medical missions to other parts of the system where people dealt with the vagaries of living on planets and moons.

He passed unbothered through corridors and down lift tubes, his white jacket and white bag with its symbolic red blood droplet on the side identifying him as a doctor. He'd entered the presidential residence through the servants' entrance and started to depart that way but paused to watch the huge screens in their break room showing the last few points of a zero-g squash game.

Superhumanly agile bodies contorted into impossible positions as the two contestants flung themselves around the enclosed court, ricocheting off the walls almost as fast as the ball. Yas knew the game well, and had played it all the way through school, but he had given up an opportunity to compete on the professional circuit to become a doctor. To become everything his parents had always expected him to be—which didn't involve bouncing off the walls of a sports court. He didn't regret channeling his energy into his career, but there were times when he missed the game, the sheer joy of unbridled athletic exertion.

The famous Donahue Dorg scored the final point, and the vid feed cut to a crowd cheering while imbibing beer and the potent sunflower-seed alcohol the station was known for.

Yas waved to the staff still watching—none of them noticed him taking his leave—and headed out the back door. As he stepped into the alley behind the residence, the street lights reflecting softly off the recycled carbon-fiber pavement, four uniformed figures strode out of the shadows to one side. Station Civil Security.

"There he is, right there."

"Get him!"

Yas looked down the alley in the other direction, certain they meant someone else. But the big men stared right at him as they broke into a run.

"I'm Dr. Yas Peshlakai." He raised his hands.

A sergeant grabbed his wrist, and meaty fingers bit into his shoulder. "We know who you are. What you just did."

"You're going to cuff him, Sergeant? He killed the president. He deserves…" A corporal pointed a DEW-Tek 900 pistol at Yas's temple.

Yas almost dropped his medical kit.

"*Killed?*" He gaped at the glaring men now surrounding him. "I was just up in her room. She's *fine*. She's recovering well. She wants ice cream."

"When Garon walked in, she was dead. You were the last one in there with her, the only one with a bag full of medical poison." The sergeant with the death grip on his shoulder reached for the flex-cuffs on his utility belt.

"No trial for him, Sarge," the corporal with the pistol said, his eyes full of rage. "Let's say he ran, and we had to take care of him, of the Kingdom sympathizer. He's a Kingdom *assassin*. He deserves death, not to weasel out of everything with some high-priced lawyer."

"No lawyer for the assassin," another corporal growled and slapped Yas's medical kit away.

It clattered to the pavement, tipped open on its side, and spilled its contents everywhere. A jet injector bounced up and hissed as it struck the sergeant's leg.

He yelped, his grip on Yas's shoulder loosening.

Yas doubted anything had pierced the man's skin, but he took advantage and broke free from his captor. He glimpsed the corporal's grip tightening on the pistol and ducked. A red bolt of energy seared a chunk of hair from Yas's scalp and slammed into the wall behind him.

He stumbled, bumped the other corporal, and shouted, "Watch out for the bag. The poison is gaseous."

As the four men's gazes lurched to the innocuous medical kit, Yas sprinted away from them. It was probably the worst thing he could have said, an implication that he was guilty, but it took them a few seconds to recover and give chase.

He lunged around a corner and down a main street away from the residence, sprinting past delivery robots and electric auto-trucks zipping along the center rail. There was nothing to hide behind alongside the thoroughfare, no crates or barrels, no parked vehicles.

Yas pumped his legs. Where could he go? Not home. They would be waiting. To the Civil Security station to talk to someone sane? Someone who grasped that suspects weren't executed on Tiamat, especially not before they'd had a trial?

The security men burst onto the street behind him. Knowing he was in their sights, Yas sprinted for another alley. Something slammed into the back of his knee, and pain roared up his leg.

He grabbed a wall, just keeping from pitching to the ground. More weapons fired with soft buzzes as the energy bolts lanced down the street. Yas lunged into the alley, his leg almost buckling every time he tried to put weight on it. He kept running, but his gait was lopsided, agonized. They would catch him soon.

Or they would *shoot* him soon.

A drone whizzed past, its camera recording him. There was nowhere to go on the station, nowhere to hide. He was miles from the docks and a ship, even if he could somehow slip past port security and stow away on an outgoing vessel.

Gritting his teeth, Yas stumbled out of the alley next to a café, outdoor tables dotting the sidewalk. A scattering of people sat in the chairs, their faces turning curiously toward him. He meant to run past them and into the café to hide, but he twisted his injured knee and tumbled to the pavement. A fresh wave of pain shot up his leg, and tears sprang to his eyes.

"There he is!" one of his pursuers cried from the alley.

Yas rolled to the side an instant before a red energy bolt skimmed past, slamming into the side of a store across the street.

Panting, he rolled again, angling toward the tables and hoping to get out of the line of sight. He bumped into a chair and tried to rise, to scramble farther away, but his leg wouldn't support him. It only sent more agony blasting through his body.

Yas raised his hands and flopped onto his back. If he appeared helpless and surrendered, maybe they wouldn't kill him. Maybe they would follow proper procedure and arrest him for a trial. This was *insane*.

As soon as the shooting had started, most of the people sitting outside the café had lunged for the door or run off down the street. But a dark-skinned woman with short black hair peered calmly down from the table right above him, one of her eyes glinting unnaturally in the lights shining through the window. A coffee cup hung poised in her gloved hand.

"Is this because we didn't tip?" She tilted her head toward Yas and quirked an eyebrow toward the man sitting opposite her at the table.

Yas assumed it was a man. He wore a cloak with a hood pulled up and some kind of mask on his face. A DEK-Tek pistol and a double-barreled SK-Ram hung in holsters from his belt.

Yas's fingers twitched. He could have reached for the Ram. But it was a weapon of deadly force, and he couldn't shoot to kill, not even to save himself.

But as footsteps thundered in the alley, a squeak of "Help?" escaped his lips before Yas could debate the wisdom of the request.

"Dr. Yas Peshlakai," the man said dispassionately, as if he were reading the name off a report. He had probably already run a quick facial identification search, the results scrolling down his contact display or whatever networked implants existed behind that hood. "A renowned surgeon and toxicology expert. Huh."

"And *not* a criminal." Yas feared the news bots were already circulating the false story.

The speaker gazed down at him, his features, his thoughts, hidden behind that mask.

The security men jogged into view, slowing as they saw Yas so close to two other people. Yas prayed they were done flinging weapons fire wantonly around, but as they stalked closer, fury in their eyes, he knew they were only getting close enough to ensure they couldn't miss. There were three of them. There was no sign of the one sane man, the sergeant who'd only wanted to arrest him.

"You'll serve me for five years if I save your life," the masked man said calmly, as if Yas wasn't a second from being shot, as if his blood wasn't staining the pavement under the table.

"Yes," Yas blurted in agreement, even though it had been a statement, rather than a question.

"Excellent."

The masked man sprang from the table and charged the security officers with the speed of a bullet. His opponents fired at him, but he somehow anticipated the shots in time to fling himself into an agile roll across the pavement, one that brought him up between the men. They tried to fan out, to find spots where they could shoot him without endangering their comrades, but he blurred around them, movements too fast to track without augmented eyes. Yas gaped as one man flew into a wall, his head striking hard enough to knock him senseless.

Someone fired wildly, and a red bolt burned through the base of a nearby table, hurling the top into the air. It landed with a resounding clatter on the pavement.

A hand grabbed Yas's shoulder. The woman.

She pulled him to his feet with a grip hard enough to hurt. His leg threatened to give way again, but she supported him, tugging him away from the melee, from the pounding of fists and cries of pain. Yas pressed his back to the wall, gasping for air and for the strength to keep his legs under him.

"Who—" Yas started to ask, but three precise shots boomed, echoing from the walls of the now-empty street. The SK-Ram, firing bullets instead of directed energy bolts.

They had an alarming finality, and all sounds of the battle ended. The masked man walked around the corner, his cloak flapping around his ankles as he holstered the Ram.

"Come, Doctor." He extended a hand toward the street. "I have a ship with a sickbay in need of a surgeon."

"What ship?" Yas asked as the woman and the man gripped him by either arm, lifting him into the air as they walked at his side, his feet dangling an inch above the ground, his injured leg leaving a trail of blood. "Who are you?"

"The *Fedallah*," the man said. "Tenebris Rache."

If Yas had been walking, his legs would have given out again.

Captain Tenebris Rache was the most notorious pirate in the Twelve Systems. And Yas had just sworn to serve him.

CHAPTER 1

"FLY, LITTLE BIRDIE, FLY," PROFESSOR CASMIR DABROWSKI WHISPERED.
He stepped back with his kludgy remote control, promising to build something better once his prototype proved successful. He tapped a button, and the robot bird sprang off his desk, delicate wings flapping furiously as it attempted to fly.

Casmir bit his lip. Would it work this time?

The bird dipped below the level of the desk, and he winced, certain it would crash. But its self-learning neuromorphic chip compensated quickly. The bird tilted slightly and adjusted its wingbeats, then slowly gained altitude.

Casmir's wince turned into a grin as it sailed toward the ceiling of his lab, swooping left and right like a songbird seeking seeds. Its flight was so natural, it made his heart ache.

It—no, she, *definitely* she—was beautiful. He couldn't wait to show her off. Maybe the media, not just the university presses, would write up the project. The news would travel through the gate network, and roboticists throughout the Twelve Systems would see his work and realize his home world of Odin *wasn't* backward, at least not in this field. No government policies held back these scientific developments.

"*That's* what you're working on now?" a familiar voice asked from the hallway. A few passing university students peered through the door around the man. "You don't find that underwhelming after three years at the Kingdom's top military research and development lab?"

Hearing the disdain from one of his former instructors made Casmir want to snatch the bird out of the air and hide it in a desk drawer. He told himself there was nothing demeaning about his project, but he couldn't keep his cheeks from warming.

"Actually, Professor Huang—" Casmir hoped his voice came out casual and self-confident, even while wondering what it would be like to actually *feel* self-confident, "—I find it morally refreshing after three years at the Kingdom's top military research and development lab." He tapped the remote to command the robot to find a perch. "I never entirely trusted King Jager's promise that my work would only be used to defend Odin and not to mow down enemies in other systems."

Technically untrue. It had taken a while for his trust to falter, for him to realize Jager wanted more than to avoid the assassination plot that had taken down his father. The king had ambitions.

"I'm sure he's not going to do that with your combat robots." Huang walked into the room, his cane clacking on the tile floor. He was known to twirl it like a pirate's rapier, prodding students who fell asleep in class. "He'll use them to make sure Odin, bless our beautiful world, is never conquered by foreigners."

"So I was told when I started working there. But you hear the same news I do. You know the pushes Jager is making, the sympathizers his agents are cultivating in other systems."

"I do my best to ignore the news, in truth. Better for the sanity."

When the bird alighted on the desk again, Huang bent to peer at it through his glasses. He murmured something, and the light of a tiny display flashed in one of the lenses. Showing magnification? Or some more in-depth analysis?

At the same time as he'd had the childhood eye surgery that had failed to fix his strabismus, Casmir had received a neural-interactive chip and contacts with an interface. A lot of the older staff preferred the removable voice-activated lenses to newer technologies.

"This is just a hobby." Casmir shrugged, as if the project didn't mean as much as it did. "My team is working on self-aware medical androids to be deployed to remote habitats and scientific outposts where there aren't human doctors. This girl—" Casmir gently touched the smooth head of his bird, "—Chaz, Simon, Asahi, and I are going to enter in a realistic-flight competition. Humans have been making drones for ages, but we've yet to create a robot that can truly emulate a bird's flight."

"Because there's not much need, eh?" Huang straightened and adjusted his glasses.

"I suppose not the need that there is for military robots, but maybe that says something distressing about our society."

"War and battling over differences has been the human norm since we first discovered fire back on Earth. Or so the history books tell us." Huang smiled and wavered his hand in acknowledgment of how much information had been lost between the time the original colony ships had left Earth, arrived in the Twelve Systems, and clawed their way back to a spacefaring level. "I'll admit it is impressive that you got Simon and Asahi to work together. I thought they were mortal enemies."

"They are, but Simon is a stellar programmer, and Asahi is a wiring genius."

"*Some* people pick teams based on compatibility of personalities rather than the brilliance of individuals."

"That sounds like a recipe for mundanity."

"But fewer explosions in the labs."

Casmir was about to point out that he'd succeeded in getting his team to finish the project, but an alert pinged on the wall console. He habitually held up two fingers in the standard hold-please-while-I-answer-a-message-or-access-the-net gesture. The display identified the caller: Kim Sato.

"Hello, Kim," Casmir answered, surprised she hadn't opted for chip-to-chip messaging rather than the city comm system.

"Did you complete your bird project?" Kim asked, no visual coming up with the audio.

"I did. It's *working*. For its preliminary flight around the lab, at least."

"Congratulations. I will see you at home."

"Wait," Casmir blurted, surprised by the abrupt end of the conversation, though he should have been accustomed to her atypical approach to social conventions by now. "Is that all you wanted?"

She paused, and he imagined her puzzling out what an appropriate response would be. He waited patiently. He was used to all types of smart, eccentric people, including Kim.

"I am placing a grocery order to be delivered by dinnertime tonight," she said. "I am considering whether to simply select our agreed-upon staples or add in a bottle of celebratory wine. There are seven varietals in stock with that adjective in the description. I assume one of them will be appropriate to honor career achievement."

"Ah." Casmir grinned, now reading her pause as a debate on whether celebratory wine should be a surprise or not.

"Do you have a preference of red or white?" she asked. "Or sparkling?"

"Red, please. Sparkles optional."

"I see an appropriate bottle. Goodbye."

Professor Huang arched his eyebrows after the comm ended.

"Girlfriend? Or android?" Huang smirked. "Or both?"

Casmir's cheeks heated again at the suggestion that he couldn't find a flesh-and-blood girlfriend if he wanted one, even if it had been over a year since he'd had a modicum of success in that department. His left eye blinked a few times of its own accord, and he grimaced, willing the obnoxious tic he'd had since childhood to stop. Contacts corrected his myopia, if not his monocular vision, and medication kept his seizures under control, but some symptoms of his flawed genes defied modern technology and pharmacology.

"Roommate," Casmir said firmly. "And not an android. She's a bacteriologist who has made many excellent contributions to the medical sciences. She's good with microbes. Humans are more problematic for her."

He shook his head, not sure why he was explaining someone Professor Huang was unlikely to ever meet. Mostly because he was still smirking. From his time as one of Huang's students, Casmir remembered well that the man had a dirty streak, especially considering he was eighty or ninety. Which was *old* on Odin. It wasn't like in some of the other systems where genetic tinkering had vastly extended the human lifespan—for those who could afford it.

"Roommate with benefits?" Huang winked.

"If you consider that she's buying me wine a benefit, then yes. As for the rest, I don't think she ever notices a man's—or woman's—anatomy unless she's poking it with a sword."

Huang's mouth drooped open. "A *sword?*"

Casmir, realizing that could be misconstrued as an innuendo, rushed to clarify. "Her father and half-brothers run a kendo dojo. The swords are real swords. Well, no, they use wooden ones, mostly, I think. Uhm—"

"Professor Dabrowski?" an unfamiliar voice from the doorway said, mangling the pronunciation of the last name.

Casmir spun toward the stranger with relief, glad for an excuse to end the conversation.

"You can call me Casmir. My students all do. I…" Casmir trailed off when he got a good look at the person standing in the doorway.

The tall, broad-shouldered man wore dark silver liquid armor that covered him from boots to neck, leaving exposed only his strong, lean face and black hair long enough to flap in the wind. Or so Casmir assumed. The knights in the animated law-enforcement posters always had breeze-ruffled long hair and an equally breeze-ruffled dark purple cloak. This man had both, though the building's ventilation system was not sufficient for ruffling.

He also wore an imposing weapon on his utility belt, what looked like an Old Earth medieval halberd on a short axe shaft. A pertundo, the legends called them, the traditional knight's weapon and far more sophisticated than they appeared. With a telescoping shaft, it could be used like a spear, but the long, sharp tip fired energy blasts similar to bolts from DEW-Tek firearms, and the blade could carve into the best combat armor in existence. At least according to the war vids.

"Can I help you?" Casmir stepped forward, silently commanding his chip to search the network for a match on the knight's face.

"I'm here to help *you*." The knight glanced both ways down the hallway before stepping inside and palming the sliding door shut. "I'm Sir Friedrich of His Majesty's royal knights."

As he said his name, Casmir's net search came back, displaying the man's face, name, and address. Daniel Friedrich, knighted eight years earlier. Residence: Drachen Castle.

"Shit, Casmir," Huang whispered. "What did you do?"

Casmir shook his head. All he could think was that this had something to do with his old job. He'd seen a couple of knights at the military research facility in his years there, but the elite defenders of the crown's interests were spread across the system, and even some of the non-Kingdom systems. They didn't stroll into the world of academia often.

The knight strode toward Casmir, his face hard and determined.

Casmir lifted his hands, fearing he was about to be arrested. But for what?

"I bring a message." Friedrich halted in front of him and glanced at Huang.

Huang leaned his hip against the desk and folded his arms around his cane, not looking like he intended to leave.

"You must flee," Friedrich said, focusing on Casmir again. "Get off the planet. Out of the entire system, if you can."

"Uh. Any particular reason?" If anyone else had been making this suggestion, Casmir would have scoffed, but if this man truly was a knight who lived in the castle… "Are you entering the robotic flight simulation contest? You're not my competition trying to get rid of me, are you?"

Friedrich gripped his arm, his lean face humorless. "This isn't a joke, Dabrowski. Knights don't get sent out for pranks."

No, Casmir knew that. But cracking jokes was easier than accepting the fear starting to roil in his gut. Fear and confusion. He was shocked a knight would have been sent out for him under *any* circumstances. Even a squire would be an oddity.

"Who sent you?" Casmir asked.

"Your mother."

Casmir would have fallen over backward if the knight hadn't still gripped him. "My… you mean my adoptive mother? Irena Dabrowski?"

"No."

Casmir opened his mouth, but he couldn't find words. He didn't know who his real mother was. His parents—his adoptive parents—hadn't told him. They'd always said they didn't know, and in the thirty-two years he'd been alive, he'd never found anything to suggest his real mother lived.

"Someone wants to ensure you do not see another sunrise," Friedrich said. "She told me to tell you to get off-world. Don't return to your house before you go. Just take what you have and find passage on a ship. Don't use your banking chip. Take your ID chip offline."

"My mother spoke to you? *Today?* I don't even know—" Casmir gripped the knight's arm back and shook it, as if he had the strength to affect the large fit man. "Who is she?"

"She—" Friedrich broke off and frowned, his eyes unfocused as he received some message. He cursed and stepped back, easily shaking off Casmir's grip. "They're coming. Two of them." He opened a rectangular pouch on his utility belt and pulled out a folded disk. "I'll do my best to delay them so you can escape."

"*Escape?* This is where I work."

"Not anymore."

Friedrich strode not toward the door but toward one of the windows. It was an old-fashioned casement window with real glass, so he could open it and peer out onto the streets and walkways of the campus eight stories below. Without pausing, he hopped onto the windowsill.

"Sir Knight." Casmir lifted a hand and started toward the man.

Friedrich looked over his shoulder, his eyes intent. "If you value your life and the lives of your friends, get off Odin now. Get out of the system altogether. *Go.*"

Friedrich sprang out the window.

For a second, Casmir could only gape in surprise as the knight disappeared from sight, the wind whipping his hair and his cloak. Casmir rushed to the window in time to see Friedrich flick his wrist and the disk unfold into a driftboard.

The knight maneuvered it under his feet as he fell, his cloak streaming above him. Scant feet from the pavement, the board's thrusters fired, and he slowed. But not for long. Board and rider zipped across the street and mag-rails, barely missing an auto-cab delivering students. On the other side, he disappeared inside the four-story cement parking garage.

"Are you going to listen to him?" Huang asked.

"I… I don't know."

As Casmir gripped the windowsill, the salty breeze of the Arashi Sea tickling his nostrils, a boom erupted from the parking garage. Flames sprang through the windows on the bottom level, and smoke flooded out through the entrances.

"Did he do that?" Huang asked.

"I don't know."

Casmir ran to his desk and waved a hand to activate the built-in computer, wondering if his staff position would get him access to the parking-garage cameras. Already, sirens wailed outside, ambulances or police coming.

"Show me the parking garage, ground level," Casmir ordered as the desktop display came to life.

"People are running out," Huang said from the window, his gaze locked on the garage. "There's smoke everywhere."

The computer took an eternity to complete a retina scan on Casmir, then showed him the hazy bottom floor of the garage. Wreckage lay everywhere, including in the stall where he'd parked his scooter that morning. He groaned. It was gone, completely destroyed.

A breeze gusted through the garage, stirring the smoke and revealing Friedrich crouched amid the wreckage. He'd put away his driftboard and drawn the pertundo, the shaft extended to more than six feet, and gripped it in both hands. In the legends, knights were always slicing and perforating enemies into bloody pulps with them, usually while balancing on train trestles over rivers or some other ludicrous place for a fight. But Friedrich wielded it like a rifle and fired green bursts of energy into the smoke.

Screams sounded, not from the display but through the window. The knight hadn't gone crazy and started shooting innocent students, had he?

Huang cursed at something outside. Casmir almost ran over to look, but on the display, the smoke cleared enough for him to see the knight's opponent.

A faceless, tarry black humanoid figure strode toward Friedrich with deadly intent. It carried no weapons—it didn't need them.

"No," Casmir whispered in horrified recognition.

The figure sprang forty feet, more like a panther than a human. Friedrich fired bolts that would have killed a man into its torso, but they bounced off. He didn't appear surprised. He shifted his grip on the weapon as his foe came into melee range.

"What *is* that?" Huang came to Casmir's side and looked at his face. "You know."

Casmir nodded mutely, unable to take his gaze from the scene playing out.

Friedrich lunged and thrust his pertundo into his attacker's black torso, the point sinking in and branches of white lightning streaking out and wrapping around it. His foe did not slow at all, merely striding forward to deliver an attack of its own.

Friedrich dodged an impossibly fast punch, the knight displaying speed and agility that would have made him a match for any human, maybe even a genetically enhanced one from another system. But this was no human, and it caught Friedrich on his second attempt to dodge, hefting him into the air.

The knight shortened his pertundo and swung it like a one-handed axe, even as he dangled, his feet well above the pavement. His foe held him at arm's reach, but one of the swipes landed, the blade cleaving deeply into its side, more lightning coursing around it.

Casmir held his breath, hoping the legendary weapon might be a match for the deadly construct. But a tarry black hand came down and yanked the blade out. The wound in its torso closed, melting together as if it were made from molten wax, and re-hardening into its original form.

Friedrich snarled and tried to land another blow, but his enemy hurled him through the smoke and into a cement wall. He struck with bone-crunching velocity.

"Casmir." Huang gripped his shoulder. "There's another one on the mag-rails outside, throwing people around as if they weigh nothing. What are they?"

Casmir swallowed. "Crushers."

"The robots you helped develop?"

"Yes."

Huang ran back to the window. "Shit, that one's coming this way. Casmir, get out of here. If they really are after you..."

"I know," he croaked numbly.

On the display, the crusher stalked toward Sir Friedrich, who was stirring, but not quickly. Casmir made himself tear his gaze away. For whatever reason, that man out there was buying him time.

He rushed around the lab in a panic, grabbing the bird robot and a bunch of tools and materials, anything that seemed like it might be useful. He stuffed them into his satchel with his lunchbox and a half-full bottle of fizzop, then laughed shortly. Almost hysterically. Was this what he was going to flee the *planet* with? He had to go home first. This was ludicrous.

"I'll tell them you went out of town if they come up here," Huang said. "Do they talk?"

"Yes, they can talk and interrogate you like a professional soldier. Professor, you need to get out of here too. Don't put yourself in danger. Don't talk to them. *Nobody* should talk to them. Try to evacuate the building." Casmir paused, looking at his desk and the work benches and his satchel. He was throwing things in without rational thought. He'd just stuffed the stapler in his bag.

"Casmir..."

"Just do it, Huang." Casmir flung his bag over his shoulder. "And be careful."

He raced for the door, half-expecting to find a crusher looming in the hallway outside.

But the hallway was empty. The knight had come in time. Maybe. Crushers could outrun an auto-cab. If they spotted him…

"*You* be careful," Huang called after him.

Casmir waved a curt acknowledgment as he ran down the hallway, already contemplating where to go to get a ride off the planet. Zamek Space Station? Would it be safe? Or would those crushers or whoever had programmed them be waiting there? Was there another place with ships that took passengers off the planet? He had no idea. He'd only been outside of the city twice—for camping trips as a boy. He got seasick and cabsick, so he'd always been certain space would be a miserable experience best left for those with iron constitutions.

He ran down the emergency stairs, accessing the net through his chip and searching for transportation options. But he halted and swore as a realization smacked him in the face like a sledgehammer.

Kim. She would be headed home from work soon if she wasn't already. If the crushers knew to look for him at his workplace, they would know his home address.

What if they were already there?

CHAPTER 2

BONITA "LASER" LOPEZ FLEXED HER LEG UNDER THE control panel in her freighter's small navigation cabin and tried to ignore the ache in her knee. She didn't have to walk to turn over the cargo and collect her pesos, just have her new assistant open the hatch and let Baum's loyalists come in and get it. Except they would pay in Kingdom crowns, she reminded herself. She would have to exchange them before leaving the system.

Having money in need of exchange would be a *good* problem. One she hadn't experienced in far too long.

Her other knee twinged.

"I'm afraid I have a lot of debt to pay off before considering surgeries," Bonita muttered to her collection of aching joints, reluctant to admit that the decades of acrobatic chases and joint-wrenching skirmishes to collect bounties were catching up with her. It was work she wished she was still doing. More honorable work than *this*.

She drummed her fingers, frowning impatiently at the large display stretching across the front of the cabin. Currently, it showed the view from the *Stellar Dragon*'s forward camera, an abandoned beach two hundred miles north of Odin's capital, moonlight shining on the waves crashing onto the sand. Farther inland, a few distant lights indicated cabins, but it was early spring and cold out. Campers strolling along the beach in the moonlight weren't likely. It was an ideal place for an exchange. If only Baum would show up.

The hatch opened behind her, and a soft *whir, whir, suck* sound came from the deck. Without looking, Bonita lifted her boots and propped them on the control panel. One of the ship's many, *many* cleaning robots whirred around her pod, vacuuming up nonexistent dirt and lint as she leaned back into the cushioned full-body seat.

The Ring of the Nibelung floated in from the corridor speakers. Bonita groaned and covered her ears as the robot swished and swept to the rise and fall of the music. She was *positive* that Viggo had no idea what the words meant in the two-thousand-year-old Earth opera. Unfortunately, that didn't keep him from playing it over and over and *over*.

"This isn't the time for housekeeping, Viggo," she said.

"Oh, I disagree," came the voice of the ship's computer. "While we're here on Odin, we must take advantage of the planet's gravity. The dust *settles*. My filtration systems are without peer, as you know, but the fans can only do so much when it comes to directing the larger particles toward the ionizer. Thank you for finally replacing the filters, by the way."

"It was the least I could do when they showed up at the cargo hatch, with a fresh charge to my bank account, a bank account that can barely afford food these days, much less air filters."

"You'll thank me later. I bet you already feel better in the mornings. I was growing concerned for your health. And Qin's, though she's admittedly sturdy in the constitution department. But if I were still flesh and blood, I'm sure I would have been coughing my way through the nights. There were mold spores on the B Deck filter. *Mold* spores, Captain Bonita."

She almost snapped at him to call her Laser, since no self-respecting bounty hunter was named Bonita, even a semi-retired one, but she'd been trying to get him to do that for almost ten years, and it hadn't stuck yet.

"Were you *really* a smuggler, Viggo?" she asked for what had to be the thousandth time.

"Certainly. I was an *excellent* smuggler."

A throat cleared in the hatchway, and Qin Liangyu walked in, giving Bonita a curious look, as if it was odd to have a conversation with the ship's computer.

Qin had only been Bonita's co-pilot for a couple of months and didn't seem to fully grasp yet that Viggo had been a human being once, before some of his enemies had caught up with him, and his doctor friend had fulfilled the then-captain's last wishes, to upload his consciousness into the *Stellar Dragon's* computer.

At least that was the story Viggo had told her. It had all happened nearly a hundred years ago, and she was the fourth owner of the ship since then, so she didn't have a way to verify it.

"I have unsecured the cargo and stacked it by the hatch. Any sign of the buyers yet, Captain?" Qin clasped her hands behind her back as she faced Bonita, her skin bronze under a light layer of fur, her black hair pulled back into a clasp, revealing pointed ears. When she smiled, fangs were visible, but she didn't smile often, not as often as a nineteen-year-old kid should.

"Still waiting." Bonita waved to the empty beach, then to the second pod in navigation.

Qin considered it but didn't sit down. She was armed, with the muzzle of a huge DEW-Tek Starhawk 5000 sticking up over her shoulder, a stunner and dagger hanging from her belt.

"Perhaps I should wait outside?" Qin asked. "Is it possible their ship already arrived and cooled down sufficiently so we're unable to read the heat signature?"

"My scanners are too advanced to be fooled by *that*," Viggo said with a sniff. "There are no ships *or* humans in the immediate vicinity. There are naknaks and numerous field mice in the grasses above the beach, an owl in a tree, and a pod of whales being trailed by two orchastas swimming parallel to the shore approximately one mile away."

"Odin got Noah's full ark, didn't it?" Bonita asked.

"Some of those creatures are native to Odin, but yes, the planet was a near-match to Earth and therefore able to sustain most of the reptiles, animals, and endothermic vertebrates that were brought on the colony ships."

"The endothermic what? Did you talk like that when you were human?"

"Naturally."

"Did you get beat up often?"

"I fail to see how that's relevant now."

The cleaning robot zoomed out on its sweepers. Leaving in a huff? Fortunately, the music grew quieter with the vacuum's departure.

Qin listened to the exchange impassively. Her genetically modified face would have been hard to read under any circumstances, but she had a knack for keeping it in a neutral expression, her yellow cat's eyes with their slitted irises changing little. A survival mechanism, probably.

"I detect an aircraft approaching," Viggo said.

"Finally." Bonita faced the display again.

"It appears to be a hawk-class hover shuttle with the markings scrubbed off."

"Not surprising. It's not like the castle would openly send knights out to pick up weapons that aren't legal yet in the Kingdom."

"Too bad," Qin said in a wistful tone. "I would like to see a knight."

"I'm afraid a knight wouldn't want to see you. They don't even let their apples get modified on Odin."

"I know. It's just that they always sound so romantic in the stories."

Bonita blinked, surprised to learn that her fierce new assistant had a romantic side or read anything but *Guns and Grenades Monthly*.

"When I was young and enduring all my training and… other things, I used to dream that one would come save me," Qin added softly.

"You don't need saving, kid. You saved yourself in the end, right?" Bonita thumped her on the shoulder. She didn't know much about Qin's history, since she'd been evasive about her past, but gathered that one of the pirate families had ordered her created and raised her to be a killer for them.

"I did escape on my own, but…"

"You don't need romance, either. Trust me. I've been married three times, and the last bastard—that *hijo de perra*…" Bonita grimaced, thinking again of her deficient bank account and the fact that this ship was all she had left, a ship with the registration taxes overdue back in Cabrakan Habitat. "Men are decent company now and then, but don't enter into a contract with any of them. You just end up screwed. Every time."

"I am now detecting heat signatures in the grass a mile up the beach," Viggo said, not commenting on her rant. It was one he'd heard countless times.

"That's not the direction Baum's shuttle is coming from, right?" Bonita asked.

"It is not."

"Maybe someone set out mouse traps for the naknaks." Bonita went back to drumming her fingers on the control panel, not liking that her deserted beach had grown busy.

"It is likely they are robots or some other type of machinery," Viggo said. "I believe they are ambulatory."

"Are they ambulating right now?"

"They are."

"Heading this way?"

"Yes."

Bonita rubbed her knee. "Wonderful."

She had expected this handoff to be easy. Baum's loyalists were supposed to be on the same side as the Kingdom, even if they had vigilante tendencies and used less than legal methods of fighting their battles. Would the Kingdom Guard or the knights truly care about them acquiring new weapons?

Lights appeared as Baum's shuttle flew over them, its thrusters hurling sand against the *Dragon's* hull. After it passed them, it rotated and lowered itself to the beach. Bonita wondered if its pilot had detected the heat signatures.

"We'll let Baum's men come to us. Qin, head back to the hold and prepare to let them in if I give the all-clear. Don't let them know it's just the two of us." Bonita wiped her palm on the leg of her galaxy suit, caught herself, and stopped. She didn't want Qin to see her nerves. She was the hardened professional, after all, a woman just shy of seventy years who'd been dealing with all types of unsavory people for more than fifty.

Normally, she wouldn't feel uneasy about this setup, but having a modded assistant on a planet that forbade genetic tinkering already had her on edge—she'd casually lied about being alone to the customs android that had chatted her up. And Viggo's ambulatory heat signatures weren't helping her nerves. The quicker she handed off the cargo and got paid, the better.

"Yes, Captain." Qin hopped through the hatchway and glided toward the ladder well, as graceful as the cat from which someone had sourced her genes.

Outside, the hatch on the side of Baum's shuttle opened, and a squad of six men in combat armor filed out, rifles slung over their shoulders, hands on pistols at their belts. They looked around warily before heading toward the *Dragon*.

"Are you planning to deal fairly or not, Mr. Baum?" Bonita wondered to herself, watching the men advance.

It was a large team, but that didn't necessarily mean Baum intended to use force. The cargo case that Bonita had pushed around by herself up in space weighed hundreds of pounds here in Odin's heavy gravity.

The comm light flashed.

"Captain *Laser*," Baum said, saying the name with the same sarcasm he'd used during their first contact.

Bonita gritted her teeth, reminding herself that she hadn't spent much time in this system. The Kingdom people didn't know her reputation well, the fact that she could shave a man's balls with a laser or any other projectile weapon known to man.

"What?" she replied.

"My sergeant has the payment. Once he inspects the goods, he'll give it to your people, and my crew will unload the cargo."

"Agreed, but you know there's a lock code on the box, right? Does your sergeant know it?"

"We know it. We ordered the weapons, after all."

"That's good, because *I* paid to pick them up, and Sayona Station wouldn't give it to me."

"You paid a balance due, a small percentage of the total, and will be compensated shortly. Baum, out."

"Ass," Bonita muttered, not caring that the channel was still open.

She closed it and switched to the ship's internal comm. "Qin, put your helmet on when you open the hatch, and don't show off your uniqueness. Baum doesn't have the Kingdom accent I expected, but if his people are from here, they're not going to like you."

"Few do," came the quiet, sad reply.

Bonita winced, wishing she'd chosen her words better. It had been a long time since she'd had to be circumspect with anyone.

"The heat signatures are close, Captain," Viggo said.

Bonita reached for the comm, intending to warn Baum in case his scanners weren't as good, but red flares of light burst out of the grass. An alarm went off as one of the attacks struck the *Dragon's* hull. The deck lurched, and rattles came from all around her.

Bonita cursed. Her freighter was better armored than most private vessels, but whatever that was had been *big*.

The red energy bolts slammed into the shuttle, and pieces of the hull blew off. The team of armored men fired into the grasses as they turned and ran back to their ship.

"No!" Bonita blurted, alarmed that the deal might not go through.

Tanks rolled out of the grass, and attack drones zipped out of the dark sky, raining down crimson energy bolts. Two of Baum's men were struck and flew sideways into the sand. The others grabbed them, dragging them toward their hatch. The hover shuttle fired its thrusters, preparing to depart.

Another blast struck the *Dragon*.

Bonita raised the ship's shields, but they were designed to deflect space trash in flight, not directed-energy weapons.

"Bonita," Viggo said. "We must abort. Those are—"

"I know, I know," she snarled, flinging herself back into the pod and pulling the neural navigator over her eye. The cool kiss of the interface pressed against her temple where her chip was embedded under the skin.

As she ordered the thrusters to fire, more energy blasts struck the hull. Her ship lurched wildly, and her pod tightened protectively, cushioning her like glass in a shipping container.

"You betrayed us," came Baum's angry cry over the comm channel.

"It wasn't me!" Bonita barked. "If you didn't want to pay for the weapons, you should have just said so."

"That's the most idiotic thing I've—"

Baum's shuttle exploded, and the channel went dead.

"Find a pod," Bonita yelled over her shoulder to Qin, not bothering to use the comm system. "If those drones follow us, we're going to be scragged."

The *Dragon* cleared the beach and accelerated over the Arashi Sea, Bonita zigzagging to make a hard target. But not hard enough. A round from one of the tanks struck them, the solid projectile tearing through the ship's hull. An alarm flashed on the engine panel. The round was lodged in the housing for the fusion drive. She prayed it wasn't an explosive that would detonate.

"Fusion drive compromised," Viggo said.

"I know that too." Bonita tried to dash sweat from her eyes, but the pod held her tight as the craft whipped about, swooping and banking and accelerating unpredictably, the framework of the old freighter creaking and groaning under the g-forces. "This night is getting to be more and more delightful."

They didn't need to fire up the fusion drive until they were in space, but there was no way they would get to the gate at the outer edge of the system without it.

The drones did not follow her out over the sea. That was one good thing, but if that robotic menagerie down there had been sent by the local law—or even the damn Kingdom knights—the *Dragon's* presence might already have been reported. And she couldn't break orbit on this backward gravity well without using the very public and very monitored launch loop.

"Captain?" Qin asked from the hatchway, gripping the jamb with strong hands and bracing herself against the erratic accelerations of the ship. "Are you all right?"

"Yes."

"Are *we* all right?" Qin's gaze shifted toward the flashing engine alarm.

After confirming that the drones had fallen out of range, Bonita steadied the ship and freed her arm from the pod's embrace so she could wipe sweat out of her eyes. "I don't know. We have to find a place that will help us with repairs and that isn't going to report us to the law."

"Do you know where that is?"

"Not yet," Bonita said grimly.

CHAPTER 3

THE HONKING, BLARING, GRINDING, AND WHIRRING OF RUSH hour in the city battered the university campus from all sides as dusk descended, but faculty housing was in a quieter interior nook. Stout oaks and prickly ciern trees lined the streets, spreading acorn-filled branches and thorny vines over the walkways. A few squirrels skittered from tree to tree, making final rounds before bedding down for the night.

Usually, Casmir found his neighborhood peaceful, but not tonight. He jumped at every student or professor riding past on a bicycle, scooter, or driftboard, and he peered into the shadows between every cottage, expecting a crusher to leap out at any second.

What was he doing coming home? This was the most obvious place for them to look.

But Kim hadn't answered any of the fifty messages he'd left. She had a chip—she wasn't one of those glasses-wearing holdouts who refused that technology—but she didn't like distractions, so she spent more time with the network receiver switched off than on.

His insides twisted and writhed as he imagined her dead inside the house, a casual flick of a wrist from a crusher the cause. How many had already died because someone had sent those two after him? He'd had the news updating, text, photos, and videos scrolling through his contact display, and the campus explosion and attack were all over it.

"Casmir?" came a call from behind him.

Even though he recognized the voice, he jumped, half flinging himself behind a tree before his brain caught up to his hyper-stimulated reflexes.

"Just like a Kingdom knight," he muttered, rolling his eyes at himself.

Kim peered around the tree, one of her braids of dark hair swinging over her shoulder. She carried her work bag in one hand and, slung over her shoulder, her exercise bag with two wooden practice swords strapped to it. *That* was where she'd been. The dojo. He'd forgotten it was her kendo night.

"Are you all right?" Kim asked. "I just checked my messages and was about to reply when I saw you walking up ahead. Where's your scooter?"

"My scooter is the *least* of my problems," Casmir said, though he grimaced, remembering the empty parking space with nothing but debris left in it. "Someone's sicced two crushers on me."

"I saw. Repeatedly." She raised her eyebrows slightly.

"Your eyebrows are judging me."

"Are they?"

"Yeah."

"It's a good thing my other body parts are neutral on the matter, or we couldn't be friends."

Casmir shook his head, though he almost laughed, mostly because he could count on Kim to stay calm. He knew she wasn't indifferent; she just didn't react much outwardly unless someone managed to fray her nerves, at which point, she snapped.

"I'm a little concerned," he said, also striving for under-reacting— or at least not hyperventilating.

"I would be too. From everything you've told me about them…" Kim looked down the street, their two-story rental cottage visible through the trees at the end of the cul-de-sac. "Was it wise to come home?"

"*No*. That's why I told you not to. We have to assume they'll check there, if they haven't already. The crushers are smart. And whoever sent them—well, I don't know yet if *they're* smart. I have no idea who they are. Or why they're picking on me."

A wheeled auto-wagon whirred past them, heading straight for the house.

"That's the grocery delivery," Kim said. "We should—"

"Leave it. I have to get off-world—out of the system, I'm told. And you… Feh, I don't know, but you can't go back there, not now. They'll question you about me, and depending on what megalomaniacal asshole programmed them, they could hurt you. A lot."

Someone else wearing wooden swords who'd been training with her father and numerous skilled athletes since childhood might have said something cocky about taking care of herself. But Kim gazed thoughtfully at the delivery wagon whirring up the street, then nodded.

"I can stay at my mother's place for a couple of days."

"Is she in town?"

"No." Kim smiled faintly. "That's why I can stay."

"Ah." Casmir considered whether she would be safe there, or if the crushers could be expected to search down the friends and *family* of everyone who knew him. The fact that Kim's mother was technically dead might throw them off, but every year there were more people who, when facing health problems that modern medicine couldn't solve, uploaded their memories and consciousness into android bodies with computer brains. For all he knew, Mrs. Kelsey-Sato still had to pay her taxes. Presumably, she had to pay the rent and utilities for the apartment her belongings occupied on her long stints hunting for interesting ruins in the Twelve Systems.

The delivery wagon left its insulated grocery box on the front stoop, and Casmir eyed it wistfully, thinking how much a bottle of celebratory wine—or alcohol of any kind—would take the edge off. But he needed all of his edges right now.

As the wagon whirred away, the front door opened. The dark body of a crusher peered down at the package.

Casmir cursed, grabbed Kim, and pulled her around the oak tree, praying the trunk was stout enough to hide them.

"They're creepy looking," Kim whispered, hunkering beside him.

"Yeah." Casmir gripped the rough bark of the tree, afraid to peek his head out to look but afraid not to. What if it was already sprinting toward them?

He peered around the trunk, and his breath caught. It stood on the stoop, looking around the neighborhood. Its featureless black head paused, pointing straight at him.

"We have to go." Casmir spun, looking for someone in a car that they could jump in. Even a car might not be fast enough.

"It's coming," Kim said as he spotted a teenager on an air bike.

"Follow me." Casmir sprinted straight at the kid, waving his arms wildly. "We need your bike."

"What? No way, Prof. This is a—"

Kim sprang past him and grabbed the teenager. The kid grunted and tried to fight, but she blocked the wild flails and dragged him off the bike.

"Sorry—it's an emergency." Casmir snatched the hovering vehicle before it could shoot off down the street without its rider.

"Run!" Kim ordered the kid, flinging a hand in the direction of the nearest house.

The crusher was halfway to them and picking up speed. Casmir leaped onto the seat as Kim smashed herself on behind him, her work bag clunking him in the ribs.

He gripped the handlebars, relieved the bike was similar to his scooter, and started to turn them around, but the crusher was scant meters away. There wasn't time.

"Hang on!" Casmir twisted the handlebars, and the bike hurtled toward a path between two houses.

Kim clamped onto him. Casmir swung the bike wide to avoid hitting trash bins and a dog kennel—much to the alarm of the dog, who barked uproariously at them. A lilac bush batted him in the face as they flew past far too fast.

Kim's grip tightened around his waist, either because she was afraid she'd fall off, or she believed his torso deserved punishment for his crazy flying.

It would only get crazier. He almost tipped them on their side as he swung into the next street and raced up it at top speed.

"It's following us," Kim reported, little emotion in her voice, even though she shouted to be heard over the roar of the engine and the whistling of the wind.

"I have no doubt." Casmir reached max speed on the bike and grimaced at the display. It wouldn't be enough.

Staff and students walking home shouted from the sides of the streets. Casmir veered around an auto-cab driving in their direction. The computer driver didn't honk, but the passenger leaned out the back window and flung a curse. Casmir whipped around a corner, only because he knew the street they were on ended up ahead, not because he had any idea where to go.

"It's gaining on us," Kim reported. "What's its max speed?"

"More than ours." Casmir could see the dark figure in the mirror, arms and legs pumping like those of a human runner, but with speed that no man, augmented or not, could ever achieve.

The wind tore at his face, threatening to rip out his contacts, and he squinted. He needed those contacts to see, not simply to display the news.

"I don't suppose you have any grenade launchers in your gym bag," he called over his shoulder.

"I have sweaty socks and a towel."

"Those might kill a human but not a crusher."

"Hilarious. Casmir, we need a plan."

Another auto-cab appeared ahead, this one crossing an intersection. Casmir cursed and jerked the handlebars to steer around it. His hair whipped into his eyes, making him wish he hadn't put off getting it cut. He dared not swipe it away. His shaking hands would never get a grip again. He'd never driven anything this fast and was amazed his poor depth perception and lackluster coordination hadn't caused a crash. Yet.

"I'm open to suggestions." Casmir was so focused on not crashing or running over anyone that he could barely process anything else. His work satchel was still slung across his body, but the tools inside were for fine motor work. There was nothing that could blow up a nearly impervious robot.

Behind them, the crusher closed the distance. It sprang at them, and he whipped the bike between two houses again. That bought them a couple of seconds as the crusher sailed past, not able to change directions until it landed. But it would catch up again quickly.

The next street over was a major artery with auto-trucks and cabs filling six busy lanes. They had come to the edge of the campus.

Casmir roared into the traffic without pausing. He was going twice the speed limit, and he weaved in and out of the larger vehicles, heading toward the heart of the city. Just where he wanted to bring a deadly killing machine.

Kim shifted behind him, keeping her vise-like grip with one arm and tugging one of her bags open with the other. Casmir couldn't believe she still had all her belongings.

"Going to try the socks?" he glanced back, not seeing the crusher in the mirrors.

For a second, he believed they had lost it, but no, it was weaving between the lanes of traffic, the same as he was. And once again, it was gaining on them.

"I have a lighter and aerosol deodorant," Kim said.

Casmir smiled. "A nice idea, but an explosion that small won't do anything to stop it."

"We'll see."

Casmir allowed himself a flicker of hope as he sped between two towering refrigerated trucks. There wasn't much room between them, and he drove as straight as possible.

Horns blared and a siren wailed behind them. Lights flashed in his mirror. Two Kingdom Guard cars sped onto the road, also weaving through traffic. Gunshots fired.

"This is *fercockt!*" Casmir blurted.

Why were the Guard officers *shooting*? Speeders weren't shot.

"They're shooting at the crusher," Kim yelled.

Of course. The officers would have seen the footage from campus by now.

"Maybe they have grenade launchers," Casmir said.

"They hit it with bullets." She looked back. "It didn't do anything. Would DEW-Tek weapons be effective?"

Casmir shook his head. "Even if they melted the liquid metal alloy, the crusher would simply rearrange the damaged molecules until it could repair them. Honestly, even grenades wouldn't destroy it, only buy us time while it fixed itself."

By all the gods in the Twelve Systems, why had he helped *invent* such a thing? Was he now going to die because he'd foolishly been honored to work for the king?

"Faster, Casmir," Kim urged, plastering herself against his back.

The crusher was so close, they could hear its pounding footsteps on the pavement over the roar of traffic.

Casmir swerved to drive in the middle of two lanes. More gunshots rang out, the Guard cars swerving and accelerating to keep up. A bullet glanced off the crusher's shoulder and whizzed past close enough that Casmir heard it.

He shook his head, too terrified to feel anything but numbness. Or maybe that was shock. This couldn't possibly end well.

Hoping vainly that he might throw the crusher off their path, he sped between a towering refrigerated truck and a hulking vehicle carrying tanks of something.

"Hydrogen," he blurted, spotting an H on the side of one of the tanks. "If we could breach—"

A bullet slammed into the tank ahead of them, and clear liquid hydrogen shot out. Kim shifted behind him.

Casmir wanted to slow down, to give her time to do something with that lighter, but the crusher appeared in his mirror, running behind the two trucks. Its arms and legs pumped so fast they blurred.

"Go, go!" Kim shouted as they drew even with the liquid spurting out.

As they passed it and sped out from between the two trucks, she shifted, and her elbow whacked him on the shoulder as she threw something.

"Was that—"

An explosion roared, drowning out his words and everything around them. A shockwave hammered their backs, and the air bike wobbled riotously as fire lit the darkening night.

Casmir fought to stay upright, fought to steady it, to keep going. In the mirror, he saw orange flames scorching the night sky. Secondary explosions roared on the back of the first as the other tanks on the truck blew. The refrigerated truck was thrown onto its side, squealing thunderously as it skidded across the pavement, blocking the lanes. Blocking everything.

Casmir licked his lips, watching the road ahead but also watching the mirror, afraid the crusher would survive that, afraid it would keep running, keep chasing them forever. Or until it caught him.

But flames roared, spewing smoke into the sky, and the wrecked trucks filled the highway. The gunfire had stopped. Did that mean the Guard officers couldn't see their target anymore?

Helicopters and Kingdom shuttles appeared in the sky, flying toward the wrecks.

Behind Casmir, Kim carefully tucked her lighter—more of a heating element, but clearly enough to produce flame—back into her work bag.

Casmir stayed on the highway for another ten miles so he could continue to fly at top speed and put distance between them and the crusher. It was possible that explosion had been enough to irreparably destroy it, especially if it had been right beside the tanks when they blew, but he wouldn't count on it. The nanites integrated into the liquid metal molecules meant every part of it was smart enough to start the repair process, to collect fresh materials to integrate if necessary. And, unless the knight had somehow managed to destroy the one in the parking garage, there was at least one more crusher out there.

It grew harder to control the bike. Casmir feared some mechanical failure was imminent, but the problem was his shaking hands. His entire body was shaking. *Gottenyu*, what if he had a seizure? He'd taken his medication that morning, but even the potent rivogabine wasn't always enough to keep his brain in equilibrium during stressful situations.

He took the next exit, terrified of what would happen to Kim if he had a seizure while he was flying, and found a park. He pulled into the vehicle lot, stopped the bike, and almost collapsed as he slid off. His stomach churned with the promise of vomit, and he stumbled toward the bushes. Maybe he would have a seizure and throw up at the same time. Wouldn't that be fun for Kim to witness?

Leaving the lights of the parking lot, he slumped against a tree. His legs gave out, and he let them, sinking to the ground, cool damp grass pricking at his palms.

Kim walked over, carrying both of her bags, and sat down next to him. She must have realized that he needed a minute, or maybe she needed a minute too, because she didn't speak right away. In the bushes, crickets chirped and czerwony bugs buzzed, the noises just audible over the roar of the highway a few blocks away. Casmir wondered if the wrecks had already been cleared.

"That ugly robot better not have bothered anything inside the house. Like my books. My real loved-and-touched physical books." For the first time, Kim's voice held emotion. Anguish. "Some of them are hundreds of years old."

"Ugly?" Casmir's voice came out far more normal than he felt it should. He wasn't shaking quite as much now. It seemed safer to talk about the robots, because he would feel like a complete ass if Kim's book collection had been destroyed. Or any of her belongings. He had no idea why this was happening, but he knew it was because of him. "I always thought the crushers were kind of elegant."

"Your bird is a lot better looking."

Reminded that he had it in his satchel, Casmir rushed to unlatch it and check on the contents. What if it had been smashed to bits in all that chaos? Ah, no. He found the robot bird intact and held it up to the parking lot lights to look for damage.

"It's certainly a more amiable creation." Casmir gently returned it to its home. "Thank you for your quick thinking back there."

"Welcome." Kim always accepted praise with a grudging mumble, as if it hurt to receive it, and she would rather shrug it off. "Thank you for not crashing. I was a little concerned when I remembered your eyes."

Casmir's left eye blinked. He sighed and rubbed it. "My vision doesn't affect my driving."

"I've seen the squash ball dangling on a string in the alley to keep you from hitting the trash bin with your scooter."

He snorted. "It *slightly* affects my depth perception. My optometrist has advised me not to take up racket sports." Not comfortable talking about his physical deficiencies, even with an old friend, he waved to Kim's belongings and asked, "Why do you keep a lighter in your gym bag?"

"It was in my work bag."

"Ah." Casmir scratched his chin. "Why do you keep a lighter in your work bag?"

"For warming the agar plates," she stated as if it was the most obvious thing in the system.

For a bacteriologist, maybe it was.

"Anything else of interest in there?" He poked her bag. "In case we need to come up with further brilliance?"

"I have several virus samples in a cold box that a colleague asked me to drop off at Mokku Park Lab tomorrow. Hisayo in immunology is working on some vaccines."

"Those won't be useful on the crushers, I fear. But I'm making a special note to keep my fingers out of your bag."

"Always wise. Women don't like men poking through their personal items."

"Like lipstick, nail files, and virus specimens?"

"Precisely." Kim gazed toward the parking lot. "How long is it going to be safe to stay here?"

"Probably not long." Casmir sighed. "Someone came to see me at work today. A knight from the castle. He said my mother, *not* my adoptive mother, sent him to warn me to leave the planet. To leave the entire *system*, he said. He wouldn't tell me who was after me."

"You couldn't wheedle the information out of him? You're good at wheedling."

"Thanks. I think. But two crushers showed up, and there wasn't time for that. I don't even know if he's still alive." Casmir's stomach churned anew at the idea that the knight might have given his life to buy him time to get away. Why would someone do that? He wasn't an important person, nobody who warranted a bodyguard. Outside of the university and the robotics circle, he was unknown. "Friedrich," he added. "That was his name. Sir Friedrich."

It seemed important never to forget that. Just in case.

"Are you going to leave?" Kim asked. "You've never been off-world, have you?"

"I've never even been off the *continent*. The one time I took the ferry over to Blume Island, I threw up." Casmir patted his delicate stomach.

"I told you I could give you some bacteria for that."

"And I told you you're nuts." Maybe because he'd always hated hospitals and feared doctors, Casmir shuddered at the idea of being one of Kim's science experiments.

"A wholly inappropriate response. Early in my career, I made a very simple strain that eats excess histamine in the body, which has been linked with motion sickness. Many antihistamine drugs reduce motion sickness, but my bacteria are a far superior option, and they've been in use in the bodies of more than five thousand test subjects for years now with no negative side effects. I'm positive you would see good results, and it would help with your allergies too. Given your numerous medical conditions, it's likely that you have impaired methylation and don't effectively clear histamines from your body."

"Another thing I'm not good at? No wonder I haven't had a date in over a year."

Kim punched him in the shoulder.

It was the correct response. Enough whining.

"Let's talk about it later." Casmir pushed himself to his feet, glad his legs supported him. "As much as I'm tempted to stay here in the city and try to get to the bottom of this, I'm terrified of those crushers taking out more people on the way to get to me, and I'm very confident in their ability to hunt me down. I've already commed my parents and sent messages to my colleagues and friends, anyone close enough that the crushers might think to question them about me. I've warned them to lie low, or get out of town for a few days, but I think it's going to be safest for all if I do as the knight said and leave Odin for a while."

Casmir had no idea where he would *go*, but if the crushers figured out he was gone—and he assumed they would—they shouldn't have a reason to hurt anyone else here.

"I need to make a quick pharmacy stop—" he didn't mention his seizure medication, even though Kim knew about it, "—and then we need to figure out how to get passage off-world without leaving an obvious trail."

"*We?*" Kim lurched to her feet. "I have to be at work tomorrow. I plated my new experimental strains and put them on warmers to start the colonization process. They'll be ready for me at nine in the morning."

Casmir hesitated. This wasn't her battle, but he feared that, as his friend and roommate for the last seven years, she would be in danger. More danger than she'd already been in.

Sirens wailed in the distance. Casmir imagined that crusher stepping out of the flames and walking down the highway looking for them.

"Call in sick, Kim. Please. Hopefully, I can get this sorted out quickly from… somewhere that's not here. A spaceship on its way out of orbit."

"A spaceship? Why would you go into space to hide? I don't know if you've noticed, but there's nothing to hide behind out there."

"There are stations, habitats, the colonized moons… I just have to get somewhere else, ideally somewhere without as many tracking and security cameras as Odin." Casmir glanced toward the parking lot, certain a traffic camera somewhere was monitoring it. If whoever was chasing him had access to the Kingdom Guard security system… "I don't think we'll have to leave the system."

"The *system*? It takes weeks just to get to the gate. My bacteria will break out and take over the world by then."

"I hope that's a joke." Casmir knew her private research laboratory had also worked with the military on a few projects that she'd never spoken much about.

"They'll run out of food and die first." A hint of sadness tinged her voice. "Look, I'll help you find a ship and get out of here, but I've got a lot of work to do. And I don't think they have decent coffee in space."

Casmir smiled faintly, aware of the coffee *and* espresso makers she used on a daily basis.

"I can take some of my work home—to my mother's flat—and nobody will think to look for me there. I'll be fine."

Casmir worried about her, but he couldn't order her to disrupt her entire life because of a threat to him. He hoped she was right, that the crushers wouldn't look too hard for her when she didn't reappear at the house.

"All right. Thanks. Any thoughts on where to go to get transport off-world where I wouldn't have to scan my chip and be on record?"

"You could probably find transport at the Shizukesa Shipyard. It's known to cater to pirate families and wealthy eccentrics who object to being tracked. But the ship would have to use the launch loop, the same as everyone else, unless it has some wicked thrusters. There aren't many ships that can break out of Odin's atmosphere on their own."

"The Shizukesa Shipyard? Is that in the city? I haven't even heard of it."

"East side, near the docks."

"How does a bacteriologist know where the pirate families lurk?"

"You forgot about my hobby."

He looked toward her wooden swords.

"My *other* hobby." Kim grinned. "The one I do for myself, not out of a sense of obligation to participate in familial bonding with my father and half-brothers."

"Oh, the novels. Are you still publishing them?"

"No, I haven't had time since I was in grad school and had my summers off, but my crime thriller continues to sell. I wish my allegorical fantasy trilogy did, but what can you do? I don't have time to learn marketing, and it's not like my pen name is available to go to book signings and readings."

"You can read to me on the way to Shizukesa Shipyard, if you like."

"You fell asleep the last time I read some of my work to you."

"It was bedtime, and I was sick," Casmir said as they headed toward the parking lot. "I thought I was *supposed* to fall asleep."

"You didn't have to be so emphatic about it."

"How does one fall asleep emphatically?"

"With moist, throaty snoring."

"That's gross."

"I know. I was there."

Maybe he didn't need to worry about her witnessing a seizure. She'd already seen him at his worst.

CHAPTER 4

MIDNIGHT APPROACHED IN THE SHIZUKESA SHIPYARD AS BONITA walked around the *Stellar Dragon*, supervising as drones and workers with welding guns went over the hull. Nobody had asked what happened, and she was relieved.

Robots and human laborers worked on three other ships parked on the spacious landing pad next to a massive warehouse full of manufacturing equipment. She hoped that meant she and the *Dragon* were nothing special and would not be remembered. Viggo had been the one to suggest the shipyard, having visited with a previous captain. Apparently, that didn't qualify Bonita for a discount.

"This is your total, Captain," the supervisor said, holding out a tablet displaying her bill in several languages. A short brown-skinned man with a pointy white goatee, he didn't look to weigh more than a hundred pounds. "I must apologize, but there will be a charge for after-hours service and a rush job."

"That's not a problem," Bonita said, though inside, she quailed at the amount.

How was she supposed to pay? Until she unloaded the cargo, she wouldn't have access to that kind of cash, and she definitely didn't have any Kingdom crowns stashed in her cabin.

"Can you translate that to System Diomedes pesos, please?" Bonita added, buying time to think. "Or Union dollars?"

Was it possible she could pay the shipyard with some of the weapons inside the cargo case? She didn't have the code to open it, but maybe she could force her way in. She'd paid for the honor to transport that cargo, after being promised she would receive quadruple her investment when she delivered it. It had been risky to sink so much of her own money into the venture, but she'd been certain she could sell off the weapons piecemeal if something went awry. She just hadn't expected to have to do it in a desperate rush. No good business was ever done that way.

"Diomedes *pesos*?" The supervisor blinked several times. "Captain, you know which planet you landed on, do you not?"

"Not a civilized one," she muttered.

"Odin is very civilized. If we were not, there would not be so many habitats and planets eager to return to the Kingdom now."

"As I've heard the news, those planets and habs are rather divided on the matter." Bonita handed the tablet back to the supervisor. "Let me scrounge inside. I'm sure I can find some crowns. I assume you take physical currency?"

"We are most pleased to accept hard crowns or gold." He smiled and bowed. "I must warn you that we test gold before accepting it. Only pure coins and bars are sufficient for payment."

"No problem."

Bonita turned toward her open hatch and almost bumped into two hulking men. They had the same face as the old supervisor but were forty years younger and two-hundred pounds heavier.

Her hand dropped automatically to the DEW-Tek 900 holstered at her hip, but she thought better of drawing. Two more hulking men that appeared to be from the same family stood to the side, cradling rifles in their arms as they watched her intently.

"We have applied a magnetic security lock to your thrusters, Captain," the supervisor said politely. "As a precautionary measure. It is not permitted to leave without paying."

"I wasn't planning on it." Bonita pushed between the big men, not flinching when she bumped against their muscled arms.

Her knee gave a twinge, reminding her how much she did not want to get into a fight with the brutes. Fortunately, they did not stop her again.

Bonita cursed under her breath as she strode toward the hatch. Damn Jake Pepper for clearing out their joint bank account and sending digital divorce papers after he'd already disappeared. She hadn't been foolish enough to commingle funds during her first two marriages, but those men hadn't been her *business* partners as well as husbands. The bastard had taken the physical currency in the ship's vault too. She was certain Jake would have taken the ship itself if he and Viggo hadn't spent the five years of Bonita's marriage sniping at each other.

When she reached the ramp, she paused. A man and a woman who didn't look like they belonged in a cash-or-gold-only shipyard were talking to someone at the hatch of the next freighter over. Someone with six pistols jammed into holsters all over his body, a silver-plated metal arm, and teeth to match.

The woman, who looked like she was on the way to an athletic competition, stood back, bags gripped in both hands, and an impassive expression on her face. Her buddy, who, with robots dancing on his rumpled shirt, looked like he was on his way to play geeky games in someone's basement, was gesticulating and smiling as he spoke to the thugly man. The thugly man did not smile back. He shook his head and waved for them to leave him alone.

Normally, Bonita wouldn't want anything to do with strangers, especially after the night she'd had, but was it possible these two were looking for passage somewhere? They both had bags, albeit not with as much luggage as one would expect if they were heading off-planet.

The man noticed her looking at them and smiled and waved cheerfully. He had pale skin, a beard shadow, and shaggy brown hair that looked like it had been cut with a bowl—three months ago. The woman, her features far more reserved, had darker skin, a stockier build, and tidy black hair back in two braids. Oddly, a couple of sticks—were those practice swords?—were attached to one of her bags.

"A little late for sightseeing," Bonita said as they approached.

"Yes," the man said, the woman once again hanging back as he came close. "Yes, it is. I'm actually in need of transportation. Would you by chance be leaving Odin and heading... anywhere?"

"Anywhere? That's a rather nonspecific destination."

"I'm a nonspecific kind of guy. Just looking for an off-world adventure. I've never been to space, you see. But I've had the itch for a long time." One of his eyes blinked a couple of times.

Was that his tell? Was he lying?

He smiled at Bonita, his eyebrows rising hopefully to go with the hopeful smile. His face wasn't roguishly handsome, but it had a charm to it. An inoffensive you-can-trust-me-because-I'm-far-too-goofy-to-be-plotting-shenanigans charm.

"You want to know what's in it for you, of course," he went on when she didn't speak. "I'm handy with tools, machines, robots, drones, and all manner of mechanical devices and objects. I can do wiring, programming, just about everything." He waved to the drones working on a breach at the top of her ship. "If you have anything that needs tuning up or even building from parts, I might be your man."

Bonita groaned. "Does that mean you can't pay?"

"I can pay. I have money. A job."

"Assuming your lab wasn't blown up," the woman muttered.

Bonita frowned—she'd barely caught that.

What kind of trouble were these two in? Or was it just him? He hadn't asked for passage for his companion. The last thing Bonita needed was more trouble on her ship.

"I have money," the man repeated, "but I'm trying to avoid using my banking chip right now." He waved his index finger, the location most people were usually chipped, in the air. "I wouldn't mind using it once we're off-planet, though if there's any possibility of barter for physical goods, that would be excellent. Have you ever seen a flying robot bird?"

Bonita stared at him, wondering if he'd escaped from some institution for the mentally unstable. Maybe that was why he didn't want to be tracked down. The wardens would show up, grab him, and throw him back into his padded cell.

"The only physical thing I would barter for would be gold." Bonita glanced at the supervisor, not surprised to see him still out on the floor and keeping an eye on her.

"I have small amounts of gold and tungsten," the man said, patting his satchel. "How much do you need?"

His female friend looked at him. "You keep gold in your work bag?"

"Yes, for the same reason you keep a lighter."

"So you can warm agar plates?"

"All right, *almost* the same reason. Gold is a highly efficient conductor of low voltage currents, and it doesn't rust, so it's ideal for electronic components. Since my current work has been interrupted, I would be willing to part with what I have." He smiled brightly at Bonita.

"Show me the gold," Bonita said. "And give me your names. Whatever names you'd like to use on this journey."

His brow furrowed, but only for a moment before he caught on. "Go ahead and call me Casmir. If I gave you a sobriquet, you would figure it out as soon as you used it and I gave you a confused look." He stuck out his hand. "I'm a mechanical engineer and specialize in robotics."

She accepted the clasp. "I'm Captain Laser Lopez."

"I see you're making much better use of a sobriquet than I would."

"Uh huh." Bonita released his grip and pointed at the woman. "And you?"

"I'm Kim. I'm a bacteriologist, and I'm not coming."

"A bacteria-what? Is that contagious?"

Kim didn't react to the attempt at a joke other than to narrow her eyes slightly. Bonita glanced at her wooden sticks and wondered if she knew how to use more deadly weapons. She seemed like someone who might be good in a fight. Too bad *he* was the one who wanted a ticket. Sobriquet. Ugh.

"As for the gold." Casmir poked into his bag. "Ah, here we go."

He withdrew a minuscule bar in a plastic baggie and held it up.

"Uh. Is that even half an ounce?" Bonita looked at Kim's bags, hoping she had the rest of their gold tucked away in one of them. A half an ounce wasn't going to cover her repair bill.

"About that. I purchased it just last month. Or rather, Zamek's higher-education institution did. It should be worth about five hundred crowns. Isn't that enough to at least get me a ride to one of the moons? I know it would buy a ticket on a commercial passenger ship."

"A commercial passenger ship full of passengers. You're trying to charter a private flight. That costs more."

"It doesn't need to be private on my account." Casmir laid a hand on his chest. "I'm very open to sharing. Kim and I have shared the same bathroom for years." His hand shifted toward her. "It's no problem at all, right?"

"You leave beard-removal gel and toothpaste all over the counter and the mirror, and at least once a month on the light fixture. It's disgusting if I go in before the cleaning robot comes through."

"See?" Casmir said to Bonita. "No problem at all."

Kim gave him a flat look.

"Are you two married?" Bonita asked.

"No," they said together.

"Because of the toothpaste?"

"No." Casmir looked at Kim. "That's not the reason, right?"

"Not the *only* reason." For the first time, Kim's dark eyes glinted with humor.

Casmir cleared his throat. "Really, Captain. Sharing is no problem, especially if it will reduce the fare. Uhm, perhaps those charming men over there would like to come." He nodded toward the thugs with the rifles.

"They're not invited," Bonita said. "Look, you're wasting my time. I need— Wait, did you say you were an engineer?"

"A mechanical engineer with a robotics specialization, yes. I teach classes and lead a research team over at the university. We're working on—"

Bonita jerked her hand up. "I don't care about that. How are you with fusion reactors?"

"Er, they rarely come into play in robotics."

"I have a breach in my core containment chamber. The reactor is offline right now, but if we can't use the fusion drive, we're not even making it to the moon anytime soon."

"Repairing the chamber sounds relatively simple," Casmir said. "I can take a look."

"If you can fix it, and you're prepared to part with that gold, you've got a deal." Bonita thought about asking if his tungsten was valuable, but she doubted the shipyard supervisor would take it, and she wasn't going to visit the local pawnbrokers.

"Excellent." Casmir planted his plastic baggie with its gold chip in Bonita's hand and strode up the ramp leading into the open hatch. He paused as soon as he got to the top. "Which way is the fusion reactor?"

"In engineering," Bonita said.

"Yes, of course." Casmir looked left and right. "And which way is that?"

Bonita dropped her face into her hand, rethinking the wisdom of letting this guy touch her equipment.

"Right." It came out as a groan. She would have Viggo run every diagnostic and analytical piece of software he had when Casmir was done. "You, Kim, was it? Does he have a clue what he's doing, or is he likely to screw up my ship?"

Normally, Bonita wouldn't ask a stranger for a reference, but after so many years in such a dangerous business, she was good at reading people. Kim struck her as someone who might be honest to a fault.

"Engines aren't his area of expertise, but he's smart. If you have a technical manual in your database, he'll be fine."

Bonita tried not to be horrified by the idea of someone using diagrams in a book as a guide to fix the most imperative part of her ship. But what other options did she have? She couldn't afford to have the shipyard repair everything. She hoped Casmir would know if he was in over his head and be intelligent enough to tell her. After all, he was about to fly off in the ship too.

Bonita nodded to herself, encouraged by the thought.

Kim hadn't moved. She was gazing at the hatchway at the top of the ramp. Casmir had disappeared, and she appeared faintly confused.

"You sure you don't want to come?" Bonita asked.

"No, absolutely not. But he didn't say goodbye, which is customary when a friend is going off into danger. I wasn't sure if I should depart now or wait or…" She shrugged again.

"We're not leaving yet. You can come inside and monitor him if you want."

"Monitor? I have a medical background. I wouldn't have the slightest idea what he was doing."

"You could make sure he doesn't leave any lubricants or gels on my light fixtures."

"I haven't succeeded at that yet."

Gunshots rang out, and Bonita jumped.

Kim whirled toward the noise, dropping her bags and landing in a fighting crouch. Bonita backed up the ramp, yanking out her pistol but wanting nothing to do with a fight. She hoped she had that option, that this didn't have anything to do with her and her illicit cargo, but she couldn't be sure.

"Get out of here," someone yelled, firing again. "No trespassing robots."

"Our bullets are bouncing off it!"

The lighting wasn't bright near the periphery of the shipyard, and Bonita squinted, trying to see what the men were firing at.

Kim cursed. "Not again."

Two dark humanoid figures strode out of the night, ignoring the workers—and the bullets ringing off their torsos. They didn't wear clothing or have distinct facial features, but they seemed to be looking straight at the *Stellar Dragon*.

One of the guards, a hulking man with arms like pylons, gave up on shooting and ran forward, using his rifle like a club. He landed a blow with the butt that would have knocked the head off a man—and most robots.

"Androids?" Bonita paused and looked down at Kim.

"Worse," she said grimly. "I have to warn Casmir."

She snatched up her bags and ran up the ramp, slipping past Bonita without bumping her.

Bonita almost reached out to stop her from boarding, but boarding looked like a good idea right now.

"Yo, supervisor!" Bonita yelled, spotting the small man running out of his office to take a look at the commotion. "We need to leave now. Here's payment for the services that were done."

She threw the baggie, glad for the natural weight of gold. It sailed across the pavement and landed at his feet.

Unfortunately, he was gaping at the intruders and not paying attention to her. What was his name? It had been on his invoice.

"Nakajima!" she yelled, and this time he looked. "Take that gold and check us out. Remove whatever locks you've got on my ship."

Bonita glanced back to see what the intruders were doing and nearly fell off the ramp. They'd broken into a run. They had passed two of the ships and would be at hers in seconds.

She sprinted inside and slammed her hands against the control panel to pull in the ramp and close the hatch.

"Viggo," she shouted from the cargo hold, "fire yourself up!"

"I am aware of the danger, Captain," the computer's voice came calmly from the speakers. "Readying for take-off now."

"Good. Are the mag-locks off?"

"Not yet."

"Not good." As Bonita raced across the hold toward the ladder leading up the two levels to navigation, a thud sounded, something striking the hull. A second thud immediately followed.

Casmir and Kim ran out of engineering.

"Crushers?" Casmir looked toward the closed hatch.

"Whatever they are, they're trying to get in." Bonita raised her voice to yell. "Qin, I need you and the biggest weapons you can find."

"Yes, Captain," came Qin's muffled reply from wherever she was.

"Can we help?" Casmir called.

"Yeah," Bonita said over her shoulder. "Stay out of the way."

Bonita left her new passengers in the hold, scrambled up the ladder, and flung herself into her pod in navigation. The piloting interface swung over as she considered the display showing the view in front of the ship. Smaller cameras fed in exterior views from the sides and the back. She groaned when she saw the two dark figures—what had Casmir called them? Crushers?—attached to the rear of the ship like ticks.

She was about to comm the supervisor outside, but the mag-locks let go without notice. Maybe he was watching and hoping she would take this trouble far, far away from his shipyard.

"Happy to." Bonita slapped the internal comm. "Everyone, hang on. We're going to pull some g's while I try to shake the sand out of our boots."

"Sand, Captain?" Viggo asked as Bonita took them into the air, blasting away from the shipyard and up the coast. She spun the ship like a barrel hurled down a long bumpy hill. "In one's boots? The very idea is making me cringe. Discomfort. Grime."

"Is it hard to cringe when you're a virtual being existing inside a computer's circuits?"

"No, I cringe extremely well. You'd just have to be another virtual being existing in the circuits to see it."

Bonita didn't answer. She stuck her tongue between her teeth and concentrated on piloting. Her pod absorbed the force of their spin, but something broke free and rattled around in one of the lower levels, clanging and clunking. There was always some damn thing that didn't get secured properly. She hoped Kim and Casmir were smart enough to find a pod and weren't flying all over the cargo hold.

When she checked the exterior camera displays, Bonita groaned. Not only had she not succeeded in shaking off the crushers, but they had advanced up the dome-shaped body of the ship, ticks moving from the ass end of the dog toward the head. And toward a hatch right behind navigation.

If they had the strength to force it open—if they were as strong as androids, they surely would—they could drop into the ship right behind her.

"Qin!" Bonita hollered. "I need you to pry some dangerous robots off the roof. Do you have your big gun yet?"

"I'm ready, Captain." Qin sprang off the ladder and stood in the short corridor, gripping a safety hook with one hand and wearing a Brockinger anti-tank 350 on a sling across her torso, the gun so big it bumped the bulkhead on either side. She grinned, pulled an explosive canister out of her bandolier, and dropped her helmet over her head.

"You definitely don't need a knight to save you," Bonita said.

"No, Captain."

"Use that closest hatch. They're almost there. Be careful not to damage the hull." Bonita grimaced, wondering if that was possible when the crushers were attached to it. "And hang on tight. I'm going to keep trying to buck them off. I don't want to lose you in the ocean."

"Understood," was all Qin said, her face turning serious.

She sprinted up the ladder that led to the roof hatch. Bonita didn't feel right sending a kid to fight her battles, but she had to fly, and Qin was far better at hand-to-hand combat than she.

A clang sounded, and Bonita could hear the rush of wind blasting past as the hatch opened. On one of the cameras, Qin appeared, rising halfway out and using her legs to brace herself on the ladder and the bulkhead as she used both hands to aim the big gun.

The crushers were closer to her than Bonita had realized—those things moved fast—and the first one rose to its feet. There was no way it should have been able to do that with the ship dipping and gyrating. It had to have powerful integrated magnets.

It lunged at Qin. For a split second, only one of its feet was attached to the hull. As Qin fired, Bonita spun the *Dragon* again.

Qin's canister slammed into the crusher's chest and blew.

"Down!" Bonita screamed, afraid the explosion would tear off Qin's head.

But she'd dropped below the hatchway before Bonita's warning. The explosion combined with the ship's spin knocked the crusher free. Its buddy turned and lifted a hand, as if to grab it, but Qin popped back out of the hatchway, distracting it.

Bonita nodded with relief as the first crusher tumbled through the air, falling a thousand feet and landing in the ocean. She hoped it rusted quickly and never made it to shore.

She steadied the ship so Qin could more easily deal with the second one.

Qin fired as it drew closer, but this one had learned from its buddy's mistakes. It flattened itself to the hull, and the canister sailed over it, exploding uselessly behind the ship.

Qin reloaded as quickly as any practiced military veteran, but it wasn't quickly enough. The crusher surged across the intervening space and grabbed her. Qin released her gun and drove her palms into her foe's chest. The blow would have sent a human being flying backward at neck-breaking speed, but she might as well have struck a six-foot-wide steel pylon.

The crusher tried to pull her through the hatchway, but Qin hooked her feet under a ladder rung. She cried out but managed to finish loading the Brockinger, the explosive canister clicking into place.

"Don't shoot when you're inside the ship!" Bonita called. "You'll blow out half the hull."

Before Qin could fire, the crusher knocked the weapon aside with so much force that the strap snapped. The Brockinger clattered down the ladder to land in the corridor.

Qin battered her enemy with a barrage of palm strikes, trying to keep it from climbing through the hatchway and getting inside. But the robotic creature did not feel pain, and it was too heavy or strong to budge. Bonita had the feeling it didn't care one iota about Qin and simply wanted to throw her outside because she was in the way. It wanted to get inside and acquire its real target.

Was that Bonita? Or her new passengers? Or the cargo? Had the same people who had killed Baum sent these things?

Metal groaned as the rung Qin's foot was hooked to threatened to give way.

"Keep us flying straight, Viggo." Bonita lunged out of her pod and ran back to help.

Qin's foot was still hooked, and she was fighting the crusher, keeping it from climbing in and getting a better grip on her. But her other leg flailed free, and the rung groaned again. The crusher would pull Qin out of the ship any second.

"Not happening," Bonita growled and snatched up the big Brockinger.

She made sure it was properly loaded and found as good a spot as possible.

"Twist free and drop down, Qin," she ordered, finger on the trigger. "I don't have a clear shot."

The ladder rung tore free. Qin did a somersault in the crusher's grip, trying to pull free, but it was too strong. It yanked her through the hatchway and flung her outside.

"No!" Bonita cried and fired.

The canister struck the crusher in the torso. It bounced off, fortunately not back into the ship. Bonita groaned again as it exploded uselessly outside the hatchway, the ship shuddering from the shockwave, and scrambled to load another round. Yellow flames lit the night. Surprisingly, even though it hadn't been a direct hit, the explosion was enough to make the crusher pause. Momentarily.

Bonita fired again.

This time, the canister struck the crusher in the head and exploded. It flew backward, out of sight of the hatchway.

Bonita charged up the ladder and stuck her head out to look around, in some vain hope that Qin hadn't fallen off. Wind roared in her ears. Cold night air smothered the hull, only the *Dragon's* running lights brightening patches here and there. As misty sea air battered Bonita's face, trying to rip her ponytail off her head, she climbed out farther.

"Qin?" she yelled. "Are you... anywhere?"

"Here," came a muffled call from behind her.

Qin crawled across the hull on hands and knees toward the hatch. She was following a seam, finding purchase where normal human fingers would never have been strong enough to do so.

Bonita reached out as soon as she was close enough, offering her hand. Qin grasped it, and they scrambled back inside together.

After the hatch was closed, the roar of the wind blocked out, Bonita slumped against the bulkhead in relief.

"Is my gun all right?" Qin looked back and forth, then spotted it where Bonita had dropped it.

"That's what you're worried about?"

"I was only able to get away from the pirates with three military-grade weapons. They're quite valuable." Qin methodically checked the function of the Brockinger.

Get away. A reminder that Qin had escaped and someone might come looking for her one day.

Qin hadn't admitted that, instead trying to imply that the pirates had no interest in her any longer, but several times, a word slip here and there had suggested otherwise.

"Let me know if you have any injuries that need patching up." Bonita patted her on the shoulder and headed back into navigation. "Someone had better fly this freighter."

Qin, frowning at a small dent on the butt of her Brockinger, did not reply.

"Really, Bonita," Viggo said. "I am perfectly capable of flying the ship. All you have to do is give me a destination. Anything short of Earth, and I can get us there."

"Last I heard, nobody remembers where Earth *is*." Bonita collapsed in the pilot's pod and did a sweep to make sure there wasn't anything else hostile attached to the hull.

"Precisely why I would have a difficult time flying you there."

A few minutes later, Qin stepped into navigation. She'd put her big gun away but still wore her combat armor, her helmet folded back to reveal a contusion swelling at her temple. Her face was flushed, and her eyes gleamed, as if she'd enjoyed herself back there. Bonita couldn't imagine.

"Thanks for getting rid of the freeloaders." Bonita jerked her thumb toward the hull. "No gold, no passage, right?"

"Seems reasonable, though I didn't bring you any gold when I came on."

"You've earned your keep." Bonita hoped her new passengers would too, especially since Kim hadn't paid anything. And didn't want to come. Bonita thought about offering to set her down somewhere, but after the night she'd had, she was too paranoid to land anywhere on Odin again.

"Thank you, Captain." Qin pressed her hands together in front of her chest and bowed.

Not for the first time, Bonita wondered what kind of crazy upbringing she'd had. She'd tried to look up Qin when she'd taken the girl on board, but all she'd found were encyclopedia references to some Ancient Chinese heroine back on Earth that she must have been named for.

Did her pirate family have descendants from that region? Some people knew where on Earth their ancestors had come from. Many more did not. Much had been lost during the years after the twenty-four colony ships had arrived in the various systems.

"Our new passengers saw me," Qin admitted quietly.

"They say anything to you?" Bonita's hackles bristled as she prepared to protect her assistant if needed. Qin could take care of herself physically, but mental attacks were harder to deflect.

"They just stared in surprise." Qin lowered her voice. "Like I was a freak."

"Well, you're not."

One of Qin's pointed ears rotated slightly.

"The Kingdom people are the only ones who bat an eye at modded humans. There are *plenty* of them roaming the rest of the systems. You're perfectly normal."

The way Qin smiled sadly suggested that hadn't been her experience, but she changed the subject instead of arguing.

"Do you think those strange robots were after us?" Qin asked. "Because of the cargo?"

"I'm not sure, but Casmir knew what they were. He called them crushers. I haven't heard of them before, but if they're trendy on Odin, that's another reason never to come back."

"I guess I won't get to see a knight."

"Trust me, you're better off this way. Go tell Casmir to fix my reactor, will you? I'm ready to leave this world."

CHAPTER 5

C ASMIR STEPPED BACK FROM THE REACTOR SHIELDING AND considered his handiwork. All it had needed was a simple patch, and he'd had his own soldering tools with him, so it hadn't taken long. The true test would come when they fired up the reactor, but he was confident it would be fine. The only problem had been a giant bullet of some kind lodged in it. A drone could have patched it up.

The bullet had been slightly alarming, suggesting that Captain Lopez had problems of her own in addition to his. Casmir appreciated that she'd given him a ride, but he would part ways from her as soon as possible.

All he wanted was to be left alone for a few hours on a station or moon base with network access so he could do some research and figure out who was after him and why. And who his *mother* was, and why she hadn't told that knight to share her name as well as her warning.

Casmir hoped that leaving Odin would mean leaving his trouble behind, but he couldn't disappear into the starry ether of space forever. Even if he did feel safe enough to use his banking chip elsewhere in the system, he only had a few months' worth of savings in his account. A few months of paying for regular stuff, like rent and food. Not tickets on spaceships and rooms in fancy space-station hotels. Even when he'd worked for the military, he hadn't made piles of money.

A cleaning robot whirred past on the deck, almost running over his boot as it vacuumed the area where he'd been working. Casmir didn't think he'd made much of a mess, but it zipped all around.

"It's working?" Kim asked from the hatchway.

Casmir jumped. He hadn't realized she was still in engineering with him.

But where else would she be? The captain was busy flying and hadn't given them cabins or a tour or even directions on where to sit. And the furry, uh, woman—Qin?—had disappeared right after the fight. The fight in which she'd almost singlehandedly kept the crushers from coming aboard. Casmir owed her thanks the next time he saw her. He vowed not to gape again. Belatedly, he'd realized that had been rude, but until now, genetically modified humans had been something he'd only read about. The Kingdom news feeds and dramas rarely showed videos of the universe outside of their carefully preserved system, and he couldn't ever remember seeing a six-foot-tall cat woman with a giant gun.

"It should be fine." Casmir put his tools away, shouldered his satchel, and walked over to join Kim.

The deck vibrated under his feet. His stomach had forced him to curl into a sick ball wedged in a corner of engineering during the wild gyrations Lopez had put the freighter through during the fight, but since then, the ride had been smooth, with cool air filtered in through a vent somewhere. That always helped. His airsickness was more likely to rear its head when he was hot and claustrophobic.

"I'm sorry you're stuck here," Casmir said.

"Me too."

"Are you pissed? I'm never quite sure with you."

"At the situation, yes, but not at you. I assume this isn't your fault unless you got into a fight with someone rich and powerful and dared him or her to throw your own creations at you."

"Yes, you know what a fighter I am." Casmir flexed his nonexistent biceps.

Kim frowned and shook her head. "You hardly ruffle anyone's feathers. What could this be about?"

"All I know so far is what the knight told me, that the mother I didn't know existed told me to flee the planet." He bit his lip. "I'm going to research assiduously as soon as…" He trailed off when Captain Lopez appeared in the hatchway.

She'd changed into a form-fitting black suit with a bulge just below the back of her neck. A galaxy suit with a Glasnax helmet that could unfold from that bulge. He only recognized it because people wore them in dramas about space pirates and invasion fleets. He grimaced at the realization that they were going somewhere where such a suit might be required.

"Progress?" Lopez jerked her chin toward the reactor.

"Yes. It's repaired."

"Already? Did you use a technical manual?"

"What?"

Kim snorted.

"Not to solder on a patch," Casmir said.

"Right. We're flying down the coast to the launch loop. Let me give you a quick tour and show you where to sit so you don't get plastered against the bulkhead when we're on the mag launcher. Or after that." Lopez waved for them to follow her.

"I guess I'm not going to get an offer to be dropped off somewhere," Kim murmured. "Do you think there's decent coffee on this ship?"

She looked around dubiously at the dented and scratched bulkheads.

Casmir patted her on the shoulder on his way out of engineering, regretting that she'd been brought against her wishes, but another concern took up more prominent real estate in his mind.

"Captain? The, uh, launch loop we're heading to—will there be an inspection there?"

"Sometimes they do a physical check, sometimes they don't. It would be better if we were taking off at a busy time rather than during the middle of the night, but I'm not inclined to linger longer on this planet." Lopez strode across the cargo hold and toward a ladder.

"I only ask," Casmir said, hurrying to catch her, "because I'm trying not to be noticed by anyone right now."

Anyone *else*, he thought, the crushers popping into mind.

"You and me both, kid." Lopez led them up the ladder to the middle of the freighter's three levels.

"I don't suppose there's any chance this ship can make it into space without using the launch loop?"

"On some planets it can. You know, nice planets with no atmosphere and a tenth the gravity of Odin."

"Ah."

They entered a corridor, and she pushed open a couple of side hatches. "Guest quarters are here and there. You can stow your gear in those cabinets—make sure you don't leave anything out. Nobody needs hairbrushes bobbing around and cracking them in the head when we're in space. You can each have your own cabin, but I'll have to ask for a fee for

Kim, since she wasn't part of the original arrangement. I've got plenty of rations, since I like to fly safe, but we don't do any free rides here."

"You could drop me off," Kim said.

"There's not much up this way except for the launch loop itself, and every time I land on this planet, I get jumped." Lopez waved into the nearest cabin. "You can strap yourself into the bunks at night, but some people sleep in the chair pods. They're designed to cushion you like an egg during extreme acceleration, but they're comfortable anytime."

Casmir rubbed a fresh bump on his head. If what they'd experienced already was an indicator of what space would be like, he would happily spend the whole trip in one of these pods.

"There are a couple of older galaxy suits in the cabinets that you can try on for further protection. They're made from SmartWeave. Gives you some defense against weapons, keeps you cool in a hundred degrees C, and keeps you warm in space. Attach one of the air tanks—" she opened a cabinet in the corridor to reveal a rack of oxygen tanks secured so they wouldn't bang around, "—to the back of the suit, double-check your helmet lock, and you're good for up to twelve hours of poking around on the hull."

"That won't be required, I hope." Casmir smiled.

"You did offer to fix things. Sometimes, the broken bits are on the outside."

"Er, right."

Casmir's stomach gave a queasy lurch as he envisioned floating around outside a spaceship in zero-g. He didn't consider himself unnaturally claustrophobic, but he'd always feared swimming because of his potential to have a seizure in the water. Having a seizure in space could be equally detrimental to his longevity. He'd picked up a two-month supply of his medicine before leaving Zamek, and it worked well in his day-to-day life, but he worried it wouldn't be up to keeping his brain functioning optimally during periods of extreme stress. Which it looked like he was going to be having a lot more of.

Lopez took a few more steps up the corridor and pushed another hatch open, revealing what looked like a combination lounge, mess, and kitchen, with all the furnishings bolted to the deck and made from a gray molded material that didn't appear comfortable. Casmir supposed pillows and cushions weren't practical for space travel.

"A couple of pods over there by that porthole." Lopez pointed. "You might as well sit for now. You can watch the launch if that excites you."

She shrugged as if she couldn't imagine it—and maybe she couldn't after as many times as she'd been into space. Her long hair was all gray, her face pale despite an olive skin tone, and he would believe she didn't spend much time in places where the sun warmed her cheeks.

"There's some exercise equipment that folds out of those walls." Lopez waved to rows of cabinets in a bulkhead behind the pods. "Not a bad idea to run and push the weight bars around if you're going to be out in space a while. We only get g's when we're accelerating and decelerating, and muscles like to get lazy if they can."

"Right." Casmir had always imagined that if he had to go to space for any reason, it would be on a transport ship large enough to spin like the big habitats did, providing a reasonable amount of artificial gravity for the passengers. He supposed if something as small as this freighter spun for that purpose, it would have to rotate so fast that it would leave them all puking. "I know I wasn't particular back at the shipyard, but do you have a destination in mind?"

The knight's warning rang in Casmir's mind, but he couldn't truly see himself fleeing the entire system. Surely, one of the moon bases or habitats that orbited Odin would be beyond the reach of the crushers, at least long enough for him to do his research and figure out what was going on. Right now, his embedded chips were offline, so he couldn't be traced, but he ached to check the news and start scouring the university and public networks.

Lopez hesitated before she said, "I haven't decided yet. I need to make a few comms. My drop-off here didn't go as planned." She waved them toward the pods. "Have a seat. You're welcome to anything in the lounge, and there's a lavatory at the end of the corridor, but don't wander around the ship and poke into things." She leveled a warning look at them. "I like my privacy."

"Naturally." Casmir smiled, hoping it would make him seem agreeable and trustworthy.

He was surprised Lopez hadn't interrogated him yet about the crushers. Was it possible she believed they had been sent because of whatever trouble *she'd* stirred up? Considering her ship had been damaged on the exterior and the interior, it seemed reasonable to believe there were also people chasing her.

"Is there a coffee maker?" Kim asked.

"There are some pre-made coffee bulbs in the mess. You can throw them in the zapbox to warm them up."

Kim gave Casmir her first scathing look of the night.

"Pre-made coffee bulbs? That you heat up in a box?" She curled a lip. "Those *can't* be drinkable."

"I'm sure they're not as good as what you're used to, but think of this as an adventure. Like camping out under the stars. This will be even better. We'll be *among* the stars."

"Without drinkable coffee. Expect me to have headaches and be grumpy."

"Will that be different from now?"

Her eyes narrowed, and her fingers twitched. She'd never throttled him before, but she appeared to be contemplating it.

"My apologies." Casmir bowed like the knights in the vids, pretending to sweep a cloak wide. "I don't know what I was thinking. I should have offered to build an espresso maker into the kitchen over there."

"And acquire fresh-roasted coffee beans and a grinder for me."

"Absolutely. I'll add that all to my priority list. Above find-out-who-my-mother-is and just below find-out-who's-trying-to-kill-me." Casmir arched his eyebrows. "Is that ordering acceptable?"

Kim waved in agreement, or simply to end the conversation, and glanced at Lopez, who'd paused at the ladder leading up to navigation and was watching impassively. Casmir had forgotten she was still there and wished he'd kept his priority list to himself.

Kim walked to the porthole and looked out to where the base of the launch loop was visible, magnetic tracks leaving from the terminal and angling up into the sky and out over the ocean. A hulking gray power plant sat next to the terminal, providing power to keep the massive structure working and accelerate ships along the tracks. Casmir had seen plenty of vessels take off on the news, usually when there was a story about how expensive the infrastructure was to maintain or how it had been damaged during a storm, but he'd never been here in person.

"Captain?" Casmir asked as Lopez started up the ladder. "When will we know if customs wants to inspect the ship before we go?"

Lopez grimaced. "Soon."

"Is there somewhere we can hide if they come aboard?"

"Hiding spots are already taken. You better find a mask if you're worried about your identity being revealed."

"I think masks only work for the pirate Tenebris Rache." Casmir waved his index finger to indicate the chip that would identify him to anyone with a scanner.

"Pirate?" Lopez asked. "To most of the rest of the systems, he's a mercenary."

"He doesn't prey fanatically on the rest of the systems' ships, outposts, and refineries."

"Guess you people did something to irk him, eh?" Lopez waved them to the pods again and disappeared into the ladder well.

The lounge wasn't a brig, but Casmir couldn't help but feel like a prisoner. How had his life turned so insane in less than twelve hours? And how had he managed to take his best friend down with him? He was glad he wasn't here alone but felt like a total ass for getting Kim involved in this. He'd intended to *protect* her, not the other way around.

Kim sat in a pod and looked out the porthole, perhaps wishing she'd had time to buy a few cases of quality coffee to bring along. He sat in the pod across from hers. It was bolted to a short track, so he could push it around and also have a view of the launch loop. He wished he could listen in on the captain's conversation with the customs agent. Were ships even allowed to take off in the middle of the night? He didn't know.

"I'm fairly certain our captain is a smuggler," Kim said.

"That's what I gathered. We knew when we headed to that special shipyard that we weren't likely to wind up with someone operating a legal business, right?"

"True. A legitimate transport wouldn't have taken us on without asking for ID."

Casmir leaned back in the pod, feeling claustrophobic as its insulated interior automatically tightened slightly to enrobe as much of his body as possible. Presumably, it got a lot tighter once they were hurtling along the tracks to build up speed to escape Odin's gravitational pull.

"The net has a record on her." Kim touched her temple to indicate she was accessing the network. "Bonita Laser Lopez from System Diomedes. She's listed as a bounty hunter, no warrants out for her arrest anywhere."

"That's promising. That she's not a known killer."

"*Known.* I wager a lot of things go unknown in the dark between the planets."

"I suppose so."

Casmir risked taking his own chip back online to access the net, not to look up their captain but to see if his name came up in any news stories. Unfortunately, he didn't know his birth mother's name, so he couldn't look her up. As a curious teenager, he'd tried to dig up information about his biological parents, but without knowing their names, it had been difficult. The agency that had placed him with his foster parents, who had eventually adopted him, had shut down a few years after the fact, leaving no contact information or records.

Casmir found his résumé and career highlights online, the papers he'd published over the years, even his grades from school. There wasn't anything in the public record about his three years working for military research, but that wasn't unexpected. That had all been classified work. The government hadn't wanted to announce the creation of the crushers. Casmir wondered how many of them existed these days. And how many were after him.

When he didn't find anything out of the ordinary on himself, he looked up the colleagues he'd worked with at the military research facility. A part of him dreaded what he would find. Had crushers also come to their doors and killed them all? He had been the team lead, but they had all contributed to the project. If he was being targeted, it seemed likely that they would be too. But by whom?

The Star Striders or Cosmic Hippies? Some group who resented mankind's warlike tendencies and tried their best to put a halt to them? The zealots from those religions usually protested terraforming and the destruction of native planets and moons, not the creation of robots. There were several anti-artificial-intelligence movements, but wouldn't it be hypocritical of them to use an AI to kill someone?

Nothing came up on the news about any of his old colleagues. Huh.

He risked sending a couple of messages to make sure they were all right. The part of him that had seen numerous spy dramas as a kid knew he should stay off the grid and not use his chip or a traceable comm system if he didn't want to be found, but the government should be the only institution with access to his chip coordinates. If *they* were after him... Well, he doubted there was anywhere he could go that would be out of the Kingdom's reach. Even if Odin and the habitats and stations in this system were the only entities under royal rule these days, King Jager had a long reach.

But one of the king's *knights* had come to warn him. So it wouldn't make sense for the government to be after him. Unless that knight had gone rogue for some reason.

He looked up Friedrich, but the first hit was an obituary. Casmir closed his eyes and dropped his face to his fist. He didn't need to scan the news stories to know what had happened. That man had given his life so Casmir would have time to escape.

But why?

"Customs is waving us through," came Lopez's relieved voice over a speaker. "We'll be on the loop in twenty minutes."

"Definitely a smuggler," Kim said, meeting Casmir's gaze, her contacts also flickering faintly with images from news feeds. "Does it bother you that we don't know where she's taking us?"

"I don't think *she* knows where she's taking us."

"Is that supposed to be reassuring?"

"Perhaps not. Would you like a hug?"

"You know my feelings on touching."

Casmir smiled. "Do you perplex your father and brothers as much as I suspect?"

He'd met her family. Her father, Haruto Sato, was a friendly, garrulous man who taught kendo and maintained the Shinto shrine in his neighborhood, leading weekly worship sessions for the community. Her half-brothers were also chatty and full of easy smiles.

"My brothers, a bit. My father just smiles understandingly and says I'm like my mother." Her mouth twisted with something bordering on distaste.

"You disagree?"

Kim shrugged. "I don't know her that well. She's always been gone on some archaeological exploration or another, trying to solve the mystery of the gate system and who built it. She's been all over the Twelve Systems. When I was a kid, I thought it was exciting and romantic and wanted to go with her." She looked out the porthole, but it was the middle of the night, and they were circling and waiting for their turn, so there wasn't much to see. "When I got older, I mostly wondered why she was never home. Why she'd bothered to have a kid if she was never going to be there to do anything with me."

"Was she flesh-and-blood when you were born?" In their previous chats regarding families, Casmir had always gotten the impression of a distant mother who hadn't quite been human even when Kim was growing up.

She shook her head. "Apparently, I was conceived ten years before I was born, before my parents split up, but she was busy with her career, so she had the embryo removed and suspended for later. Then she contracted a rare bacterial infection while on some water world that turned out to have life native to the system under the ice. Humans hadn't known about it prior to that and didn't know how to kill it. It was fascinating."

"Your suspended-embryo-self thought that?"

She shot him a dirty look. "I studied it later. When I was old enough to be interested in bacteria and the medical field."

"So, like ten?"

"I was seven, actually, when I first started studying the bacteria that killed her. Her body. The bacteria didn't pass the blood-brain barrier, so she was fully *compos mentis* when she uploaded her brain into her new... robot body. I guess you can't call it an android when it's only thirty pounds and has fur."

"Ah." Casmir had wondered if the woman might have been mentally compromised when she'd made that decision. "It's a monkey body, isn't it?"

"Don't remind me. She's weird."

"And your father says you're like her?"

"Kind of him, isn't it?"

Casmir scratched his jaw. "Maybe he means it to be. He doesn't seem like the type to insult people."

"I suppose not. Like I said, I never got to know her well. She once admitted that when she was dying, she regretted not having had her baby. That's why she rented an artificial womb and decided to have me even though she wasn't human anymore. Kingdom law forbade it—and my father was stunned that she wanted that, since they'd broken up years before—so she had me on Zhizhu Station in System Hind. I lived there with her until I was three, but her colleagues interested her in some new find, and she brought me back to live with my father, so she could go off cavorting around the galaxy. She visits some but..." She shrugged again.

Casmir thought that was as much as she would reveal—it was more than she'd ever told him before—but she spoke again.

"I should be over it by now, shouldn't I? I turned thirty-one last month, after all."

"Yes, I remember the celebratory wine." He smiled and waved a hand. "I guess, be glad that you've got your father and half-brothers, right?"

She spread her hand. "They are accepting, but you're the only one who doesn't think I'm odd."

He grinned. "Have you seen some of the people I work with? Wickmayer makes you answer trivia questions about spaceships before he'll talk to you. Chang only eats green foods. Simon writes love poems about prime numbers. Or maybe *to* prime numbers. You're one of the most normal people I know."

"I think that means you're a magnet for odd people, not that I'm normal."

"This is possible. But hey, other than the mother-in-a-monkey-body, I don't know if your background would be considered that unusual in the rest of the systems. They say you can find everything from marriages between twenty people to humans engineered to have both sex parts to people giving genius brains to their dogs and marrying *them*." Casmir didn't think he was the typical conservative Kingdom subject, but he wasn't quite open-minded enough not to find some of that strange. "And you know I can't judge the circumstances of anyone's birth when I don't know my own."

He was still floored by the idea that his true mother might be alive somewhere—and care enough to warn him about danger. Maybe. If she'd truly cared about him, why hadn't she ever come and seen him?

"So your mother could also be a monkey, and you just don't know it yet," Kim said.

"Exactly. Perhaps we could set up a mathematical experiment later to calculate the probabilities."

"Pod up, passengers," Lopez said over the comm. "We're up next."

"Off to see the odd rest of the galaxy," Casmir murmured as the ship shifted slightly and a *ker-chunk* emanated from somewhere below them. He could no longer see the launch loop from their porthole, so he assumed they were on it.

"What will the appropriate response be if we meet someone married to their dog?" Kim asked.

"I'm not worldly enough—galactic enough—to tell you."

His pod tightened automatically, a shield coming down to protect his head and padding molding to and pressing against his face. A surge of claustrophobia rushed through him. He sucked in a big breath, fear of being suffocated rearing within him. But he found he could breathe through the padding. And even see somewhat.

He had the sense of the ship moving along the tracks, but it was some time before he felt what had to be their acceleration. There was nothing to see out the porthole, which was good because his view of it was poor now. They climbed into the sky, fifty miles and more, then leveled off and shot along the track stretching high above the ocean, picking up speed with each passing second.

A slight feeling of pressure touched his chest but nothing like the three times Odin's gravity that he'd expected. He closed his eyes, waiting for the ship to escape the atmosphere and for his journey to truly begin.

"Another ship got onto the tracks right behind us," came Lopez's voice over the speaker, a little muffled by her own pod.

Casmir wanted to ask if that was typical or if they had something to worry about, but he simply closed his eyes and held on.

CHAPTER 6

DR. YAS PESHLAKAI PACED NEXT TO THE AIRLOCK, his medical bag in hand, his magnetic boots clanging faintly on the smooth metal deck of Captain Rache's ship, the *Fedallah.*

Usually, the vessel's spin gave it almost as much gravity as his home—his *former* home—on Tiamat Station, but it was stationary now, just outside the gravity well of the gas giant Saga and docked to Saga Kingdom Refinery Number 1. It was the first of two refineries the pirates—or respectable mercenaries, as the crew had often assured Yas they were during the last three months—had supposedly been hired to blow up.

He had no idea if any digital money would exchange bank accounts. From what he'd seen of Rache so far, the captain pillaged from Kingdom ships and stations at whim, leaving piles of dead bodies behind whenever he attacked. Military warships sent after him were either destroyed or simply never found him. Vessels from the rest of the systems did their best to avoid him.

At least the refineries were unmanned, automated robots and machinery the only possible recipients of the mercenaries' DEW-Tek bolts and explosives.

Yas shook his head, trying not to think about how he'd promised to do his best to keep these people alive for five years. Four years, nine months, and three days, now. Numerous times, he'd been tempted to go back on his word, to escape at the first chance, even wondering if the pirate captain might have set everything up that eventful night in order to acquire Yas as a doctor. But at the few ports they'd visited, Rache hadn't given Yas any chances to wander off on his own. Besides, Yas didn't have anywhere to go. According to all the news articles written about President Bakas's death, he had done it. He'd poisoned her and then run, proving his guilt. And now there was a bounty out for him, wanted alive or dead.

If Yas had remained on Tiamat Station, or even in the same system, maybe he could have hunted for the true murderer and tried to clear his name, but how could he do that from a hundred light years away? In five years, when his term with Rache was up, would anybody still care about President Bakas's death? Would there be any clues left to follow then?

A yellow light on the airlock control panel flashed, and the hatch hissed as it opened.

"Out of the way, Doc," one of the mercenary sergeants growled, stomping through the hatchway in full combat armor, a helmet shrouding his features.

He and the man behind him carried a pair of large cylindrical tanks that barely fit inside the airlock chamber. Yas stepped to the side to make room.

"Where's the captain? I saw that he was injured." Yas flicked a finger toward the display in the bulkhead. It showed Lieutenant Moon's camera feed as he walked next to Rache and several other men.

"Don't worry, Doc. If the captain dies, we'll let you live. You've got uses, even if you won't pick up a gun." The sergeant patted him on the shoulder as he stepped into the corridor. Actually, it was more of a punch.

Yas braced himself, not fazed by the abuse from the mercenaries. He'd suffered worse on the various sport teams he'd played on in his youth. What fazed him was that his life had gone to shit, and he was stuck out here with these ignorant jackasses, working for a man who'd made a career of killing people. What had he done to deserve this?

"Here, Doc," the corporal who stepped out behind the sergeant said. "Make yourself useful until we bring you someone to patch up."

He and the sergeant thrust the tanks at him. Yas juggled his medical kit so he could catch them, glad for the non-existent gravity.

"What are these?" Yas asked.

"What do you think they are, Dr. Genius?" The sergeant laughed as he and the corporal headed back into the airlock.

"Helium? We're stealing from the refinery?" Even as he objected, Yas realized how silly it sounded. Why not take some of the valuable gas before they blew it out of Saga's orbit?

"We're salvaging fuel from a wreck."

"It's not a wreck. It's a—"

"Oh, it'll be a wreck in about five minutes. What are you? One of King Jager's knights? We don't need any moral righteousness out here. Besides, we're making it easy on everyone. Merc ships need gas, the same as anyone else, but people get a little nervous when we show up at their fuel station. We—" The sergeant's helmet spun. "Shit. Cycle the lock, Varma."

The hatch clanged shut in front of Yas, and the light on the control panel flashed again. Yas looked toward the display.

Before, still, dark rooms full of machinery and tanks had stretched ahead of the main force. Now, huge boxy security robots with thrusters jetted toward Rache's team. Lieutenant Moon's helmet cam had provided a stable feed, but now, it jerked dizzily as he and the others ran for cover, firing at their mechanical enemies. Mechanical enemies that fired back, defending the refinery.

A shot struck one of the men in the shoulder, and his boots came free of the deck. He started to float away in the zero-gravity environment, but one of the other mercenaries grabbed him and pulled him back down. He was the smallest of the group, and Yas recognized him even though they all wore the featureless helmets and black armor.

Captain Rache.

He fired a grenade launcher toward the charging robot defenders. It detonated when it clanged off, and light flashed, the effect underwhelming in zero gravity. Six androids jetted down from above, landing in the middle of the mercs.

The captain spun and leaped at one with cybernetically enhanced speed and strength. He punched, thrusting one android into a tank, but another lunged in and wrapped powerful arms around his torso. Rache drove an elbow into his foe's chest, ducking and twisting free. A lightning-fast kick hurled the android toward the approaching robots. It bounced off, twisting to stop its momentum and jet back into the fray.

The lieutenant's helmet jerked and jumped as an android grabbed him and shook him. Yas looked away from the display, the battle too confusing to follow like that.

He tapped the chest controls on his suit. His helmet unfolded from its slot between his shoulders, spread over his head, and snapped to the rest of his suit. That gave him access to the combat channel. And a lot of cursing.

"...weren't supposed to be this many defenses!"

"We're fucked."

"The captain was shot!"

Yas bit his lip. Should he go over there and try to help? He started to push a hand through his hair, but his fingers bumped the thin, nearly impervious Glasnax of his helmet. He didn't have any weapons, and nothing in his medkit would stop robots or androids.

"Look out, sir!" someone cried.

A tangle of curses came from several mouths.

Yas closed his eyes, waiting for the comm ordering him to come help Rache. Or maybe a comm saying it was too late to help Rache.

It was selfish, but Yas's main concern was what these mercenaries would do to him if the captain died. He hadn't won a lot of friends thus far, refusing to engage the thuggish brutes in conversation. Few of them had educations or followed the news, and their favorite topics were excrement, masturbation, and how many women they were going to bang during their next shore leave.

Rache was different, with a cultured way of speaking and a tendency to reference classic books and recent articles on science and technology, but he didn't deign to converse with Yas or anyone else often. To call him a companion would be a grave presumption. He was the leader of the ship, and that was it. His presence ended arguments whenever he entered a room, and Yas had little doubt that he was the sole reason any order existed among the rough mercenaries.

Someone's scream echoed through the helmet speaker, and the audio feed ended abruptly. The display on the wall went black.

Yas stared at the hatch, wondering if anyone would make it back.

"Bridge?" Yas asked, switching to the ship's internal comm channel. "Are they still alive over there?"

"Shit, Doc, that you? Cowering in the corridor instead of over there helping them?"

"The captain told me to stay here."

The comm officer grunted and didn't respond. Or give an update.

Yas was on the verge of going up to the bridge when the airlock light flashed again. Still holding the tanks, if only to keep them from floating away, he stepped out of the way.

"Dodger," the captain's voice sounded over the channel, ridiculously calm. "We're cycling in. Get ready to depart. Quickly. We've set timed charges."

"Understood, Captain," the ship's pilot said.

The hatch swung open, and the first six men in the boarding party strode out.

"Doc, I got a hangnail," one announced. "Need you to fix it."

The man behind him punched him. "Moon's dead. Shut your hole."

"Mercs die. That's how it is. Ought to kiss the captain's ass that it doesn't happen that often on this ship."

The men strode past, ignoring Yas, nobody offering to take the tanks. The hatch shut automatically so the airlock could cycle for the second half of the team.

"If you need help," Yas called after them, "head to sickbay. I'll be there shortly."

Nobody acknowledged him.

When the hatch opened again, the captain strode out with four more men. One less than had gone over. Skin and blood showed through a hole in the captain's armor. Yas gaped, wondering what had struck him that could pierce the strong alloy.

"Pod up," the captain ordered his men. "We're not sticking around to watch the fireworks."

Several curt renditions of "Yes, sir" sounded, and his men strode away.

"Chief," Rache said over the ship channel, "got some fuel here for you to pick up."

Chief Engineer Khonsari's distracted, "Yes, sir," came in response.

"Lieutenant Moon?" Yas asked when only he and the captain remained in the corridor.

"A round blew his head off," Rache said matter-of-factly. "Even you couldn't have saved him."

"Was it worth it?" Yas looked at the captain's injured shoulder and waved for him to head to sickbay.

Rache didn't move. His voice turned uncharacteristically savage when he said, "It's always worth it to strike against the Kingdom. I am noting for the future that Jager has drastically increased security in his unmanned refineries. He must have been expecting trouble. We shouldn't have lost anyone on a job like this." His jaw might have clenched inside the helmet. He definitely sounded pissed. Because he cared about losing a man? Or was he merely irked that he'd made a mistake and lost one of the pawns on his chess board?

"You know," Yas said carefully, probing a little, "most of the Twelve Systems aren't particularly worried about King Jager's ambitions."

"Then they'll be all the easier for him to surprise and take advantage of when he makes his move. Do you not believe he had a hand in your president's death?"

Yas almost mentioned that he'd wondered if *Rache* was the one whose hand had been involved in that, but he caught himself in time.

"It's possible that Kingdom supporters were behind it," Yas said, "but they're naive if they think our station or any other station or world in our system would give up their independence and succumb to Kingdom rule again."

Or was *he* the naive one to believe that? He thought of the short discussion he'd had with President Bakas the last time he'd seen her alive. *Someone* wanted back in the Kingdom badly enough to have ordered a good woman assassinated.

"Don't be so certain, Doctor. The universe has become a strange place. Many people long for the old ways, for a time when the worlds around them made more sense, and what it meant to be human was more clear cut." Rache started up the corridor, the helmet on his armor folding back, but not his mask. Never his mask.

Yas had never seen Rache's face, nor did he have a medical record on him in sickbay.

A lot of the crew's records didn't contain detailed background information, but they at least listed blood types, drug usage, and biological and cybernetic implants. Yas knew nothing about the captain. As far as he'd heard, none of the crew did.

They reached the intersection where one could turn toward sickbay and engineering or toward the bridge. Rache strode toward the bridge.

"Sir?" Yas pointed toward sickbay. "There are droplets of blood floating away from your shoulder."

Rache looked at the wound. "It's not that bad. I'll have the chief fix my suit."

"Not that bad? It looks like a spear went clean through your shoulder." He peered around to Rache's back, but the suit hadn't been pierced on that side. That didn't mean his statement wasn't correct.

"It will heal."

"Not unless you come to sickbay and let me clean that and glue it shut. Punctures get infected easily."

"I paid for regenerative wound-healing enhancements and the best immune system you can buy."

"At least let me give you a painkiller."

Rache hesitated. His injury *had* to hurt. Had he pulled whatever spike or lance had made it out on his own?

"I've got my own. A couple of the other men will be waiting for you." Rache nodded toward sickbay, then strode toward the bridge.

"Your doctor advises against self-medication and treatment," Yas called after him.

"Noted," Rache said without looking back or slowing down.

Yas watched his back, wondering what secrets he was hiding. Why didn't he want his new doctor to help him? Because he thought Yas would take a sample of his blood and identify him?

"Who are you, Captain Rache?" Yas murmured softly.

The ship accelerated away from the refinery, the force pushing him against a bulkhead. He would have to find a pod soon.

He glanced back at the bulkhead. The display showed a feed again, this time from one of the ship's exterior cameras. It was focused on the blocky gray contours of the refinery as they flew away, the planet Saga's huge, cloudy blue surface and pale rings visible beyond it.

Then the refinery blew up, not as impressively as it would have in an oxygen-rich atmosphere, but enough to leave no doubt that it had been utterly destroyed. Another strike against the Kingdom.

Bonita waited until they'd escaped Odin's gravity and were sailing away from the planet before sending messages and trying to find someone who wanted to buy state-of-the-art weapons at a reasonable price. Delivery included, anywhere in the system.

Probably.

She glanced at the gauge showing her hydrogen reserves and grimaced. The fusion drive was working, which was good, but her tanks were low. She'd expected to get paid on Odin and be able to buy fuel before leaving the system again.

Qin stepped into the hatchway. "Captain?"

"Yes?"

"Do you think it's all right if I talk to the passengers?"

Bonita frowned over her shoulder. "They're not wandering around, are they?"

The *Stellar Dragon* had escaped Odin's atmosphere, and their current acceleration gave them about a third of the planet's gravity. If Kim and Casmir had spent as much of their lives on the planet as Bonita suspected, they would be marveling at the sensation of feeling significantly lighter than usual.

"They're still in the lounge, I think. I just wanted to ask them about knights. I've been curious, and who better to know than someone from Odin?"

"About knights?" Bonita asked. "Why?"

The last thing Bonita wanted was to hear about the Kingdom's uptight law enforcers. She glanced at her scanner display, aware of the ship that had come off the launch loop right after them. It made her uneasy that it was heading in the same direction as the *Stellar Dragon*, especially since Bonita hadn't programmed in a course yet.

"Like I said, I've never seen a knight, except in vids. I was hoping I would get a chance while we were on Odin, but our visit was so short." Qin's feline face took on a fully human and wistful visage.

"I thought we discussed this." Bonita made her voice gentle. "A Kingdom knight isn't going to… approve of what you are. You're better off avoiding them."

"Maybe one would understand that this—" Qin gestured to her body, "—wasn't my choice. And he would be nice about it. And noble. In the stories, knights are always noble and gentlemanly to women." There was that wistful sigh again.

"I think you should stop reading romances. Try some thrillers. Or cozy mysteries. Have you heard of Debra Croon? She's a hundred and eighty years old, or something close, and has written more than two hundred novels in her Moons of Pegasus series. The same sentient cats have been helping her heroine solve crimes for all that time."

Qin wrinkled her nose. "Sounds kind of boring."

"*I* like them." Bonita waved toward the corridor. "I'd wait a few days to let our guests get settled in and used to… things, but go ahead and talk to them if you like. Just don't mention our cargo."

"I won't."

"And don't get too upset if they treat you like an oddity."

"I won't." Qin skipped off down the corridor.

Skipped. Bonita's hired killing machine skipped. Well, so long as she blew crushers off the ship when needed, that was fine.

Bonita returned to sending messages. Unfortunately, since this wasn't a system she traveled through often, and this wasn't her preferred kind of work, she didn't have many contacts here. She envisioned herself standing at an intersection at one of the space stations, trying to sell the weapons one by one out of a trench coat. That would *not* be ideal.

After she sent her messages, she grabbed pictures of her new passengers from the ship's internal cameras and fed them into a network search. She *should* have researched them before taking them on board, but that liftoff had been far hastier than expected.

"Casmir Dabrowski," she read as his face and bio came up in a corner of the star-filled navigation display. "Professor and robotics team lead at Zamek University."

As she skimmed through, she decided he was exactly what he'd claimed to be. A few news stories popped up after the initial entry, and she saw something about an explosion at his workplace and the fact that he hadn't been seen since then.

"An explosion caused by crushers?" It didn't say specifically, but Bonita's jaw clenched as her suspicion grew. If those robots had been here for Casmir, and he hadn't thought to mention it to her, she would be very irritated.

She didn't know how ubiquitous the crushers were on Odin, but when she searched specifically for them, she didn't find anything. She began to suspect they hadn't had anything to do with the *Stellar Dragon* or its cargo.

There weren't any interesting news stories about Kim Sato, other than one from a few months earlier that mentioned her along with a couple of other scientists in an article on advancements in creating human-implantable bacteria capable of consuming radiation. Trials were supposedly being conducted by the military now.

Bonita touched a hand to her stomach, uneasy at the mention of a human-implantable bacteria, but she knew a lot of spacers who'd died to some cancer or another over the years. Sometimes they were curable, and sometimes not. Sometimes, it was the seventh or eighth one that got a person. No matter how much shielding a ship got, it wasn't as good at keeping out radiation as a planet with a magnetosphere. Or even a habitat buried in an asteroid under miles of rock.

"Perhaps it is fortunate that you have acquired these individuals," Viggo said, no doubt monitoring her search.

"How so?"

"If we run into Kingdom law enforcers who are irked that you tried to sell a stockpile of weapons to revolutionaries on their planet—"

"Baum said he was a *loyalist*, not a revolutionary." Which she no longer believed, since he'd been attacked by what had likely been Kingdom Guard robots and drones.

"—you could use the passengers to barter for passage out of the system," Viggo finished, ignoring her interruption.

"Use them like hostages, you mean?" Bonita asked. "I'd like to think I'm more honorable than that."

Though it was admittedly easier to be honorable when one's bank account and fuel tanks weren't running on fumes.

"One must take care of oneself out in the wide expanse of space." As Viggo spoke, one of his cleaning robots zipped in, climbed the bulkhead to reach the control console, and started vacuuming between the switches.

"Especially when it comes to germs?"

"Precisely so. But I was thinking of other dangers today. Did you notice that ship is still following us?"

"I noticed that it hasn't set a course yet, the same as we haven't set a course."

"From what I remember of being human, there's not much appeal to ambling aimlessly through space. Courses are set, usually with great intention, to take advantage of the gravitational pull of other orbiting bodies in the system."

"I know, Viggo. I'm watching it."

A ping sounded, the first response to one of her messages. Diego from one of the system's pirate families. Dealing with pirates wasn't ideal, but at least he was originally from System Diomedes, the same as she, and they'd crossed paths before. Admittedly, she would sell to just about anyone now.

"Laser Lopez," the mustachioed man who appeared on the display said, "you still between the stars?"

"Rarely these ones."

She waited, expecting a delay. The comm said he was calling from Forseti Station, the system trade hub, shipyard, and fuel depot orbiting between the gas giants Freyja and Freyr. She suspected he was rerouting the comm to make it appear that it came from the station but that his family's ships were lurking within the murky layers of clouds on one of those planets. Only the most elite and wealthiest of the pirate families could afford slydar stealth technology that hid their ships' heat signatures. Others made do with what nature offered.

"I understand you have some cargo you're looking to sell cheap," Diego said.

"I don't remember mentioning that it would be cheap. This is prime, top-of-the-line equipment, straight out of the pristine labs of Sayona Station. There's not a speck of dust on any of it." She ignored the cleaning robot now defying what modest gravity the ship currently had by vacuuming up the side of the bulkhead.

"But your original deal went south, no? And you need to hit the gate out of the Kingdom's lovely system?"

"Odd, none of that was in my comm."

"I can read between the words, señora. You send a full list of the contents of your cargo, and I'll make you an offer. How long until you reach Forseti?"

"Viggo?" Bonita asked.

"Due to the current favorable alignment of Odin with the gas giants, only a week and a half."

"You hear that, Diego?" Bonita didn't like the idea of sending exactly what she had, especially since she hadn't seen inside the big case to verify its contents, but she couldn't expect Diego to make the trip without knowing what he was buying. She also knew the pirate families wouldn't report to the Kingdom Guard or any other government agency. They might report to other pirates... but she had to take that risk. The weapons were cutting edge, but they weren't so unique or proprietary that criminals should flock after her for them.

She assumed. A glance at that other ship on her scanner made her question that assumption.

"I heard. Some of my people will be there to make an offer." Diego smiled. "If everything is as top-of-the-line and dust free as you say."

The vacuum rolled across the ceiling above Bonita's head. "It's *definitely* dust free."

"See you soon, *señora*."

As soon as his face disappeared from the display, Bonita thumped her fist on the console. "Really, Viggo? Your little robots need to clean while I'm on the comm?"

"They clean all the time, just not always in the cabin you're in. One must keep ahead of dirt and grime to ensure enough for an avalanche does not form."

"How could an avalanche of grime *possibly* form on the ceiling over my head? Program in the best course for Forseti, please."

"Yes, Captain. Do you believe your pirate contact intends to deal fairly?"

"*Fairly?* No. But predictably, I suspect so."

Fortunately, she didn't need a fair deal. Baum had paid for most of the merchandise. She only needed to cover what she'd paid to pick it up—the balance he'd owed—and what it had cost her to make the trip. It would be nice to make a profit, but at this point, she would be delighted to break even.

As Viggo altered the ship's course, pointing them out toward the distant points of light that represented the gas giants, Bonita watched the other ship. It was going to be telling if it set a course to follow them.

CHAPTER 7

CASMIR GRIMACED WHEN KIM THWACKED HIM IN THE thigh with her wooden sword.

"Stop bouncing so much," Kim ordered. "You're making yourself an easy target. And putting yourself in danger of hitting your head on the ceiling. Again."

"Sorry, the low gravity is weird."

His stomach agreed. He'd been lying down for much of the last three days, wishing the motion-sickness tablets he'd consumed had helped more than they had.

This was the first day he'd felt reasonably normal. He'd made the mistake of coming to the lounge where he'd found Kim jogging on a treadmill with straps that pulled her down, simulating the higher gravity of Odin. An odd glee had entered her eyes when she spotted him, and she'd pounced, thrusting a sword at him and offering to teach him a few moves. Assuming she was bored without her work, Casmir had agreed. His battered thighs assured him that had been a mistake, but at least it had kept his mind off his problems for an hour. He was frustrated by his lack of progress in finding out who had sent the crushers.

"Doesn't it bother you?" he asked.

"Some. I'm getting used to it. It's better than the near-zero-g of Gjoll Station."

"Oh, right. I'd forgotten you had to spend a couple of months at the orbital station."

"For my early work on radiation-eating bacteria. Since it was designed to live inside space-faring humans, I had to make sure microgravity wouldn't negatively affect it. I suggested to my advisor that I could simply send instructions and samples up to the research scientists already working up there, but Dr. Yamada always liked to torment me." Kim lowered her sword and stared at the diamond gridding of the deck. "I haven't sent any messages to my colleagues because I haven't wanted to lead anyone to you, but I have a number of worried inquiries in my inbox. People are wondering what happened to me, and I feel bad letting them believe… I'm not sure what they believe. I am known for not responding to messages for a few days, but it's not like me to miss work."

"Kim, return your messages, please. Before we get so far out that the network is flaky." Casmir didn't know if that ever truly became a problem, as there were relay satellites throughout the system, but at the least, there would be a long time delay as they flew farther from Odin. "I appreciate you not wanting to help them—whoever they are—find me, but I don't want your family and friends to think you got sucked into a robotic trash compacter on the way home from work."

"You haven't figured out who *they* are, yet?" Kim sounded surprised.

Because she assumed he was a decent researcher? He wasn't horrible, but scouring the public and university networks hadn't given him any clues, and it wasn't as if he had access to government databases or could comm the king and ask to speak with friends of the late Sir Friedrich. The elusive knights were notorious for not publishing their personal contact information.

Casmir shrugged helplessly. "No. I keep checking the capital's news and searching for mentions of myself. I have been reported missing, and the parking-garage fire and knight's death were covered. None of the major networks spoke specifically of the crushers, but I found some footage on a conspiracy node. I'm guessing the government is squelching the stuff it has control over, since the crushers are supposed to be a secret weapon for the military."

"No mention of our rental? I hope that means the house is still standing. With all my books unmolested."

"Me too. The conspiracy node, which may or may not be a reliable resource, reported that a group of knights have been assigned to find out where the crushers came from and who's responsible for them. Apparently, a few went missing from a military facility a couple of months ago, which implies… I'm not sure. Maybe that someone has been gunning for me for a while? I've been raking through the compost heap of my brain and trying to guess what I might know or have done that would have prompted someone to try to kill me."

"Multiple times."

"Technically, I believe that was all part of one mission, the crushers being programmed to assassinate me. And keep coming after me until they succeeded."

"Lovely."

"I'm assuming at this point that it's *not* the government. The king shouldn't have any reason to hate me. He never came to our research lab. I doubt he even knows that I exist."

"There are numerous arms and factions within the government."

"True."

"And King Jager's focus is reputed to be outward now, not inward."

Casmir nodded. Maybe he shouldn't rule out anyone yet.

Kim looked out the porthole to the black blanket filled with stars, the white dots far brighter and crisper than they were when filtered through Odin's atmosphere. "Have you talked to the captain about our destination? We passed Odin's moon and orbital stations the first day."

Casmir hated to admit that, until today, his stomach had kept him in his bunk and disinterested in caring what their destination was. He'd managed his net searches in between bouts of nausea and vertigo. Kim knew most of his weaknesses, so it wasn't like it mattered, but he hated to remind her of them. He hated to remind *himself.*

"I haven't. I was just so glad to get away…" His eye blinked a few times of its own accord. "I'll talk to her soon. She's feeding us, or allowing us access to the boxed rations, so I don't think she means to kill us, but we shouldn't trust her blindly."

"Clearly, you haven't tried the coffee bulbs." Kim gave him a baleful look. Most of the time, her face was impassive, but substandard caffeine options brought out her vitriolic side.

"My stomach hasn't been requesting acidic beverages."

"There are twenty-seven ingredients in the coffee-and-cream bulb. The shelf-life is fifty years. I don't think *radiation* is the reason why people get cancer out here."

"Maybe you can create a nice intestinal bacteria to help digest strange preservatives."

Kim lowered her sword and stepped closer to him. Fortunately, not to thwack him again. She glanced toward the ceiling. Had she spotted cameras up there?

"Will you talk to her? You know I'm not any good at…" She spread her fingers and shrugged.

"People?"

Her eyelids drooped. "I was looking for a word that conveyed my inability to grasp when individuals are lying to me. And also that I struggle to persuade them to tell me things."

"I think I got the right word." He grinned.

"Fine, fine. But if she's heading for the gate to take us to another system, I want to know about it. So we can figure out a way to stop her. If she doesn't get rid of us soon, it's going to be obvious she has some profit motive for keeping us. Otherwise, why wouldn't she have dropped us off at the moon base?"

"I don't know, but if that's not her destination, it would have taken her hours to land and take off again. And that ship was following us." He realized he didn't know if that was still true. He *did* need to talk to the captain.

"Maybe, but, Casmir, I refuse to be kidnapped. I'm not going to just disappear from my work and my *life* for months." Kim stabbed agitatedly at the air with her sword.

The hatch opened, and Casmir whirled, worried Lopez had been listening in and wasn't pleased about what she'd heard. Normally, he wouldn't be that concerned about his safety on a ship run by two women, but he'd watched the footage of Qin wrestling with that crusher. No normal human being of either sex would have been able to hold out that long against the powerful robot.

It was Qin, not Lopez, who stepped inside and looked curiously at them. Her face was mostly human, and elegantly human at that, but the pointed ears that perked out of her black hair were definitely not human.

She didn't come farther into the cabin, pausing with… uncertainty?

Casmir, afraid he'd been staring, smiled and gave her a cheerful, "Hello, ma'am. Have you come to tell us where we're going?"

"Ma'am?" She appeared bemused at the address.

Casmir wondered how old she was.

"You can call me Liangyu. Or Qin. That seems easier for everyone."

"Qin is your surname, right?" Kim asked, then, when Qin nodded, asked a few words in one of the old Earth languages. Chinese?

Qin shrugged helplessly. "I don't know any other languages except System Trade. I was born in a lab and don't have any parents, any culture, anything but my name to suggest what all was spliced together to create me. I think the geneticist mostly looked in the fridge and pulled out all of his leftovers."

Casmir stared at her. "That's... a joke?"

"Uhm, sort of."

"Sorry, I don't know much about genetic engineering."

"I wish I didn't," Qin said softly.

"You probably know it's one of a handful of sciences that the Kingdom forbids. We're supposed to be humanity's seed bank. Tamper-free. They don't even gene-clean newborns with issues." His eye blinked, and he sighed at his body's willingness to demonstrate his genetic eccentricities.

Kim nudged him in the back. "If you *do* end up hiding out in another system, that might be a good time for you to see what can be done to you as an adult."

"Yeah," Casmir said noncommittally.

If he'd wanted that badly enough, he could have set aside the time and money to make a trip to an off-world hospital at some point, but he feared that any surgeries would come with side effects or that things would end up worse, that his brain wouldn't be able to adjust its circuits after thirty-odd years of operating one way. And, as always, he feared hospitals, of something going horribly wrong, or of them finding some worse malady lurking in his blood.

"Might be better for you than the brain surgery," Kim murmured.

"Yeah," Casmir repeated, not without a shudder.

His doctor had once suggested an operation to install a responsive neurostimulation device to stop his seizures, but that would have involved opening up his *skull*.

Qin tilted her head, probably hearing every murmured word with those unique ears. "Would you be permitted to return to Odin if your genes were altered? We were scanned to ensure we did not bring produce with viable seeds to your world." She smiled. "The captain was worried about the wea— about something else being discovered in the scan, but your customs officers only cared about seeds."

"People are permitted to leave and have medical issues addressed," Casmir said, "so long as it's not done in such a way that genetic changes will be passed on to your offspring."

"Because it would be horrible if you had children born without defects," Kim said dryly.

"You should be happy they let you do the work they do," Casmir told her. "I've never quite understood why it's acceptable to tinker with bacteria but not with food or human or animal embryos."

"Because the king wants those radiation-eating bacteria perfected for our cancer-prone, space-faring military officers."

"Do you know any knights?" Qin asked.

Casmir tried to tie that into their previous conversation but decided there was no tie. Maybe she had grown bored of talk of genes.

"I've met a few in passing." Casmir tried not to think about Sir Friedrich. Kim shook her head.

"That's disappointing," Qin said. "I was hoping—well, I thought they might be all over on Odin. We didn't get much time to stay."

"They're not all over. With few exceptions, you have to be of noble blood to become a knight, and even then, there's an extensive training program that has a high dropout rate. The Kingdom Guard and municipal police handle most crime on the planet."

"Oh." She seemed disappointed.

"Qin, do you know where we're going?" Casmir asked. "The captain didn't tell me."

"You've been in your cabin the whole trip."

"My horizontal position didn't make me less curious about where we're going."

"Forseti Station," Qin said with a shrug, as if there was no reason to lie or for him not to know.

Casmir found that reassuring. Kim's talk of kidnapping and profit motives had made him uneasy.

He hoped he would have better luck with his research on a big hub like Forseti. If he still couldn't find anything on the net, maybe he could hire a private investigator. How much did that cost? Maybe Kim had researched it for one of her novels and knew.

Lopez jumped through the open hatch. "Qin, we're going to have company. Help me make sure everything vital is hidden. We're going to push out some of our supplies in the hope that they'll believe that's all we're carrying."

"Yes, Captain," Qin said, as Casmir blurted, "Company? What *kind* of company?"

"The kind that's been following us since the launch loop on Odin." Lopez pinned him with an accusing stare.

Casmir gripped the bar of the fold-out treadmill.

"You think they're coming for your cargo?" he asked, though that stare suggested she thought he was the cause of the trouble again.

Was he? If those two crushers had survived their drop into the ocean and made it to shore, they could have taken a ship. Or they could have uploaded the details of their chase to someone's server. They'd seen which ship Casmir had gotten on, so if they knew where the *Stellar Dragon* was, they knew where he was. Now, he wished he had asked Lopez to drop them off after the skirmish, so he could have found passage on another ship, but his finances wouldn't have allowed for that, even if she'd agreed. He'd given all the gold he had to her.

"It's possible," Lopez said, "but I think it's more possible they're after *you*."

"Oh." Casmir decided it would be unmanly to hide from her wrath behind one of the pods.

"You can't outrun them?" Kim asked.

"No. Trust me, I've tried. Whatever's driving that ship—it's a new dolphin-class dreadnought out of Yug Daegu Shipyard—it's got more power than we do. They matched our acceleration the first day, and they've been creeping closer ever since."

Kim looked at Casmir, maybe thinking what he was, that it would have been nice if Lopez had updated them earlier.

"The *Stellar Dragon* has a railgun we can take potshots at them with, but in the end, we're just a freighter. They have a lot more weapons. I'd rather not get blown to pieces over this."

Over *him*. She didn't say it, but that cool stare was leveled Casmir's way again.

He dropped his gaze to the deck, not surprised that she was displeased. He had asked for passage without giving her any indication that someone was pursuing him. That had been rude and disingenuous. It hadn't occurred to him at the time that he was being duplicitous; he'd just believed he had escaped the crushers and would be able to get away before they caught up again.

"You two better finding a hiding spot," Lopez said.

Qin had already disappeared. Lopez ducked into the corridor and headed for the cargo hold.

"At least it doesn't sound like she intends to turn us over to that ship." Casmir wondered if crushers were piloting it, or if he would finally get a chance to talk to human beings, human beings who might be schmoozed into explaining why they were after him.

"I doubt she'd tell us if she did." Kim pushed the exercise equipment back into the wall and closed the cabinet door.

"I better talk to them." Casmir headed for the hatch.

"To who? Qin and the captain?"

"No, whoever's following us."

"That's not how you hide, Casmir."

"I could interface my chip with the ship's communications computer so I could talk to them from under my bunk, but I'm not sure that would be more effective."

Kim gave him a disgusted look, but she followed him to navigation.

It was empty. Clangs and thumps echoed up from the bottom level of the ship as Qin and Lopez moved things around in the cargo hold. A rear camera showed a black pyramid-shaped cruiser coming up behind them, the tip ready to ram them in the backside. Or more likely, the ship would come alongside them for a forced boarding. Casmir's mind boggled at the idea of doing that at the speed the ships were going, but he'd seen it in news vids before. The computer systems for coordinating airlock attachments had to be extremely sophisticated.

He looked for the comm panel among equipment that hadn't been built to Kingdom standards and was labeled in a language he didn't recognize. No doubt, it belonged to whatever culture had thought building a sauna and a salt-crystal room in the ship's lavatory was a normal thing.

He poked a couple of buttons under the universal symbol for network-to-network contact.

"Maybe you should ask the captain before comming them," Kim said. "Or randomly pushing buttons on her console."

"Always a wise idea," a bland voice said.

Casmir whirled, thinking some new crew member had appeared behind them, but the words had come from a speaker.

"As the operating system, automatic pilot, and resident wit for the *Stellar Dragon*," the voice said, "I'm afraid I can't let you tinker or comm other ships without Bonita's permission."

"Bonita?" Casmir mouthed.

"I like Laser better," Kim said.

"Thanks so much for sharing my name with strangers, Viggo," Lopez said, stepping into navigation and frowning at Kim and Casmir. The pistol that usually hung in her holster was in her hand. "What are you two doing up here? I believe I said *hide*, not take over the ship."

Casmir lifted his hands. "That wasn't our intent. We want to talk to the people on the other ship."

"We?" Kim also lifted her hands, but her frown was for him, not Lopez.

"*I*," Casmir corrected. "I, I, I. If it's I—me that they want, I'm going to let them know they can have me. I don't want you or Qin to get into any more trouble on my account, Captain."

"Noble," Lopez said sarcastically. "But I've already tried comming them. I've tried numerous times in the last three days. They're not answering."

"If they're looking for me, maybe they would answer me."

Lopez waved her pistol at the comm panel. "If you want to see if you're special, go right ahead."

She didn't holster her weapon, but Casmir felt more comfortable when it was pointed at the deck instead of his chest.

"Comm them, Viggo."

"Certainly, Captain." After a few seconds, the computer added, "I'm attempting to get through now. If you wish to send a message, you may do so."

Lopez eyed Casmir, and he nodded and said, "This is Casmir Dabrowski. If you're looking for me, I'm prepared to turn myself over without a fight if you leave this ship alone."

Silence stretched. Lopez yawned and used the tip of her pistol barrel to scratch the side of her head. A few more clangs drifted up from the levels below. How much illicit cargo was there for Qin to move around?

"Are you *sure* they're after me?" Casmir asked Lopez.

"No, but they've had a long flight just to retrieve fifty thousand Union dollars in weapons if that's what they want."

"You think I'm more valuable than fifty thousand Union dollars? I'm flattered. If I'm doing the exchange calculation correctly, it takes me almost a year to earn that much at home."

"I don't know what you're worth, kid. We might be about to find out."

Casmir, who hadn't been called *kid* in years, eyed the hulking pyramid ship. He got more of a feel for its size as it came alongside the *Dragon*.

It was easily ten times larger than the freighter, so he was surprised it had fit on the Odin launch loop. Four humongous thrusters jutted out of the back end. He would have guessed the ship could reach orbital escape velocity without the assistance of the loop, but maybe they'd wanted to save their fuel. Or maybe they'd wanted to stay close to him.

"They are preparing to extend docking clamps and an airlock tube, Captain," Viggo said. "Do you wish to cooperate or shall I object to their familiarity?"

"I'd love to object, but look at the guns on that thing. And those are missile launchers. They've probably got nukes nestled up in there." Lopez shook her head. "I'm going to head to the airlock and greet them. Politely. You never know. They may be interested in buying some weapons and willing to pay more than Diego."

"Given their size and rude silence thus far," Viggo said, "it seems unlikely that they would be willing to pay for anything that they can take."

"They can try." Lopez stuffed her pistol in its holster and strode out of navigation.

Casmir started after her, but Kim stopped him with a hand.

"Where are you going?" she asked.

"With her. I'll stand next to her and give myself up if I'm what they want. But you should hide up here somewhere. Nobody should want you."

"Thanks so much."

"You know what I mean." Casmir looked at the massive ship on the display. "But do me a favor, will you? Look up the schematics for that ship. If we can get the layout, maybe we can do something."

"Like what?"

Casmir picked up a cleaning robot that was circling the pods. Suction treads on the bottom of its frame accounted for its ability to climb walls and maneuver across the ceiling.

"I'm not sure yet. But keep this for me, please." He handed the robot to Kim and jogged after Lopez.

"If you want souvenirs, I'm sure the Forseti Station gift shop has something less dented," Kim called after him.

"I'm not positive we'll ever make it there."

"Wonderful."

CHAPTER 8

ONITA STOOD NEXT TO THE AIRLOCK HATCH, HER arms folded over her chest and her pistol in a holster on her belt. Qin was hiding, the cargo was hiding, and if the two nuisances she'd picked up on Odin were smart, they were hiding too. Qin wouldn't *stay* hidden if there was a fight, but Bonita would prefer to have her as a secret weapon rather than starting the game with that card face-up.

She did not like that the other ship hadn't communicated with them before presuming to lock up, and she had been tempted to raid her small armory for explosives that could hurt even armored soldiers. But the last thing she wanted was to fight a battle in her own cargo hold and have the intruders blow holes in the side of her ship. This trip would end for her extremely quickly if that happened.

As much as it galled her, it would be better to pretend to be helpless and let them have what they wished. Especially if that was Casmir. She didn't owe him anything, and it would be a relief to get him off her ship before more of those crushers showed up. With luck, the intruders would leave her alone once they had him.

A faint *clunk-ting* emanated from the airlock chamber. They were coming.

Casmir jogged out of the corridor and across the hold to join her. He didn't have any weapons, which wasn't surprising since he hadn't arrived with any. She was a little surprised he hadn't asked to borrow something, but she was glad. A passenger on her own ship could blow holes in the hull as easily as an intruder.

"What are you doing?" Bonita asked.

"Preparing to give myself up to prevent you and your ship from being troubled further."

She squinted at him. She wasn't positive that was truly what he'd been planning when she'd caught him in navigation earlier. If he was smart enough to build robots, he was probably smart enough to make up a story on the fly. Was it possible he knew more about who was following them than he'd let on?

"How was my hand-raising earlier?" Casmir lifted his hands over his head, empty palms open. "Sufficient to appease criminals? I want to get it right." He lowered them, then raised them again, as if she were some cartoon bank robber with a gun poked against his spine.

"Are you more dangerous than you seem?" Bonita asked him. "Or are you truly a doofus?"

"I don't think anyone has ever called me dangerous, but a doofus? I'd like to keep looking for adjectives, if it's all the same to you."

A knock more like the bang of rifle fire came from the hatch. The mirrored faceplate of a helmet and the gray airlock tube extending toward the other ship were all she could see through the small round window. A gloved hand came up, showing a Tac-75 explosive, detonator ready to be set if she didn't open the hatch.

Bonita released the lock and stepped back, not bothering to draw her pistol. She had no idea how many enemies were about to stomp onto her ship, but that first one was in heavy combat armor. Her galaxy suit was rated to take some damage, but that man could walk through a field of flying bullets and energy bolts while yawning and scratching his armpit, and he would feel nothing.

The hatch swung open, and six armored figures strode into the hold.

Casmir scurried back, lest his foot be stepped on, but he also peered into the airlock chamber and down the tube attaching them to the other ship. Bonita imagined some doofus-counterpart of his leaning out and waving from the other end. Though that was unlikely. Why would pirates, or whatever these people were, tote civilian engineers along on a mission?

"No, no," Bonita said as the armored men spread out. "Come right in, I insist."

She wouldn't draw a weapon, but she doubted her situation would get any worse if she drew sarcasm.

"Captain Lopez," one of the men said, his voice filtered through a speaker in his helmet. "You made a mistake."

"How rare for me. And you are?" Bonita didn't like that these people knew her name when she had no idea who they were. Nothing had come up when she'd searched for information on their ship. She'd found the layout and specs for the model but nothing about that specific vessel. It didn't have an ident chip, so that lent credence to her notion of pirates. She wondered who they'd bribed to get on the Odin launch loop.

"People who will fight to keep advanced weapons out of the Kingdom's hands. The rest of the galaxy is not going to suffer under their oppressive rule again."

"I wasn't taking any weapons to the Kingdom," Bonita lied easily, though unease tapped a discouraging beat in her stomach. Maybe they weren't here for Casmir, after all.

"Weapons?" Casmir tilted his head. "Does that mean you're not here for…"

Bonita willed the kid to shut up. He should have hidden.

"Are you Casmir Dabrowski?" the speaker asked.

"Yes."

"It was thoughtful of you to introduce yourself. I don't know who you are yet, but I asked the lieutenant to look you up and see if there's a reward."

When Casmir arched his eyebrows, they disappeared under his shaggy bangs. "If there is, would you let me know? Because it's been an extremely confusing week."

The helmeted figure stared at him. Maybe he was also trying to decide if Casmir was dangerous or a doofus. Not that the two had to be mutually exclusive.

"Where are the weapons, Captain?" a second figure asked, a woman.

That surprised Bonita because the armored intruders were all well over six feet tall. Maybe she was augmented, which was a disturbing thought, because that meant these people might all be the equivalent of Qin.

"I'm afraid you're mistaken about weapons," Bonita said. "There's nothing like that here. I had a small cargo that I delivered in Odin—I never saw what was inside—but it's long gone. I can give you the name of the buyer, if you wish."

She wondered if her unwelcome visitors were responsible for the robots that had blown Baum's shuttle out of the sky. She'd assumed the Kingdom Guard had sent those, but maybe not. If the people on this ship *had* been behind that, would they believe she'd had time since then to unload the cargo?

"Everything I have now is hooked to that bulkhead over there. You're welcome to search the crates, but I'd appreciate it if you *not* take them, as they're the ship's necessities, not a cargo for delivery." Bonita waved to a prominent crate labeled *vacuum toilet parts*. She'd put that one in front to discourage interest. "Like I said, I've nothing left from the other cargo."

"Of course not," the woman murmured. "Stavros, Taylor, search the ship. Thoroughly. These freighters are known to have secret compartments, but they never seem to be mentioned in the factory specs."

"Because smugglers add them afterward."

Stavros, Taylor. Bonita burned the names into her mind in case she had a chance to look them up later, to figure out who she was dealing with. Vigilantes? Mercenaries? Could these be some of Captain Tenebris Rache's people? The last she'd heard, he was a one-ship operation, and that wasn't his ship out there, but maybe things had changed. He was known to loathe the Kingdom, though stopping a shipment of weapons seemed like a small-time job for him.

"We questioning her?" the man asked. "Easier than having our men tear the paneling off all over the ship."

"We should question that one." The woman pointed at Casmir. "He looks like he'd crack like a Radkin melon left all summer to dry in the sun."

"He also looks like he doesn't know anything."

"That would be true," Casmir said.

"And if he's valuable, whoever wants him might not want his pretty face mutilated."

"We could just mutilate some fingers. Nobody minds fingers much, even if they're missing altogether."

Casmir lifted his arms but appeared torn between hiding his hands behind his back and raising them overhead, as he'd practiced. Bonita felt a little sorry for him, even if he had brought trouble with him. It wasn't the *current* trouble, it seemed.

"Who are you?" she asked the thugs.

Information always had value. Maybe she would get lucky and they would chat.

"Somebody who doesn't want to see the genophobic Kingdom government in charge of anything more than its own planet," the man growled. "And maybe not even that."

"Genophobic?" Casmir asked. "Afraid of sexual relations? I haven't met the king, but he does have the three princes *and* a princess, so that seems unlikely. If you mean that we're uncomfortable with genetic engineering, then yes, that has been the policy for centuries."

"Shut up." One of the other men reached for him, while two more stepped toward Bonita.

Bonita jumped back, her pistol finding its way into her hand by instinct. The armored men laughed when she pointed it at one of their chests.

"You *will* tell us where the weapons are," the leader said. "Nobody cares if *you* get mutilated."

She sprang back again when they advanced, her knee twinging even in low gravity, but the intruders were too quick. Even if they hadn't been augmented humans, that armor gave them extra speed and strength. She fired, hoping to get lucky, that her energy bolt would find a seam, but it only clanged off a helmet. An armored hand blurred in and clamped down on hers, squeezing.

She cried out, unable to keep hold of her pistol.

It clattered to the deck, and she found herself hoisted into the air. She fought, more out of instinct and desperation than because she had a chance at escaping. A hand curled around her throat, and that cut through her panic. She grew very still.

"Where are the weapons?" the leader asked, his fingers tightening.

Pain flared at the pressure, and Bonita couldn't keep tears from springing to her eyes. She hoped they looked like tears of defiance, not tears that suggested she was on the verge of giving in.

"Already... told you..." she spat out the best she could with her voice box being crushed. And her windpipe.

Why hadn't she at least put the helmet up on her galaxy suit? That would have offered some protection from *this*. Already, her breaths were more difficult to draw up her windpipe from her lungs. Would they kill her if she didn't talk? Or if she did?

Normally, she would have simply accepted the loss of the cargo as the cost of working in a risky business, but she couldn't afford to dump it, not anymore. Damn Jake Pepper for being such an ass and leaving her in this desperate a situation, and damn her for not reading him better, for not seeing his betrayal coming.

The fingers tightened further. "You *will* tell us where the cargo is, or you will die. Nobody needs you. We've got pilots aplenty, pilots who can fly this ship for us. Which we just might claim for ourselves. After all, if we found a ship adrift, it would be within our right to claim it for the war effort."

Nobody needs you. It was a strange time for the words to penetrate deeply and for Bonita to realize how accurate they were. Her parents were long gone, and she'd never had children. Who would even miss her if these thugs killed her?

"War? What war? Nobody's at war yet." That was Casmir.

He sounded like he was hanging upside down in someone's grip, but Bonita couldn't focus on anything other than her fear and the darkness encroaching on her vision. She grasped the single armored arm holding her up and tried to pry the fingers away, but they might as well have been made from graphene.

"If you believe that," someone replied to Casmir, "then your news service is even more censored than we thought. Only the Kingdom wouldn't tell its own people that they killed President Bakas, and now half of the systems are gunning for them." The man laughed.

"Let's make a deal," Bonita rasped, clawing for a brilliant plan. "Maybe I can go back to Odin and retrieve the cargo for you."

The man shook her by the neck. "We *know* you have it here."

Desperate, she kicked out, her boot striking her assailant in the armored groin. It did nothing but hurt her toes.

"Last time I'm asking, Captain," the man said. "*Where* are the weapons?"

She closed her eyes, aware of hot tears leaking down her cheeks, even as her body used the last of its air. If she passed out, she might not wake again. If she didn't tell them...

"Kill her," the woman ordered before Bonita had finished deciding.

"No!" Casmir shouted. "I can show you the weapons."

The fingers loosened. Her captor didn't release her, and her feet still dangled three inches off the deck, but she was able to suck in a deep breath through her bruised throat.

She turned her head as much as she could, intending to shoot Casmir a dirty look—she was positive he didn't know where they'd hidden the cargo—but she glimpsed Qin crouching in the corridor, her Brockinger anti-tank 350 aimed at Bonita's captor, as if she'd been about to fire.

The intruders hadn't seen her yet. Should Bonita give her the go ahead? The problem was that even with that gun—which might or might not do anything against their armor—Qin was only one person to their six. Further, the explosive round might tear a giant hole in the hull.

"I mean, I can find them," Casmir corrected as all the armored faceplates turned toward him. He was, indeed, dangling from one ankle, his hair brushing the deck as he twisted, looking up at people. "She didn't confide their location to me, because I'm not a trusted member of her crew, or perhaps because I spent the last three days dealing with airsickness—technically, is it airsickness in space where there is no air? Make that space-sickness."

The one holding him shook him. "You know where they are or not?"

"I can find them," Casmir repeated. "I'm a robotics engineer. There are robots all over the ship for cleaning and various tasks. I can modify one with an infrared camera and have it zip around the ship, looking for spots in the paneling that are cooler than they should be, indicating a lack of insulation behind it."

"How long would that take?"

"Oh, not long at all. The programming would be a breeze. An hour, perhaps, assuming I can get my tools. And be stood upright. A table and some space to work would be ideal, but the upright thing is paramount."

In the corridor, Qin raised her eyebrows, seeming to ask if she should wait or start a firefight. If she did the latter, Bonita was highly aware that she and Casmir would end up in the crossfire. They wore their galaxy suits, but neither had their helmets on.

Not wanting to draw the intruders' attention to Qin, Bonita only made a slight negative hand gesture. Better that Qin wait until she could leap from hiding and ambush the intruders, ideally one on one. And if Casmir was successful in buying time…

"He *is* a robotics engineer," one of the men said. "The lieutenant said she didn't see a bounty out for him, but there were a bunch of recent news stories from Odin about him being missing and his university's parking garage blowing up."

"Fine," the leader sighed. "Throw him in a room where he can work, and round up any other crew members you find, but keep most of our guys looking for the weapons. Easier if we just get them ourselves. I don't want to be hooked up to this garbage barge all day."

"Garbage barge?" came Viggo's indignant voice from a speaker.

Someone snorted. "There's one crew member."

"Actually, that's the ship's computer," Bonita said.

"We'll see." The man waved for his team to spread out and search.

Good, they were splitting up. Maybe Qin would have a chance to set up ambushes.

The man holding Casmir turned him right side up and dropped his feet to the deck. His face was red, and one of his eyes kept blinking, but he managed a bleary smile for Bonita when their captors trooped them off toward the lounge.

"If you think I'll thank you for this," she growled at him, "you're wrong."

His smile grew sad. "I thought you might not."

CHAPTER 9

CASMIR ALTERNATED BETWEEN TINKERING WITH THE TWO CLEANING robots open in front of him, their circuit boards and wiring exposed, and putting tools in and out of his satchel. He'd already reprogrammed the vacuums—that had been simple—but he lacked something important that he needed, and he didn't know how to get it.

He sat in the lounge with a sullen Captain Lopez across the table from him and an armored man looming by the hatch, keeping an eye on them. Or so Casmir assumed. Thanks to those mirrored faceplates, their guard could have been sleeping or watching a porno vid and they wouldn't have known it.

As far as Casmir knew, the intruders hadn't yet found Qin or Kim. That was a little surprising. Maybe this freighter was better at hiding things—and people—than he would have guessed. The trick he'd promised he could pull off might not have worked even if that was what he'd truly programmed the robots to do.

He needed an explosive, and sadly, Kim hadn't left her lighter and deodorant out on the table.

If he could hunt around in the mess cabinets, he might be able to find some chemicals that could work, though what would be perfect were some of the canisters from that anti-tank gun Qin carried around. Wherever she was.

"You're wasting your time," Lopez said, her voice harsh. "Everybody is. There's nothing for you—or *them*—to find." She glared at the impassive guard.

"Well, if you ever need to search the hidden holds of other ships, you might find it handy to have a robot for the purpose." Casmir smiled and tapped one of the vacuums, though he wished he could convey that he'd only been trying to save her life. He hadn't been convinced that thug had only been scaring her. Her face had been purple, and he swore he'd heard something snap in her neck. This scheme was the first thing he'd come up with, but as he'd selected robots from the impressive collection of cleaning devices in a closet in engineering, he'd come up with a better idea.

"*I* don't invade other people's ships and steal their hard-won goods."

The hatch opened, and the guard swung toward it, his rifle pointing into what turned out to be an empty corridor. Lopez jumped to her feet.

The guard glanced back at her, but her weapons had been removed, and she couldn't do anything but crouch, ready in case... what?

Casmir tried to see around the guard, who was now poking his head into the corridor. Something flew above his helmet and into the lounge. A canister.

Casmir lunged in the opposite direction. He'd wanted an explosive, but not like this.

The guard spun toward it as it started spewing smoke.

Was it some noxious knock-out gas? No, that wouldn't affect someone in combat armor.

Casmir covered his mouth and backed farther from the table. It *would* affect him.

The soldier stomped out into the corridor, and the *bzzzt* of a DEW-Tek rifle firing sounded. Lopez ran out after him only to have him spin back toward her, pointing his weapon at her chest. She lifted her hands as Casmir had done earlier and backed into the lounge again.

Smoke swirled about her ankles. It stung Casmir's eyes, but he couldn't yet tell if it would do anything more inimical. He did his best not to inhale.

Something slammed into the armored guard from behind, hard enough to make him stumble forward. A hand appeared, tossing a weapon to Lopez, and a boom sounded as someone—Qin?—fired a weapon that could have blown a hole in the hull of the ship. But it struck the guard in the back, hurling him across the lounge. He crashed shoulder-first into the far wall. It left a dent. Both in his armor and in the wall.

Unfortunately, he found his feet and fired back. Qin and Lopez leaped into the corridor and used the jamb for cover.

"Qin!" Casmir called, torn between wanting to hide his unarmored body under the table and needing one of her explosives.

She glanced at him as she leaned around the jamb to return the guard's fire. Perhaps realizing the threat to the hull of the ship, she'd switched to bullets, but they didn't do anything to hurt the armored thug. And he realized that. He strode toward them.

"I need one of your things," he yelled, deliberately vague, hoping the guard wouldn't remember.

When she glanced again, he waved at her bandolier and pointed to the explosive shells. Would she see? That smoke kept spewing into the room, creating a thick green haze in the air.

The guard roared and charged, spraying his rifle fire and leaving scorch marks in the bulkhead opposite the hatchway. He disappeared into the corridor. Footsteps rang out. Qin and Lopez running from him? Or had more of the intruders heard the noise and come to help their man?

A few oddly quiet seconds passed before an armored man stuck his head into the lounge. Casmir didn't know if it was the same guy as before or a new one. He thrust his hands into the air and tried to appear as innocent as he could.

The mirrored faceplate looked from him to the table full of parts and back to him. "Stay here. Keep working on that thing."

The guard left, clanging the hatch shut behind him.

"If I don't pass out first." Casmir coughed at the smoke stinging his eyes and scouring his throat.

He ran to the source, grabbed it, and threw it into the garbage chute. He sanitized his gloved hands under the kitchen spritzer and wiped them vigorously on a towel. He flapped at the air with that towel, hunted until he found a vent fan for the ship's small stove, and turned it on.

As the smoke curled toward it, he decided he didn't have the urge to pass out. It seemed that Qin had only thrown a weapon designed to cloud the air. Maybe it did something to whatever scanners the men had built into their armor.

Casmir headed toward the table but noticed something just inside the hatch. One of Qin's explosive shells lay on the deck nestled against the wall.

"Perfect," he crooned, carefully picking it up with both hands.

A clank came from the back of the lounge, and he jumped, almost dropping his prize. He clutched it to his chest as if it were an egg.

One of the exercise cabinet doors opened, and Kim stuck her head out through a three-foot-high opening. She peered around the lounge and flinched when she saw Casmir. Her brow smoothed when she realized he was alone.

"You were in there the whole time?" he whispered. "Didn't they search in here?"

"They searched. Someone opened my cabinet, and I thought they would spot me, with some technology if not their eyes, but I think the cabinet doors and interior walls are designed to scramble scanners. I was behind the exercise cycle and their equipment didn't tell them." She pointed her thumb into the depths of her cabinet. "Also, they were busy arguing while they looked. I gathered they were more interested in finding what they thought would be large crates of some illicit cargo rather than human beings."

"That's good. I'm not sure when they'll be back, so you may want to stay in there."

Kim couldn't have made a more sour face if she were sucking a Devarian lemon.

"Or come out and risk getting caught." Casmir slid into his seat so he could continue working. "You can hold my tools for me."

"A cornucopia of delightful options." Kim slithered out of her cabinet, gripped her back, and grimaced as she stretched. "I don't suppose there's a way to lock the hatch?" she asked as she walked to the table.

"They might get suspicious if I lock it."

"Are you working on something for *them*? Who are they, anyway? Pirates?"

"They neglected to introduce themselves."

"That's rude."

"I thought so. I haven't seen any faces yet, so I can't run a network search. I'm afraid you know as much as I do." Casmir made a bracket to secure the explosive inside his chosen robot. Now to work on a detonator. A remote one would be ideal, rather than a simple timer. "Though I did learn that there's not a bounty on my head or a warrant out for my arrest."

"They checked?"

"Yes, because of the message I sent, they thought I might be worth kidnapping. I'm pleased to learn that I'm not. But still puzzled."

"What are you making?" Kim asked.

"It's a…" Casmir glanced toward the speakers, not sure if there were cameras in the walls and if the intruders were monitoring them. Or if they were busy playing hide, seek, and attack with Qin and Lopez. "Device to detect things hidden in the walls. They're having trouble finding the captain's contraband, and I'd like to live, so I offered to help."

Kim raised her eyebrows. She might not be good at telling if strangers were lying, but he suspected she knew him well enough to decipher deceit. She didn't call him on it.

"Can I help?" She made a grasping motion in the air, maybe indicating that she felt useless.

Casmir knew the feeling well. He was used to teaching and working with his team on projects every day. He'd never been good at taking days off. That was why he ended up making robotic birds in his spare time.

"Sure. Screw the lid back on that one. He's going to be our decoy."

Casmir secured a remote-control chip in the vacuum before pushing it toward Kim. Then he set one up inside of the second robot. If this worked, he would lose some of his spare parts forever, but if they survived and reached Forseti Station, he could buy new parts.

Assuming he deemed it safe enough to use his banking chip. He still needed to figure out who was after him, but he felt reassured that this mess was about something else. Maybe he'd left his pursuers back on Odin. Of course, if he got himself killed here, flying along in the middle of nowhere, it wouldn't matter that he had successfully eluded those crushers.

"Let's see if they're ready." Casmir grabbed the remote and set the two robots on the deck.

He succeeded at moving them left and right, forward and back, and he'd given them both tiny cameras on their fronts. He was able to toggle between the two on his remote's tiny display, which offered him slightly different views of the closed hatch.

"I'd be impressed," Kim said, "but they did all that *before* you started tinkering. I saw one vacuuming inside one of the kitchen cabinets this morning."

"Not on orders from my remote. And not with cameras."

"Because normal people don't want a close-up of what's being vacuumed."

"I might find it entertaining."

"That doesn't negate my statement."

Casmir grinned at her. "Did you get a chance to look up the layout of that ship?"

"Yes. The bridge and briefing rooms are at the top of the pyramid, cabins and lounges, a rifle range and a gym in the five middle decks, and then engineering, environmental controls, and cargo on the largest, bottom level. The airlock is extended from there."

"Is there a lift going up to the bridge?"

"Ladders, I think."

"Aren't spaceships supposed to be accessible for people with injuries or disabilities?"

"I don't imagine a lot of pirates roll around in wheelchairs."

"Did you get a map downloaded?" Casmir asked.

"It's just in my head."

"All right. Stand next to me while I drive them, please." Casmir opened the hatch, listened for a moment, and grimaced at the sounds of fighting. They came from the hold down below, not from the corridor outside, but that would still be problematic. He had to navigate the vacuums through the hold and to the airlock. Maybe he would get lucky, and everyone would be too busy to notice what he was doing.

"Drive them where?" Kim asked.

Casmir set the robots in the corridor, nudged the remote, and they rolled toward the ladder well. Fortunately, they had no trouble navigating vertical walls. "Let's hope that the signal is strong enough to get them the whole way there."

"Whole way where? The enemy ship?"

"You'll see." He grinned at her again.

"Has anyone told you that engineers are annoying?"

"Engineers? No. I've been told *I'm* annoying."

"Good."

Bonita crouched behind the crates in the cargo hold, exchanging fire with one of the intruders. Qin had raced to the armory and was supposed to get her a weapon that would have a chance against their armor. She'd meant to select something herself, but they had her pinned down. Four of them. She didn't know where the other two had gone.

A crimson energy bolt slammed into one of the crates, hurling it backward. The lid flew open, and prepackaged meals flew about the cargo hold. Bonita ducked lower.

One of the men strode straight toward her meager cover. She leaned out and fired four times with her pistol. Her bolts ricocheted off his chest plate, not even leaving scorch marks.

"Qin," Bonita shouted. "Now would be good."

She appreciated that Qin had come to the lounge to rescue her but wished she'd had more of a plan than sprinting into the cargo hold and hiding. The guard had been too close behind, and another intruder had been waiting by the airlock. There'd been no chance to hide.

The man's stride turned into a run, and he sprinted toward her crate. Bonita fired again, for all the good it did, and scrambled backward.

He would have slammed into her, but Qin sprang over Bonita's head and landed in front of her. She lunged and crashed into the man, taking him to the deck despite his armor. She landed astride him and slammed her helmet into his.

For a second, he seemed stunned, and Qin used that pause to fire her Brockinger at a second man rushing toward them.

Bonita winced at the explosion in the middle of her cargo hold, but it took the man in the chest, knocking him backward and peeling his armor open like a sardine can.

The man under Qin recovered and slammed two armored fists into her chest. Though her galaxy suit insulated her somewhat, she gasped in pain. Only the grip she had on him with her legs kept her from flying up to the ceiling. She tried to load another round in her Brockinger, but he grabbed the big gun, attempting to wrest it from her.

Bonita realized Qin had brought a Starhawk 5000 out for her and dropped it on the deck when she attacked. She snatched it up and rushed toward the grappling combatants.

Even though the rifle had more power than her pistol, it was no Brockinger. Bonita didn't bother to shoot but instead used the butt end, slamming it into the man's faceplate over and over. That had to distract him, if nothing else.

He roared and bucked Qin into the air. She flew backward, her helmet slamming into a crate. Hard.

Bonita pointed the rifle at his chest but saw four determined intruders striding toward her. Only one was down, the one Qin had fired an explosive at. It had torn open his chest armor, but it had also blown a crater in her deck, revealing conduits and insulation underneath. Her cargo hold couldn't take more abuse.

Four rifles pointed at Bonita's chest. She had no delusions about her galaxy suit repelling them all.

The entire boarding party was down in the cargo hold again. That meant nobody was watching Casmir, but if all he was doing was building a robot to help her enemies, Bonita hardly cared. This escape had been pointless.

Qin groaned faintly. She lay on her back under the crate, the fingers of one hand twitching. She must have struck it like a pile driver.

"Qin," Bonita whispered under her breath, trusting Qin's enhanced hearing to catch it. She lowered her weapon to the deck and spread her arms. "Stop fighting. Pretend you're knocked out. Until we get a better chance."

From the way Qin's twitching fingers stilled and her helmet did not move, Bonita feared she truly *was* knocked out. Or worse.

CHAPTER 10

THIS IS REMARKABLE WORKMANSHIP," YAS SAID, EYEING THE brain scan of Chief Engineer Jessamine Khonsari, the woman who'd been having coffee with the captain when he first met Rache—by collapsing in an injured mess at the base of their table.

Now, she sat on one of the sickbay beds, rotating her shoulder and grimacing as she gripped one of the handholds to keep herself from floating away.

"I knew about your arm and eyes and synthetic joints from your record," he added, "but I hadn't seen the full body scan. I didn't realize you had circuitry integrated seamlessly into your brain."

"Yes, I'm a modern wonder. Drugs, Doctor. I'm here for some drugs."

Yas arched his eyebrows, the magnetic boots of his suit keeping him attached to the deck. The ship had docked at a second refinery orbiting Saga, so they were without gravity again.

"You might have torn a ligament, Jessamine. Let me take a look."

"Might as well call me Jess, Doc. Seeing as how we're getting intimate." She pushed a hand through her short, curly black hair, then maneuvered the top half of her suit down to her waist. She stopped moving her shoulder so he could examine it with his fingers and a quick Hexscan.

"Intimate? I suppose I'd be amenable to the offer..." Yas smiled, though he doubted she had anything sexual in mind. "But I'm only planning to scan your shoulder."

"You looked at my brain circuits, Doc. I don't let many people do that."

"I hope that doesn't mean you plan to kill me after I give you your medication. To keep me silent."

"Nah. I only kill people who try to blow up my engines. I'm a lady."

"Clearly." He kept his tone dry and made a point of only examining her shoulder and none of her *lady* attributes. He hadn't been here long enough to get desperate and horny and start hitting on the crew. Further, he was a professional, even if his world had been taken away from him. "Yes, a torn ligament. It shouldn't need to be immobilized, but let me give you something to speed up the healing."

"Sparring with these men is *not* healthy." Jessamine eyed the injector he extracted from his kit.

"I imagine not. Two-thirds of the crewmen are enhanced with various legal and illegal implants. The ones that aren't look to have been born hulking trolls."

"It's not a profession that attracts beauty-pageant winners."

"With rare exceptions?" Yas raised his eyebrows.

Nobody would call Jessamine a troll, not with those arched cheekbones, full lips, and elegant facial features. Despite all of the surgery she'd had done, Yas could tell from her scans that it had all been for medical purposes, likely to repair her body after a brutal accident, rather than to enhance strength and speed.

She looked away from what he'd meant to be a compliment and said, "No. No exceptions."

Maybe she was self-conscious about the prosthetics.

As the jet injector hissed, the captain's voice sounded over the speakers. "Dr. Peshlakai, I need you on the refinery."

Yas frowned. After the mess at the last refinery, he had no desire to visit this one.

"Is someone injured?" he asked.

"Someone is dead."

"I can't help you with that, Captain."

"Get over here. *Now.*"

The ice in the captain's tone chilled Yas, and he started packing his medical kit. He hadn't seen Rache lose his temper yet, but he *had* witnessed him shoot one of his mercenaries in cold blood when the man had been discovered transmitting the ship's coordinates to a Kingdom military outpost. Somehow, that frigid, remorseless calculation seemed worse than if he'd lost his temper and killed the man in a fit of rage.

"I'm on my way, sir." Yas selected a few extra scanners, a scalpel, and syringes for taking blood samples.

All he could guess was that there was something strange about the dead man and Rache would want an autopsy and answers. He hadn't mentioned which crew member it was.

"Have fun," Jess said. "See the sights. Don't forget my drugs when you get back. The last doc always gave me trylochanix."

"For... injuries from sparring? That's a very strong and addictive analgesic. And an antidepressant." He arched his eyebrows. Jess, with her easygoing smiles, hardly seemed like someone in need of that aspect of the drug.

"Yeah, it's what they gave me after my surgery. It was the only thing that helped with the pain and the neuropathy I got from my body getting jury-rigged back together. Doc Otero kept it in that cabinet right there." Jess smiled and pointed at the main enclosure for the ship's medications. It was out along the wall and without a lock on it, something Yas intended to change when he could requisition the help to move it somewhere more secure. He'd already walked in on one of the mercenaries helping himself.

"Do you still have neuropathy? Your record says the surgery was two years ago."

"Yup, sometimes. Especially when other things get knocked out of alignment." Jess waved at her shoulder. "Everything hurts like fire then too."

She was casual as she spoke, but she also avoided looking him in the eye. That made him uneasy, as did the idea of simply handing her something so addictive without having done an examination or being more familiar with her history. But when he looked at Dr. Otero's notes— nobody had yet explained to Yas what happened to his predecessor, and he was afraid to ask—Yas did see that he'd given her a legitimate prescription for trylochanix whenever she'd suffered injuries.

And there seemed to be *numerous* injuries. She got hurt sparring or at work often.

Simply a byproduct of being part of this crew and going on dangerous missions? Or was it possible she intentionally got hurt so she could get more trylochanix?

"Have you tried other medicines?" Yas asked.

"Yeah, but nothing works as well. It's fine, Doc. I only take it when I need it. You know, when something short circuits." She held up her prosthetic hand and her pinky twitched a few times.

He was fairly certain that was an intentional motion rather than a short circuit. He was also fairly certain trylochanix wouldn't do anything to help with mechanical issues. Dulling neuropathic pain, however, *was* a legitimate use.

"I see. We should schedule a full examination when you have time—and when *I* have time." Yas remembered that the captain was waiting for him. "Let's discuss this further when I get back."

"Gosh, Doc, if you want to go on a date, just ask."

"That would be delightful, but we should probably keep things professional."

"Sounds boring."

"I'm going to give you a simple analgesic for now, and you let me know if it's not enough." Yas selected something strong but basic and non-addictive from the cabinet. "We can reevaluate after an exam."

Jess frowned but didn't object, merely accepting the tabs and hopping off the table with a, "Thanks, Doc," before heading back to engineering.

Yas grabbed one of the oxygen tanks from a locker of emergency air, rations, and water in the corner. Sickbay was one of a handful of independently powered areas in the ship that could be isolated from the main environmental system and act as a safe haven if primary power or life support went out. He almost grabbed one of the DEW-Tek pistols in the cabinet but opted for a tranquilizer gun from a drawer instead.

"Do I get a guide, Captain?" Yas asked over the comm as he headed through the corridors of the ship to the airlock.

Nobody answered him.

He hadn't been off the *Fedallah* since first stepping on—the captain had denied him the freedom to take leave, even with an escort—but he'd had the mandatory space-evacuation training on Tiamat Station and attended the yearly drills, so he felt comfortable heading out an airlock. Walking through a station full of robotic security sentries without a bodyguard was another matter.

When the airlock cycled and the hatch to the dark station opened, he shivered at the vast emptiness ahead of him. His helmet light came on automatically, a beam piercing an open bay and playing over dark tanks, pipes, and machinery. A single unnamed mining ship was also docked to the big bay, and robots worked with hoses and pipes to unload helium, methane, and the various other gases that would have been scooped out of Saga's atmosphere.

None of the robots reacted to Yas's presence, and he walked slowly into the bay, careful to keep at least one magnetic boot attached to the deck. Ahead of him, a figure appeared in the mouth of a corridor. Yas's gloved hand twitched toward his tranquilizer gun. What he thought that would do against a robot or android, he didn't know, but as soon as his flashlight beam shifted, he recognized the black combat armor of one of Rache's men.

"This way, Doctor," Rache himself said over the comm.

Yas hurried to join him, and they meandered through an eerie high-ceilinged maze of giant tanks and processing equipment, and pipes bigger around than he was. A mutilated security robot floated limply in the air a few feet above the floor.

"You've cleared the refinery of dangers?" Yas asked.

Rache's faceplate turned toward him for a long moment. "You're here to determine that, Doctor."

"Oh, good."

Eight of Rache's mercenaries waited in a control room full of gauges and panels displaying numbers that meant nothing to Yas. Some of the men stood. Others sat cross-legged above the floor, tilted at odd angles and thinking nothing of it.

All manner of clothing and personal belongings floated among them. A toothbrush dangled near Yas's eyes. To one side, a couple of camp beds were strung between pipes, the straps designed to keep people from floating away while they slept, but nobody was in the beds now. Two more were attached on the other side of the room, also empty.

"Someone has been living here?" Yas thought of the docking bay with only the automated mining ship attached. If someone *had* been camped here, wouldn't there have been another ship? He spotted a few magnetic crates attached to the deck in a corner, the lids thrown open, and he realized the mercenaries must have been searching for valuables. "But they left the refinery and abandoned their belongings?" Yas guessed.

"They didn't abandon anything." Rache tilted his helmet back enough for his headlamp to shine on the ceiling.

Yas sucked in a startled breath. Four bodies floated up there, snugged into the corners by the walls.

Someone chuckled at his reaction, but most of the mercenaries were oddly quiet.

The four unmoving bodies were all in suits, helmets still in place, with oxygen tanks attached to their backs. Had they been stuck on the refinery and run out of air?

"Grab a corpse for the doctor, Chains," Rache said.

"Yes, sir." Corporal Chains pushed off the deck, maneuvering past dangling shirts and hairbrushes, and grabbed a leg. He rotated and pushed off the ceiling, dragging his load down to the floor with him.

"We haven't taken them out of their suits, and I have no intention of bringing the bodies onto my ship." Rache gripped a shoulder, pulling the corpse toward Yas. "But I want to know what killed them before we leave, and if there's any danger to us. It doesn't look like exposure to space, and none of their tanks are completely empty. Close, but they still had air when they died." Rache waved at the floating belongings. "These were like this when we got here. At first, I assumed someone jumped their camp and killed them, but there aren't signs of injuries on their faces, and there's no damage to their suits."

"Your people didn't tear the stuff out of the crates?" Yas asked.

"Not us," Chains said. "I walked right into those blue panties there when I came in."

"On purpose," another mercenary said and guffawed. "Closest he's gotten to a woman in... ever."

"Don't know what you're talking about, Baker. I screwed your mom just last month."

Ignoring the crude barbs, Yas peered through the dead man's faceplate. Rache was right. There were no indications of petechial hemorrhaging from asphyxiation or contusions that might have hinted at brain damage, but the man did have a pained expression on his face, so Yas doubted he had died peacefully in his sleep.

"There are two men and two women," Rache said. "These aren't military spacesuits. It looks like a civilian team."

"Captain, I found a couple more bodies," someone said over the comm. "Two more men. Older."

"Did they die the same way?"

"No. One pulled off his helmet and died of exposure. The other has a medical injector sticking out of his galaxy suit's leg port. Looks like he stabbed himself with some drug. Dyoxynoran, it says on the side of the injector."

Yas swallowed, about to describe the drug and that it was used in hospitals when a patient wanted a quick end, but Rache nodded, apparently already familiar with it.

"Want us to bring the bodies back, sir?"

"No," Rache said. "We're not taking them on board the ship."

Yas stirred. "I need to be able to take them out of their suits to perform an autopsy, Captain. If that's what you want."

"We're not taking them on board my ship," Rache repeated coolly. "You can't make any guesses? Narrow things down?"

Yas spread a helpless hand. What did the man want? These people could have died of a million things, and he couldn't make educated guesses with them shut up inside their spacesuits. "There are no weals, so it's not the Great Plague."

"Helpful."

It had been a joke, if a poor one, since a hereditary vaccine had been created and distributed to most of the Twelve Systems almost two hundred years ago. The Great Plague rarely made an appearance these days. The captain did not sound amused.

"I'm sorry, sir. I can instruct the men on how to set up a proper quarantine if you want me to examine these people here or on the ship, but I need to take at least one of the bodies out of its suit. Does your airlock chamber have a decontamination program in case we're dealing with a disease?" Yas didn't know of many biological organisms that could survive in the cold vacuum of space, but there were a few natural ones and more than a few manmade ones that could. Further, his helmet display told him it wasn't as cold in the refinery as it was outside. Presumably, the machinery couldn't operate at -250 Celsius. And he knew of plenty of organisms that didn't need oxygen to live.

Rache gazed thoughtfully at the bodies. Deciding whether to examine them further or simply walk away from the mystery and blow up the station?

Yas admitted to curiosity and wanting to explore further. The mercenaries' combat armor was as good as a biohazard suit when it came to protecting them from bacteria and viruses, and if the ship had a good decontamination system, the threat of bringing something deadly on board ought to be minimal. Even so, he wouldn't blame the captain if he wanted to be safe and avoid further contact with whatever had caused this.

"It looks like everything valuable was taken, sir," the sergeant searching the cases said, "but there are some broken scanners and archaeology equipment. I turned this one on, and the screen says it's for cataloging and dating wrecks."

"What wrecks would you find on a refinery?" Chains asked.

"Maybe they were down on one of the moons and came here because…" The sergeant shrugged and looked at Rache. "Someone was chasing them? Their ship was damaged and they needed someplace to wait for help?"

"Anything else in there?" Rache waved at the case without commenting on the speculation.

"Uhm, there are also some storage chips," the sergeant said. "This one has a sleeve with—I'm not sure. Are these gate coordinates scribbled on it?" He held it up, showing clusters of constellations.

"Yes." Rache held out his hand.

The sergeant handed over the chips and grinned. "Maybe they contain the long-lost secrets to who built the gates and what happened to Earth."

Yas knew it was a joke, but it *was* the kind of thing archaeology teams researched. Time had fuzzed the details around the twelve gates that connected the systems, and how their Earth ancestors had originally discovered them and figured out how to send colony ships halfway across the galaxy to make use of them. No evidence of alien civilizations had ever been found by astronomers, but that didn't keep those with imaginations from speculating about dead or hidden races that could be out there. Some also hypothesized that there was a thirteenth gate somewhere within reach, one that led back to Earth. It was just waiting to be discovered, so humanity could use it to visit their home world again and find out what had happened.

"Gather anything else that might be valuable or informative and prepare to bring it with us," Rache said. "But not until after the doctor runs his autopsy. Set up a lab right here, Doctor. I want to know what killed these men and if it's a threat to us." He waved to indicate the refinery they'd all been walking around in.

"Yes, sir."

Casmir bit his tongue as he guided the robots through the airlock tube extended from the other ship. Sweat dribbled down the side of his face. Given the firefight going on in the cargo hold, he could hardly believe he'd managed to get them across it without notice. The little robots were slow and methodical. Twice, he'd had to override their hardwired program to vacuum as they went.

The enemy ship's airlock hatchway had a raised lip, but the robots handled it without trouble with their suction-cup treads. He guided them one after the other into the corridor beyond it, the tiny display on the remote showing the route ahead of them. The left side opened up to the cargo hold Kim had mentioned and also a shuttle bay. A bulkhead sealed off whatever lay to the right.

"Engineering should be to the right at the first door," Kim said, leaning over his shoulder to better see the display.

"Good."

Casmir watched for the crew as he guided the robots along. All it would take was one pirate spotting the small intruders and shooting them. Dust wasn't likely expected to fight back, so the robot vacuums didn't have any armor.

He rolled them into engineering, then tucked them against the wall inside the hatchway while he spun one slowly to pan the cavernous room. And cursed when he spotted a man standing in front of a console between their main engine and the huge fusion reactor. His back was to the robots, for the moment.

The grainy camera didn't show a lot of detail, but Casmir thought a pair of heavy pistols hung from the man's belt. He wasn't wearing combat armor, but he also wasn't wearing a uniform. Pirates seemed as good a guess as any for these guys, but would pirates care about who sold what weapons to whom in a war?

War. His mind still boggled at that notion.

He'd heard stirrings and seen news reports about colonies and governments in other systems fighting with each other, some eager to retain their freedom and others wanting to return to the old days when the Kingdom had ruled and set laws over all, but he hadn't thought anything was far enough along to be considered a war. Odin was safe, and their system was stable and always had been, unless one counted the assassination of King Jager's father more than thirty years earlier. But, Casmir realized, the Kingdom had always controlled System Lion, so of course it wouldn't be in flux now. It was the only system that hadn't broken up and pulled away after the century of Golden Rule, as the Kingdom referred to the brief era when it had controlled the entirety of the Twelve Systems.

"Are you going to just stare at that guy's butt?" Kim waved at the small screen on the remote as she glanced toward the hatch in the lounge. "Or do you have a plan?"

"Butt-staring can't be a plan?"

"Not when our lives are in danger."

"But at other times?"

"*Casmir.*"

"I'm looking for a vulnerable spot to plant the one with the explosive. On the engine housing? Or their reactor? A reactor breach would be easy for them to repair, but if we got lucky with the engine, we might mangle something that requires spare parts. Spare parts that they don't have."

"Do people go into space without the ability to manufacture new parts?" Kim asked. "I know our military takes materials printers along even on short voyages."

"Maybe pirates aren't as prepared. At the least, it'll take them time to make and install replacement parts. We can change course slightly and hope they don't know where we're heading."

Casmir made sure the crewmember's back was still turned, then navigated his robot toward the engine. He wished he knew more about spaceships. He accessed his chip, did his best to capture the view the robot was giving him, then ran a search for information on the particular engine.

They weren't close to Odin anymore, but most of the planet's encyclopedias and academic databases were on redundant servers on satellites throughout the system, so it only took a few seconds for a response to come back. The schematic of the engine appeared on his contact.

"Perfect," he whispered, easing the robot up the side of the housing. "What's the other one going to do?"

"Be a distraction."

After he placed the first robot, hopefully in a spot where the engineer wouldn't notice it in the next five minutes, Casmir toggled to the second one. He guided it back into the corridor and located the ladder well Kim had mentioned. His robot couldn't climb rungs, but it had no problem walking up the wall opposite them. Not quickly, unfortunately.

"A distraction on the bridge?" Kim guessed.

"Yes, I'm hoping to—"

Muffled voices came from the corridor outside the lounge.

Casmir cursed and lunged for the far side of the table. Numerous tools and robot parts were scattered across the top. He sat in the chair and tucked his arms under the table to hide the remote.

Kim ran toward the cabinets, but the hatch opened before she reached the latch. She spun, pressing her shoulder to them and crossing her arms over her chest, as if she'd meant to be found all along.

Two armored men strode in dragging Qin and Lopez. Lopez glowered in Casmir's direction. Qin appeared to be unconscious.

Casmir stared bleakly at them. He'd hoped he could set off his distraction before he was caught, or that he wouldn't be caught at all.

The men dumped the women on the deck and looked at Casmir.

"The sergeant said to get…" One man's faceplate tilted toward the tool-littered table. "There was supposed to be a robot."

"Yes." Casmir smiled cheerfully and gestured with one hand toward the mess. "I'm working on it."

Under the table, he manipulated the robot out of the ladder well and headed it toward the bridge.

"That's just a bunch of junk." The man looked at his colleague. "Can we shoot them? Shoot *all* of them?"

Fortunately, his buddy was too busy staring at Kim to answer. "Where did *she* come from?"

"It looks like you need all manner of assistance when it comes to searching for things," Casmir said.

Qin groaned and shifted on the deck.

One of the men planted an armored boot on her back and pressed the muzzle of his rifle to her neck. "Don't think about it, freak."

"Freak?" his buddy asked. "She's better looking than some of the modded *things* out there. Sometimes, I don't think the Kingdom's laws are all that draconian. I mean, they are, but some things shouldn't exist."

"Don't forget whose side you're working for."

"The side that pays me best."

While they were giving more attention to each other than Casmir or Kim, Casmir pushed the handle on the remote and navigated his distraction robot onto their ship's bridge. It was six times the size of the *Dragon's* navigation cabin, but only two men occupied stations inside. Casmir allowed himself to hope that meant there wasn't a large crew on the enemy ship. Maybe if he made enough trouble over there, the six armored thugs would be called back to help with it.

"Tie up that woman." One of the men pointed at Kim. "I don't know where she came from, but we don't need trouble roaming free. We'll tie them all up and apply some pressure to help with finding the cargo. Especially if this idiot can't patch those parts together into something useful."

Casmir smiled. Under the table, he set the distraction robot to squeal like a hundred terrified pigs. Then he set it loose on turbo vacuum mode so that it darted all around the deck. He glimpsed the bridge crew whirling to look for it as it caromed around the stations, and fought back a grin. It wouldn't do any damage or take them long to nullify—one of the brutes would likely shoot it—but maybe they would be slow to react to a problem in engineering because of it.

One of the armored men frowned at Casmir. "You doing something under the table?"

"Nothing I want you to know about."

The man strode toward him.

Casmir toggled to the robot in engineering, but the system lagged, and he didn't gain access quickly enough. Damn it. He needed more time.

"Playing with robots gets me excited," Casmir blurted and tried to smirk, though he was too busy panicking to manage any acting flair.

The man had been reaching for his arm, but his hand halted in midair. "You telling me you're yanking your stick?"

He jerked his hand back.

"That's disgusting," Kim said, either to help make them believe that or as an honest comment. A disapproving I-can't-believe-you-said-that look accompanied it.

The video finally resolved so Casmir once again viewed engineering from the camera of the robot on the engine housing. Nobody had moved it. He hit the button, ordering it to detonate the explosive.

The display went black and so did his view of engineering. Had it worked? He'd thought they might hear something since the ships were connected through the airlock umbilical cord.

He checked on the robot on the bridge where he still had a connection. The two men must have heard the explosion in engineering, for they raced out, leaving the area empty of crew.

Maybe Casmir could take advantage and tinker further. For some reason, the grumpy intruder hadn't reached for his arm again.

Casmir sent the bridge robot climbing up the side of the environmental-controls station.

The two men in the lounge with him spun to look toward the hatch. Casmir didn't know if they had heard shouts or something over their helmet comm units.

"Stay here and watch them!" one man barked and ran out.

His buddy, whose boot was still on the back of Qin's neck, scowled suspiciously at Casmir.

Shouts came from the cargo hold of the *Dragon*. Casmir couldn't decipher them, but he hoped the men were being ordered back to deal with an attacker on their own ship.

The remaining guard abandoned Qin and strode toward him. "Let's see what you're really doing under the table."

Casmir looked down at his lap—and the remote—and feigned innocence, but he also got a few more commands in. The robot didn't have any kind of hand or grasper, but he managed to bump one of the vacuum nozzles against the control for the lights. The bridge went dim. Hopefully, the lights on their entire ship did.

The man grasped his arm and yanked it up with so much force he pulled Casmir from the seat—and the deck. Once again, he dangled in the air, a flash of agony in his shoulder as his captor almost twisted it out of the socket. The man tore the remote from his fingers and smashed it in a steel grip. Dozens of tiny pieces tinkled to the deck.

"What did you—"

An arm snaked around the man's helmet and yanked him backward, halting his words.

Qin.

She leaped onto his back and wrapped her legs around his waist, one arm around his throat. That throat was armored, but the man still dropped Casmir and whirled to deal with her.

As Casmir rolled away, hoping to avoid the skirmish—and being crushed by giant combat boots—Qin slammed her free fist into the man's faceplate. If a normal human had done that, nothing would have happened, but Casmir heard a faint crack. Was she strong enough to shatter Glasnax? He hadn't thought that was even possible.

Lopez rose to her feet and rushed to the kitchen area. The man tried unsuccessfully to tear Qin off his back. Even though his armor enhanced his strength, she had much better leverage.

As Casmir joined Kim beyond the far side of the table, Lopez leaped up and ran to Qin's side. Orange light flared—a blowtorch.

"Hold him still," Lopez barked.

"Easier said than done," Qin replied as the man ran to a bulkhead and spun to ram her against it.

Lopez followed and held the blowtorch to one of his thigh seams. He didn't seem to feel the heat, but if she had time, it might melt through his armor.

After a few seconds, the man shrieked. He'd been too busy wrestling with Qin to pay attention to Lopez, but now he released Qin's arms and lunged for the blowtorch.

Qin took advantage of his distraction and rearranged her grip to hook a leg over his shoulder and pin one of his arms. She was like a spider, immobilizing him from behind. A massive crack sounded.

Qin moved so quickly that Casmir didn't see what happened until the man's helmet was bouncing across the deck, the faceplate shattered. He cursed and bucked, flailing to try to get rid of her and the blowtorch burning its way into his thigh seam.

With his head exposed, Lopez shifted the blowtorch to his face, holding the flame an inch from his eyes. He froze.

"Strip," she ordered.

A shudder went through the deck. Casmir grimaced. He hoped the damage he'd done to the other ship wouldn't cause its course to shift. If it ricocheted off them at the speed they were going... the explosion would be the last thing any of them ever saw. Nothing but shrapnel would arrive at Forseti Station.

The man's eyes bulged as he stared at the blowtorch.

"Strip!" Lopez said again. "Or we'll do it for you."

"Get your she-cat off my back," he growled. "I'm not a damn scratching post."

Lopez's eyes were icier than a comet as she brushed the blowtorch flame across the man's cheek.

He screamed and jerked his head back, clunking it against the bulkhead. "All right, all right, you bitch."

"Tranq him," Lopez told Qin.

Qin sprang off his back—neither of them appeared as wounded as Casmir had thought they were when they'd been dumped in here—and ran to a cabinet that he'd assumed was part of the pantry. She pulled out a first-aid kit with a jet injector, loaded a cartridge, and ran back and jammed it against the man's neck. A soft hiss sounded. He was in the middle of removing his torso piece, per Lopez's order to strip, but he swore and grabbed his neck.

"What the—" He only had time to glower at them before tipping to the deck, unconscious.

"In retrospect," Lopez said, "we should have waited for him to get the rest of the armor off before tranqing him."

Despite the words, the two women set upon the unconscious man and soon had him out of the rest of his gear.

As they patted him down, removing everything from grenades to daggers to malleable explosive material, Casmir asked, "Did you get them to dump you in here on purpose, knowing there was a blowtorch in the kitchen cabinet?"

"That was the idea."

"And, uhm, *why* was there a blowtorch in the kitchen cabinet? Are there any weapons in the breadbox or refrigerator that we should know about?"

"It's a tortilla keeper."

"What?" Casmir asked.

"That's not a breadbox; it's a tortilla keeper. And no, there are no more weapons. The blowtorch is there because now and then, I take a break from my standbys of chocolate and orejas—and chocolate-dipped orejas—and make a crème brûlée." Lopez grabbed twine from a drawer and started tying their prisoner's hands behind his back.

Casmir, deciding he didn't believe her, wondered if the twine was for trussing roasts, or for this precise purpose.

"What happened to get them all riled up?" Lopez asked when she was done. "Half their team ran back to their ship."

"I believe a robot exploded in an inconvenient location in engineering," Casmir said. "Perhaps you should take advantage of the chaos."

"Right." Lopez waved for Qin to follow, and they ran out, the hatch clanging shut behind them.

"You're welcome," Casmir called.

He looked sadly down at the shards on the deck, all that remained of his remote. By now, he wagered that was all that remained of the robots on the other ship too. The one in engineering must have blown into a million pieces. One of the crew—had they implied they were mercenaries?—might have blown the one on the bridge into a similar state.

"So…" Kim eyed the unconscious man. She was still leaning against the cabinets. "Are you worried we've gotten ourselves involved with people in even more trouble than you are?"

"I don't know. Crushers were trying to kill me. What degree of trouble would be worse than that?"

"These people were talking about a war, which tends to involve mass killing and the annihilation of entire cities. Or planets." Kim grimaced.

Casmir did find the talk of war alarming, but he was preoccupied with his own problem now, so he had no trouble staying focused on that. Kim's eyes were troubled though—maybe she was thinking of her family back home.

"You're not worried about your book collection again, are you?" He smiled, hoping to distract her from dark thoughts. He doubted Odin was in danger of an invasion anytime soon.

"I haven't *stopped* worrying about that. If those crushers molested my shelves, I'm going to find whoever sent them and force them to replace every missing book." Her eyes widened at some new thought. "What if we're not back in time to pay next month's rent? What if the landlord takes all our stuff and sells it? At some sidewalk sale? My first editions could be pawned off on teenagers for pennies."

"That won't happen." Casmir winced. He'd meant to make her feel better, not worse. "The rent is taken out of my account automatically every month."

"You think the university is going to keep depositing money in that account if you're not at work?"

"One would hope I'd get a paid leave of absence, at least for a while."

"You have to put in for that, don't you? If you skip town—or the planet—it doesn't just automatically come."

"Have I mentioned how cheerful and inspiring it is to travel with you?" Now Casmir was worried about more than the crushers.

"No."

CHAPTER 11

A FAINT HUM REVERBERATED THROUGH THE DECK AS THE *Stellar Dragon* increased its acceleration. Taking advantage of the commotion, Bonita and Qin had captured the second mercenary that had been left behind to guard them. The rest had all charged back to their ship to deal with the problem over there. Bonita had forcefully removed their airlock docking tube and shut the *Dragon's* hatch before rushing to navigation, her knees aching every step of the way. She prayed she was done with running and twisting and lunging for her life for a while.

She slung herself into the piloting pod, wanting to put distance between her freighter and their ship. With luck, whatever had happened over there would force the mercenaries to stop to fix it, but she couldn't count on that.

"What *did* happen?" she asked aloud.

With her pod sealed around her, she couldn't look at Qin but knew she had claimed the other seat.

"What made them run back to their ship?" Bonita added.

Casmir had said something as she and Qin ran off to deal with the other intruder, but she'd barely heard it.

Viggo was the one to answer her. Qin, who had been feigning unconsciousness alongside Bonita, probably didn't know any more than she did.

"Two of my newer model cleaning robots were *utterly* destroyed," Viggo said. "Do not be surprised to find a charge to your account when I order replacements on Forseti Station."

"That didn't answer my question as much as you seemed to think it would."

Bonita remembered Casmir promising the mercenaries that he would modify a robot to help find the hidden cargo. Had that been a ruse? She'd been ready to knock his head off when he'd said that.

"At his request, I left one of my 350 rounds behind for Casmir," Qin said.

"Which he installed in one of my cleaning robots along with a detonator," Viggo said, "and remote-controlled it over to the other ship. I could not see where it went once it left, but, judging by the sudden surge of heat in their engineering section, it was somewhere crucial to the ship's operation."

Bonita grimaced. "Does that mean I owe him? I *hate* owing people."

"You helped him escape the trouble that was following him on Odin," Qin said. "Perhaps that means you're now even and don't owe him anything."

"*You* helped him escape that. He probably owes *you* something."

"I was going to ask him more about knights and if they're as noble as the stories say, but we were interrupted."

"Maybe he'll kiss your hand later," Bonita said. "Even the non-knights from Odin have notions of chivalry."

"I'm not sure he's... my type."

"It's the hair. Nobody could daydream about a man with such shaggy hair." Bonita ordered her pod to release her. "I'm going to make sure the men we knocked out aren't going to escape my makeshift brig and find their armor. Let me know if anything up here demands my attention."

"I am already searching the catalog of a small-robots dealer on Forseti Station," Viggo said. "I shall inform you promptly if I find robots suitable for insertion into my maligned cadre of troops."

"That's *not* the anything I imagined demanding my attention." Bonita headed into the corridor. "You must have thirty of those things. Why worry about two?"

"Cleaning efficiency will go down."

"There's not so much as a speck of dust anywhere on this ship."

"*Now.*"

Bonita dropped down the ladder to the next level and paused at the closed hatch to the lounge. She ought to thank Casmir, but maybe a nod of gratitude and a handshake when he departed would do.

She continued past the lounge and checked on her prisoners, as she'd said she would. They were both sedated, and she might leave them that way for the rest of the trip. She doubted it would kill them, and she didn't want to risk having to deal with any heroic escape attempts from them.

After that, she swung into the mid-level lavatory. The *Dragon* could carry a crew of ten, plus passengers, so there were enough amenities to accommodate a few people at a time. The amenities weren't what interested her now; rather the bulkhead behind the toilets held her attention. She found the secret sensor at the edge of the panel and leaned in for a retina scan.

After the beam verified her identity, the panel slid open. She tapped a button, and layers of insulation receded, revealing an eight-foot-long by four-foot-wide case. She carefully tugged it out. There was no way she could have hefted it on Odin or another high-gravity planet, but she managed to manhandle it to the deck where she considered the computerized lock thoughtfully.

The dealer on Sayona Station had given her the case without the code. At the time, she hadn't thought much about it, since it was Baum's merchandise, and he'd paid most of the purchase price. Most of it but not *all* of it. Now that he was gone and nobody from his organization had contacted her, she considered it hers to sell as she wished. There was just the problem of the code. And the fact that she was starting to wonder if state-of-the-art weapons were truly what lay nestled inside. The items on the list of contents she'd been given seemed like they would fit in this size case, but a lot of other things could be nestled in there too.

Until those thugs had boarded the ship, she'd assumed that list of merchandise accurate. But now...

"If you are wondering if the mercenaries found the cargo," Viggo said, "you could have asked."

Bonita jumped, clunking her elbow on one of the wash stations.

"Viggo. We've had this conversation before. You're not to speak with me when I'm in the lav."

"But you're not doing the things people do in a lavatory. Things that I can't say I miss having to be concerned with. I do miss food and eating. Do enjoy that whenever you get a chance."

"Thanks for the tip."

Bonita ran her hand over the lock pad panel. It lit up with a request for a code. The display formed into a keyboard with letters, symbols, and numbers, creating more combination possibilities than she could imagine. She pulled out a handheld scanner, but it couldn't read anything through the case's hard exterior.

"Any chance your big computer brain can open this, Viggo?"

"Perhaps if there were a means for me to interface with it and run a few code-breaking routines, I could, but I don't see an access port, and it's not responding to my wireless signal. It appears to be fully self-contained. Perhaps your new ally would have some ideas."

Her first thought was that he meant Qin, since she'd only been aboard a couple of months. "You mean Dabrowski? He's not an ally. He didn't even pay a full enough fare for where we're taking him. And his not-wife didn't pay anything at all."

Not that Kim had technically wanted to come.

"He was astute and swift at reprogramming my robots." Viggo still sounded indignant about the loss. "Perhaps he'll have ideas for opening this, if that is what you want to do. I note that it's been on board for six weeks, and you haven't attempted to gain access previously."

"That's because I previously thought it was a batch of high-end guns."

"You no longer believe that?"

"Who sends a mercenary ship to collect guns? Yes, anything from Sayona Station is going to be cutting-edge technology and higher quality than you can find on Odin, but they're supposed to be handguns and rifles, and that's it. I only paid ten thousand Union dollars, and I think Baum paid fifty. That's a lot to *me*, especially right now, but nobody sends ships full of mercs to mine such small asteroids."

Bonita ran a hand along the fine seam between the top and bottom of the case. Was it possible her blowtorch would work? Maybe, but then she risked heating up whatever was inside. The last thing she needed to do was cause an explosion in her lavatory. She already had craters in the deck plating of her cargo hold, thanks to that skirmish.

The hatch opened, and Bonita whipped her pistol out and pointed it at the intruder.

Casmir ambled in before he saw her, the pistol, and the case. He halted, his jaw dropping halfway to the deck.

He whirled, lifting his hands in the air. "If that's your illicit cargo, I didn't see a thing."

"I know you didn't, because it's still locked in its case. I haven't seen it either."

"Uhm, right. Is that a problem?"

"That I haven't seen inside? It wasn't, until those mercs showed up and shot up my ship."

Bonita waited for him to leave. He kept standing there with his hands up.

"I apologize for coming in without knocking," Casmir said. "I didn't realize anyone was in here. I had to... you know."

"By all means, use the facilities. Your half ounce of gold entitles you to all the toilet paper you need."

Casmir didn't move. Probably because he didn't know if her sarcasm could be taken at face value.

She gave him an exasperated sigh. "Put your hands down. I'm not going to shoot you." She realized she was still pointing her pistol at him and holstered it. "Especially if you really do need to use the lav. Shooting someone with a full bladder could result in a mess."

"That is possible. I encourage you to aim lower if you ever need to shoot me. Legs seem relatively repairable and, even if not, are unlikely to affect my ability to do my job. I'd be even more willing to sacrifice a foot." He lowered his hands and pointed to the corridor. "I'll wait out there until you're done."

Bonita eyed the case and thought of Viggo's suggestion. It wasn't a bad one, but did she want some goofy stranger—and she did mean *goofy*—to know her secrets? Yes, he had helped them escape those mercs, but he was just looking out for his own life.

"Casmir," Bonita said, stopping him before he closed the hatch. "Do you think you could open this?"

She hoped she wasn't making a mistake. Both by enlisting his aid and by trying to look inside the sealed case. But if something that wasn't on the packing list was hidden in there and she tried to pawn it off on Diego, she could make an enemy of the pirate family.

Shouldn't she be old enough by now to stop making stupid mistakes? No, her last marriage was a testament to that.

Casmir stepped inside and crouched for a closer look, scrutinizing the seams as she'd done and also the keypad. He tapped the keyboard integrated into the display, eliciting a soft beep.

"What are you *doing*?" she snarled, her hand twitching toward her pistol again.

He noticed the gesture and leaned back in alarm, his eye blinking. "Seeing what I'm dealing with?"

Bonita forced herself to lower her hand. "Can't you do that without touching it? What happens if you don't finish entering the combination? It could shoot out flames or poison gas or who knows what."

"Flames? That seems an extreme response to an incorrect code entry. And unlikely given the size of the object and the likelihood that people who purchase such safes want most of the interior space for storing goods. Still, I accede to your point. It is likely that we'd be locked out after a certain number of incorrect tries. I simply wanted to know if it required a physical touch or if an electronic signal might work for activating the keys, because I do know of software for cracking systems like this. I would have to build something to interface with it. Hm, I don't see any kind of port."

"Yes, Viggo mentioned that being a problem."

"Perhaps electronic pulses..." Casmir tilted his head thoughtfully.

Thinking? Or waiting for input from the ship's computer?

Bonita waved toward the ceiling. "Viggo?"

"You told me not to speak with you in the lavatory."

She rolled her eyes.

"It is generally a relaxing sanctuary where one prefers not to be disturbed," Casmir said. "Though I have noticed that the differences in the equipment on a spaceship are rather pronounced and require more concentration than relaxation."

"Wait until you try it in zero-g."

Casmir grimaced, his hand drifting toward his belt before he caught it. "I'll see what I can build while I'm downloading a cracking program."

"How does a robotics researcher know about cracking programs?" Bonita called after him.

"I am also a teacher of teenagers. All good teachers have to be aware of the various methods students use to breach secure files, virtual and physical, in an attempt to alter test scores."

Qin appeared in the hatchway, looking over her shoulder as Casmir's footsteps retreated. She turned her curious eyes toward the case.

"Problem?" Bonita doubted Qin would openly question her choice to include Casmir in her snooping, but she preemptively changed the subject just in case.

"The mercenary ship is falling farther behind."

"Good."

"But they sent a communication ahead to Forseti Station."

"That's less good. Were you able to intercept it?"

Qin shook her head. "No, it was on a tight beam."

"So, if they have allies on the station, they could be waiting for us when we arrive."

"Should we consider changing course?"

"I'm sure we should, but I already told Diego we'd meet him there. And sell him this." Bonita eyed the case. "Whatever it is."

Qin arched her eyebrows. "We could ask our captured mercenaries if they know what it is. One would assume they had some knowledge, so they wouldn't be duped and accept a lesser prize."

"I don't have any eslevoamytal along," Bonita said. "It's an expensive drug, and I haven't had a reason to do interrogations for a while."

"I could question them without a drug." Qin didn't appear excited by the prospect, but something about the grim set of her eyes said she had done it before and could again.

For the first time, Bonita was tempted to ask for more details about Qin's past. She had a policy of not prying—most people in her line of work didn't appreciate nosy questions about their personal history—and she'd gotten the gist over the last couple of months.

"Here we go," Casmir announced in the corridor.

Qin stepped aside, and he entered with a portable keyboard attached to a little black box with a wire and a magnet or sensor or who knew what dangling from the end.

"You made your thing for interfacing?" Bonita asked.

"And running a software-cracking program, yes." Casmir knelt beside the case and attached the magnet to the keypad.

"It takes me longer than that to make a sandwich."

"Oh? Do you make the pickles from scratch?" Casmir tapped a few commands on his keyboard—Bonita watched intently in case she ever needed to replicate the actions—then let it hang next to the case while he waited for the program to run. "One of my colleagues does that. He's pickled everything from lemons to garlic to cauliflower to blueberries. Oh, and cured bacon. That was odd. His concoctions do make for an interesting aroma in the lunchroom when he brings them in. And he's never happy unless everyone samples them."

A beep came from Casmir's device, saving Bonita from having to come up with a response to the question—there *had* been a question in there, hadn't there?

"That's a shorter code than I expected." Casmir reached for the keypad on the case but paused. "Do you want to stand back? In case it's wrong and you were right about the flames?"

"Just press it. I can yank you in front of me quickly if need be."

"I see. You're not willing to shoot a man with a full bladder, but you'll push him in front of an inferno without hesitation."

"To protect myself from incineration? Yes, I'll risk wet boots."

"Ew," Qin said.

"I guess it's a good thing I only needed two of your cleaning robots earlier. I'd hate to leave you with a mess."

Qin's *ew* turned into a giggle. It was a strange sound coming from someone who'd just been talking about interrogating prisoners. Maybe she was rethinking Casmir's knightly potential.

He tapped in a code, using a mix of letters, symbols, and numbers, and settled back on his heels. A reassuring beep came from the case, and the lid popped.

Bonita eyed it warily, half-expecting a trap to be triggered. Casmir did not reach for the lid right away. She pulled out her scanner again. It still couldn't read much with the case open only an inch, but it didn't detect any heat or radiation.

Casmir extended a hand toward it. "It's your illicit case."

"Good. Thanks. Give me that." She pointed to the contraption he'd used to open the lock. Whatever was in here, she wanted to be the person to have control over opening and closing it in the future.

His brows lifted, but he handed her the device. Then backed up to the hatch, but he didn't leave the room. He had to be curious.

Should she make him go?

She shrugged and pulled the lid up, standing away from the opening, but no traps sprang. His code must have been deemed acceptable.

Bonita was disappointed but not surprised that the case wasn't full of the various handheld weapons that had been on the list. It took her a moment to figure out what it *was* full of. A disassembled rocket in an insulated mold that would keep it from being jostled around in zero gravity. Several rows of vials lay next to it in insulated pockets. A slight vapor came off them, and she realized that section of the case was refrigerated. The vials had labels, but the print was too small to read without removing them.

When Bonita reached for one, Casmir said, "I wouldn't."

"Do you know what they are?"

"I think Kim might," he said grimly.

"Oh, good. I wanted to have more people aware of the secret cargo stashed on my ship."

"You know I was going to tell her about everything anyway, right?" Casmir smiled, but the gesture only drew attention to his one-eyed blink. Was he nervous about what they'd unearthed?

Bonita waved. "Go get her."

He tripped over nothing as he hurried away. He *was* nervous. Considering he had remained relatively calm while being manhandled by mercenaries, Bonita worried she should be nervous too.

Kim appeared in the hatchway. She'd been wearing her borrowed galaxy suit all along, as Bonita had advised on the first day, but now she had the gloves on and the helmet in place.

That alone made Bonita take several large steps back from the case. What had Casmir told her?

As Kim gazed down at the case, she didn't react with a gape or any of Casmir's signs of nerves, but when she stepped inside and crouched in front of the vials, it was with slow and deliberate care. She picked up one of the vials, read the label, and examined the seal. She set it back in its pocket and picked up another one.

Bonita watched her eyes through her faceplate, but she might as well have been watching an android. Kim methodically examined several of the vials. She barely glanced at the rocket. Bonita had seen a few of those in her day and thought it looked state-of-the-art but unspectacular. It was simply a tool for delivering and dispersing the vials, she wagered.

But delivering and dispersing them where? A space station? A *planet*?

"There are four strains," Kim said. "With extras for... redundancy, I suppose. They're all lab-grown and extremely customized—nothing existing in nature—so I can only make guesses based on the scientific naming conventions. And the presence of a delivery mechanism," she added dryly, waving toward the rocket.

"A bioweapon, I assume," Casmir said from the doorway, his helmet also on now. "That's an XR-7 Heavy Stinger—I know thanks to Professor Petrov's fascination with model rockets. If it were detonated high enough in the atmosphere, it's got the power to spread its payload over a continent."

"That would result in too much dilution, even for something extremely potent," Kim said. "These vials aren't very large. But a city might be targeted."

"A city with millions of people?" Casmir asked. "Like Zamek?"

"Yes. And if those bacteria are self-replicating once they find a host, far more than a city could end up affected."

"Those are designed to kill people?" Bonita asked. "Is that what they would do?"

"That's my guess from the names." Kim eyed the vials. "I'd love to have a look at the strains in my lab under my microscope. Well, maybe not in *my* lab. In the Biosafety Level Four lab at the back of our campus."

"You're going to make me hyperventilate, Kim." Casmir waved at the case. "I've been sleeping next door to that bulkhead. And taking a leak right under it." His voice *did* have a hysterical edge to it, but he gulped and cleared his throat. "How about we close up Pandora's box there, eh? Would that case be sufficient to keep the bacteria in if something happened to one of those vials? Like it broke?"

Kim snorted. "Doubtful. Shipping this is even more illegal than making it. There should have been all manner of biohazard warning and fragile stickers covering this case, and the vials should have a containment field around them, not some completely ineffective padding. But, if the proper precautions had been taken, I suppose someone couldn't have been tricked into delivering it then." Kim gazed at Bonita.

"I wasn't tricked," Bonita snapped, more out of reflex than because it was true.

"If you *knowingly* brought this on board your own ship, you're even more of an idiot than I think you are right now."

Bonita clenched her teeth, her fingers twitching toward her pistol.

"Easy, my friends," Casmir said, lifting his hands, ambling non-threateningly into the room, and standing between them. "I think this is a time for us to come together in problem-solving camaraderie rather than in insult-throwing angst that could lead to unfortunate mishaps. Such as bullets being fired next to horrible biological weapons that might be able to melt us into piles of radioactive waste from the inside out."

"Shit." Bonita hadn't truly intended to pull out her pistol—she just had that instinct when she was being threatened—but the idea that a little mistake could do what Casmir described... "Yeah, let's close it up and put it away."

"Put it away?" Kim asked. "If you're *not* an idiot, you'll space that. *Now.* While we're out in the middle of nowhere, and it's unlikely to ever be found again."

Bonita carefully lowered the lid while considering her options. She *could* space the case. But she had Diego waiting to buy non-existent weapons, and crazy mercenaries that knew she had it—and whoever their employers were had to know too.

She could apologize to Diego and tell him the deal was off—she would have to, since she didn't have what he'd agreed to buy. But what about the mercs? They knew where she'd come from, and they knew where she was heading. If she spaced it, they might be able to retrace her route and find it. Even if the case didn't have any kind of heat signature, a metallic object would still be detectable on scanners.

She could space it and blow it up with the railgun, but if her pursuers caught up with her again, they might not believe she'd destroyed it, at least not at first, not until they'd tortured her to death for its location. That would be an unpleasant way to go.

Her life had been so much easier when she'd been a bounty hunter. She vowed to go back to that if she survived this hellish month. If she had to compete with young pups for bounties, so be it. She knew how to find people and take them down. This... This was too much.

"Would that truly work?" Casmir asked Kim. "Someone knows she has it and could simply retrace our route to find it. And then what? Some unscrupulous bad guys have this weapon in our system. Unscrupulous bad guys who could be gunning for Odin."

Bonita nodded, glad he'd had similar thoughts, so she wouldn't have to explain. Even if her concerns were more about her own life than the ramifications of the weapon being unleashed on a planet. She would worry about that *after* this was off her ship.

"Space it and destroy it, then. Does this freighter have guns? If not, maybe one of Qin's explosives and a remote detonator?" Kim looked at Casmir.

"We're not destroying it until we're someplace with witnesses who will swear they saw me destroy it," Bonita said. "Help me put this back in the cubby, Qin."

Bonita had carefully and with painstaking thoroughness closed the lid, and she gently lifted one side of the case.

Qin hesitated before coming inside—it was the first time Bonita recalled her hesitating to follow an order. She ordered her helmet to affix itself before stepping close and gingerly picking up the other side.

"Are we safe if we keep our suits on, Kim?" Qin asked as she helped Bonita return the case to its hiding spot. "You can go out in space in them. They're airtight." Qin looked at Bonita, the grim young woman willing to torture men gone and a scared teenager peering out through those cat's eyes. "Right?"

"They could protect us from a bacterial infection," Kim said, "but I'd hazard a guess that any protection would only be temporary. A couple of those labels mentioned acids, and I've heard of plenty of bioweapons with the ability to eat through hazmat suits as well as flesh and muscle. The vile people who make these things don't want them to be easily defeated."

Casmir held up a gloved finger. "Easy, Kim. You've seen me hyperventilate before. You don't want to deal with the consequences."

Kim shook her head at the joke—or maybe it wasn't a joke—and watched Bonita secure the panel, the case now tucked back into the hidden compartment.

"What are you going to do?" Kim asked.

"I don't know yet." Bonita rubbed her face. "I don't know."

CHAPTER 12

CASMIR WILLED HIS STOMACH TO STAY CALM AND enjoy the motion-sickness pill he'd taken as he gripped a handhold built into the wall near the porthole and looked at what he could see of Forseti Station—so far, only the asteroid exterior that protected it from radiation and space trash.

He'd had to remove his helmet for long enough to refill his suit's water reservoir and pop the pill into his mouth, and his rush to affix it again had made Kim smile. He'd been careful to stay fully ensconced as much as possible since their little discovery. It had been days, but he hadn't slept much since then. He'd been too busy imagining some horrible manmade disease eating him from the inside out before it ate everyone else on Odin from the inside out. He couldn't keep from glancing uneasily in the direction of the lavatory ten times an hour.

"As far as we know, it's still contained," Kim said after one of his glances.

"Which should make me feel much better, I know, but I keep worrying about it. I can't even go in to use the facilities on this level, because I'm afraid if I flush too hard and rattle the bulkhead, one of those vials will break, and we'll all die horrifically."

His boots lifted slightly from the deck, and his stomach lurched with queasiness at the strange sensation of almost floating. Two days earlier, the ship had flipped over, and they had been decelerating toward their destination since then. Now that they were almost there and barely moving, there wasn't a force in play to keep their feet, or anything else, on the deck.

His toolkit was on the verge of floating off the table. He scrambled over to get it, half walking, half pushing off the wall and furniture bolted to the deck.

"Exactly what are you doing when you flush those toilets?" Kim asked. "It sounds like you have an oddly vigorous technique."

"How can you be so calm? If anything happens to that stuff, we'll die. If Lopez sells it to pirates who decide to unleash it on the station, we'll die. If the people who originally ordered it show up and take it back to its original destination of Odin, where it was presumably to be used, everybody we know and love could die."

Casmir thought of all his friends at work and of his parents. And of the mother he'd never met but who had cared enough to leave money sufficient to fund his education—and who'd sent a knight to warn him to get off-world. She probably hadn't meant for him to get off-world in a ship carrying a genocidal bioweapon.

"I'm not pleased about the situation, I assure you," Kim said. "Especially since I don't trust the captain."

"I think she's decent—she hasn't threatened to kidnap us and ransom us back to our families, so I can overlook that she's a smuggler. She helped me out of an uncomfortable situation, whether she intended to or not. But she hasn't said what she's going to do now that she knows what she's got." Casmir, toolkit in hand, made his way back to the porthole where Kim also hung on to a handhold. "With that kind of threat, she could inadvertently cause something awful to happen. An *accident* could cause something awful to happen. And that's making me nervous. I packed my meager belongings, under the assumption that she'll ask us to get off here—and I think I should figure things out from somewhere with more resources before fleeing farther out of the system—but can we just walk off the ship knowing what we know? That a horrific weapon is stashed in here, possibly available to the highest bidder?"

"I was thinking of..." Kim glanced toward the speakers on the walls. She activated her chip and sent him a text message that scrolled through his vision. *I considered sneaking in there and taking the vials to dispose of myself, but with the ship's computer aware of everything that goes on, I assumed it—he—would alert her. And then she would shoot me. She has a twitchy gun hand.*

I noticed, Casmir messaged back.

My current plan is to walk straight off the ship and find the Kingdom Guard station, or whoever handles law enforcement here. I have enough experience to advise, if necessary, but dealing with containment isn't my area of expertise. With luck, they'll have an expert trained to handle infectious diseases and threats like this since a fully enclosed station is a place where something could run rampant and kill the entire population.

I'm sure a space station has an amazing filtration and air-scrubbing system in place.

That might or might not be enough. Something designed to thrive in human hosts could hunker down and pass from person to person through contact. Kim shrugged. *With luck, it'll be a non-issue, because they'll find the shipment and dispose of it properly.*

I could use some luck.

The *Stellar Dragon* sailed closer to one of the asteroid's poles, over banks and banks of solar panels attached to the rocky surface, and into a massive tunnel. Bright lights illuminated the manmade passage, and they flew past a couple of passenger transports on their way out. Their freighter navigated around a few turns, and one of the circular ends of the station came into view, reminding Casmir of the top of a fizzop can. A miles-wide, spinning fizzop can.

All along the rim of the can, numerous sets of hangar doors were set into the surface, as well as banks of airlocks and the massive open bays of repair facilities. Flashing signs promised the availability of various types of fuels, cheap hotel rooms, reasonably priced repair facilities, and all-you-can-eat buffets. Dozens of ships were docked at the airlocks, which were tiny compared to the mass of the station. They reminded Casmir of little barnacles attached to the side of a sea-going ship. He hoped the size and population of the station meant it would be easy to disappear inside and that few people would notice the arrival of the *Stellar Dragon*.

"Let's hope we don't run into any of your friends here," Kim said, switching back to voice.

"I wonder if it's better for us to leave right away or wait a few hours and depart in the middle of the night." Casmir wondered how days worked on the station, if there was perpetual artificial light, or if there were day and night cycles.

A knock sounded before the hatch to the lounge opened. Qin stuck her helmeted head inside.

"Captain says it's been nice knowing you and to grab your stuff and be ready to depart as soon as we lock up."

"Thank you, Qin," Casmir said.

Kim snorted. "Apparently, we're leaving right away."

Qin shut the hatch again without mentioning the case or what Lopez intended to do with it.

"So it seems," Casmir said.

He hoped Kim's plan to visit the Kingdom Guard office would be easy to implement. Maybe he could make inquiries about his own problem there. Would the local authorities have access to the Odin systems? Maybe by now, someone had figured out who sent the crushers.

A clang reverberated through the freighter as they docked. Casmir's feet clunked down to the deck, and a wave of nausea came over him. They were piggybacking off the station's spin gravity now that they were attached. He did his best not to think of them twirling around in space like kids on the playground pushing a merry-go-round to spin faster and faster. Horrific devices. Of course, he'd had a seizure and fallen off one once, so that hadn't helped him fall in love with them. That had been the year before his doctor had found a more effective medication for him.

Now, if he could just find a more effective medication for motion sickness.

"Easy, stomach," Casmir murmured, patting it. "Enjoy your drugs and ignore the craziness of our new reality."

"Does talking to it make it less queasy?" Kim headed for the corridor.

"It hasn't yet, but I'm an optimist."

"I've noticed."

After Casmir collected his gear, he headed up the ladder well instead of down.

"Where are you going?" Kim had already started down to the cargo hold, but she paused.

"To say goodbye and thank the captain for her hospitality."

She squinted at him. "You're trying to figure out what she's going to do with the case, aren't you?"

"Certainly." He hadn't considered it—the idea of letting the authorities handle it sounded stellar to him—but it sounded silly to admit that his parents had always insisted on good manners from him.

He gave Kim a knightly bow from the ladder, then climbed out and wobbled to navigation. The gravity was steady, but it was still different from what he'd grown accustomed to the last couple of days.

The hatch stood open, Lopez in her pod, the sides peeled back so he could see her profile.

"Captain?"

She looked warily over her shoulder.

Casmir repeated the bow, this time offering a more genuine version. "Thank you for bringing Kim and me along to the station. I know you hadn't planned on us being here and sucking down your food, and I regret that I can't offer you more money, but even when I dare access my banking chip, it's not connected to a great deal of wealth."

"Tell me about it."

For a confused moment, he misinterpreted her sarcasm and thought she referred to his situation. But that wasn't it.

"Funds are short for you as well?" he asked.

"I wouldn't have gotten myself into this mess if they weren't." Lopez flung a hand in the direction of the lavatory. "Don't get married, kid. Especially not to a conniving ass of a man who's oh-so-good at making you believe his dreams are your dreams, and then disappears with everything in your savings account and all of your clients."

The openness of the rant surprised Casmir, and he wondered if she had been drinking. Having an awful bioweapon on one's ship probably warranted alcohol, but she had also been piloting her freighter into dock, so he hoped for soberness.

"I'll keep that advice in mind, Captain. Though I don't have plans to marry a man, so perhaps I'm saved on that front. That's not allowed on Odin, you know."

"It's a backward little planet."

"I've heard that often, but it works for the backward individuals on it. At least these days, there are other options for those who don't fit in." He spread a hand, thinking of how often he, as a kid, had dreamed of escaping to another system, one where hulking masculinity was considered a suggestion of simian ancestors rather than a desirable trait, and where beautiful women fantasized about smart scientists and engineers rather than knights and sports stars. But he'd never been positive such a place truly existed or that modifications and augmentations did anything to change human nature. "Regardless, I do hope that you find a solution for your financial woes. I'm sure it's very difficult to start over. I fear I may be about to find that out personally, if I can't get to the bottom of my own problems so I can go home again."

All he received was an indifferent grunt.

Casmir thought about doing as Kim had suggested and asking what Lopez intended to do with the bioweapon, but he doubted Lopez would answer, and he might rouse her suspicions if he pried.

"Goodbye, Captain."

She flicked her fingers in what was either a vague farewell wave or an attempt to remove a booger.

Kim was waiting for Casmir in the cargo hold, her bags over her shoulder, the wooden swords once again affixed to one. They found Qin waiting at the airlock hatch, her hands clasped behind her back.

Lopez's voice floated down the ladder well from above. "Don't let them forget to leave my suits."

Casmir touched his helmet, reluctant to take it off, much less leave it behind. He could think of all manner of situations where a self-contained suit might be useful on a space station, and he wagered most of the residents had their own tucked away in emergency lockers.

He almost asked if they could borrow them and send them back, but Kim was already removing her suit and helmet.

"Right," Casmir muttered and shed his own.

Even though they were older models, they were probably worth more than he'd paid for passage.

"It was interesting to meet you." Qin stuck her hand out to exchange grips with them. "It was great how you disabled the merc ship, Casmir. You're smart, and I wish you were staying on."

"Thank you," Casmir said, surprised but pleased by her words.

Now, he wished he'd gotten a chance to know the young woman better. Despite her fearsome looks, she was a far more amenable soul than the captain.

"Be very careful with that case," Kim told Qin for her parting. "*Very* careful."

"I understand. I'm sure we can get rid of it in a way that it won't be put to horrible use on anyone."

"Good." Kim nodded.

Qin tapped a control panel, and the hatch swung open, revealing a short walk to the station's also-open hatch.

Casmir crossed first, vowing to keep his eyes open for threats. He accessed the network and called up a map of the station as well as the location of the nearest Kingdom Guard office. The idea of sending uniformed men to the captain's door as a thank-you for her help made him squirm with guilt, but they couldn't ignore the threat on her ship.

All of the airlocks funneled their crews out into a tiered concourse bustling with people, exotic food smells, and thousands of noises from conversations to robot vendors hawking their wares to the rings and clangs of gambling machines. Booths and shops ranged from the practical—food and fuel stores— to the whimsical—robotic squirrels that rode on a person's shoulder—to the salacious—hotel rooms with men, women, and androids for rent by the hour. Casmir had heard that such offerings were tame in System Lion and that one could find far more exotic sexual entertainment in the other systems.

He started into the concourse but noticed Kim hesitating in the airlock chamber. Hesitating and grimacing as if she were in pain.

"Are you all right?" Casmir asked.

"Yes." Kim took a breath and visibly collected herself. "It's just noisy." She waved at the concourse. "Let's hurry through, please, and find someplace less... *less*."

"Right." He remembered her once admitting that she got headaches and had a hard time focusing on conversations if there was a lot of other stimulation around. As someone whose seizures were sometimes triggered by flashing lights, he could empathize completely.

They strode into the concourse, and Casmir headed toward a Kingdom Guard office identified on his map, though his eye was drawn to the robot squirrels. He wondered how realistic their ambulatory range was in comparison to the flesh-and-fur creatures that had inspired them. As he drifted toward that shop, simply to ask the merchant for confirmation on how to get to the Guard station, of course, he was so busy looking at the robots and the tools along the back wall that he almost missed the tall figure striding purposefully toward them.

"Casmir." Kim elbowed him.

A large blond man in dark silver liquid armor and a purple cloak veered out of the traffic to walk beside Casmir. His stomach knotted for reasons that had nothing to do with gravity. A knight.

Would he deliver another warning? Had the crushers beat Casmir to the station?

The knight kept facing ahead, not speaking at first. He showed them his pertundo, the telescoping halberd currently in a compact form that hung from his belt, as if to prove his identity. Or maybe he was simply showing he was ready in case he needed to put it to use.

Casmir thought of the knight who'd died for him, and the urge to apologize profusely to this man swarmed over him. He opened his mouth to ask if he had known Sir Friedrich, but the knight spoke first.

"The ship you stepped off is carrying something dangerous." The knight looked at Casmir and Kim out of the corner of his eye.

"Yes!" Casmir blurted, relieved the authorities already knew. "Someone needs to—"

"Not here. Come with me." The knight unclipped his pertundo, twitched it for emphasis, and pointed the sharp tip toward doors at the end of the open mall area.

Casmir realized the man wasn't using the weapon to identify himself. It was a veiled threat. Comply or else.

Casmir was so startled he almost tripped. Why would a knight feel he had to even subtly threaten *him*? He looked at Kim. Her grave expression said she'd already figured out the threat.

We may be considered guilty by association, her text message floated through his vision.

Casmir held back a groan as the knight ushered them into a room.

Two uniformed Kingdom Guard officers stood behind a table inside, wearing the same blue-and-gray uniforms that the Guard wore on Odin. Their hands rested on stunners in holsters, and their faces were icy.

A sign on the back wall of the room read *Customs Interrogation.* Casmir doubted they were about to be searched for smuggled fruit.

"Hello, officers." Casmir waved and did his best to sound cheery, not like a man with something to hide. "And Sir Knight, I didn't get your name. I'm Casmir Dabrowski."

He looked to Kim to see if she wanted to do her own introduction. Her mouth was sealed shut.

"This is my friend," he offered, smiling. "Can we help you?"

"Sir Russo," the knight said shortly.

Casmir bowed and said, "It's been an extremely eventful week, and I'm hoping to get home as soon as possible, but I fear it's not safe. Uh, how much do you know about that?"

"We know who you are and that good men died on the day you mysteriously disappeared from campus, Mr. Dabrowski." The senior officer, an inspector, his badge said, leaned his fists on the table. "Tell us about the contents of that safe."

You mysteriously disappeared? Casmir didn't like the accusatory sound of that. In his absence, had he somehow gone from being a victim to being a suspect for something? Who could have possibly come to that conclusion?

"Safe? If you mean the case holding the rocket, it's about this big by this long." Casmir demonstrated with gestures. "And the other contents are—" he looked at Kim to see if she wanted to explain, but she had adopted a stay-silent-unless-questioned position, "—alarming."

"There *is* a rocket." The knight sucked in an alarmed breath. "And it was on Odin. Dear God."

"It could end up back there if we're not careful," the inspector said. "Dabrowski, how many people are on that freighter? The official dossier says it's just the captain, but we know there's at least one other crew member, some modded freak the captain didn't report when she came to Odin. But for all we know, there are twenty armored men in there. Too many for even a knight to handle."

The inspector shot Sir Russo a firm look, and the knight's lips pinched into an annoyed expression, suggesting they had argued about this earlier. Had Russo intended to charge straight onto the freighter?

"Well, there aren't twenty people." Casmir paused, feeling another twinge of guilt, this time because it seemed like it would be a betrayal to help these men storm the *Stellar Dragon.*

He wanted the authorities to know about and get rid of the bioweapon, the same as Kim, but what if Lopez and Qin were hurt or killed in the process? Lopez hadn't been willing to give up the case to the mercenaries. Would she try to hide it from the Kingdom Guard? How much money did she have tied up in that cargo?

Casmir shifted uneasily, remembering her admission that her funds were low.

"For what capacity did the captain recruit you, Dabrowski?" Russo asked. "Advice on the rocket? We already know why Sato was there." He frowned at Kim as he waved at her. "I trust you tested the samples and found them viable."

Kim's eyebrows flew up.

"I assume you were careful," Russo added, "but is there any possibility of leakage? Do we need to quarantine the ship, or is it safe to retrieve the vials?"

"They were sealed when I saw them." Kim looked at Casmir. Was she as bewildered by this line of questioning as he?

"Er, advice on the rocket?" Casmir asked, struggling to get his head above the quicksand burbling up around them. How could these people know so much but be so wrong about everything? "I happened to know the model and its capabilities, but my specialty is robotics. That must have come up in your research."

"We know your specialties," the investigator said coolly. "And we know you've published papers on rockets as well as robotics."

"I haven't published anything on rockets..."

He trailed off as the investigator flicked a tablet on and slid it across the table so he could see the article on the display.

"Oh, that was for a ballistics class that was required for graduation. There was an opportunity to earn extra credit and some leeway on the final exam if we wrote a couple of research papers and submitted them to periodicals. I was honored that mine was published, but I was mostly pleased to get full marks from crusty old Professora Langbottom. I was worried about my grade-point-average in those days, you understand."

The investigator and the knight exchanged long looks.

Casmir wondered if *they* were messaging each other back and forth. The second Guard, an imposingly tall and broad constable with rolled-up sleeves displaying meaty arms, merely watched everything. He'd walked around the table to stand between Casmir and Kim and the exit.

As if Casmir would try to flee from a *knight*. Where could he even flee to on a space station?

"There are two people on the crew," Kim said, "Captain Lopez and a modded woman with extra strength and likely other attributes we didn't see demonstrated. Neither we nor they learned the truth about their cargo until we were en route. My understanding is that Lopez was trying to deliver what she believed were guns. Then we were attacked by a mercenary ship and barely got away. After that, she snooped and learned she'd been duped. As you deduced, I'm a bacteriologist, and I would be happy to advise your experts on how best to dispose of the bioweapon once you acquire it. Neither Casmir nor I went aboard that ship to help commit a crime. We were fleeing the crushers that were chasing and trying to kill him. Any chance you or one of your colleagues on Odin knows who's trying to kill him?"

Casmir nodded, grateful to Kim for parsing it so clearly for the men. That should help.

But the constable snorted with disbelief, and the inspector and the knight exchanged another long look. Casmir kept himself from pointing out that typically only lovers gazed into each other's eyes for such unwavering lengths of time.

Sir Russo jerked his head toward the door.

The inspector nodded and said, "We're going to talk to our superiors. Constable Davis, search them for weapons and keep them here."

"Gladly." The constable cracked his knuckles and eyed Casmir like a tasty morsel.

Casmir couldn't keep from grimacing—or maybe cringing. He'd dealt with enough bullies in his life to recognize the type, the eager gleam in the eye of someone who enjoyed having power over others. And putting that power to use.

"Let's see those pockets, you treasonous deadbeats," the constable said, striding forward as soon as his colleagues left, the door shutting behind them.

Kim scowled. "We haven't betrayed anyone."

"Don't much care." The constable cracked his knuckles again.

There was only one high window in the wall next to the door. Was the glass insulated so the people shopping in the concourse wouldn't hear them scream? Casmir decided it would be a shame if his wails of agony interrupted the purchase of someone's robot squirrel.

Yas walked past the bridge and toward the captain's briefing room and quarters, glancing out a porthole that he passed. The ship had undocked from the refinery, but Rache hadn't yet given the order to blow it up. Maybe he was waiting for the autopsy results. Yas wished he had found more.

He looked down at the small opaque capsule that he'd cleaned off assiduously before heading up here and hoped it contained something that would distract Rache from the fact that Yas had no idea what had killed those people.

The double doors opened as he approached, and he found Rache standing in the briefing room, his hands clasped behind his back as he gazed at news footage on a screen. When Yas walked in, Rache paused the playback, the display freezing on the face of a man with shaggy brown hair, a lazy eye, and a grin that didn't seem appropriate for the headline flashing over his head.

Odin robotics professor chased by military robots, almost killed in explosion.

"What did you find?" Rache looked at Yas's hand.

"As I told Corporal Chains before he would let me back on the ship, the body had no sign of a viral infection, no hint that the immune system had sensed a threat and responded, and nothing to suggest poisoning." Yas had checked and rechecked for symptoms of toxic exposure, since poisoning would have explained deaths without outward signs of violence or illness. "There was a great deal of cellular damage throughout the body, and I believe that's what killed them. Just looking at the cells, I would have assumed they belonged to very old individuals who died from the deteriorative diseases of age."

"They didn't look that old."

"No. I believe this may have happened quickly. I might have thought acute radiation exposure, but I've seen plenty of that when dealing with space-faring peoples, and this wasn't the same. Usually, acute radiation exposure causes outward signs such as bruising, bleeding from the orifices, hair loss, ulcers, etc. But you saw these bodies. They were unblemished. Further, we should have been able to detect radiation on their suits, and I tested the bodies and also the refinery for exposure. The refinery isn't particularly well-insulated from cosmic radiation, which isn't surprising since no humans work there, but that's not what killed those people." Yas spread his hands. "I'm sorry I don't know what did."

"I see." Rache didn't sound pleased.

Yas didn't know if it was with him or with the situation. Even though Rache's features were hidden behind that mask, Yas suspected the captain didn't like excuses—and wasn't hiding the fact.

"I did find something else that may be useful." Yas held up the capsule between his thumb and forefinger. "It was strategically hidden inside the body of the man I autopsied. I almost missed it."

"Strategically hidden? What does that mean? He shoved it up his ass?"

"Close. He swallowed it. It was on its way through his gastrointestinal system, the protective shell keeping it intact."

Rache didn't speak for several long moments. "It seems that these archaeologists found something someone thought was worth killing for."

"We don't know that someone else killed them yet, I'm afraid." Yas shrugged apologetically for the vagueness of his findings.

"Actually, we do. I suppose we don't know what exactly happened to the people on the refinery yet, but someone blew up their ship. I had Trotter do a scan of the area, and he found wreckage. We also found video footage from exterior cameras on the refinery and were able to access it. Three days ago, an unmarked cargo ship modified with dozens of extra weapons chased a shuttle from an Odinese research vessel in this direction. The shuttle was damaged. As it passed extremely close to the refinery, a team of six people with crates took a spacewalk out its hatch to one of the airlocks here."

Rache waved toward a porthole and the refinery outside.

"Their shuttle continued past," he went on, "accelerating toward the gate. It wasn't a long-range craft, so they either hoped to gain assistance from the Kingdom warship that's always stationed at the gate, or they wanted it to *look* like that's what they were doing. It's possible the entire crew went on that spacewalk, and it was on autopilot. The unmarked cargo ship continued after the shuttle without slowing down at the refinery. It's likely they didn't see the people depart. Both ships flew out of the refinery's camera range shortly after, but the wreckage we found was in the direction they were heading. It was so pulverized as to be unidentifiable, but it's likely it was the remains of the shuttle."

"Where did the shuttle originally come from? A research vessel, you said?"

"Yes. Our scanners picked up the matching vessel in orbit around one of Saga's moons—Skadi—which is currently on the far side of the planet from us. A Zamek newspaper article from a couple of months ago mentioned it and a large team of archaeologists and scientists heading out on a mission. It didn't discuss what they were researching." Rache pointed at the capsule. "How long ago would that have been ingested?"

"Ah, transit time would have varied depending on stress, hydration, and other factors, but perhaps a day before he died, and I gauge they died no more than a day before we found the bodies. We have to assume that if they spacewalked from their shuttle to the refinery, some time passed between when they arrived and when they died."

"So, the archaeologist may have swallowed it before his team left their shuttle, assuming their attempt to hide wouldn't work and they would be captured."

"Yes," Yas said. "He also could have swallowed it when they got to the refinery. If he knew he would die and believed whoever was chasing them would find their bodies and their belongings..."

"Destroying whatever is in there—" Rache pointed to the capsule, "—would have been a surer way to hide it."

"Maybe he hoped someone friendly would find them, at which point, he would want to share the contents."

"Did you look inside?" Rache's tone grew cooler, and he held out his hand for the capsule.

Yas couldn't tell from that tone if he would be in danger if he had. "I didn't open the capsule, no. I scanned it to see what it contained—there's a storage chip inside—but that's it."

Rache carefully broke open the capsule, then retreated into his quarters on the far side of the room. Yas didn't know if he was hunting for something to read the chip—he didn't recognize the connector or know what could interface with it—or if he meant to leave Yas in the dark while he examined it.

But Rache soon returned with a suitable transfer cable and plugged it into the display on the wall. The robotics professor's face was replaced with shaky video footage. A recording made from a helmet cam?

Rache leaned his hip against the table and watched.

"That doesn't look like the refinery," Yas said, not sure if he should offer to leave or not. His curiosity kept his feet rooted.

"No."

"It looks like the corridors of a very old ship. Or a station. Sort of. Is that daylight pouring in?"

Rache looked at him silently, then back to the footage.

Yas clamped his mouth shut. The back of someone's spacesuit came into view for a moment. It looked like a civilian suit, not military or

Kingdom Guard. And then it was gone. The operator of the camera passed under a gaping hole in the ceiling of the corridor, wan sunlight entering, shining on a mound of snow and ice that he had to climb over.

"They're down on a moon or a planet," Yas murmured. "With at least some gravity."

The video stopped and restarted in what might have been an engine room. Yas didn't recognize the design of the ship or even the style of architecture. Gray and black unpainted metal walls. Exposed circuits not covered by panels. Pale dust—or was that frost?—over everything.

A monkey bounded into view, and Yas almost pitched over, startled. The brown furry creature held a panel or maybe a circuit board in its hands, its tail whipping about as it bounced up and down.

If the sight of the creature surprised the person operating the helmet camera, no twitch or jerk of surprise showed up in the feed. Rache also didn't react.

"A robot?" Yas guessed, able to think of no other explanation for a monkey on an archaeological mission.

"Or a loaded droid."

"Oh, right." Yas knew dying people occasionally uploaded their consciousness into androids, but he hadn't met a monkey version. "Too bad there's no sound."

The camera came closer to the monkey and the frosty circuit board in its hands. Rache sucked in a surprised breath as the details on the surface sharpened.

Yas didn't recognize anything on the board. It looked like something out of a computer, but what kind of computer, he couldn't guess.

The video stopped and didn't switch to anything else.

Rache looked at the date stamp. "Six Odin days ago. The farthest away they could be and have had time to come to the refinery and die— or be killed—is one of Saga's thirteen moons. We can't assume it was Skadi and that the research ship has been orbiting it the whole time, but Skadi *is* a frozen hunk of ice. I believe it's the only one of Saga's moons with a surface that you could walk around on, but I'll double check."

"Are you going to forgo your refinery-destroying mission to go exploring?" Yas was careful to keep judgment out of his voice. He didn't know Rache well enough yet to be certain his life wouldn't be in danger if he irked the man.

Rache gripped his chin, the mask malleable enough to allow it. It was more of a hood than a mask, Yas decided, and it covered his hair as well as his face. Whatever the black mesh-like fabric was made from, it didn't keep Rache from seeing through it.

"Forgo? No. I've already been paid, and I will complete my mission. But if what I think those people found is still down on that moon, I would prefer it if Jager wasn't the one to get it. That research ship is registered to a university on Odin, so it's possible the Kingdom government sanctioned the mission. Jager might have sent them personally." The ice had returned to Rache's tone, as cold as the pile of snow they'd seen on the video. He looked at Yas. "Did you ID that body while you were poking through its cells?"

"Yes. His ident chip was still implanted. He was a spaceship-engineering professor named Kinyar Boehm from South Zamek University."

"An engineer? That's not what I expected. Though maybe they needed someone with mechanical expertise on their team." Rache looked back to the display, perhaps thinking of the circuit board.

He held up a finger. While he ran a network inquiry?

"The only loaded monkey-droid working in the archaeology field in any of the systems is a Dr. Erin Kelsey-Sato," Rache said. "She's also from Odin."

"Ah," Yas said neutrally.

Even if it turned out that some Kingdom operative had been responsible for killing his president and framing him, Yas couldn't manage the blanket hatred that Rache seemed to feel toward all of King Jager's subjects.

Rache must have sent a command to the screen, for the display switched back to the roboticist.

Huge swaths of text accompanied the man's photo. Rache flipped through a few more photos and more text. Yas couldn't read the words from across the room, but the pictures all seemed to be about the roboticist. Casmir Dabrowski, as he was identified in one headline. On the run and currently missing. One photo showed a blown-up parking garage on Odin. Another looked to be from a traffic camera that had caught the man with a woman riding behind him on an airbike as a tanker blew up on a highway behind them.

Rache zoomed in on the woman. Two names flashed as the computer identified the faces. Dabrowski and Kim Sato.

"A still-living relative of the monkey?" Yas scratched his head, wondering how Rache had known to pull up this story before Yas had walked in with the camera footage. Had he found something in the crates his men had been searching?

"Daughter. Or so the net tells me. Huh."

"Is that... useful to you?" Yas felt lost, but he hoped the captain didn't have anything inimical planned for the two refugees. They looked far more like scientists than criminal masterminds, and Yas would rather speak to such people than shoot them. The crew of this ship made him dearly miss intelligent discourse.

"Perhaps. Perhaps not. The net says she's a bacteriologist, so she may know nothing of her mother's work."

"They seem like unlikely people to be caught up in—what *are* they caught up in?"

"Nobody seems to know for sure yet. At least, it hasn't been released to the media." Rache flipped back to the photo of the roboticist, then gripped his chin again as he studied it or maybe the text—the man's résumé and professional accolades. "Though I have a hypothesis about why this man may be a target."

"Are you going to tell me?" Yas asked.

"No, Doctor. Let me know if you find out anything more about the body."

That would be hard since the captain had forced him to leave the bodies on the refinery, not even permitting him to bring a blood sample on board, but Yas said, "Yes, Captain," and turned toward the door.

"And, Doctor?" Rache said, making him pause.

"Sir?"

"Tell no one of this. If you made a copy of the chip—"

"I didn't."

"—destroy it."

Rache stared at him through his mask, and Yas had the urge to squirm, even though he truly hadn't made a copy and knew very little about what was going on. He held up his hands defensively, resenting that he was so unsure of himself here and that he had to fear for his life, but he couldn't help it. This wasn't his world any longer, and he had no idea how to navigate it without acting like some mindless sycophant.

"You're dismissed," Rache said.

Yas hurried out, his mouth dry.

CHAPTER 13

THE COMM PANEL IN NAVIGATION BEEPED. BONITA STOPPED pacing in the tiny space behind the piloting pods, faced the display, and took a bracing breath. Diego's scowling face popped up.

"As I said in my message, Diego," she said, hoping to head off a tirade, "my circumstances have changed, and I won't be able to sell you those weapons. I apologize for the inconvenience."

"Inconvenience? *¿Qué chingados?* We almost got hammered by a ship full of knights. What'd you do? Comm them to let them know we were coming?"

"No, of course not. I—"

"Because they were damn sure we were coming to pick up something from you, and they were willing to nuke us rather than let that happen. I thought those uptight bastards were supposed to be noble. Nuking people isn't noble."

"I didn't—"

"You're lucky we had something to throw out to intercept their attack and then the slydar to slip into nothing on their scanners. If we'd been killed, my family would have made sure you died a horrible *painful* death. Don't contact me again."

The screen went black.

Bonita slumped into her pod. This week kept getting worse and worse, and that didn't look like it would change soon. It wasn't as if she could sell that case to anyone now, not unless she sold it to a psychopath who planned to *use* it on people. She wasn't a saint, but she couldn't live with that.

She'd spent the majority of her life obeying the law, even working to put criminals in jail. It was only in the last year that she'd been forced to take some sketchy delivery jobs to make ends meet. But smuggling weapons, biotech, and drugs here and there wasn't the same as helping someone set up mass genocide. She couldn't do that.

But damn it, she was tired of getting screwed out of money. Could she take the case back to Sayona Station and get her money back? Unfortunately, that was weeks of travel and a gate-jump away, and she had no idea if they would give even a partial refund. Sayona Station didn't have a reputation for exemplary customer service. Few businesses in System Cerberus did.

It was a moot point right now, since she didn't have enough fuel to reach the gate. As much as she hated to admit it, she would have to accept the loss and turn over the bioweapon to the authorities here. She wagered those knights already knew what she had. It would be better to voluntarily give it to them than wait for them to take it forcefully.

And then... Hell, she didn't know what then. She needed to buy some helium-3 and deuterium to have more options. She wasn't sure she had enough fuel to even make it back to Odin now. Not that she wanted to return to that benighted planet.

Maybe she could find some minor bounty to collect here on Forseti Station. She could make a few Kingdom crowns and refuel.

"Viggo, will you check the posted bounties for me? See if anything new has popped up this week. Ideally, someone who might be lurking on this very station and who we could capture and turn in quickly."

Her knee twinged at the idea of chasing down some criminal, reminding her of one of the reasons she was semi-retired from the demanding business, but she could take a few painkillers and do a job. She had Qin to help now too.

"I will check." One of Viggo's vacuums rolled into navigation, humming happily as it slurped up nonexistent lint and dust.

"And don't order any deliveries until we get paid for something," Bonita said. "You don't need more vacuums."

"Really, Captain. My fleet has been decimated."

"Removing two from a fleet of thirty hardly qualifies as decimated."

"Actually, since one was already inoperable—you wouldn't allow me to order parts last month, you may recall—it precisely qualifies under the historical definition of decimated, in which one in every group of ten soldiers was killed as punishment to the whole group."

"Your robot vacuums are not soldiers, Viggo."

"And yet, performance is suffering due to their inability to implement full coverage during every day cycle, as is recommended for maintaining an optimal environment for crew and passengers. I fear this ship is turning into a pigsty."

"Yeah, it looks like a helium-hogger exploded all over a refinery." Bonita gestured to the as-always-immaculate navigation cabin, then reached for the comm to call the authorities. An incoming signal flashed first. "This station is a chatty area."

"Forseti is the largest and most populous station in System Lion. There are more than eighty levels, fifty hotels and resorts, two shipyards, and a vast industrial area responsible for the manufacture of seventy percent of the mining equipment produced in the system."

"Thanks for the encyclopedia entry."

"There is an excellent robotics shop in the concourse that has three aisles of self-propelling vacuums."

"You're *not* getting more vacuums."

As she slapped the comm to answer, an alarm flashed on the far side of the control panel, and a faint clank reverberated through the ship. A man wearing a blue-and-gray Kingdom Guard uniform appeared on the display, and she didn't have time to check the alert.

"Captain Lopez here."

The man's scowl announced his displeasure before he said a word. "Lopez, your ship is being held and a quarantine enforced until such time as it's deemed safe for my men to come aboard and collect the highly illegal biological weapons you're carrying."

"Ah, and your name is?" Damn, so much for her idea of preemptively contacting the law so she wouldn't get in trouble.

"Guard Chief Wu. If you cooperate fully with my people, your sentence *may* be more lenient."

"My sentence? I haven't—"

Wu cut the channel, and the blackness of space returned to the display.

"That clank you heard was a dock-lock being secured to the ship," Viggo said. "We won't be able to leave until it's released."

"I guessed." Bonita slumped back into her chair. *Sentence?* Had anyone even proven she'd committed a crime yet? "Why, Viggo, why did you let me agree to carry this cargo without looking inside?"

"You didn't ask for my agreement."

"An error."

"Usually, yes. But I have good news. There have been new bounties issued since we came through a couple of weeks ago, and I can guarantee at least one of the subjects is on the station."

"Not much I can do about it now. We're trapped."

"Technically, I'm trapped," Viggo said. "You could walk off through the airlock."

"Where I'd be apprehended. Or shot."

"That is possible."

Bonita stared at the stars without seeing them. Was it possible she could sneak off, collect a bounty, and bribe someone in Lock Control to release her ship?

Fleeing would make her look guilty, and she would end up with a warrant out for her arrest, but it would only be in the Kingdom. She would have absolutely no problem avoiding this system for the rest of her life. She didn't know if that would be enough, that they would refrain from issuing a systems-wide bounty for her, but she had to hope they wouldn't bother. Not for smuggling. Admittedly, she was smuggling the worst thing she could have possibly smuggled...

"Show me the bounties," Bonita said. "The one for the guy on this station."

"Yes, Captain."

Casmir's face came up on the display, along with his full name, occupation, and last-known place of employment and residence.

"Are you yanking my oxygen tank?" Bonita asked.

"No, Captain. It's extremely fresh. It appeared in the system three hours ago."

"We hadn't been docked yet three hours ago."

"It was sent out system-wide, not specifically to this station. It's possible that whoever's looking for him doesn't know where he is."

"This is making me wish I'd asked you to check on bounties *two* hours ago." Before she'd booted Casmir off the ship. "But it would feel weird to..."

"Collect a bounty on someone who assisted you numerous times on our voyage?" Viggo suggested.

"No," Bonita said, even though that was exactly what she was thinking. The kid was weird, but he *had* helped, and the idea of turning him over to some lowlife who might torture all the robotics secrets out of his brain didn't sit well with her. "And it was only two times."

"It is possible those mercenaries would have left you dead and taken your cargo if he hadn't damaged their ship."

"And how horrible it would have been if they'd taken that cargo."

"Would you not have found your death inconvenient?"

"It would solve my current problems," she grumbled, then ordered the display to scroll for the rest of the information on Casmir. Such as who wanted him and how much they were paying.

If he had committed a Kingdom crime and all she had to do was turn him over to the Guard station, that wouldn't be a betrayal, surely. If he was a criminal, he deserved their punishment.

She snorted at the irony. She was hardly in a position to judge someone. But still, it wouldn't be the same as handing him off to some pirate family or angry group of anarchists who wanted to shake classified information out of his innocent brain.

Assuming he *knew* classified information. Did he? She had no idea.

"Two hundred thousand Kingdom crowns?" Bonita gaped, forgetting to look at who had issued the bounty when her eyes locked onto that. "Holy stars, I've never gotten that much money for a bounty in my life. I've only *seen* a few for that much. I remember a shoot-out between bounty hunters where three of them killed each other in their eagerness to collect on a lucrative target like that." She shook her head. "Shit, he's probably already caught. I doubt he made it to the first elevator."

"The bounty is still active."

"That just means someone hasn't turned him in. They probably have him."

Bonita closed her eyes. As impractical as it was, she couldn't help but think of what she could do with that much money. Repair everything that needed repairing on the *Stellar Dragon,* pay off the loans she'd had to take out to keep the ship running after Pepper left, get caught up on the registration taxes, and still have money left to fund her retirement. Oh, maybe she would work a few jobs on the side, but nothing like this.

She could rescue tourists kidnapped from Balneario del Mar on Tlaloc. Something low-key. Easy.

"I will alert you if the bounty is removed, Captain."

"Thank you," she murmured, then remembered she hadn't looked at who had issued it. "Pequod Holding Company? Never heard of it. Viggo?"

"It's not publicly traded, and there's little information on it. It makes investments on the stock and commodities exchanges. Nothing about profits or capitalization size."

"Nothing about what they're worth then?"

"Correct."

"So a business is looking for Casmir, huh?" That was unexpected, but Bonita could see it fitting in with her idea that someone wanted research secrets from him. It was hard to imagine him earning the ire of some torture-happy pirate family, but maybe his robotics work was cutting-edge stuff. "Of course, we have no idea what this business does or if it's even real."

"That was my thought," Viggo said. "Given the minimal information on the company, it looks like a front."

"Where do they want him delivered?" Bonita didn't see that detail in the listing. If she could somehow make this work—and she had no idea how yet—she would have to be careful with the exchange, make sure to set up protection. She didn't need to talk to any of her old bounty-hunter contacts to know that this company had never paid a bounty before. With no history, they couldn't be trusted. They would have had to dump some money in an escrow account to make the listing on the hunter exchange, but... lawyers could figure out ways to take that money back without issuing a single crown.

"There's a network contact listed," Viggo said. "That's it. You would have to comm them and ask."

She stroked her chin. It wouldn't hurt to ask, right? It wasn't as if she could do anything about it even if Casmir was to be delivered to a corporate office three levels down.

"There are armed men now stationed outside your airlock tube," Viggo reported.

"Are they staying on the station?"

"For now. Shall I lock the hatch door? Qin did not do so before leaving."

"Leaving? Qin *left*?" Bonita hadn't forbidden it, but Qin hadn't told her she was going, so she was surprised. But this could be an opportunity. If Qin wasn't stuck on the ship, she could look for Casmir.

"Yes. She told me she wanted to see if there were any knights on the station, so she could see one in the flesh before leaving the system. In case we didn't ever return."

Bonita almost laughed. Her nineteen-year-old super soldier seemed more like a nine-year-old girl at times.

"Qin?" Bonita commed her.

"Yes?"

"Where are you now?"

Qin hesitated before replying. "I'm looking for a knight, Captain. Just to see. I'm sure he won't talk to me, but I'm wearing a hood, so people won't stare. I won't get in trouble. Are you mad that I left without asking for permission?"

"No, you're my crewman—woman—not my indentured servant. Look, I need you to find Casmir... and capture him."

Bonita wasn't surprised at the long pause.

"Capture?"

"A bounty has been put out, and if someone hasn't already gotten to him, we're going to collect it. Once you have him, don't bring him back to the ship. Wait for me to comm."

"But I like him, Captain."

"I don't think it's for his head. His death, that is. I think some business wants what's *in* his head."

"Like what?"

"How should I know? Robotics secrets. Just get him, Qin." Bonita put an edge in her voice, not wanting to argue further, though she always felt bad snapping at Qin. She always had the sense that Qin had already been snapped at—and worse—enough in her life.

"Yes, Captain," came the whispered reply before the channel closed.

"Viggo, do some deeper research on that holding company, please. There must be some clues out there. I want to know who the CEO is. In the meantime..." Bonita called up the contact information on the bounty poster so she could find out where they wanted Casmir delivered.

Casmir clenched his jaw as Constable Meat Paws dug through his satchel, tossing valuable tools and his prized robot bird to the floor without a thought. The man had already turned out Casmir's pockets, his rough pat-down leaving numerous burgeoning bruises.

Casmir's cheeks flamed with heat such as he hadn't felt since he'd been a scrawny kid in school, being humiliated and pushed around by bullies. He hadn't had it as bad as some of his equally scrawny friends, because he'd always been quick to crack a joke and he'd had some success at making people want to laugh at him instead of punching him, but he'd endured a lot before finding his place at a university so competitive that nobody had time to pick on anybody else. There'd been too many assignments, too many tests to study for. Thank God.

"Useless crap," Meat Paws announced, tossing the satchel on the floor with the rest of his stuff.

"Look out!" Casmir blurted, lunging to keep him from stepping on the bird.

He bent to pick it up, but Meat Paws planted a hand on his chest and shoved him hard enough to send him tumbling into the table. His hip smacked hard against it.

"Is that yours?" Meat Paws pointed down at the bird.

"Yes. Just let me pick it up. Please. That took my team weeks to get working right, and it's a prototype right now."

Casmir spotted Kim moving toward the man out of the corner of his eye. She looked like she would beat the snot out of the constable. Afraid that would get her in trouble, Casmir stepped forward and lifted placating hands, hoping to resolve the situation himself. Unfortunately, his mind was devoid of jokes or clever questions that might have distracted the man.

"Please. It's just a little—"

The constable stepped on it before Kim or Casmir reached him. Fragile components crunched under his heavy boot.

"Might have had a transmitter in it," the constable drawled, grinning at Casmir's distress.

"Asshole," Kim said.

"What've you got in *your* bag, girlie?" He leered at Kim and turned toward her.

Casmir's jaw clenched harder. He couldn't believe the Kingdom Guard willingly employed this thug. Had nepotism been involved in the hire? Bribes? Blackmail?

Kim stood over her bags, her stance wide, her arms crossed over her chest, and she didn't answer. She'd endured the same search that Casmir had, though the bully had been more inclined to grope her than punch her. Casmir doubted that was any better. He knew Kim well enough to be certain that his calm, unflappable friend was a split hair away from losing her temper and pummeling the guy.

"Those sticks—what are they? Swords?" Meat Paws grabbed her bag, the wooden swords strapped to the outside. "You have a permit to carry weapons on Forseti, girlie?"

A gunshot rang out in the concourse, and shouts and screams erupted.

The constable whipped his head up and sprang to the window.

Dread filled Casmir's gut, and he met Kim's eyes, finding a similar emotion there. After all the insanity of the last week, what were the odds that this had nothing to do with them?

The constable cursed. "What *are* they?"

They?

Casmir shook his head, hoping his creations hadn't made another appearance.

"Maybe you should go check, Constable." Wishing he were taller, Casmir rose on tiptoes to peer out the window, but the man blocked it, his nose pressed to the glass. More gunshots fired, and the squeal of some other weapon hurt Casmir's ears. "It sounds like your friends need you."

The constable whirled on him. "Are you responsible for that? Some diversion so you can escape?" He thrust his finger toward the door. "Innocent people are getting hurt."

Casmir lifted his hands. "I don't even know what's going on out there."

A scream of agony pierced the door.

The constable squinted, his fingers curling into fists, and strode toward Casmir.

Casmir skittered back, kicking one of his tools and sending it careening off a wall. Kim slipped behind the constable and pulled herself up so she could see out the high window. She dropped down immediately.

"Two crushers," she said.

Casmir cursed violently, both at the crushers and at Meat Paws, who was determined to grab him and maybe throttle him to death. He ducked and only avoided being caught because the constable clipped his hip on the table. Casmir ran around it, trying to keep the man on the opposite side from him.

The constable whipped out a stunner and pointed it at Casmir's eyes. "You tell me right now if you're responsible for that. Because if you are..." His finger tightened on the trigger.

Casmir dropped to the floor. He couldn't let himself be stunned. Those crushers had to be here looking for him.

Again.

A crack boomed in the room, and he thought the constable had fired a gun—a real gun.

"You bitch," the man snarled.

Kim.

Casmir sprang to his feet in time to see her crack him again with one of her wooden swords. It rapped against his knuckles, and he dropped the stunner. She waded into him, the two practice blades a blur as she pounded them into his flesh. He blocked a few strikes with his arms, bellowing at the pain the blunt blows caused, then roared and charged at her.

She sidestepped him, and he thundered past and slammed into the wall. She pounced before he'd recovered, and she landed a solid blow on the back of his head. Rare fury burned in her eyes—or maybe that was desperation, for she glanced at the window.

"Stun him." Casmir pointed at the constable's fallen weapon, hoping they would get in less trouble if the man wasn't seriously injured.

Casmir ran around the table to grab it, but Kim beat him to it and fired as the constable readied himself to charge again. He pitched to the floor, his cheek landing in the broken pieces of Casmir's robot.

Kim tossed his weapon on top of him. "Don't call me girlie."

"I'm glad you're on my side." Casmir rose on tiptoes again so he could peer out the window, then yanked his head down. "You're right. Two crushers. I can't tell if it's the same two. They all look the same. They're striding down the concourse, hurling aside anyone who gets in their way." He swallowed, his brief glimpse burned in his mind. "I saw some Guards that looked like—at least one couldn't be alive. Not with his neck twisted like that."

"We have to get out of this room without them seeing us."

"And go where? We can't lead this trouble back to the *Dragon*. Even if we could escape that way, I bet the Guard has Lopez's ship locked down."

"I don't know, Casmir." Kim moved around the room, snatching up their belongings and returning them to the correct bags with swift precision. "You made these things. How do we kill them? Or reprogram them? Because it's clear they're not going to stop hunting you."

"You need a physical key to program them. I made sure they couldn't be tampered with remotely. They don't even have wifi receivers in their metal molecules. And you've seen how impervious they are. I mean, if we could get our hands on explosives or a rocket launcher, we might be able to destroy them. But we couldn't fire such a thing on a space station without risking blowing a hole in the exterior. A thousand alarms probably go off if you even remove the safety on a weapon like that."

Kim finished packing the bags and thrust his satchel at him, sans the robot bird that was beyond repair. He gave it a sad nod, whispered, "*Zikhronah livrakha,*" then pushed it out of his mind. There wasn't time to be sentimental.

"There has to be a way to get them off your back," Kim said. "We don't let bullies run our lives, right? Human *or* robot. You're smart, and this is your world. Come on, Casmir. Think of something."

Her encouragement helped. He *was* smart, damn it. And this *was* his world. He'd made those crushers. Who better than he to defeat one? Except that he'd designed them to be difficult to defeat. What he truly needed was a crusher of his own to fend off the other ones.

He froze halfway through the motion of slinging his satchel over his shoulder, and it clunked him in the back. "Could that work?"

"Yes," Kim said.

"You have no idea what I'm talking about."

More gunshots fired, more screams. They were closer, louder. Farther up the concourse toward this room.

"I trust you," Kim said, "and we're out of time."

Casmir ran to the fallen constable and snatched the stunner that Kim had dropped. It wouldn't do a thing to the crushers, but he might need it to convince people to let him in someplace with tools and the materials he would need for the work. Work that would take hours and hours, even with the finest manufacturing equipment, and even if he could find the exact materials he needed. The schematics he'd designed and programs he'd written were stored in his chip, if not hardwired into his brain, but he feared that wouldn't be enough.

But he had to try.

"All right. We're going to build our own crusher," Casmir said. "But we can't do it here. Any thoughts about how we can get out of here without them seeing us? I know you read all those stories about ninjas as a kid."

"Ninjas didn't spend a lot of time skulking through space stations. Ancient Japan was purportedly full of forests."

"There were some artificial plants next to the robot squirrel kiosk."

Kim peered out the window. "We can go now."

"What? They left the concourse?" Casmir sprang to the window to check for himself.

"No."

Casmir groaned. They were walking into the airlock hatch that led to the *Dragon.*

He ran for the door. "We have to help Captain Lopez."

"No." Kim gripped his shoulder. Hard. "Lopez has Qin. She's better than you or me for combat. You build your robot, and then maybe you'll have a chance to play hero."

Casmir knew she was right, but it stung his heart to run the other way when people he knew were in trouble. By the time he built a robot, it would be far too late to help Lopez and Qin if they weren't able to handle the crushers themselves.

"My map—" Kim pointed to her contacts, "—shows several levels devoted to manufacturing ships and asteroid-mining equipment. Would they have the tools and materials you need?"

Casmir jerked out a nod. "They might. All right, let's go."

The crushers were gone when he opened the door and slipped out, but he stumbled at the sight of so much carnage, so many broken tables, plants, kiosks... people. There had to be more than a dozen men and women down on the deck, not moving. Others cried and groaned, grasping injuries.

The knight who'd been questioning them—Sir Russo—appeared, leading twenty men in combat armor. Casmir halted and tried to blend into the wall. Russo didn't notice him. He ran toward the *Dragon's* airlock tube with his pertundo extended in one hand and a rifle the size of a cannon in the other.

Casmir was tempted to shout a warning, a reminder about the bioweapon—they dared not blow open that bulkhead in the lavatory—but Kim squeezed his shoulder again.

He forced his legs to run away from the interrogation room and the concourse and deeper into the station. He couldn't help until he had more than his puny hands to offer.

CHAPTER 14

BONITA HEADED TO THE LAVATORY TO RETRIEVE THE case, so she could walk it into the station and hand it to the authorities. She was surprised they hadn't barged in yet. They had mentioned quarantining her ship, and she knew the airlock hatch on her end was closed, but she couldn't believe they wouldn't send in Guard officers in combat armor.

"We have a problem, Bonita," Viggo said.

She froze with her hand halfway to the latch. "Another one? I'm maxed out. I refuse to accept any more."

"Sorry. I've tied in to the public station feeds, and two of those crushers appeared in the concourse. They're knocking everyone aside."

"Shit. They're after Casmir?"

"They actually just turned toward our airlock hatch."

"Ours? *Why?*" That word came out as a plaintive whine. She couldn't help it. Why was the universe flinging so much crap at her this month?

"Unknown. Perhaps the bioweapon was always what they wanted, and Casmir mistakenly believed they were after him."

"They can have it. I'm not defending that death trap anymore, and I'm not risking them shooting up my ship to get it." Bonita spun around, debating on hiding places. If she wasn't in their way, would she be safe? If she hid, that might help ensure that. "What kind of scanners do those crushers have? Do you know? Do they find their targets by sensing heat?"

"I know nothing about them other than the name that Casmir supplied. There aren't any public records on them."

"Of course not."

"They've reached our airlock hatch. A knight and several armored men are shooting at them and trying to stop them. Ineffectually."

"Wonderful." Bonita sprinted down to the cargo hold and flung up a floor panel that appeared identical to the hundred others.

It led to a freezer that was designed for carrying food for the crew and frozen cargo rather than smuggling anything, but it might be ideal for avoiding heat-sensing robots.

A horrific wrenching came from the airlock, followed by a clatter, and Bonita envisioned the crushers ripping her hatch off and flinging it across the concourse. She slipped down the textured metal steps, careful not to make a sound. Her galaxy suit adjusted immediately to the temperature, keeping her body warm, but without her helmet up, she felt the icy bite of cold air on her neck and face.

Bonita pulled the overhead panel into place, careful not to scrape it or make any noise. The frozen darkness of a coffin swallowed her, but she didn't mind. It was better than what was coming.

She crouched, her back to a box of vat steaks, as ominous thuds reverberated through the deck above her. She touched her helmet controls, and it unfurled and *snicked* into place. That tiny noise seemed to boom in her ears, and she held her breath, hoping the crushers hadn't heard it.

The helmet display gave her night vision, but there was little to see. Crates of frozen food boxed her in from all sides.

The footsteps came across the deck of the cargo hold, two sets, heavy.

Shouts drowned them out. Firearms roared, and bullets clanged off something in the hold. Bonita winced, imagining more damage to her ship. She and Viggo could handle simple repairs, but if those people blew holes in the hull, the *Dragon* wasn't going anywhere, even if she *could* bribe someone to release the docking clamps.

A foot slammed down right above her. The thick metal warped, denting before her eyes.

She lurched back, trying to wedge herself into a gap between two crates. Not that their meager protection would help if the crushers tore open the panel. They were sure to see her.

More clumps and thumps sounded over her head, then a thunderous bang as something was hurled into a wall.

"Viggo?" she whispered, trusting her helmet to patch her through to the ship, even if there wasn't a pickup in the freezer. "Do I want to ask what's going on?"

"I believe not, Captain." His voice came softly through the helmet speaker next to her ear.

"Who's winning?"

"I would say a stalemate at this time. One crusher is keeping a knight and eight armored law enforcers from going deeper into the ship. Another one is searching the ship. I have put my cleaning robots in hibernation so they won't be damaged."

Gunshots fired in rapid succession, followed by a crash.

"I'm more worried about the *ship* being damaged," Bonita said. "Has it been?"

"There are two punctures in the hull currently."

Another crash sounded.

"And numerous dents," Viggo added with disapproval.

Bonita clenched her fist with *more* than disapproval. Frustration coursed down her arm, and she squeezed so hard an alarm flashed on her helmet display.

A cacophonous boom pounded her ears, and the deck lurched. *Now* how many punctures were there? And was the case with the bioweapon still safe?

"The Kingdom Guard team has managed to down one of the crushers," Viggo said. "The head was torn off. Mostly. It's hanging on by a strand. Ah, never mind. The head is melting and reaffixing itself. I'm not certain melting is the correct term."

Bonita groaned. "What *are* these things?"

"Now, they've grabbed the crusher."

Footsteps thundered in sync, the panels vibrating.

"They're running toward... oh, the forward hatch," Viggo said. "It's starting to fight back, but if they're able to, yes, they've opened the hatch. I'll have to burn a lot of the oxygen mix later to refill the ship with air. But the crusher was blown out into space. As was one of their people."

"Someone in full armor with a tank, I hope." Bonita didn't care that much. She wanted them all off her ship, crushers, knights, and Kingdom Guard officers included.

"Armor with a limited oxygen supply likely. They've closed the hatch so nobody else will be blown out. My exterior cameras show the crusher tumbling away from the station. It doesn't appear to have any means of propulsion to reverse its direction."

"Good. *Finally*, a weakness."

"The Kingdom Guard officer has jet boots. He's angling toward a hatch on the side of the station."

"What's the other crusher doing? Is it damaged?"

"No. It's methodically searching the ship. The Guard officers are looking for it now. It is not attempting to hide. Its mind appears to have but one track."

"Fine with me. I don't want to deal with killer robots that get philosophical."

Gunshots fired from higher up in the ship, closer to navigation. Bonita grimaced as she imagined more damage being done to the hull and equipment.

Footfalls returned to the cargo hold, heavy and ringing as they struck the deck. She knew it was the remaining crusher before Viggo warned her.

"Don't move," he whispered.

She froze, not planning on it.

Shouts came from the corridor. A muffled, "There it is!" reached her ears.

Guns fired, and bullets clanged off something over her head. The crusher?

"Is it *leaving*?" she breathed.

"It didn't get anything."

"Not that we can see. It could have hidden something in its body. If it can reattach its head…"

"It couldn't hide a whole rocket," Viggo said.

More gunshots fired, the clangs coming from near the airlock now.

Bonita's knees ached, and her thighs burned from crouching. She willed everyone to leave her ship.

"Inspector," a man said as he paced above Bonita. "We dealt with one of the robot-things, but the other is heading back into the station. It's looking for something, but we don't think it found the bioweapon."

Bonita didn't hear the response.

"Right. We'll keep searching the ship. If it's here, we'll find it."

Another pause.

"Haven't seen her. We'll find her."

Bonita grimaced again as the footsteps receded. She had no doubt who *her* was.

"What now, Viggo?" she whispered once the cargo hold fell silent.

"Unknown, Captain."

"Are there still men standing guard in the concourse?" She hoped vainly that they had all taken off after the crusher and that she could walk off the ship while nobody was looking. But to what end? She didn't want to be stranded on Forseti Station. She wanted to fix her ship, get rid of those vials, and get out of the system.

"Many left in pursuit of the crusher, but two remain. I believe they have orders to keep anyone from coming or going."

Bonita leaned her helmeted head against a box of frozen cauliflower. "How do I get these people off my ship, Viggo?"

"Perhaps if you show yourself, explain the situation, and help them find the case, they will be lenient."

"They've already condemned me. What kind of lenience can I expect? Twenty years in prison instead of a life sentence? And what would happen to my ship if they sent me off to some mining asteroid to serve my time. What would happen to *you*?"

"Twenty years is not as long to me as it is to you, but I believe I would find not having you aboard to be boring."

"Thanks."

"It's also unlikely that someone else would order me new vacuums."

"Figure out how to get me out of this situation, and I'll buy you a cadre of vacuums." Granted, she would have to collect Casmir's bounty to be able to afford even a cadre of salt shakers, but if she could get off this station, there would be hope.

"A tempting offer, Captain. If I think of a solution, I will let you know."

"Are they all wearing self-contained suits or armor?" Bonita asked, mulling over ideas.

"All except for the knight. I am uncertain whether a helmet folds out of his armor, but currently, his head is unprotected."

"Is there air on all of the levels or was it vented?"

"There is sufficient air. The hatch was only open for a few seconds."

"If he's unprotected..." Bonita drummed her fingers on a crate of frozen juice bulbs. Did she have anything in small glass containers? Or what looked like glass containers? *Breakable* glass containers. "Minced garlic in a cube. You'll have to do." She tore into a box full of fresh-frozen herbs.

"What do you plan, Captain?" Viggo asked warily.

"I'm going to attempt to do what you suggested, but if they try to get me off the ship to arrest me, I'm going to bluff."

"That may not go well."

"That's normal for me these days."

Sneaking into the huge machine shop on Deck 17B was easier than Casmir had anticipated. Almost everything on the furnace and manufacturing levels was automated, so once they'd gotten past the keycard reader, they hadn't been questioned by anyone. Even with the battered remains of his tool collection, he'd managed to make a card that fooled the simple system. Casmir gathered that theft wasn't a big problem when it came to shipbuilding equipment that weighed tons.

Finding and collecting the sophisticated nanites he needed to program and integrate into the molecules of the liquid metal alloy he was about to make had been more difficult. He'd been about to give up and send Kim to sneak into the hospital, in the hope that their medical nanites would work in his matrix, but then he'd found a molecular manufacturing laboratory that supplied materials to a nearby zero-g semiconductor plant, and he'd been in heaven.

"Do you want me to do anything?" Kim asked as he set up the tools he would need to reprogram the nanites in the back of a shop.

An electric smelting furnace that he would use later blocked them from view from the main doorway, but that didn't make Casmir feel safe. He was sure there were security cameras all over the station, documenting his trespassing and theft. He could only hope that once he had some protection, he could more easily get to the bottom of his problem and get his life back. His life where he went to work, was paid, and could in turn pay for the parts he was using today. Admittedly, he would have to work for a year to earn enough to pay for the expensive materials.

"Just watch the door, please," Casmir said as he set to work.

He'd chosen a shop with a back door so they could run if they had to, but if the crushers were the ones to stomp in, hunting him down, it might not matter. There wasn't an airbike here that he could steal.

"Already doing that." Kim had stopped ten feet away in a spot where she could see the door, and stood ready to spring into action.

"I should have known. Sorry."

"You don't have to be sorry. Just build that robot. Or even better, build an army of them, so we can survive the day."

"I won't have the time or materials to build an army, but I'll see what I can do with this one."

After a few minutes, Kim glanced his way. "I'm sorry, Casmir."

"For what? I'm the one who got us in trouble. And who should have thought of this back on Odin. Not that I had time there to build anything." He glanced at a digital clock on the wall, though it wasn't as if the crushers had given him a schedule of when they planned to find him next. Was it delusional to hope the ones that had appeared on the station hadn't been looking for him? That someone had sent them after the bioweapons? Probably. He suspected they'd gone to the *Stellar Dragon* because it was the last location they knew he'd been.

"For snapping at you. And for being cranky."

"If you're cranky—and I'm not saying that you are, because my mother told me never to accuse a woman of being cranky or emotional, *especially* not that—it's definitely not without reason." He worked while he spoke, afraid to take the time to glance over at her. Fortunately, the nanites were fresh from the manufacturer and a blank slate, so he didn't have to hack through any security measures to start uploading the code. The code the military didn't realize he still had on his chip. "You shouldn't be here, and it's my fault that you are. And I can't even wish that you weren't here, because I'd probably be dead by now if I was alone."

"I think you could have figured out a way to get the better of Constable Braindead on your own."

"Is that what you were calling him? I'd decided on Constable Meat Paws. I'm afraid I'm better at being the distraction than the deliverer of death by a thousand blows of wooden sticks."

"I stunned him. It's hard to knock someone out with *bokuto*."

"Is it?" Casmir asked. "You left him nicely purpled. Like a ripe eggplant."

"Are you supposed to sound so approving when you talk about violence?"

"If the violence is being done to bullies, it's acceptable."

"He was doing his job." Kim sounded like she regretted thumping the man. She didn't lose her temper often, but it was like a switch flipping when she did.

Casmir thought Constable Whatever had deserved it. It was a lot less than the crushers would have done to the man if he'd been in their way.

"In a bullying way," he said firmly, feeling a twinge of regret for his lost bird.

Kim snorted.

"*You* probably didn't get bullied in school, so you don't recognize their hateful kind. Sometimes, they're chameleons, friendly and charming in front of authorities, and then utter assholes when there's no chance of repercussions for their actions. Admittedly, that constable was more of a red-headed rock agama than a chameleon."

"A what?"

"A red-headed rock agama. They're lizards with brilliant red heads and electric-blue bodies, and they're super territorial. They challenge intruding males by puffing out their throat pouches and bobbing their heads like they're doing drunken pushups. Tell me that doesn't remind you of our constable tormentor."

"I didn't notice a throat pouch."

"He was probably hiding it. If you've never seen those lizards, they're beautiful. You should visit the reptile museum in the capital, or go see them in nature on Karudera Continent. They thrive down there. It's supposed to be like Africa on Old Earth. Did you know Odin supposedly has all the species that existed on Earth, even some that were extinct by the time the colony ships left? Apparently, we brought..." He caught himself rambling while he worked and glanced at Kim. "I believe I went on a tangent. What were we talking about?"

"Bullies," she said dryly. "Why do you think they never bothered me?"

"Well, you have those sticks. And didn't you once say that your brothers picked you up after school in the van for the dojo? With the logo on the side? The one with a slim, unassuming man breaking a log with his fist?"

"Yes, but girls don't usually beat each other up. I wish they did. It's easier to dodge a punch than gossip and insults."

"For *you* maybe." Casmir tossed her a lopsided smile.

"You *are* better at talking than punching. You would have made a good girl." She said it as if she were stating a fact, not delivering a taunt. "Maybe we should have traded places in school."

"Would I have learned how to break a log with my knuckles?"

"Of course not. Everybody knows you have to use a palm strike on a log."

"Palms are still impressive."

"I'll let my father know. That's him on the logo."

"Lacking the knowledge to properly use my palms," Casmir said, "I had to build my own robot bodyguard in school. Ralphie, I named him. He helped me survive the middle grades."

"I'm surprised it took you this long to realize you should do the same thing here."

"Me too. I guess I've gotten used to being moderately respected by my peers at work and being surrounded by people far more inclined to banter about academia than pick fights."

They fell silent, and Casmir didn't know how much time passed as he worked, finishing with the nanites, and then venturing out for the metals he needed. He felt the pressure of trying to replicate in hours something that had taken his team six months to make back in the military research lab. But that had included days and days of experimenting and testing, failing, going back to the drawing board, then building and testing again. Now, he could essentially work from a blueprint.

Sometime near the start of the station's day cycle, Casmir yawned and rubbed his eyes, even though he knew he shouldn't with his contacts in. They were gritty, watery, and likely bloodshot. He glanced at the clock again, worried that more people would come into the manufacturing area with the start of a new shift.

"I'm following the station news," Kim said quietly. "Everything is on lockdown, and citizens and visitors are being ordered to stay in their homes and hotel rooms. From what footage I could find, two crushers walked onto the *Stellar Dragon*, followed by the knight who questioned us and many armored men. One crusher walked off about twenty minutes later."

"Where did it go?"

"The station cameras lost track of it. News reporters are asking for updates from any citizen that sees it."

"Why do I have a feeling it's looking for me?" Casmir asked.

"Because it left the ship without the rocket?"

"It probably doesn't care about the rocket. It just wants me." He surveyed his work, wishing it was further along. "If you're bored, you could spend some time trying to research who sent these after me."

"I have been."

"And you haven't found anything either?"

"Not about you or the crushers. There's a fresh report that terrorists broke into a military research lab on Odin this week but nothing about what they stole, if anything." Kim shrugged. "It's interesting, but there's not anything definitive to link it to the previous break-in and the missing crushers."

"Terrorists? What kind of terrorists?"

"The article was vague, and I can't access the government databases to run searches there."

"No, I can't either anymore," Casmir said. "I had limited access even when I worked for them. Since we're at a dead-end with what's available in the public records, all I can think to do is destroy the crushers the person or organization that's after me obtained. Then they'll have to come themselves to get me."

"You think that'll be an improvement?"

"Maybe I'll learn why they want me dead."

"Hopefully not the instant before they shoot you," Kim said.

"Hopefully not."

CHAPTER 15

BONITA WAITED UNTIL IT WAS QUIET IN THE cargo hold before easing out of hiding.

"The knight is alone," Viggo informed her. "He's in the lavatory."

She strode that way, wanting to get this over with as soon as possible. "Using it or searching?"

"He's running his hands over the wall panels. He's done that in several cabins, so it may simply be luck that he's in there. The others are searching in engineering, navigation, and the environmental-control room, currently. The two mercenaries you had in the brig were removed and taken onto the station."

"Thank you."

Bonita looked at the two tiny cubes in her gloved hands, a thin gelatin layer keeping the contents together. One held crushed garlic, the other frozen basil. They looked nothing like the laboratory vials that Kim had lifted from the case to examine, but Bonita was hoping the knight didn't know anything about horrific custom-made bacteria or what kinds of containers one used to transport them. She would do her best to keep him from getting a good look at her cubes.

The lavatory hatch was open when she reached it. The knight heard her approach and spun toward her before she stepped inside. His hand tightened on his telescoping halberd, the shaft extending to give him the long version of the weapon.

Probably because she hadn't grown up in this system and consumed all those stories about knights and their amazing combat prowess as a kid, Bonita would have been more concerned about a DEW-Tek rifle pointing at her chest. Nonetheless, she stopped in the corridor outside the hatchway.

"Despite what you think, Sir Knight," Bonita said, forcing herself to use the respectful title they preferred, "I am not your enemy. I didn't know what I was getting when I agreed to transport that case, and I will happily give it to you now, presuming you plan to take the weapon out and destroy it."

He gazed at her, studying her eyes. There were stories about knights having telepathy and a knack for reading minds, but as far as she knew, even the colonies that adored tinkering with the human genome hadn't managed to create brains with such abilities.

She was aware of clunks and clangs from elsewhere in the ship as his men searched. She could also hear a faint hiss of air escaping from the *Dragon*. Viggo had his repair robots out, working on fixing the leaks, but they must not have had time to patch the hull everywhere yet. She hoped the exchange tubes were hooked up to the station, and they were getting free water and oxygen while they were stuck here.

"Show me the bioweapon," the knight finally said, "and I will make sure it is destroyed. You have my word that I don't want to see that used on any human beings. It is true that King Jager has ambitions to extend the reach of the Kingdom again, but not through killing innocent people. What point would there be in bringing a habitat or station under one's rule when there's nobody left alive inside?"

That was more information than she had expected—and she wasn't warmed by the plain admission that his king wanted to expand—but she found she believed it, that the knight didn't want to sell this to someone else or use it. She believed he would destroy it.

"I'll show it to you, but I would like to negotiate for my release afterward. As I said, taking it was an accident. I don't deserve to go to jail over it, especially if I help you get rid of it now."

His chin came up. "You are a smuggler. It's not my fault that you inadvertently smuggled something more dangerous than you believed. In the Kingdom, smuggling involves a sentence of no less than ten years."

"I'm not a Kingdom citizen. Your laws—"

"Apply to anyone traveling through our space. We will find the case, whether you help us or not."

"Why not let me make it easy? I fetch it for you right now, and you turn your back and let me go. If not, who knows when that crusher will be back?"

His eyes sharpened. "How do you know what they're called?"

"It's not my first time seeing one."

"They haven't been deployed in combat yet."

Yet. Wouldn't it be wondrous fun when the Kingdom sent out armies of them?

"Maybe not," she said, "but you had a recent outbreak of them on Odin, and I've met two."

As he opened his mouth to reply, someone farther up the corridor asked, "Uh, Sir Russo?"

Two of the armored men had climbed down the ladder from navigation and were staring at Bonita. Shit.

"Get her," the knight said and strode toward her.

The armored men also stalked toward her.

"Don't!" Bonita lifted her arms, one of the cubes between thumb and forefinger in each hand. "Look, I tried to be friendly, but you're not hauling me off to some prison. I'll die first, and I'll take anyone on my ship down with me. From what the bacteria scientist said, this would be a particularly horrific way to die."

Actually, Kim hadn't said anything about what the gunk in the vials might do, but Bonita thought it was a safe guess.

The men stopped moving. The knight, the only one without a helmet on, squinted at the cubes.

"Stop," he called to the others, then scrutinized Bonita, holding her gaze again. "Your sentence will go the other way now that you've threatened us. You'll spend the rest of your life in a detention center."

"I'd been wondering how I would finance my retirement. I guess that would make it a moot problem." She smiled, trying to appear confident—and hide the tremor in her hands. Had she just sealed her fate? Gone from smuggler to terrorist? "Get off my ship, Sir Knight. You and all of your men, or I drop these. The green one can eat right through galaxy suits and combat armor, I understand. Before it eats through your flesh, muscle, and organs, leaving nothing but a steaming pile of brown goo on the deck. I'm not sure what the white one does. I guess we can find out together."

She glanced at the armored men to make sure they weren't moving and also to see if her words had any effect. It was hard to tell through their faceplates, but they exchanged looks with each other.

More guards stepped out of the environmental-control room at the other end of the corridor. Bonita tried not to panic. Nothing like being trapped.

Any of the men could have sprung and tackled her before she could get out of the way, but she would drop the cubes on the deck if they did. And then they would break open. The men had to be calculating the odds now, wondering if they could reach her *and* keep her from dropping the cubes?

"You expect me to believe you would subject yourself to that fate?" The knight spoke quietly and took a subtle step forward.

"Stop!" Bonita jerked her arms up higher, as if she meant to throw the cubes.

He stopped.

"Get off my ship." She backed up to make room for him to leave the lav. Then, not wanting the ones in the corridor at her back, she eased across the way and into the lounge. "Now."

"Do it," the knight said.

"But, sir—" one of the men said.

"Don't argue," the knight snapped and strode into the corridor, his purple cape flapping around his armored calves.

He didn't throw her a backward glance or a threat; he merely stalked to the ladder, his back rigid, and descended. The men exchanged more looks with each other before following him down to the cargo hold.

Bonita didn't trail them. She would get an update from Viggo. If they were setting a trap, he would know.

A clang echoed up from the cargo hold. The hatch shutting.

"How many did they leave behind, prepared to ambush me, Viggo?"

"None, Captain. They all left. Well played."

Bonita lowered the cubes, the gelatin tacky from handling. "I wish I could agree. I think I'm just compounding my mistakes. All I want now is to get out of this system as quickly as possible and never return."

"That does seem advisable."

A faint *clink-clank* reverberated through the ship.

She almost dropped the cubes in surprise. "Was that the airlock clamp?"

"Yes, they've released us. I need to repair the damage to the hull before we can depart. And I assume you'll want to recall Qin."

Bonita tossed the herb cubes into the sink and wiped the gunk off her gloves. "They're not going to let us go."

"They *have* let us go."

"Maybe they're letting us leave their airlock concourse because a crazy captain is waving around deadly biological weapons, but they're not going to let us go far. How much do you want to bet that the plan is to let us get twenty miles away from the station and then launch nukes at us? Destroy us and obliterate the bioweapon while they're at it. Does this station have nukes?"

"According to the description on the network, it's fully capable of defending itself and also extending solar sails to fly to different parts of the system if necessary."

"So they can move out of the neighborhood if some of the bacteria survive the nuke. Good for them." Bonita gripped the edge of the counter, staring bleakly at the pulped garlic in the bottom of the sink and trying not to see it as a symbol for her life.

"Two armed men have been left to guard our airlock on the station," Viggo reported.

"Meaning they'll shoot me if I try to leave." Bonita activated her comm. "Qin, what are you up to?"

A long pause followed, and Bonita worried Qin had already been captured. Or she'd run into that remaining crusher and hadn't come out on top.

"Searching for Casmir, Captain," Qin whispered, the channel finally opening. The rumble of machinery sounded in the background.

"You're a good crew member. But I need you to—" Bonita stopped. She'd been about to abort her attempt to collect his bounty, but her underlying problem hadn't changed, even if she'd piled new ones on top of it.

She still didn't have money to buy enough fuel to get out of the system. In theory, she could snag what she needed from one of the gas giants on the way to the gate, but she didn't have an efficient means of collecting helium-3 from a planet's atmosphere. She envisioned leaning out the hatch, trying to scoop up gas in a jar. She wagered Casmir could jury-rig something more practical.

"Stick to your mission," Bonita said. "Find Casmir, but don't let him know we aim to collect the bounty. Let him believe we *learned* about the bounty and the crushers, and we were worried about him. We're offering to take him out of the system, and all we ask is for him to help us collect fuel along the way."

"You want me to lie to him?" Genuine chagrin accompanied Qin's words.

"If it makes you feel better, you can tell him that's what *I* said." Maybe Bonita should have made up that story to tell Qin from the start. When her assistant didn't respond right away, Bonita added, "We're in a precarious situation, Qin. The local authorities have let the *Dragon* go, but I'm positive it's because they plan to blow us out of the stars as soon as it's safe enough for them to do so without damaging their station. If you *can't* find Casmir…"

She swallowed as unexpected emotion thickened her throat. Regret for getting herself into this situation. Regret for risking her ship and endangering Qin.

"You better stay on the station," Bonita finished. "They shouldn't have a qualm with you. With your skills, you can find another captain to take you on, easy."

"Not a Kingdom captain," Qin whispered, the words almost inaudible over the background rumble of wherever she was. "I've already… My hood slipped a couple of times. The people acted like I was some mutant carrying a contagious disease. A mother hurried her kids out of the lift when I got on it."

"I'm sorry, Qin."

"But I wouldn't leave you anyway. That's not right. I'll find Casmir. I bet he can help. Maybe he knows how to disable the station's weapons long enough for us to escape."

Bonita didn't know if a robotics scientist would have that kind of knowledge, but she let a tendril of hope creep into her body. If Casmir could hack into the system, that would be easier than bribing someone with nonexistent money.

"Good plan," Bonita said. "If he's willing, do that."

Unfortunately, she feared Casmir would balk. Even if he was being chased by those crazy robots, she doubted he had ever done anything criminal in his life.

"If he's not willing," Qin asked in a soft, uncertain voice, "do I force him to?"

"Just explain that we're his only way out of the system. Anyone else who offers him a ride will only be looking to collect his bounty."

Bonita waited for Qin to say that was what *they* were planning to do. "Understood, Captain. I'll find him."

As soon as the channel closed, Viggo spoke. "You have a comm message, Captain."

"Oh, I don't doubt it. Threats from the Kingdom Guard office, I presume?"

"No. A response from Pequod Holding Company."

For some reason, her blood chilled. She didn't know why. It wasn't as if her life could get any worse right now.

Dread and curiosity mingled in her gut as she raced to navigation to check the response. It was a simple text message, no video.

Refinery 2, Saga.

"That's it?" Bonita tried to scroll for more, but there was no more.

"That is the entire message. There is no truncation, no data loss."

"Saga is one of the gas giants on the way to the gate, isn't it?" If her memory served, it was the last planet in the system and, at its current position in its century-plus-long orbit of the sun, not that far from the gate.

"It would be appropriate to classify it as an ice giant or a gas giant," Viggo said. "Most of its mass is comprised of a dense icy fluid of materials over a small rocky core. It has thirteen moons, none of which are inhabited, even by robotic mining systems. Winds gust more than a thousand miles an hour, and the average temperature is just below -200 Celsius."

"So, it's a nice place to visit."

"It has two refineries that deliver gas by the tankful from collectors traversing a huge orbital ring that lets them dip into the planet's atmosphere to gather helium-3, molecular hydrogen, methane, and other useful gases."

Bonita's ears perked. "Helium-3, you say? Do we have enough fuel to get there?"

Viggo's long pause wasn't reassuring. Bonita assumed he was checking and rechecking calculations, since he wasn't one for dramatic flair.

"If we have no mishaps along the way, we could *just* reach Saga," Viggo said. "We would not have enough fuel to return to Forseti Station or anywhere else."

Bonita's palms broke into a sweat at the idea of being stupid enough to sail off without enough fuel for a return trip. Her gloves sensed the heat of her hands and cooled a few degrees. As if that would keep her from sweating.

She licked her lips, then almost laughed because she was more nervous about this idea than about being shot at by the station or having a warrant for a life sentence placed on her head. That was because she'd been stranded before, and she knew how terrifying it was to be without fuel to run the engines, engines that not only powered the propulsion but drove the life-support systems. She remembered lying on her bunk alone and watching the condensation of her breath accumulate on the metal frame of the bunk above hers as oxygen slowly depleted and carbon dioxide built in the air…

Bonita shook away the memory, surprised at how vivid it was after twenty years. She'd survived that situation, and she would survive this one.

"As long as we can make it, we'll be fine," she said firmly. "The meeting point is a *refinery*. That's perfect. We'll drop off Casmir and pick up a tank of helium at the gift shop on the way out."

"The refinery is populated only by robots. I deem a gift shop unlikely."

"What, robots don't have birthdays and anniversaries?"

"Not that they celebrate."

"I'm sure we'll be able to find some fuel in a refinery." Bonita slid into her pod to answer the message, to let them know she had Casmir, and that she was coming. If fate turned her into a liar, she would be dead, and it wouldn't matter.

"What do you think?" Casmir asked.

"It looks unnervingly like the other ones." Kim covered a yawn as she walked around his finished product, the metal alloy giving it the same tarry black hue as the other crushers.

It towered six-and-a-half feet tall, six inches larger than the military models. Casmir hadn't dared divert much from the known-good pattern of the previous ones, but he had given his slightly more mass, in case it helped. He had only been able to scrounge enough materials to build one, and he was well aware that two had shown up every time they had come after him.

"You couldn't have made it look a little friendlier?" Kim asked. "Or at least used a less villainous color?"

"A color can't be villainous."

"Of course it can. That's why all villains throughout history have worn black. Tenebris Rache wears a black mask."

"You can't rely on a mercenary for insight into fashion trends."

"You can when it comes to fashion trends for villains. King Jager has declared him a pirate, not a mercenary, and an especially heinous enemy of the crown."

Casmir yawned and waved away the argument. There hadn't been any metal dye in the shop, and the color of his crusher was the least of his concerns. There might come a time when it would be useful if it could blend in with the regular ones, at least at first glance.

"What do we call it?" Kim asked.

"I am a Z-6000, programmed to protect Kim Sato and Casmir Dabrowski," the crusher announced in a flat monotone.

Kim jumped back. "They *speak*?"

"Yes, they're similar to androids in intelligence and linguistics ability."

"None of the other ones spoke."

"You didn't ask them any questions."

"It must have slipped my mind while they were trying to kill us."

Casmir yawned again. The day cycle had returned to the station, the rooms and corridors brightening to simulate morning light on Odin, but all he wanted to do was find a place to take out his contacts, put in some eye drops, and take a long nap. But first, they needed to figure out—

A clank rang out, and the machinery rumbling in the other work areas sounded louder as a door opened. It must have shut again because the noise grew muffled once again.

"People coming to work?" Kim whispered.

"Let's hope that's all it is." Casmir stepped up beside her so he could see the doorway leading into their room.

Kim had been watching it all night, never dozing off or faltering in her guard duty. Nothing had come in. Yet. The doorway lacked an actual door, so they couldn't simply lock out intruders.

Footsteps boomed in the hall. They were too loud, too heavy, to belong to a human.

Casmir glanced toward the back way out of their workroom and took a step in that direction, but then he halted. He had a weapon to use now.

"Go take care of it, please, Zee." Casmir pointed.

Without a word, his new crusher strode toward the front doorway.

"You have to say please to it when you give orders?" Kim asked.

"I like to be polite to robots. You never know when another Verloren Moon situation will arise," he said, naming the ice moon that a large portion of computers and robots had taken over after gaining intelligence and liberating themselves in the last century. All of humanity, at least all of humanity living in the Twelve Systems, was glad they hadn't shown any interest in spreading out from there.

"True. But we're—" A crusher appeared in the doorway, and Kim whispered, "Never mind."

Zee sprang, slamming into it so hard they struck the far corridor wall and crashed through it.

Kim gaped. "Do we help or…"

"No." Casmir grabbed her arm and jerked his head toward the back exit. "We get out of here. It'll find me."

"I'm not sure yet whether to be comforted by that."

Casmir didn't try to convince her. Only time would do that.

He led the way out the back door and into a labyrinth filled with huge molds and covered vats of molten ore—a foundry. Heat rolled off the machinery and blasted their faces. A few voices mingled with the clashes, thunks, whirs, and grinding noises emanating from large alcoves, and the sounds from the fight soon fell behind.

Doubt filled Casmir as they ran farther away. There was nothing he could do to help, but what if his creation wasn't up to the very first task he'd given it? What if the military had made modifications to his original design in the last year and the crushers were better killers now? Or what if it ended up as a stalemate with both machines destroying each other?

He tried to tell himself that it only represented twelve hours of work this time, not the months and years he'd put into the original project, but he couldn't help but feel distressed at the idea of losing his creation before he'd even gotten to know it. What if—

Kim grabbed his arm, pulling him to a hard stop.

She pointed in front of them, down the wide aisle they were following, then tugged him into the shadows between two giant empty crucibles. A hooded figure walked toward them, a huge gun in hand.

"I think that's Qin," Casmir whispered, though he wasn't sure. The hood shadowed her face.

Kim pulled him farther back. "Are we sure we want her to find us?"

"I... don't know. We didn't part on bad terms."

It took Kim's words to make him wonder *why* Qin would be looking for them. He couldn't imagine any other task would have brought her down to this level of the station.

A scream rang from the walls, from back the way they'd come. Casmir's heart crumbled. His crusher wouldn't be hurting people—he had programmed it to defend *only*. That had to mean that his crusher hadn't made it.

"Shit," Qin said, only a few feet from their hiding spot.

She lifted her big anti-tank weapon. Casmir stepped out, just in case he was wrong.

A crusher strode toward them. Which one was it? He squinted. It was hard to tell if this was the six-foot or the six-and-a-half-foot one without another beside it for comparison.

Qin fired.

Belatedly, Casmir lunged over and pushed her arm away. The crusher saw the shot coming in time to react, dropping into a fluid crouch. The shell blasted over its head and slammed into a machine at the end of the walkway. It exploded, hurling shrapnel everywhere.

"What are you doing?" Qin barked. "Run. Get out of here. I'll delay it."

The crusher leaped back up. It did not sprint toward them. It looked at Casmir.

"I am a Z-6000, programmed to protect Kim Sato and Casmir Dabrowski."

Casmir grabbed his chest. Thank God.

Qin hadn't lowered her gun. "*What* is going *on*?"

"That one's mine." Casmir stepped in front of her as the crusher approached. "Uhm, Zee. Someone screamed. You didn't cause that, did you?"

"My appearance alarmed several workers. They ran away."

"I told you everyone knows black is villainous." Kim stepped out of the shadows. "You should have made him pink."

"What happened to the other crusher, Zee?" Casmir asked.

"It will reassemble itself soon. I do not know how to permanently destroy it."

"According to the captain, the Kingdom Guards threw one out a hatch," Qin said, backing away as the crusher strode closer.

Casmir nodded. "That would work. They can't morph into anything they don't have the base materials for—no making jet boots and rocket fuel. Zee, if you get a chance, throw that crusher out an airlock, please."

"I will attempt to do so."

An ominous bang came from beyond the vats, followed by the jarring booms of a pneumatic hammer.

"Let's go," Qin said, gesturing for them to follow.

Kim hesitated.

"Come on." Casmir jogged after Qin, waving for both of his allies to follow. They could question Qin once they'd put fifty levels of the station between them and the other crusher.

She led them past two banks of passenger lifts and to a larger maintenance elevator full of paint brushes, buckets, drop cloths, and brush drones. They stepped in and she hit the button for a floor several levels above the airlock concourse.

"Did the captain make it?" Casmir asked. "We saw... We were being questioned when the crushers showed up. We saw them head to the ship."

"She lay low while the authorities fought it, so she's fine for the moment." Qin pointed at him. "But you are not."

"This is not news." Casmir felt better with the big crusher looming behind him, but Zee wasn't a solution to all of his problems.

"How about the fact that there's a bounty on your head?"

"Uh, are you sure? I recall those mercenaries looking me up and saying there wasn't one."

"That was five days ago. This popped up yesterday."

"Are you *sure* you can't make an army of these?" Kim poked the crusher's arm and seemed surprised that it had no give.

"I could if I had time, access to that machine shop down there, and someone to deliver more materials. But I didn't pay for the raw materials I used. Someone is going to figure that out eventually. And probably send a bill to the house."

"The captain is still in trouble," Qin said. "Casmir, we need you to figure out how to disable the station's weapons. Just temporarily."

Casmir gaped at her. "That's illegal."

"Not if they don't figure out you did it."

"No, I'm pretty sure it's still illegal."

"In exchange, the captain says she'll take you out of the system. You're not going to be able to stay here with a bounty on your head. And it looks like you can't go back to your planet yet, right?"

"Unfortunately, that's correct."

Kim shook her head bleakly.

The lift came to a stop, but Qin pressed a button to hold it.

"Are you in?" Qin asked. "I've been wandering the station all night looking for you. I passed the airlock and shuttle bay traffic-control center, so I can show you how to get there. Before, I thought maybe you could remotely hack into their computer from a closet somewhere, but between me and your new friend, maybe you could simply barge in and deal with anyone who objects."

"They'll definitely be able to figure out who did it if we take that route." Casmir pushed a hand through his hair. The idea that he could hack into a secure government traffic computer from a random closet was ludicrous. Everything about this was ludicrous. "Why does Lopez need the weapons turned off? She's not—" He dropped his hand. "She still has the bioweapon, doesn't she?"

"Not intentionally. I wasn't there, but I gathered things got out of hand. Her only hope now is to flee to another system where the Kingdom doesn't have any jurisdiction. And she's offering to take you with her. It'll take whoever is chasing you a lot longer to find you then. The gate can go to any of the eleven other systems without leaving any trace of a ship's passage."

"I know how the gate system works," Casmir grumbled. "As much as most people know, anyway. Which is admittedly not much."

He met Kim's gaze, wondering what she thought about this. She'd been silent, watching the exchange through slitted eyes. She was always suspicious of strangers or anyone who seemed to want something. He was quick to trust, wishing to believe the best in people, and knowing from experience that people performed better when they knew they were valued and trusted. But Qin wasn't one of the young engineers on his robotics team. She was a warrior loyal to Captain Lopez who was, as far as he knew, loyal only to herself.

"Isn't your captain a bounty hunter?" Kim asked Qin.

Qin shrugged. "She used to be. She hasn't collected a bounty in as long as I've been with her. I assume she retired because it got too dangerous."

"Whereas smuggling is like an afternoon sunning yourself in Castle Park."

Qin shrugged again. "If you want to stay here, we'll figure something out. I can try to force the airlock-control officers into helping, or keep them distracted while my captain escapes."

She nodded, as if she'd already decided to sacrifice herself.

If Casmir had to pick one of them to escape and one not, he would have chosen the other way around. Lopez was jaded and hard to like. Qin could probably break his neck by blowing fiercely, but she was a more amenable soul.

"Let me pull up a map," he said with a sigh.

"I can take you to—"

"I want to find out where the weapons are physically located and fired from. It would be easier to tamper with them than hack into a secured system. From a closet."

Qin beamed a smile at him, the gesture sincere if alarming, since it displayed her fangs. Maybe she knew that, because the smile faded quickly, and she gave him a more formal nod. "Good. Thank you."

"Wait until we see what I can actually do," Casmir said.

Kim had a finger to her lips, and when he met her gaze, she shook her head slowly.

Because she thought Qin was lying? Or because he was about to do something that would get him into more trouble with the law?

Judging by the graveness of her expression, probably both.

CHAPTER 16

T HE HEAVY SLIDING DOOR TO THE WEAPONS ROOM was locked, the control panel beside it requiring a retina scan for entry. An eyeball was a lot harder to forge than a keycard.

"This is the place?" Qin asked, watching the corridor in both directions with her hulking gun in her arms.

Casmir expected a squad of Kingdom Guards to rush in to apprehend them at any moment. Their odd little group hadn't gone unnoticed. They had been forced to stun two guards who'd tried to stop them on the way out of the lift on this level. Even though they'd tied up the man and woman and stuffed them into a server closet, it was only a matter of time before someone raised an alarm.

"It's one of two torpedo rooms, according to the station's schematic." Casmir waved toward his temple, where he was keeping his embedded chip offline most of the time, out of fear that security could use it to track him. "I dug up and downloaded that instead of the map for the general public. It's proving accurate so far."

"Smart." Qin smiled at him.

Casmir made himself bob his head in thanks for the compliment, though he was skeptical that they were truly on the same side.

"Shall I blow it open?" Qin patted her big gun.

"That sounds noisy," Kim said.

She hadn't spoken much since Qin explained the plan in the lift, and Casmir ached to pull her aside for a private chat. But there hadn't been a chance. Qin hadn't threatened them, but her mere existence next to them with that gun and her enhanced muscles was a threat, if a silent one. Casmir could sic Zee at her if he needed to, and he and Kim could run, but then he might lose the only asset he had. Whoever had placed a bounty on his head—and he didn't doubt Qin about that—and sent the crushers… it wasn't Qin or Lopez.

"Zee?" Casmir waved at the door. "Could you open this, please? Ideally without making a lot of noise."

"What would a human consider a lot of noise?" Zee asked.

"Uh, below seventy-five decibels would be good."

"How do you know how loud that is?" Qin whispered.

"Kim's coffee grinder has a warning label on the side that lists its output."

"My coffee grinder," Kim murmured. "How I miss it."

Zee reshaped his arm from its human dimensions into something akin to a mattock, then slid the sharp wedge under the door and heaved upward. Metal crunched and snapped, and the door rose. Casmir winced at the noise, though it was far less than Qin would have created with an explosive round—and probably not any louder than Kim's coffee grinder.

"Secure the area, please." Casmir pointed inside. "No killing," he added, though it shouldn't have been necessary, as he'd instilled that in the crusher's programming, to defend without killing if at all possible. He had wanted to program that into the original military crushers, but the knight-general overseeing the project had laughed and vehemently denied his request. That had been one of Casmir's first inklings that he was building robots for more than defensive purposes.

Zee strode into the room. DEW bolts shot out of flush-mounted weapons in the wall, weapons they hadn't been able to see from the door.

Casmir jumped and blurted a useless warning as red beams sliced into the crusher. Zee turned toward one of the weapons, sprang, and smashed a fist into the control panel. The bolts halted abruptly. He repeated the action with the panel on the other side of the door.

The energy bolts left holes in his torso, but they re-formed into a solid mass within seconds. Zee strode around the room, seeking more threats.

"Handy," Kim remarked from the door. "Was the robot bodyguard you made as a kid like this?"

"No." Casmir laughed at the idea. "My knowledge of robotics was a little more rudimentary then, and I only had access to the building materials I could scrounge around the apartment. Kitchen pans were involved."

"I'm sure your mother was delighted."

"Do delighted people usually scream at you and threaten to withhold dinner?"

"That hasn't been my experience."

"Then that may not be the correct adjective."

"The threats have been eliminated," Zee announced.

Casmir jogged in and found the four torpedo bays and a locker full of warheads. The station didn't appear to house nuclear weapons, but the charges in the warheads could easily destroy a ship. It would take too long to sabotage the torpedoes themselves—and his eye twitched at the thought of handling explosives when he didn't have experience working with them—so he headed straight for the launch tubes. He hoped it wouldn't take much to disable *them*.

A weapon buzzed behind him, and he sucked in a startled breath.

"Just disabling the cameras," Qin said, waving a pistol. "Keep working."

"Yes, ma'am." As Casmir removed an access panel, again thankful that he'd managed to retain his toolkit through all this, he wondered how much the cameras had caught before she zapped them. How many corridor cameras along the way had recorded their passing?

He thought about the way they had been walking, with Qin leading and Zee following behind them. To an outsider, might it look like Kim and Casmir had been hostages? Forced to go along with this scheme? Someone smart would probably figure out that Casmir was the only one of them who could have built a crusher, but he could have also been forced to do that. It sure would be nice if someone on the outside would decide that he was innocent and that all he'd been doing since fleeing his home was trying to stay alive.

But was that true at this point? Maybe up *until* this point. If he disabled the weapons and escaped on the *Dragon* with Lopez and Qin, he would be sealing his fate.

The station authorities already believed he was part of a crime revolving around the bioweapon, but wasn't it possible that if he went to them and *helped* them, his name might be cleared?

Whereas if he followed his current trajectory, he would be digging himself deeper into the icy core of a comet from which he'd never escape.

He kept working as the bleak thoughts spun around in his mind, his hands slow and methodical and almost without input from his brain, but he couldn't stop worrying. He considered again the cameras and how things might look to an observer. Even now, with Qin and Zee standing near the door, alternating between watching the corridor and watching him work, it might appear that they were his captors rather than his allies.

What if he left a message while he was tampering? A simple text note informing whoever found it that he hadn't been acting of his own free will. Might that save him when the law eventually—and what seemed inevitably—caught up with them? Or was it already too late?

He wished he knew if Lopez actually intended to do what she'd relayed to Qin. Did she plan to help him get out of the system? Or was it a ruse so she could collect his bounty herself? And who had put a bounty on his head? Was it the same person who'd been sending the crushers?

A morbidly curious part of him wondered how much it was for. How much was his head *worth*?

"Is there anything I can do to help?" Kim crouched next to him, her back to Qin.

He almost said no but realized she might want to talk. Unfortunately, Qin probably wasn't far enough away for them to speak privately. If she had normal ears, she would be, but Casmir remembered some childhood trivia about house cats being able to hear things four or five times farther away than humans.

He shook his head slightly but pointed to the tiny display that he'd tampered with while disabling the first torpedo launcher.

My apologies, station personnel, but I am being forced to temporarily disable your weapons. Full control will return in twelve hours, if you do not override the programming sooner. I have been chased and shot at since leaving Odin. Please see Sir Friedrich at the castle in the capital for details, as he knows far more than I do.

Kim's brow furrowed—she hadn't met Friedrich, but he had probably told her the man had died fighting the crusher in the parking garage—but all she did was nod slightly.

Casmir hoped the authorities had no way to know that *he* knew Friedrich was dead. He hoped that if he sent them sniffing around the knight's death, they would find someone else close to Friedrich that knew the truth. Like his *mother*. Whoever and wherever she was.

As Casmir replaced the panel, hiding the condemning message from Qin's eyes, he worried he was adding evidence to the list of crimes that had to be mounting against Captain Lopez. That made him feel guilty—no matter what Lopez planned in the next few days, she had let him and Kim onto her ship, and they might not have escaped the crushers if she hadn't.

That guilt didn't keep him from programming the same message into the rest of the torpedo launchers.

Yas finished cleaning and organizing every tool and piece of equipment in sickbay, and he completed a list of items he needed restocked to keep the mercenaries alive. He needed to send it to Rache, since the captain handled the outfit's finances himself, but he was reluctant to disturb him.

The ship hadn't left the refinery, and Rache had been scarce outside of his quarters. Was he buried in research? Whatever that archaeology team had found seemed significant, and Yas worried Rache would decide he didn't like it that his new doctor had watched the video diary with him.

The sickbay door opened, and Yas spun toward it, thinking the captain might have come for a chat about that very thing. But Chief Jess Khonsari strolled in with an easy smile, her hands in the pockets of her greasy coveralls.

Yas glanced at the case that held sickbay's various medications, wondering if she would try to angle for trylochanix again. And if she did, what would he do? Demand she have an examination first and that they try a number of less potent—and less addictive—medications before going back to that? Or simply assume that the previous doctor had done all that and had known his trade? Yas wasn't a surgeon in a hospital with rules governing the distribution of prescription drugs, not anymore. He was a thug with a scalpel, a criminal among more criminals.

"How's the shoulder?" he asked, deciding not to cast judgment yet.

"Oh, it's doing fine, Doc." Jess rotated it to demonstrate a full range of motion and gave him a radiant smile. "I came up because I lost the draw."

"The what?"

"To see who in engineering would come talk to you. The grunts were in on it too. Oh, and Chaplain."

"This ship has a chaplain?" He'd had no idea.

Jess wavered a hand in the air. "Sort of. He was studying in some monastery, went crazy, and killed everybody there, or so the stories say. He's one of Rache's assassins now. Good at it too." She ambled over and leaned against the medicine case. "The crew calls him Chaplain. I'm not sure you want to confess any sins to him." Her forehead screwed up. "Is that the right religion for that? I get so confused with all of the options these days."

"I take it you're not overly theistic."

"Not overly, no. A friend suggested I become an astroshaman now—" she waved her prosthetic hand and gestured to her cybernetic eyes, "—but I'm not interested in meditating until I can spiritually fuse my human and cyborg bits." Her mouth twisted in a dismissive expression.

"What did these various venerable people wish to speak with me about?" Yas asked, not wanting to get into a discussion of the merits of the new and old religions out there.

"We were all wondering if you knew why we're still here. Seeing as you're buddies with the captain now."

"*Buddies?*" Yas hadn't spoken to the captain in days—and infrequently before then.

"Sure. He saved your life. And he told the guys not to pummel you or he would pummel *them*."

Yas blinked slowly. "When did he do that?"

"Right after you came aboard with your nose up in the air like you were better than everyone here."

"I didn't intend to convey that message."

"Well, Ox and Chains and Chaplain thought they'd help you see the error of your ways. The captain said no, and nobody crosses him. He may not be as big as a lot of the men, but he's dangerous."

"Given his reputation, I would assume so."

"Anyway. The refinery. We're still here, and we haven't blown it up like we did the other one. Usually, we're in and out. Lingering in one spot for long isn't a good idea, even with the slydar hull plating. An hour ago, our lookout spotted three Kingdom warships on course for Saga."

"How far away are they?"

"Four days, but it's possible they'll realize we're loitering in the area. If they get a hint that it's actually possible to catch Rache this time, I bet they'll divert forces from the gate. One of *those* ships could be here in just over a day."

"Do you think they're aware that the first refinery was destroyed? It was all automated. Maybe those ships are just making a supply run."

"Oh, they're aware. Odin is considered backward because of its stance on genetic engineering, but it has the same tech as the rest of the systems. Some knight with a telescope in Jager's castle is probably counting the zits on your butt right now."

Yas's hand strayed to his backside. "I use an antibacterial soap that keeps those to a minimum."

"I'll let the guys know. Especially Moretti. He's about given up on his fantasy of the captain jumping his wrench after a vigorous sparring session in the gym. Maybe he'll shift his attention to you." Jess winked.

Yas had no idea what to say. This conversation had taken an alarming turn.

"Whatever the men think, I'm not the captain's confidant."

Yas could have spoken of the autopsy and the footage he'd seen, but Rache had been clear that he didn't want that information getting out into the wild. Though the idea of intentionally ingratiating himself to the captain turned his stomach, it occurred to him that if Rache *did* treat him differently than he did the rest of the crew, Yas shouldn't snub that. If he could stomach it, maybe he should attempt to cultivate a friendship with the man. Rache had considerable resources for a criminal. Maybe it was possible he could one day help Yas clear his name.

"That's disappointing," Jess said. "You should offer him some of that special soap."

The comm chimed.

"Doctor Peshlakai," the captain said. "Is there a DNA sequencer in sickbay?"

"There is, actually. I just completed an inventory and was surprised at some of the equipment in the storage room here." Specifically, Yas had wondered if the mercenaries had raided a medical laboratory somewhere and let their last doctor shop gleefully through the haul before selling off the remains.

"Good. Dust it off."

Yas couldn't imagine what on the refinery Rache had found that he wanted sequenced. They had already identified the bodies of those who had died.

"Yes, sir," was all he said, certain Rache wouldn't appreciate prying. The comm clicked off.

"What are we sequencing?" Jess had moved to the door, but her eyes were bright with curiosity. Had it truly been some lost bet that had sent her up here to gather intel?

"I don't know."

"Will you tell me when you do?"

"Not unless the captain says I can."

Her lips twisted. "You're no fun, Doc. But I should have known that when you started talking about butt soap."

She waved and left sickbay before he could find a decent response.

Yas headed toward the equipment storage room but paused, glancing toward the medicine case. He hadn't been watching Jess when the captain had been speaking. A part of him didn't want to look, to see if the number of foil trylochanix packets matched the number he'd just recorded on his inventory, but his feet took him over there, regardless. He opened the case and counted. Several packets were missing.

He rubbed the back of his head, pushing his fingers through hair that had grown shaggy in the last three months. What was the protocol for something like this? Did the mercenary ship have a rule book? Should he tell the captain? Or talk to Jess? For all he knew, half the mercs were jacked up on some drug or another. Was it within his purview to question these people's life choices?

Yas pushed the quandary to the back of his mind to consider further later and went into the storage room to dig out the DNA sequencer he would never have expected to find on a mercenary ship. Or be asked to use.

CHAPTER 17

WHEN THE *STELLAR DRAGON* RELEASED ITS DOCKING CLAMPS, Forseti's airlock attachments seemed to give the freighter an extra push. Bonita imagined the station very much wanted to get rid of them.

Qin sat in the co-pilot's seat, and Kim and Casmir stood just inside the hatchway to navigation, watching the display with tense faces. She wasn't sure how they had made it back to the ship in one piece, especially when they weren't wearing armor or galaxy suits, but she suspected Qin and the hulking crusher that had strode on board with them accounted for it.

Kim had acquired a stunner somewhere, and Bonita took note of it. Before they reached the refinery, she would have to take it and any other weapons they might have acquired. In the bounty-hunting business, it was bad form to hand over armed captives. She had no idea how she would take the crusher from them.

She'd almost wet herself when that had walked on board. Whether Casmir had reprogrammed one of the others or built one from scratch, she didn't know, but it added a big complication. Handing over a captive with a killer robot at his back was even worse form.

"I hope we got them all," Qin whispered, her eyes locked on the display.

Bonita nibbled on the inside of her cheek as they sailed away from the asteroid protecting the station. She didn't know how long Forseti would wait to fire—or attempt to fire.

An incoming courier ship sailed past them on its way to the station. Bonita realized that even if the torpedoes were all disabled, if Forseti's traffic-control officers acted quickly enough, they could send ships with working weapons after the *Dragon*.

"Everything that was on the builders' schematic," Casmir said.

"What's the deal with your new friend?" Bonita asked casually, hoping Casmir would get chatty, as he tended to do, and explain it in great detail, especially whether it needed to plug itself in and take a nap at night.

"I got tired of being bullied," was all he said.

He smiled but also peered into her eyes, as if to ask, *Are you also a bully I need to protect myself from?*

"I can believe that," Bonita said and faced forward again, adjusting a couple of controls that didn't need adjusting.

She doubted he would find any duplicity in her eyes, as she had plenty of experience at bluffing and keeping her thoughts masked, but there was no need to take the risk. Even if he was goofy, she reminded herself that he was also smart. She'd met engineers and programmers who were good with their tech and far less so with people, but she didn't think he fell into that category. The fact that she felt guilty about what she was planning attested to that. She wouldn't say he'd won her over, but she already regretted her choice. She just didn't see any other options now.

An alarm beeped on the control panel, and she tensed. A warning about weapons firing?

No, it was the fuel indicator.

"We're being warned that the ship doesn't have enough fuel to get us back to Odin or to the gate and beyond," Qin said.

Kim and Casmir exchanged alarmed looks.

"I know," Bonita said. "Viggo and I already chatted about that. We're going to stop at Saga on the way out and either collect some helium-3 ourselves or see if we can borrow a tank from one of the orbital refineries."

"*Borrow?*" Kim asked.

"I'd say barter for one," Bonita said, "but I don't think there are any people stationed on those refineries, and I don't know how to barter with robots."

"They tend toward the practical," Casmir said, "but I don't believe there are any self-aware robots out there. Just automation. Most of the systems learned from the Verloren Moon incident that creating artificial intelligence comes with a lot of risks."

"No kidding." Bonita got the shivers every time she flew within a light year of the computer-run moon. She'd heard the whole thing had once been covered in ice. Now, it was covered in the gray of metal and circuit boards, an entire world turned into a giant computer, or at least it seemed that way from the outside. As far as she knew, no humans ever went there, other than the cyborg nuts who started to believe they *were* computers. "If you all are feeling bad about taking fuel without paying, maybe we can leave your crusher in trade." She smirked at Casmir—that would be one way to get rid of it. "What do those go for on the open market?"

Casmir didn't return the smirk. "They're not on the open market. The Odin military holds all the patents since the work was done in their labs. I'm breaking another law by making one, since I no longer work there." His shoulders slumped. "I no longer work anywhere."

He looked so forlorn and dejected that Bonita had the urge to give him a pat and say that things would work out. But she didn't. Thanks to her, things probably *wouldn't* work out for him.

The comm panel chimed. The entire station was visible on the display now, meaning the *Dragon* was likely far enough away that it could be blown out of the stars without causing collateral damage.

"It's station security," Viggo said.

Bonita was tempted to accelerate into their course and ignore them, but curiosity made her take the comm. "Captain Lopez."

"You are ordered by Knight-Colonel Dresdark to halt your ship and prepare to be boarded by a hazardous materials team that will deal with your quarantined cargo."

Bonita muted the comm. "I'm guessing that means they tried to fire at us and found out they couldn't."

"If they had wanted to send a team over," Viggo said, "they would have tried again while we were still attached."

"How much do you want to bet that they want us to wait while they ready a ship with enough firepower to blow us up?" Bonita asked.

"I would not take that bet," Viggo said.

Casmir shifted uneasily behind them. Kim merely watched with her typical flat expression.

The message repeated, followed by a terse, "Respond, Captain Lopez."

Bonita unmuted the comm. "I think you want to blow up my ship, so I'm going to pass on your offer."

She programmed in the course for Refinery 2 in Saga's orbit.

"It was not an offer; it was an order."

"Since I never served in the military," she said, "I get those two mixed up."

A new voice came over the comm, a man's deep baritone. Was this Knight-Colonel Dresdark himself? "If you keep flying, Lopez, you'll never be welcome in our system again."

"Trust me—I'm not planning to come back." Bonita ended the comm and faced Kim and Casmir. "You two better pod yourselves in." She waved toward the lounge. "We're about to accelerate out of here as fast as our engines can take us."

Casmir hesitated but nodded. "Let me know if you need help building a helium-3 collector for Saga. I could make something to pick up and isolate enough for your needs, so we wouldn't have to borrow anything."

"I'll keep that in mind." Bonita waved them out of navigation, feeling a twinge of an emotion she couldn't quite identify. He'd offered exactly what she'd thought he might. She wasn't sure when she'd started wanting to hire him rather than collect his bounty, but it was inconvenient.

After Kim and Casmir disappeared down the ladder well, Qin whispered, "I don't want to turn him in, Captain. He's done everything we've asked. Cheerfully."

"I know, but we can't keep him, Qin. Someone is hunting him. Someone rich and powerful. We have problems enough without him on board."

"That doesn't mean we have to be the ones to turn him in."

"Qin, we need the money."

"If we gather free fuel…"

"We'll *still* need money. I owe money on the ship, have nothing left to buy food and parts with, and after this fiasco, I'm not even sure I'm going to be able to keep flying. The Kingdom is known to hold grudges. Flying off to another system may not be enough to escape their reach.

I'm probably going to have to fling bribes around left and right and maybe do a complete overhaul and ID change of the *Dragon* if I want to survive the year."

"But—"

Bonita jerked up a hand. "I won't drag you along with me. I'll stop at the first station we come to and drop you off with your pay. You've been good enough not to point out that it's been two months since I've been able to pay you. After this, I'll be able to. And you can find another gig. With a captain who's more…" More what? Smarter? Younger? Better connected? Bonita rubbed her eyes, irritated to find moisture there. "Just more."

"I'd rather go on not being paid if that means not turning them over to someone who may kill them."

"That's not an option."

"Captain—"

"It's *not* an option, Qin," Bonita growled, spearing her with a glare. "If you can't drop it, get out of navigation." ·

Qin's face closed up, and she left her pod without another word, clanging the hatch shut behind her.

Bonita sighed and almost asked Viggo if she was doing the right thing. But she knew she wasn't. She was doing the desperate thing, as she'd been doing all year. One desperate thing after another. What were the odds that she would survive her choices and live to see her next birthday?

"I can't believe you're fixing her things," Kim said from the treadmill she had pushed out of the equipment cabinet.

They were alone in the lounge, three days into their flight to Saga, a horrifically inhospitable planet that had starred in no tourist brochure ever. Casmir was surprised there wasn't a prison set up there, but it would cost a fortune to build something that could survive the railing winds that scoured the gas giant. As with most planets, it was easier to build a habitat in orbit than to combat the elements inside the atmosphere.

"I like to keep my hands busy." Casmir sat cross-legged on the deck, spare parts and things never meant to be parts mounded to either side of his knees as he attempted to build a couple of cleaning robots to replace the ones he had sacrificed on the mercenary ship.

"Why don't you busy your hands hacking into the comm system to see why Lopez is *really* taking us to Saga?" Kim pounded along on the treadmill, the steady thumps creating a rhythm.

"I don't think that's wise." Casmir tapped his temple and glanced upward to remind her that the sentient ship could hear and see them from anywhere on board. He activated his chip in case she wanted to communicate silently.

Because they'll retaliate? Kim messaged. *Or because you'd rather keep your head in the sand like those giant ostriches in the zoo in the capital?*

It's not that. I just don't see how we could change our fate right now.

We could take over the ship. Your big robot has been nothing but a dust collector for the last three days. Kim waved a hand to where Zee stood in a corner, watching the hatch.

I assure you, he's not dusty. I saw one of the ship's cleaning robots crawling up his leg earlier.

Why not put him to use? Kim asked. *If we could take over the ship, we could control our fate.*

What would change? At this point, we're closer to Saga than we are to Forseti Station or anywhere else in the system. And it doesn't sound like we could go many other places on the fuel the ship has. One of Saga's moons, maybe, but none of them are inhabited. Nothing out this far is.

Kim shook her head. *You've succumbed to this, Casmir. We're not wearing shackles. We're not helpless. Yet. That could change if we do nothing. I bet you a hundred crowns and a pound of my favorite dark roast that someone is waiting for us—for you—on that refinery.*

Maybe, maybe not. Why are you so sure Lopez and Qin are lying to us?

Why are you so sure they're not?

I'm not. I'm just optimistic.

Well, knock it off. At least hack into the ship's comm and read up on your bounty. We don't even truly know if there is one yet, do we?

I checked, and it's not on the public network. I assume there's some private bounty-hunters-only club that you join to get job notifications, but wouldn't you like the details? And to see if Lopez has been in communication with the person who posted it? Or anyone else?

Casmir exhaled slowly, pretending to be engrossed in his work, but he couldn't argue against Kim's logic. *I wouldn't be opposed to checking on that information, but I doubt I can hack into the comm system without Viggo knowing about it. He would tell Lopez, and she might stun or tranq us for the rest of the trip.*

With your looming bodyguard watching?

She could gas us through the vents.

For an optimist, you sure know how to worry about all the negative possibilities. Look, if they act against us, we'll take over the ship. You send your robot against Qin, and you and I will figure out a way to stun Lopez and deal with the ship.

I can't threaten to kill anyone, Kim.

I'm irked enough that I can. I want to be in control, at least of myself, by the time we dock at that refinery. If we're not, you could be shot the second you step out of the hatch.

Casmir held up a hand. *All right, let's find out first if there's truly someone waiting for me.*

You'll hack into the comm system?

Let me try something less incendiary first. Casmir got up and headed for the hatch.

Kim slowed her run. *Where are you going?*

To visit Qin.

Kim unstrapped herself from the treadmill and caught up to him at the hatch to Qin's cabin. Neither of them had been inside before.

When Casmir knocked, a polite "Come in" sounded.

Not sure what to expect from the room of a deadly killer who could hold her own in a fight with a crusher, he pulled the hatch open and stepped inside. Then blinked. Several times.

The cabin was pink, purple, and frilly. There were posters of famous knights, sports stars, and vid actors on the walls, and a glass case held shelves of books packed tightly so they wouldn't shift around in zero gravity. Other cases held sculptures—or were those wax candles?—of mythological creatures such as griffons, dragons, unicorns, and minotaurs.

"Hello," Qin said, the word half greeting, half question.

She lay on her stomach on her bunk, flipping through a physical magazine with glossy pictures of musicians. A song that reminded Casmir of a smithy's hammer on a rampage in a room full of anvils played from the speakers.

"Sorry for the intrusion," Casmir said, waving around the room.

"It's all right. You can come in. I never get visitors, not nice visitors." Qin sat up and crossed her legs. "The pirates used to come, but they only wanted sex."

"I—what?" Casmir stared at her, realizing he knew nothing of her background.

Qin shrugged and waved away the question, then hopped to her feet. "Do you want to see my candles? I was never allowed to buy anything on the pirate ship, so I bought all this stuff with my first pay from the captain." She grinned, removed the dragon from its case, and showed it off. "You can burn it, but I never would want to melt the sculpture."

"You bought this all with one pay deposit?" Casmir asked, bemused. The girl must love shopping. Though now that he surveyed the collection again, he could see that everything had likely come from a couple of shops in some space-station concourse.

"My room and board are covered, so I don't have a lot of expenses. The captain even does my claws for free. See?" She lifted her hands, revealing blue paint dotted with white stars.

Casmir stepped back involuntarily at the sight of her long razor claws. He hadn't realized they retracted and extended.

Qin noticed the response, and her face fell. She lowered her hands and hid them behind her back.

"Sorry," Casmir blurted. "I'm on edge around deadly weapons lately. For no particular reason. The fingernail, uhm, claw paint is very nice."

"Thank you." Her smile returned. "You're very chivalrous."

Kim snorted.

"Like a knight," Qin added. "Did you ever think of trying to become one? There's an academy that you can apply to, isn't there?"

"If your grades are good enough, if you can pass the athletic exams, and if you have noble blood. I only would have qualified in one of those areas." His mind boggled at the notion of him walking around in knight's armor with one of those purple cloaks flapping in the breeze. He would probably trip over the halberd every time he extended it.

"You have to have noble blood?" Qin wrinkled her nose. "That's weird. That just means that some ancestor of yours kissed up to a king, right?"

Casmir almost laughed. "Typically, someone did a great deed, but since it had to be noticed by the king, I suppose ass-kissing might have been involved. Some people were simply so heroic and monumental in history that the populace demanded they be made knights and nobles, blood and education notwithstanding. Like Admiral Mikita, the great warrior-leader who helped King Dieter and Princess Sophie unite the Twelve Systems and create the original Star Kingdom."

He didn't know if someone from another system would be that familiar with Odin's historical figures, even if Mikita had effected change throughout all the systems, but Qin nodded.

"Yeah, my makers made me read all about him. To learn military strategy." She wrinkled her nose again, suggesting unicorns and dragons might have been of more interest to her, but then tapped a claw to her lips thoughtfully as she scrutinized his face. "You kind of look like him."

This time, Casmir *did* laugh, and he heard another snort from Kim. She'd moved over to examine the titles on the bookshelf but clearly hadn't stopped listening.

"That's the first time I've heard that." Casmir smiled gently, since Qin appeared puzzled. "There are a lot of pictures of Mikita in our textbooks. In all of them, he's about eight feet tall with shoulders like mountains, a granite jaw, and the muscles to rip trees out by the roots. I am…" As he waved self-deprecatingly at his five foot seven inches, narrow shoulders, and scrawny build, his eye blinked a couple of times to further demonstrate his lack of heroic attributes. "Not those things," he finished.

"Huh, those don't sound like the same pictures I've seen. He's in my boxed set of *Great Leaders of Earth* and *Great Leaders of the Twelve Systems*. Kim, do you like books? I have a lot of fairy tales. And the Confucian classics."

Casmir arched his eyebrows. Maybe Qin knew more about the history and culture of her namesake than she'd let on.

"Oh, and some romances," Qin added. "The romances are silly. As if sex is anything like they describe in those books, but the System Boar fairy tales especially are full of symbolism and some of them make you think."

"I've read a number of these, yes." Kim waved to the shelves.

"The fairy tales or the inaccurate-sex romances?" Casmir asked.

"You know my feelings on sex." She sent a message along with the words. *Please tell me we came here for something greater than this discussion.*

"That it's messy, unpleasant, and achieves nothing that a laboratory and an artificial womb can't accomplish, I seem to recall," Casmir said.

"Precisely. Should one even wish to procreate."

"Kim is not eager to have children," Casmir explained, since Qin's forehead was crinkled. "I, on the other hand, think it would be delightful to have a little boy or girl to build robots with. Someday. If I survive. How much did you say the bounty on my head is?"

"Two hundred thousand Kingdom crowns." Qin clapped a hand over her mouth as soon as the words came out.

"Were you not supposed to tell me?" Casmir kept his voice gentle and devoid of accusation, though it depressed him to verify that Kim had been right. Qin hadn't admitted that yet, but she wouldn't have reacted that way if they weren't up to something. "Because the captain is planning to collect it? Do you get a reasonable cut? What will you buy? I'm sure you can only fit so many candles in this cabin."

Qin turned her back to them.

"You tricked me," she whispered.

"Did I? I just asked a question." It was true, but her response made Casmir feel like a heel. He *had* meant to lower her guard so she would answer honestly. "I don't blame you. We've been in a crazy situation, and sometimes when the adrenaline is coursing through people's veins, unwise decisions are made."

He doubted that had happened to Lopez, though, at least when it came to the decision to collect his bounty. She might have gotten in over her head with the bioweapon, but this had been a calculated choice. She'd had a lot of time to change her mind, all night on the station while Qin had been looking for him, and she hadn't.

"I didn't want to do it," Qin said, her back still to them, "but the captain… she was divorced, and her husband took everything, and left her in debt. Don't tell her I said this, but I know she's desperate. It's why we're running on next to nothing. It's why she's taken risks she wouldn't normally take. She's had nothing but trouble since I joined her, and she's not… I know she would prefer to do the right thing."

"That's good to know," Casmir said, trying to keep his tone neutral. He wondered if there was a chance that he could lure Qin over to their side. "I don't suppose you can tell me *who* is offering that bounty? I've been running for weeks now and had crushers try to kill me numerous times, but I still have no idea who is after me and why."

Qin gazed at the wall without answering. Maybe that was all he would get from her. She probably saw it as a betrayal to speak to him, but he had a hard time giving up. Her silence seemed to mean that she knew. He stared at the back of her head, groping for something clever to say to entice the answer from her.

"Please, Qin," was what came out, a soft pleading whisper.

Her chin drooped. "Pequod Holding Company."

Kim looked sharply at her.

The name didn't mean anything to Casmir, but he hoped Kim had some information.

"Viggo couldn't find much about them," Qin added. "It's not a publicly traded company, and there weren't any officers or board members listed. No home planet or habitat."

"Thank you for that, Qin."

She twitched one shoulder and continued to face the wall.

"Is there any chance you would help us turn things around?" Casmir asked.

Qin was shaking her head before he finished the sentence.

"I don't want to hurt you or see you hurt, but I can't go against her." Qin turned around, her chin up, her eyes determined. "She's my captain, and I agreed to follow her orders. A soldier who can't follow orders has no place in the unit. No place anywhere, because that means she can't be trusted to do her job."

"To see what is right, and not to do it, is want of courage or of principle," Kim said, waving toward one of the books she was presumably quoting.

Qin's eyes tightened at the corners. "Please leave now."

Casmir frowned. Qin had already helped by sharing what he'd needed to know. He didn't want to make her feel bad just because she wouldn't betray her captain.

"Of course." Casmir waved Kim toward the hatch. "I'm sorry we disturbed you, Qin. And that I tricked you. It's just... It's my life. I want to keep living it. I hope you'll pardon my selfishness."

She scowled and turned her back on them again.

As Casmir and Kim stepped into the corridor, she messaged him again. *Pequod* is the name of Captain Ahab's ship in Moby Dick.

The who in the what? He glanced back at her.

She frowned. *Didn't you read any books without schematics in them at the university?*

I did my best to avoid classes that made use of such odious things.

Well, you may remember that I took as many classes as I could get away with on classical literature from Earth. In the novel, Captain Ahab loses his leg in an encounter with a whale and vows revenge on it. He spends the whole book trying to find it, and when they do, they fight a big battle and lose. Ahab and his ship, the Pequod, *are destroyed. For the last three thousand years, the name* Pequod *has been associated with doom and failure.*

For those who read the book.

Someone who wants you dead apparently did.

Maybe it's a coincidence. That's a pretty obscure reference, don't you think?

Kim shrugged. *Whether it's a coincidence or not, I don't want to meet the people trying to kill you.*

No, I'm not eager to either. Not in person, at least. Perhaps over a video chat from three planets away where we can work out our differences without touching.

You're not going to get that if we continue on our current trajectory. Kim spread her palm toward the ceiling. *Are you ready to take over the ship yet?*

We'd have to figure out a way to get Viggo on our side or a way to disable him, and then we'd still be in a logjam, because neither of us is a pilot. We'd need him to fly the ship. Or Lopez.

What if we hold Lopez and Qin hostage and force him to help us? Or at least not to impede us?

Please tell me you're not thinking of getting out one of those vials, Casmir replied.

No. One of the first things I'd do if I had control of the ship is to throw those out the airlock, get some distance between them and the ship, and launch every weapon the Dragon *has at them.*

Good.

I was thinking of something that will scare Qin and Lopez but won't be deadly.

Such as?

"I have a dreadful headache," Kim said aloud, stopping in the corridor instead of heading back into the lounge. "I'm going to see if there are painkillers in the sickbay."

Casmir assumed that was for Viggo's sake. The ship's computer might have already reported the conversation in Qin's room.

Am I following? Casmir messaged her.

No. I'm enacting a plan. You go back to the lounge and finish building Viggo his robots. Maybe he'll think more kindly of you then. And maybe he'll pay more attention to what you're doing than what I'm doing.

Let's hope. Out loud, he said, "Grab me some more motion-sickness pills while you're there, please," as Kim headed down the corridor. "One can never have too many."

"It's possible to overdose on those, you know."

"I'll take my chances."

As Casmir headed into the lounge, he wondered if he should be worried or optimistic about whatever Kim had in mind. Probably worried. After all, she'd told him to knock off his optimism.

CHAPTER 18

BONITA GRIPPED THE CONSOLE IN NAVIGATION AS ANOTHER wave of nausea assaulted her. Sweat beaded on her forehead, her face was flushed, and no amount of water could quench her thirst.

The *Stellar Dragon* was finishing its deceleration, with Saga's blue cloudy sphere filling the display ahead of them, so gravity was almost nonexistent, but she was used to zero-g. Zero-g didn't give her a fever.

"Viggo?"

Speaking made her stomach worse, and she groaned and released herself from her pod, then half ran and half pushed herself off the walls to the lavatory. Space toilets were obnoxious under any circumstances, even for a seasoned traveler, but they weren't designed for puke. She made a mess, then collapsed on the deck, her cheek pressed against the cool textured metal.

Two of Viggo's cleaning robots roamed around, whirring softly. For once, she didn't mind their constant presence. She wouldn't want to clean up the mess she'd just made herself. And her stomach still wasn't appeased. She sensed that if she tried to get up, she would puke again.

"Viggo?" she rasped, dragging her sleeve across her mouth.

"Yes, Captain. Are you allowing me to break your rule about contacting you in the lavatory?"

"Don't get funny with me. I'm not in the mood." Bonita closed her eyes. She ought to be in navigation to pilot them into the refinery and find a docking spot, but she feared she would have to let Viggo handle it.

"Yes, Captain. Your body temperature is elevated. It appears you are sick."

She watched as one of the vacuums whirred past in front of her eyes, sucking up the proof of that. "Good guess. Tell Qin to head to navigation and check for other ships before we dock. If we need to dock at all. I'm sure whoever is picking up Casmir doesn't live in the refinery."

"Qin is also incapacitated by illness. She is in a similar state in the other lavatory."

A bead of sweat trickled down Bonita's jaw as she worried that over. It wasn't that uncommon to catch a virus after visiting a station, habitat, or some other population center, but she wouldn't have guessed that her genetically engineered assistant could be afflicted by something so simple. She could have sworn Qin had once mentioned having an enhanced immune system.

"There's no chance one of those vials in the case broke, is there?" Her belly quivered with terror as she envisioned soon feeling much, much worse.

"I am unable to scan the contents, as you may recall, but the case is still secured behind the panel, and nobody has gone in to tamper with it."

That didn't mean it was impossible that something had happened. Could the contents of those vials leak out through the seams in that case? Kim had said something about acids that could help bioweapons eat through combat armor and space suits.

"Kim," Bonita rasped, suspicion leaping to mind. "What about our passengers? Are they sick?"

"They appear to be fine. They have not left the lounge since yesterday."

"Not even to sleep? Why, because they knew the air is contaminated? Or *we* were contaminated?" Bonita tried to lurch to a sitting position, wanting to rush down to strangle those two and see if they'd done something.

"The air on the *Stellar Dragon* is most certainly *not* contaminated," Viggo said stiffly. "Even if it had briefly been so, all of the air on the ship cycles through the filters and CO_2 scrubbers every hour. All particles larger than .01 microns are captured and incinerated."

"Are any viruses smaller than that?"

"Few."

"So *some*?" Bonita vomited again and flopped onto her back on the deck. "I feel like I'm going to die. You're *sure* those two didn't sneak into the lavatory and grab one of those vials?"

"I am positive. However, it's possible that they did something else. I believe they know about the bounty and that I am capable of monitoring them. They are speaking approximately 74% less than they did on the first leg of our journey, so I assume they are communicating chip-to-chip."

"Qin might have told them." Bonita closed her eyes again. She'd worried about that, that Qin might even turn on her and help them escape. Maybe she should have locked everyone in the brig three days ago. But Qin could probably break down the cell door. And then there was the matter of Casmir's new pet. "I think I botched this, Viggo."

"We are less than a half hour from the refinery. The scanners show several docking spots available. Two are in use by automated mining ships, but there are no manned vessels attached currently. It appears that we can dock without a passcode, though it is possible the refinery interior has defense systems to keep passersby from raiding its processed gases."

As if Bonita could raid anything right now.

"Do you wish me to dock?" Viggo asked.

"Are there any other ships in range of your scanners? Besides those mining tankers? You're positive nobody is inside those?"

"Correct. Neither the mining ships nor the refinery have air pressure or oxygen. You'll need your suit and tank to visit."

Bonita had assumed a ship would be here waiting and that she wouldn't *have* to visit. Maybe someone was on the way.

"There is a large civilian vessel orbiting one of the moons on the far side of Saga's orbit from us," Viggo added. "It would take twelve hours to reach it. I see nothing else in the vicinity besides satellites."

"Meaning we're early or someone has stealth technology. Go ahead and dock. We're going to need to get fuel one way or another eventually." Bonita didn't know how she would manage that while she was sick, but it would be better to have full tanks before Casmir's buyer showed up. Just in case things went supernova.

"Yes, Captain. You have visitors coming."

"Kim and Casmir?" She groaned again as she watched one of the vacuums traipse across the ceiling.

"Yes."

"Are they armed?"

Bonita patted her side where her holster was usually attached to her suit, but it wasn't there. It was hanging over the back of her pod in navigation where she'd draped it that morning. Damn it. She was supposed to be more competent than this.

"Kim has a stunner and Casmir is walking behind the crusher."

And Bonita and Qin were on their backs in separate lavatories. Fantastic.

A soft knock sounded at the hatch. Such polite mutineers.

Except they weren't mutineers. They were prisoners. Escaped prisoners.

"From now on, all prisoners ride in the brig, Viggo."

"Yes, a wise policy. Though Casmir did make two new cleaning robots for me out of spare parts."

Was *that* why Viggo hadn't paid that much attention to what those two had been concocting? Casmir, the only man in the system who knew how to win over computers.

The hatch opened. Bonita peeled one eyelid up, saw the crusher stride in, and lowered it again.

She'd often imagined bravely facing death with her eyes open. She'd failed to imagine herself lying in vomitus, too weak to lift a hand. How shortsighted.

"Hello, Captain Lopez," Casmir said politely, his footsteps coming to a stop near her head.

She wanted to strangle his polite throat.

"I apologize for the little virus Kim coerced back to life in order to incapacitate you, but we were worried you would send us to this Pequod Holding Company in flex-cuffs, and we'd like to go with our hands free and more options available. We'd prefer not to go at all, but your actions have made it clear that we're not safe staying with you. If circumstances somehow play out favorably, I'll try to arrange for some helium-3 to find its way into your cargo hold, but I've recently been told I'm overly optimistic, so that may not be possible. However, Kim says you should recover from your illness in short order, and then you can retrieve it yourself."

Bonita didn't say anything. She didn't even open her eyes.

"Again, I apologize for your discomfort," Casmir said. "I just didn't think you were open to reason. Ah, I don't suppose you'd care to tell me when your Pequod contact is showing up? They aren't in the refinery, are they? We didn't see a ship…"

"Go to hell," Bonita rasped, then rolled over and threw up again.

Casmir gripped a handhold in navigation as the *Stellar Dragon* eased toward a bank of airlocks on the side of the refinery. Saga's massive blue body filled most of the view beyond the sprawling structure, swirling angry clouds streaking across its gaseous atmosphere at hundreds of miles an hour.

The long-range scanners showed a civilian research ship orbiting one of the planet's thirteen moons, but when Casmir tried to comm it, the panel locked up. It seemed Viggo wasn't going to let him send outgoing communications. The research ship was a twelve-hour flight away, so the crew probably wouldn't have dropped what it was doing to come help him with his problem, but he wouldn't have minded asking. Cajoling. Begging. Pleading…

Unfortunately, it looked like Casmir and Kim were alone in dealing with whoever was coming. Unless they could *avoid* dealing with them somehow.

He eyed a pair of automated mining ships that were docked at the refinery.

"Viggo is taking us all the way in, huh?" Kim pushed herself into navigation to stand beside Casmir. "Any chance we can change the course and *not* go where these people will be waiting?"

Zee was anchored in the corridor, watching their backs in case Qin or Lopez recovered enough to rush them.

"All the controls are locked down." Casmir hadn't even been able to sit down in the pilot's pod. Its sides had tightened into a ball, denying him access.

He had some hacking knowledge, but he was skeptical about successfully getting around the security measures while the intelligent computer entity inside was watching everything he did.

Once again, he eyed the mining ships and then looked to the scanner display showing the distant research vessel.

He switched to chip-to-chip messaging to speak to Kim. *There's a research vessel orbiting Skadi Moon. I wonder what they're studying. There's not an atmosphere or much of value down there.*

Why are you worried about what they're studying right now? Kim frowned at him.

I thought they might be more inclined to accept us on board as temporary passengers if either of our expertise would be useful to them.

Kim's frown turned to an expression of enlightenment. *You want to take one of the mining ships over there?*

If we can get to one and figure out a way to override its automated programming. Those ships should have plenty of fuel. What they might not have is oxygen, since there's no human crew. But if we take a couple of air tanks for these suits... Casmir pointed his thumb toward the supply cabinet in the corridor. *My concerns are that the captain of that ship will say no and, even if he or she says yes, that we might be endangering the crew. The* Stellar Dragon's *scanner doesn't show any weapons on their ship.*

Maybe we could talk them into giving us a ride somewhere civilized before this Pequod Holding Company shows up.

That would be nice. Dare he be that hopeful?

"I believe I'm being quite lenient in letting you live when you infected my crew with a virus when I wasn't paying attention," Viggo said, belatedly replying to their conversation. Maybe he had been busy discussing something with Lopez. "It is only because you promised they would recover soon that I haven't reacted in a vengeful manner. And because you repaired vacuums that I believed beyond repair."

"Vengeful?" Kim murmured. "Do you think he could kill us?"

Maybe she realized she had taken more of a risk than she believed.

"All he would have to do is seal the rooms with Lopez and Qin, then open an exterior hatch and vent the ship's atmosphere."

She elbowed him in the ribs. "Don't give him ideas."

"I'm sure he has plenty of his own ideas already."

"A great many," Viggo said agreeably. "How long until Qin and Bonita recover?"

"I spoke truthfully to them," Kim said. "They'll be weak for a few days, but they should be feeling better in a matter of hours."

Casmir was glad. Lopez had been so sweat-slathered and miserable. He hadn't realized Kim's virus collection would contain anything that virulent.

Viggo issued a noise akin to a *harrumph*.

Are we leaving the ship as soon as it docks? Kim asked silently as the *Dragon* glided closer to an empty slot.

Yes, the sooner we get to one of the mining ships, the better. It'll take time to figure out how to override the autopilot.

Are you sure Viggo will let us leave?

No. Let's find out.

Casmir left navigation, giving Zee a pat on the way by, and headed for the cabinet with the oxygen tanks. Kim was also in a galaxy suit, so it wouldn't take them long to prepare to leave.

"The captain wants you to wait here until our contact arrives," Viggo said as Casmir reached for the cabinet.

"She doesn't want us to wait on the refinery for whoever's coming?" Casmir slowly withdrew two oxygen tanks, wondering if Viggo would keep the hatch locked so they couldn't walk off the ship. He thought of that blowtorch in the kitchen.

"No," Viggo said.

"She wants to make sure she gets paid and we don't just walk ourselves into a trap," Kim muttered.

If Casmir and Kim were still on board when Lopez recovered, he didn't know how she would respond. Maybe Lopez would shoot him herself and hand his dead body over to Pequod Holding Company. Casmir hadn't thought to ask if his bounty specified he be alive or dead at delivery. Given his experience with all those crushers, he assumed these people wanted him dead.

"Is there any chance you can tell us when the Pequod ship arrives, Viggo?" Casmir handed one of the tanks to Kim and fastened another onto his own suit. He was tempted to take extras, but Viggo would guess their plan right away if they did. "Captain Lopez was disinclined to share that information."

"The captain does not know. She was given this location but no date and time. She never spoke to anyone."

"So we could be here for a month?" Kim attached the tank to her suit and pointed at two others nestled inside the locker.

Before Casmir could decide whether to grab them, Viggo said, "Another ship just appeared on my scanners. Oh dear."

For a computer, he could convey dread in his words quite well.

Casmir ran back into navigation, checked the scanner display, and flinched at how close the new ship was. It had to have twenty layers of slydar on the hull because there was no way it should have been able to sneak up on them without Viggo detecting it.

"I am putting an image on the display," Viggo said. "And informing the captain that we have company."

The display, which had previously shown the side of the refinery, shifted to a camera on the other side of the ship. A black vessel approached like the shadow of death. Sleek and angular and bristling weapons like a porcupine bristled quills. It had no running lights, and its edges seemed to blur and blend in with the stars behind it. One could look right at it and miss seeing it. Just as the computer's scanners had, until the last minute.

The longer Casmir looked at the approaching vessel, the more certain he became that he'd seen it before on news reports. It was possible there were many of that model and that this wasn't the same ship that was always featured in those horrific news stories, but he doubted it.

"You've identified it, Viggo?" Casmir asked.

"It does not have an ID chip such as Kingdom ships are required to have," Viggo said, "but I do recognize it. The *Fedallah*."

"Let me guess," Kim said. "The captain calls himself Ahab."

Casmir looked curiously at her.

"Fedallah is the crazy prophetic harpooner in the book who foresees Captain Ahab's death. Aren't you excited to be captured by a fan of the classics, Casmir?"

"The captain of the *Fedallah* is Tenebris Rache," Viggo said.

"The pirate who's destroyed dozens of Kingdom ships, military outposts, and research laboratories in the last ten years," Casmir said numbly, wishing he were back on Odin where the nefarious captain's exploits had been disturbing but distant. A single ship didn't have the might to bother Odin and its orbital defenses, but the rest of the system seemed to be fair game. "No, I can't say that I'm excited by his reading hobby."

Kim's sarcasm faded, replaced by open-mouthed shock, her eyes widening with alarm. She recovered enough to mask her fear and say, "He probably just read the comic book."

Casmir couldn't manage a response. He pushed shaking hands through his hair. Tenebris Rache. Was this the man who'd wanted him dead all along? *Why?*

Because he'd made robots for the military, and Rache loathed the Kingdom and King Jager and all he stood for? How would such a man even have gotten hold of crushers to reprogram them and send them to hunt down Casmir? His ship never went anywhere near Odin; if it did, the military would hunt him down relentlessly. No, the pirate skulked about near the gate and the gas giants, striking and then leaving the system anytime the military got close. Nobody was sure how he got past the guard ships at the gate, but he did. Over and over. He'd even attacked and disabled them a few times.

The bristly black ship glided toward the airlock hatch adjacent to the *Stellar Dragon*.

"I have to get out of here." Casmir checked to make sure the mining ships were still docked. "Viggo, you have to let me go. Please. I'm not asking for any help. Just open the hatch so I can leave."

"Do it," came a weak rasp from behind them.

Lopez hung in the air behind Zee, her gray braid floating free around her head, the crusher's arm keeping her from advancing farther. Her shoulder slumped against the wall, her face was ashen, and her legs looked like they would have given out if they'd had to support her weight.

"Pardon, Captain?" Viggo said.

"Let them go." Lopez met Casmir's eyes. "I didn't know who it was. I thought that company was some business that wanted you for your brain, to question you or make you work for them, not..."

"My brain isn't that valuable, I'm afraid," Casmir said bleakly.

Lopez's gaze shifted toward the *Fedallah* on the display. "Nobody deserves that fate. To be tortured by a sadistic madman and killed." Her voice dropped to a whisper. "I didn't know."

"As you wish, Captain," Viggo said. "We are docked, and I am unlocking the airlock hatch."

Casmir nodded to Lopez. "Thank you."

He kept himself from pointing out that he wouldn't be in this situation if she hadn't tricked him, but there was no time for voicing grievances. The pirate ship would be docked within minutes. Casmir didn't know what the inside of the refinery looked like, but he assumed it would only take the pirates a few seconds to walk from one airlock to the next.

He tapped the button on his chest plate to bring his helmet over his head and pulled himself past Lopez and Zee toward the ladder well using the handholds on the bulkhead.

"Come with me, please, Zee," he said, though he needn't have bothered. The crusher strode after him, its soles magnetized as effectively as Casmir's boots.

Kim also came after him, but Casmir lifted a hand. "You better stay here." He switched to chip-to-chip messaging to add, *I'm still going to try to enact my plan, but it's going to be an extreme long shot now to get to the mining ship and escape.* "If he only wants me, you should be safe staying on the *Dragon*."

"I'm from the Kingdom. If the news stories are even remotely accurate, he would shoot me simply because I was born on Odin."

"Lopez can hide you."

Kim looked over her shoulder. Lopez dangled limply in the corridor, her head lolled against a wall.

"Just stay here and promise me you'll speak fondly of me when they hold my funeral back on Odin. And have a wonderful career, and find a new roommate who can get ready in the morning without making a mess. And who doesn't leave pieces of projects all over the coffee table."

"Casmir, I'm not—"

"Don't worry. I'm not giving up. But I don't want to get you killed." He hugged her, his helmet clunking against hers. "Stay here and hide. Promise me!"

She did not.

Casmir rushed down the ladder and into the cargo hold while thinking about how he would get away now. Even if he made it to the mining ship, it was a *Kingdom* mining ship. Rache would have no problem blowing it into a million pieces.

An image of a news story from five years earlier popped into his head, video footage of Kingdom soldiers shot dead all over the cargo hold of their own ship, of two of the king's most loyal knights strung up and staked to makeshift crosses where they'd been stripped and tortured and left to die.

Captain Rache was pure evil, and he wanted Casmir.

Willing his hands to remain steady, Casmir hit the button to open the airlock hatch. His helmet display had automatically synched with his chip, and his contact scrolled the environment outside, along with his medical stats. His blood pressure and heart rate competed for the position of most alarming stat, and he tried to remember if he had taken his seizure medication that morning or if he was thinking of the day before. Would Rache shoot him if he was in the middle of convulsing in midair? That would be a delightful way to go.

He stepped into the small airlock chamber with Zee and started to close the hatch behind him, but Kim stuck her arm out to halt him.

"What are you doing?" Casmir asked.

She pulled herself inside, a stunner and a borrowed Starhawk rifle in her hands, and closed the hatch. "Coming with you."

"Kim, I'm trying to nobly sacrifice myself so you can get away. You're making that difficult."

"You said you had a plan, not that you were going to fling yourself at the guy's feet."

"My plan has a low probability of success."

"Well, now it's improved." She stuck the stunner in his hand.

"You think your kendo skills will make a difference against a fleet of sadistic pirates?"

"No, but if we're captured, I bet I can engage the captain in a literary discussion of *Moby Dick* while you think of a way to get out of trouble. I wrote a paper on it."

"What was it about?"

"Penises."

"Uhm, what?"

"To be specific, the social and homoerotic bonds between the male characters in the story."

"Just the sort of discussion a psychopathic killer should find fascinating."

"He might."

The air finished draining out of the chamber, and a green light signaled the outer door ready to open.

Aware that Rache's killers might already be in their own airlock chamber, Casmir fired his jet boots to hurry down the short connection tube to the refinery's hatch. It was locked. He tried a few buttons, but it asked for a code. He should have known that any stranger with a ship wouldn't be permitted to stroll onto a government refinery.

"Zee, can you open that?" Casmir realized they were in a vacuum now and that sound wouldn't travel. He pointed at the hatch and mimicked forcing it, hoping he'd given the crusher enough intuitive reasoning to grasp what he wanted.

While he was demonstrating, Kim stepped forward with the rifle and blasted the hatch controls. Casmir cursed and scrambled out of the way, his boots firing him into the side of the tube.

"You're going to get me killed before Rache even finds us," he blurted over their shared comm.

"You and your robot were taking too much time."

Kim stopped firing—she'd melted a hole around the latching mechanism—and yanked on the hatch. It opened easily. Fortunately, there wasn't an inner hatch, and they flowed out into a bay full of pipes and lined with rows of hulking storage tanks. There wasn't any light inside, other than a few flashing yellow and blue indicators on bulkheads, and a flashlight beam activated on Casmir's helmet.

Kim only took three seconds to look around before hurrying toward the other airlocks, all visible farther down the outer wall of the bay. Casmir hurried after her, but he shone his light around as he and Zee navigated over the pipes. If he could find some inspiration here, he wasn't too set in his plan to improvise.

He spotted the mangled remains of what appeared to have been robot sentries. Warped and charred, they'd been struck by DEW rifles, or maybe explosives.

He must have made a startled noise because Kim glanced back.

"What?" she asked.

"I think Rache was here before." Casmir waved at the debris.

"Setting a trap?"

"I don't know."

With few other options, they continued toward the mining ships. In the shadows up ahead, undamaged robots moved about. They were unhooking equipment for draining the ships' tanks. Did that mean they were almost done, and those ships would leave?

Casmir fired his jet boots to pick up his pace. None of the robots reacted as they passed.

A red light flashed behind them on the airlock panel where the mercenary ship was docked.

"Go," Casmir said, panic gripping his heart. "They're coming."

He and Kim jetted past the last of the robots and to the closest mining ship.

"At least the door is open," Kim said.

Yes, the hatch was open, an airlock tube in place, and drones zipped in and out of the ship. A porthole showed numerous hookups between the vessel and the refinery. Different gases being transferred inside? All Casmir knew was that it would take time to disconnect everything and launch the ship. Time they didn't have.

As he was about to push himself into the tube, a hand gripped him from behind. Zee. His mouth moved as he said something, but Casmir couldn't hear it. The mining ship and transfer tube were as devoid of air as the refinery.

Zee pushed him aside and maneuvered himself to go first, and Casmir got the gist.

"Your noble bodyguard," Kim said.

"Everybody should have one."

"I doubt the military would agree."

As Casmir followed Zee through the airlock tube, he tapped into the network, grimacing at the lag, and called up a layout of the mining ship. He threw in a few searches to see if anything came up related to overriding automatic controls.

"Casmir," a voice said over his helmet comm—Viggo.

"Yes?" Casmir magnetized his boots and set them down on the deck inside the ship's hold. It was even more full of tanks than the refinery bay had been, and there was nowhere to go but straight down a long aisle toward a distant hatch.

"My scanners show heat signatures in the refinery now. A team of ten men in combat armor is in the bay."

"Thank you," Casmir whispered, even though there was no chance of his voice carrying anywhere. Unless the pirates had hacked into their comm system and were listening in. A depressing thought.

He strode down the aisle as quickly as he could while keeping at least one boot attached to the deck. He activated a rear helmet cam, though he wasn't sure he wanted to see the pirates when they charged up behind them.

Interior hatches opened automatically as Casmir and Kim hurried into navigation at the front of the ship. Instead of a digital display, three large portholes showed Saga and part of the black bristly hull of the *Fedallah*.

The pilot's seat wasn't nearly as fancy as the pods in the *Dragon*, having merely a seat back and a seat belt for protection. Casmir worried that meant the ship had a ridiculously slow drive and it would take twelve days to reach that moon instead of twelve hours.

"They are not boarding the *Stellar Dragon*," Viggo announced.

"I would say that was good news." Casmir tugged himself into the seat, securing the belt clasp to keep from floating away. "But I'm afraid that means they've figured out where we are."

"They have." Kim stood in the hatchway, her rifle pointed rearward.

Casmir reached for the controls, hoping he could very quickly figure out how to override the automated system and fly them away. He should have brought Lopez along. A pilot would have had a better chance at this.

"They're coming," Kim barked.

She started to close the hatch to navigation, but Zee rushed out past her. She closed it after he left.

"That might buy us some time, but it looked like the whole group of ten back there, all in combat armor." Kim looked at him. "Casmir, even if we get the ship going, *they're* already on it."

"I know, I know." He tapped buttons furiously, hoping vainly... There, that looked like the override.

A message came up on a screen. *Manual control activated.*

"Hah!" It was something. Now if he could—

Light strobed outside the portholes, and Casmir jerked his head up in surprise before the back of his mind cried, *No, don't look!*

It was his last thought before he lost control of his body and awareness of his brain.

CHAPTER 19

CAPTAIN?" VIGGO ASKED.

"Yeah?" Bonita knew she was floating in the middle of the corridor beside navigation, but she couldn't summon the energy to move. She had stopped throwing up, but she still felt like one of the mystery clumps clogging up the innards of one of Viggo's vacuums.

"Neither the refinery nor the mercenary ship has cameras that I can access, but I was monitoring heat signatures on the station and the mining ship that Casmir and Kim attempted to commandeer."

"Ah?"

Was that what they had been doing?

"It appears that they were captured and taken into the mercenary vessel," Viggo said.

"The *Fedallah*."

Bonita had never had a run-in with the infamous mercenary ship, but she knew its reputation well, and she knew to avoid it. Captain Rache might be known for hating the Kingdom and terrorizing its ships, but he'd partaken in plenty of deadly missions in other systems too. Anything, the rumors said, that would help his people hone their skills. Their skills at killing.

Unexpected tears pricked at her eyes. She would never have brought Casmir here if she'd known Rache was the one who'd placed that bounty. Nobody deserved that man's wrath. She couldn't even imagine what the kid had done to earn it. She feared he'd simply been born on the wrong planet and chosen the wrong profession. Maybe one of his crushers had been used on Rache's ship and killed someone he cared about. Assuming the hardened mercenary cared about anyone.

"If you plan to contact them in regard to the bounty," Viggo said, "you may wish to do so soon."

Bonita snorted. "You think that bastard is going to pay me? I should have known better, should never have contemplated working for an unproven client. The money was too good, too tempting. It would have solved too many problems." A tear floated away, and she wiped her eyes. "Even if Rache was going to pay, I can't, Viggo. I can't make this trade. Casmir doesn't deserve this, no matter what he invented."

"What do you propose?" Viggo didn't object. Even though that much money would buy him all the robot vacuums and ship upgrades he could ever want, he didn't object.

Because he also thought she'd done the wrong thing?

With the help of a handhold, Bonita pushed herself into a semblance of an upright position. "Where's Qin? Still in the lav?"

"She crawled to her bunk a little while ago."

"Where's the merc ship? Still docked next to us?"

"Yes."

"Qin?" Bonita said over the ship's comm. "How would you like to plan a rescue?"

"Captain?" came the weak and uncertain response. But it also seemed to hold hope.

"We're next door to Tenebris Rache, and he's got Casmir and Kim. I've... realized I've made a mistake." Why was it so hard to admit that? "I want to help them escape."

"I'm coming up."

"Captain," Viggo said, "should I point out how outmatched we would be in either a battle between ships or a battle between crews?"

"No."

"Should I point out that you're in a weakened state?"

"*Definitely* no."

Bonita pulled herself into navigation. She didn't plan to get into a fight with the mercenaries—that would be pure suicide. But if she could provide a distraction, maybe Casmir and Kim could figure out a way to escape on their own. They'd proven their resourcefulness a number of times already—if Casmir actually wanted to hurt anyone, he could be extremely dangerous. That crusher. She shuddered. "Wait, where *is* his crusher? Did the mercs destroy it?"

"Unknown, Captain. It left with them, but it has no heat signature, so my scanners can't find it."

Bonita tugged herself into her pod, and it wrapped comfortingly around her, cushioning her and keeping her secure.

"Still coming, Captain," came Qin's weak call. "Almost there..."

Bonita grimaced in sympathy, knowing just how much effort it was to move right now. There was no way they could fight even one mercenary. Whatever distraction they planned, it would have to be something clever, something that used brainpower rather than brawn.

"You said they made it to that mining ship, Viggo?" Bonita pointed to the scanner display since the cameras couldn't show them anything on the other side of the hulking mercenary ship.

"Yes."

"So the crusher might be there and damaged. I wonder if it would be worth retrieving. I also wonder if there's anything we could use on the refinery to cause a problem for Rache's ship."

Qin made it into navigation and grabbed the back of the co-pilot's pod to sit down, but she froze. "We're going to fight Tenebris Rache?"

Bonita had never heard fear in her young assistant's voice. She heard it now.

"We're going to distract him so Casmir and Kim can escape," Bonita said. "I'm still working out the how. Either we or Casmir and Kim will have to disable his ship to give us long enough to fly out of here. And— shit. We still need fuel. All right, we're going to have to take a field trip into that refinery anyway, so we might as well look for the crusher. And hope the mercs are too busy with Casmir to have men roaming around over there. If we *can't* disable their ship, they'll come after us and blow us out of the stars. Even if we can disable them, we'll have to plot a course very carefully that keeps the refinery between them and us for as long as possible, or they'll still be able to blow us out of the stars. Did you see all the weapons that thing has?"

Qin looked toward the ship looming at the edge of their display, but her haunted eyes didn't seem to see much. It was as if they were locked on some past event.

"You haven't met him before, have you?" Bonita asked.

"I saw him once, when I was twelve and being trained by my then-new pirate owners. We were at a gathering on one of the neutral moons in System Cerberus with some of the related pirate families. There was a nice lake and trees and little cabins and trails and ducks and *qoypods*. I'd never lived anywhere except a spaceship or space station, and I remember thinking how delightful it was. And then he strode up with some of his men. He wasn't invited; none of them were. He argued with one of the pirate heads. I was too far away to hear what they were talking about, but later, it came out that one of the pirate families was on retainer for King Jager. They were infiltrating us, in a way, but we didn't know that then. All Rache said was that he didn't like Jager's sycophants. They ended up drawing weapons, the pirate a pistol, him a long dagger.

"He should have lost, but he was fast. Enhanced. Cyborg, I think. But maybe he's not human at all. Some say he isn't. He wears that mask, so who knows? Rache sliced the leader's head off. Others tried to jump him, but his men lunged in, and they were as ruthless as he was. What had been essentially a family picnic turned into a blood bath. Those who were smart stayed out of it. My captain pulled me back. A lot of people weren't that smart. They should have had him and his men outnumbered, but they didn't come out on top. All of the mercenaries walked away. Fifty, sixty pirates didn't. I remember him looking around at the end, seeing if anyone else would come forward to challenge him, to try to stop him. His oily black mask looked right at me. Even though I couldn't see his eyes, it scared me so much that I had nightmares for months afterward. I… never wanted to see the man again."

Bonita was empathetic, but now she worried her only advantage would go into shock if she actually came face to face with Rache.

"I'll go to the refinery alone then," Bonita said. "See if I can figure something out while I'm collecting fuel."

"No." Qin drew a shaky breath. "I'll do it. I can handle—"

The comm beeped. It was the *Fedallah*.

Bonita stared at the panel. Should she answer it when she planned mayhem? Yes, she had better answer it, *because* she planned mayhem.

"Captain Lopez," she answered, striving for nonchalance.

"Captain," a rich cultured voice said, "we generally expect prisoners to be handed over to us in flex-cuffs, not armed and dangerous with killer robot bodyguards."

"I'm reasonably sure there was only *one* robot."

Who was she talking to? Rache? Or some lackey? If it was Rache, he ought to sound far eviler, perhaps with a scratchy rasp from when someone had tried to garrote him once. She had no idea if that had ever happened, but that mask had to hide *something*.

"It was an inordinately difficult one to deal with."

"Those *prisoners* were inordinately difficult to deal with." Maybe she shouldn't warn him of that, but it sounded like he'd figured it out by now. "You should have offered *four* hundred thousand for Dabrowski and Sato."

"I didn't ask for Sato. And—" his voice took on an icy edge, "—we are not renegotiating at this juncture."

Bonita stared at the comm panel. There was no video, so she couldn't attempt to read body language, but did that imply he actually meant to *pay* her? She'd assumed he wouldn't. Where would a mercenary get that kind of money? Admittedly, he was an infamous mercenary and probably got paid well to blow up Kingdom assets.

"I am, however, interested in a cargo I've learned you carry," the man added.

A chill went through her fevered body. Thanks to her preoccupation with her sickness, she'd forgotten about the bioweapon.

"I don't have anything else that's for sale. Shall I transmit my bank account information to your finance officer for the transfer of funds for Dabrowski?"

"Do so. I will transfer two hundred thousand, as agreed, for... Dabrowski." Why the pause? That was odd. Almost making it sound like that wasn't the kid's real name? "And also the fifty thousand that a Mr. Baum agreed to pay you for that case. I understand that deal fell through and that it's available."

Shakes that had nothing to do with her fever racked her body. The man knew about the bioweapon, no doubt. And she was positive now that she was dealing with Rache personally, not some lackey.

There was no way she could give him the bioweapon. He'd take it to Odin and use it for exactly what it was designed for.

Bonita closed her eyes and gripped the edge of the console hard enough to hurt. "I'm afraid I can't sell you that. When I learned what was inside, I jettisoned it into the nearest gas giant. The extreme temperatures there will have destroyed it."

"You're a poor liar for such an experienced bounty hunter."

Asshole.

"What can I say? I've been sick. Make sure to search Sato for petri dishes full of viruses, or she'll do in your crew too."

"Interesting."

Bonita rubbed her sweaty forehead. She needed time to think. She was probably making things worse for Kim and Casmir, not better. How could she end this conversation?

"I'm transmitting my account information now," she said as cheerfully as she could and closed the channel.

Qin hadn't said a word or even reacted during the conversation—her face had an eerie frozen stillness. But she looked over in surprise when the channel closed.

"You can't hang up on him," she squeaked.

"You recognized his voice? That was Rache, right?"

"Yeah. Are you... going to send your banking information?"

Bonita exhaled slowly. Was she?

If she accepted payment and then tried to rescue Casmir, she would truly piss off the mercenary. But she would piss him off, regardless, if she attempted a rescue. Except she wasn't going to rescue anyone, right? She was only going to arrange a distraction and hope Casmir could get himself out of there on his own.

Not caring if it was cheeky, Bonita leaned forward and transmitted her banking details. She would see if the merc actually sent the money before worrying about moral implications and consequences.

"Wait a second." Bonita thumped her hand on the console. "You said Rache is a cyborg, right? Enhanced muscles and the like?"

"Probably bones too, either reinforced or replaced to support the stress of what enhanced muscles can do." Qin's brow creased.

"But he'd likely still have a human immune system. Human organs. Skin. Brain. Things susceptible to..." She looked over her shoulder significantly.

"You want to send over those vials in such a way that they'll blow open on the mercenary ship?" Qin stared at her.

"I wonder if there's a reward for killing Rache. I've never had the audacity to look, but King Jager must have something out there. The problem is that we couldn't unleash it while Casmir and Kim were on board."

"And how would *we* escape if we broke open the vials on their ship?" Qin asked.

"I've got some Tac-75 in the armory. We could set a timed charge, give them long enough to—"

An alert scrolled down Bonita's contact, letting her know that money had been transferred into her account. Two hundred and fifty thousand Kingdom crowns.

"Damn. I didn't think he'd actually pay."

Since Rache was bullying her into giving him the case, Bonita felt a little better about trying to screw him, but she still wondered if she was going to survive the day. Maybe she would go out in a fiery blaze. Then she wouldn't have to worry about financing her retirement.

"How much did he pay?"

"Two-fifty."

Qin looked gravely at her. "Then he's going to send men over for the case."

"Not if we offer to bring it to him." Bonita tapped the comm to open the channel again. "Captain Rache? This is Captain Lopez."

"Captain Rache is unavailable," a woman said.

A woman? Somehow, Bonita had never imagined women on the fearsome mercenary's ship. Maybe she was as cyborged-up as the men.

"I need to speak with him, please. About our deal."

"He's unavailable," the woman said firmly.

Because he was interrogating Casmir?

"Fine," Bonita said. "Let him know we're getting the case out of the safe and that I'll have someone bring it over."

"I'll tell him. Chen, out."

Once the channel was closed, Bonita asked, "Will you do me a favor, Qin?"

"You're my captain and commander. For however much longer you live." Qin's lips quirked into a smile, but it was a fleeting one.

"Find some drugs in sickbay to make you feel better, and go out there and get me some fuel, just in case we're able to pull away from this refinery in one piece. Look for whatever remains of the crusher too. If there's any chance it's still ambulatory and I can convince it to take an order from me... we'll send *it* to deliver the case."

Casmir woke up groggy and confused and in a different place than he expected.

The wall beside him and ceiling above him were white. Everything on the mining ship had been gray and blue. His helmet was off, but his body was restrained, strapped to a bed. For *what*? Some mercenary's medical experiments?

Panic surged through him, cortisol and adrenaline clearing his brain from the after effects of the seizure. Yes, the seizure. He recognized what it had been, even if it had been a couple of years since his last one. But seizures didn't knock out his brain for more than a couple of minutes. Not long enough to be moved to another ship. At least they never had before.

"Are you awake?" Kim asked from somewhere underneath him.

Casmir turned his head, grimacing at the dizziness that washed over him. His hair floated around his face, in need of cutting. In need of gravity to stay put. Were they still docked to the refinery? They were somewhere with air and heat.

"Yes," he rasped. "What happened?"

"You had a seizure."

"I know about *that* part." His words sounded a little off as they came out, not quite right to his ear, and he made himself focus on articulation. "What happened after that? Why was I out for so long? How did we get here?"

"They got through your robot in short order—I think a couple of them stayed back to fight it while the others stormed navigation. One of them ripped the hatch right off the hinges. From what I've seen, they've got some cyborgs here, so add superhuman strength to whatever their combat armor gives them. They ran in, and I didn't get a chance to bring up the literary merits of *Moby Dick* before they stabbed a needle bigger than a katana through our suits and drugged us. My suit has patched itself back up, but my shoulder hasn't. It stings like crazy."

As he grew more aware of his body, Casmir realized he'd also taken a puncture in the shoulder. He was too numb to do more than acknowledge the pain. He felt lucky that whatever they had given him hadn't started a cascade of seizures. But that was the only thing he felt lucky about.

He craned his neck to look around and spotted two empty bunks on the opposite wall. Thick silver-blue bars and a gate barred the exit from what he realized was a brig cell. He couldn't see Kim. She had to be strapped to a bunk below him. His fear of medical experiments appeared to be groundless—as if mercenaries were into neuroscience research. They'd simply been strapped to the bunks because of the lack of gravity. How thoughtful of their captors to care that they stay in one place instead of floating up to the ceiling.

Casmir wondered why Rache hadn't killed him outright. Was he the one who'd issued the bounty? Or was he some middleman? No, if Kim was right, Pequod Holding Company had to be linked to Rache's ship, the *Fedallah*. But why would mercenaries want *him*?

"I have a headache," Casmir announced.

"From the seizure?"

"Among other things."

"Someone flashed those lights on purpose," she said.

Casmir swallowed. "Yeah, they did, didn't they?"

He hadn't had time to consider what it was or why it was happening then, but it wasn't as if a mining ship had a reason to flash bright lights before departing. He supposed it was a possible feature, like a truck on Odin buzzing before it backed up, but he'd never heard of such a thing. It was more like—

"Someone knows your weaknesses," Kim said.

"You don't think it was chance?" His voice came out small, and that was how he felt. Small and scared. He couldn't imagine what he'd ever done to deserve some bloodthirsty mercenary's attention. But it seemed this Captain Rache had decided to add him to his list of hated Kingdom subjects.

"No."

He closed his eyes and tried to slow his breathing, to calm his body. A therapist he'd had as a kid, before the doctors had found better medication to control his seizures, had suggested that he do that whenever he felt stressed, since stress and fatigue had been triggers for him. Little good that did when someone flashed lights in his eyes.

A clang sounded somewhere, and the distant thud of footfalls followed, magnetic boots clomping on the metal deck.

"I wish you'd stayed on the *Dragon*, Kim," Casmir said.

"You'd be bored if you were stuck in a cell by yourself."

"It doesn't sound like I'm going to be here long enough to get bored."

"They may just be coming to feed us. Or to unstrap us so we can pee."

"Somehow, I doubt mercenaries care about the biological needs of their prisoners."

"Whichever one is responsible for cleaning the cells does."

Two armored figures stepped into view. Since Casmir could see their scarred and cruel faces, he assumed neither one was Captain Rache. The media had never managed to get a photograph of him, but they spoke often about the mask he wore. Like some tortured villain from one of Kim's classics.

"Greetings, fellows," Casmir said with as much cheer as he could muster. "We were just debating how to attend to our biological needs. Are you here to assist?"

"I'm also available to debate penises and symbolism in ancient Earth texts," Kim said.

The men looked at each other.

"Why do we always get the failed comedy teams?" one asked.

"Lack of seniority."

One of them slapped a control panel that Casmir couldn't see, and the gate swung open. One guard stayed in the corridor, his rifle pointed loosely toward Casmir, and the other approached his bunk. Neither glanced at Kim. On the one hand, that might be a good thing—maybe they would decide they had no reason to bother her and would let her go—but on the other, she could be extremely useful if an escape opportunity presented itself. Maybe she could even win over Captain Psychopath by talking books with him. Or at least gain some lenience.

"Are we going somewhere?" Casmir asked as the guard unstrapped his legs.

"For a chat with the captain."

"Will maiming and torture be involved?"

"Seeing as how you've got a Kingdom accent, that seems likely."

The guard unstrapped his arms and tugged Casmir off the bunk. He still wore his galaxy suit, with the helmet retracted, but they had taken his belongings, including his borrowed oxygen tank. No chance of him stomping on a guard's foot and escaping out an airlock. Not that foot-stomping was likely to work in zero-g.

The guard dragged him into the corridor and started to close the gate. He must have received a message on his chip because he paused, glancing back into the cell.

"Captain wants her too," he said.

"Yeah? She's kind of cute. Can we grope her on the way?"

Casmir clenched his jaw, wishing he had the strength to fight the armored brute. With only two of them, there might never be a better chance to escape.

"*You* can ask Rache that if you want."

"That might not be healthy."

"Irking him rarely is."

The guard unstrapped Kim without groping her. One small mercy.

Casmir did his best to look around for inspiration as his captors strode up a corridor to a lift, up uncounted levels, and down another corridor. It was hard because the guard stuffed him under his armpit, limiting his view along with his feelings of masculinity. It was even more distressing to know the cybernetically enhanced brute could have managed the same maneuver in full gravity.

They passed an open area full of stations—the bridge—with men and women secured by pods like the ones on the *Dragon*. They all looked over, many of their faces scarred or modded with tattoos, piercings, and more exotic deformities. Casmir couldn't tell if they'd paid for them or if they'd been inflicted during a torture session. A couple of the men didn't even look human. One had a half-machine face with a red camera-lens eye. Another was covered in fur that made Qin's fur accents seem like a light dusting.

Despite the harsh, almost inhuman features of many of the crew, curiosity shone through all of their eyes as they regarded Casmir's passing. Did that mean Rache didn't put out bounties for Kingdom roboticists that often?

"Why are they looking at us like *we're* the freaks here?" Kim muttered when the guards paused to wait in front of a pair of sliding doors. Her face wasn't far from Casmir's.

"I don't know, but I get that look more often than you'd think."

The doors opened. The guards walked into an empty conference room. Another set of double doors was on the other side.

Casmir's guard pulled out flex-cuffs and snapped one around his ankle, then clipped him to a bolt in the deck near a wall. Kim was clipped in a similar fashion.

As Casmir struggled to arrange himself in an upright position, the back doors slid open. The guards snapped to a rigid attention stance.

The figure that appeared in the doorway wore black combat armor with sidearms and daggers thrust into a utility belt of the same color. He did not have a helmet on, but a hood and mesh mask covered his hair and face. It was also black.

Casmir looked at Kim and rolled his eyes.

"I *know*," she mouthed back.

"Sir," the guards said in unison.

"We've secured the prisoners," one added, rather obviously.

"Good. You're dismissed."

The guards snapped salutes—Kingdom military salutes—and walked out. Casmir gaped at that. Were salutes the same throughout the various systems' armies? If so, that startled him, given all the cultural differences out there. But someone who hated the Kingdom wouldn't adopt their methods, surely.

Their hands weren't bound, and Kim swatted him. She mouthed something else, but he wasn't sure what it was this time. Ascent? Accent?

Accent.

Yes, if that was Rache, he had a Kingdom accent. He sounded like everybody else Casmir knew from the capital.

"Let me know when you two are done trading whispers," Rache said, hooking a foot under one of the conference table seats to stay in place while he faced them. "So we can talk. Actually, wait." He tilted his head slightly. Sending a message? "My doctor is on the way."

That sounded ominous. Maybe there *would* be medical experiments. Casmir's eye blinked.

"Are you not feeling well, Captain?" he asked in his best conscientious voice, willing his eye to knock it off. "Because we'd be happy to delay our torture session until you're fully capable of enjoying it."

The mask stared at him. How was he supposed to read the man through that?

The stare lasted so long that he found himself fighting not to squirm. No doubt, that was why Rache did it. For some reason, he was completely focused on Casmir. Kim, he remembered, had been an afterthought. What had prompted Rache to remove her from the cell at the last minute?

"I don't think this guy is going to appreciate your wit, Casmir," Kim muttered.

"You're welcome to start discussing penises with him any time."

If Rache's eyebrows twitched under that mask, Casmir couldn't tell.

"Uhm," Kim said. "All right. I see you're a *Moby Dick* fan, Captain Rache. Why did you pick Rache for your sobriquet, by the way? Surely, Ahab would have been more in theme. If a bit on the nose. I suppose that would have been an odd choice, given Ahab's obsession leading him to a dreadful end. Rache conveys the desire for revenge without necessarily hinting of certain death."

"What book is Rache from?" Casmir whispered.

Kim shook her head. "It's an old German word that means revenge. It was also a type of hunting dog."

"You think he's furry under the mask? Like the guy on the bridge?"

"Should I be flattered that you're that fascinated by my name choices?" Rache's tone was dry.

Casmir tried to decide if that was better than furious. Maybe, maybe not. Rache probably killed people left and right without ever losing his temper. That was typical of psychopaths, wasn't it?

"If you knew Kim, you would definitely be flattered," Casmir said. "Usually, she's not interested in anything with more than one cell."

"Is that right." Rache offered Kim a fluid bow. Impressively graceful for zero gravity. "As to my namesake, Ahab would have been fine, as far as his fate goes, but I disliked the biblical connotations. Any of my more well-read soldiers might have believed it indicated I am a poor leader."

"You believe your actions will lead to your death then?" Kim asked, then glanced at Casmir. "If so, why travel down the path you're on?"

Right, the plan was for Casmir to come up with something clever while Kim distracted the captain. Unfortunately, Casmir couldn't reach the wall, the table, or anything else. The guards had removed his tool satchel and everything from his interior pockets, including his medications. He might end up having a lot more seizures soon if they didn't return those. At least his allergies had been better in space. It wasn't as if there was any pollen up here. Though the furry dog-man outside could be problematic.

"We all die eventually, Ms. Sato. Even the life-extension technologies only get you so far." Rache faced her fully. "Unless one uploads her consciousness into a computer, though many argue that the essence of one's humanity is lost without the ability to experience the senses or to have one's thoughts and actions affected by hormonal changes. What do you think?"

Kim hesitated and glanced at Casmir.

Could Rache know about her mother?

"I've got a relative I can ask about that later, if you're curious," Kim said. "In fact, if you let us go, I'll send her a note right away and get her opinion."

"I don't think she's able to receive messages right now."

Kim's face lost all expression—and much of its color. Casmir frowned and clenched a fist. He didn't know what this brute was implying, but he didn't like it.

The outer door opened, and another mercenary floated in wearing a galaxy suit instead of combat armor. Maybe he wasn't one of Rache's men. His skin seemed too bronze for someone who spent his life in space, and he had a handsome, clean-shaven face lacking in tattoos, piercings, or other modifications. He carried a white medical kit.

"Yes, Captain?" he asked.

"Doctor, take a blood sample from the male." Rache pointed.

"Casmir," Casmir offered. "Casmir Dabrowski, if you wish, though that's more syllables. Some find it a mouthful. I went by Caz for a while, but it prompted people to spell my first name incorrectly, with a Z rather than the S. And Cas has a different sound, so that's not quite right. I like Casmir."

Rache ignored him, and so did the doctor. Kim gave him a sympathetic look. She knew he babbled when he was nervous.

"Yes, sir." The doctor opened one of the cases. All of the tools inside were secured so they wouldn't float out.

Casmir glimpsed a needle and swallowed. He'd had blood drawn often enough that he wasn't too alarmed by the sight, but he *was* alarmed that mercenaries wanted his blood. *Why?*

"What is it that you're looking for?" Casmir asked Rache. "It's clear you're already familiar with my medical issues. I assume you ordered the lights flashed outside?"

"Yes," Rache said, not explaining further.

The doctor approached with the needle. Casmir thought about flailing and trying to knock it out of his hand, but Rache watched intently. Rache who, according to legend, was part cyborg. Maybe his face was entirely metal underneath the mask, the skin seared off by some horrible plasma burn earlier in his life.

The galaxy suit defied the doctor's attempt at taking his blood through his sleeve, and Casmir almost laughed.

"Are you as inexperienced in space as I am, Doctor?" He tried to sound friendly rather than mocking. Finding an ally here wouldn't be a bad idea.

"I've been out here for three months. Usually, people take their clothes off for me. In sickbay, I mean. Not because I enjoy seeing these people naked." The doctor glanced at Rache.

These people. That did seem to imply that the good doctor wasn't a mercenary by choice. Casmir definitely wanted to chat with him, maybe without his looming captain watching. Not that Rache truly loomed. He wasn't nearly as tall as Casmir had expected from his reputation.

"Just stab him in the neck." Rache waved at Casmir's throat.

"Right," the doctor said as if that wasn't a big deal.

Maybe it wasn't—Kim didn't look concerned, and she knew far more about medical stuff than Casmir. Still, Casmir couldn't keep his eyes from going wide with concern as the needle approached his jugular.

Aware of Rache watching him, he strove for nonchalance. "This wasn't how I imagined the torture going."

"I can get you paper and a pen if you want to write a request list."

Kim snorted.

"You're not supposed to laugh at *his* wit," Casmir said as the cold needle bit into his vein. "He's the villain."

"It wasn't a laugh. It was a snort."

"From you, that's a riot of emotion."

The doctor finished the blood draw, then pulled out a tube of Skinfill and dabbed a smear to Casmir's throat. The conscientiousness almost made Casmir laugh. He wondered if Rache was rolling his eyes behind his mask.

"Done?" Rache asked after the doctor secured the vial in his case.

"Yes, sir."

"Now, take mine."

"*What?*" The doctor gawked. He might have fallen over if there had been any gravity to tip him in that direction.

"You heard me." Rather than tugging up the hood that might have revealed his face, he removed the torso and arm pieces of his armor and pushed up the thin sleeve underneath.

His muscled arm was pale, the veins easily visible thanks to a body fat percentage akin to that of a marble statue. There were a few scars, but they appeared medically induced rather than a result of a lost fight. Spots where cyborg implants had been inserted?

"Today, Doctor," Rache said.

His still-gaping doctor hadn't moved.

"I expect that woman to try something," Rache added, glancing at Casmir. "She didn't want to give up her other cargo."

A fresh new fear flushed Casmir's veins. Rache could only be referring to Lopez and the bioweapon. How had the mercenary found out about *that*? For that matter, how had Rache found out about *him*?

Despite his surprise, the doctor's hands were steady as he gripped the captain's forearm and inserted a new needle. When he'd drawn the blood and tucked his vial away, Rache gripped his shoulder, his fingers digging in. Not enough to make the doctor wince, but Rache did have his undivided attention.

"Run a DNA test on both. Send me the results. Then delete them. Tell no one what you found."

"Yes, sir."

Rache released the man with a push that sent him toward the door. The doctor hurried out.

"Ms. Sato." Rache unhooked his foot and pushed himself toward her.

Kim leaned back, wariness narrowing her eyes.

He stopped his gentle drift by gripping her shoulder and sticking his leg out, foot bumping the wall. "There's something I'd like you to view in my quarters."

"I'm not interested in your collection of sex toys," Kim said.

"What about my collection of books?"

She hesitated. "Am I allowed to use them to psychoanalyze you?"

"Haven't you already done that?"

Kim looked at Casmir.

He clenched his fists again, worried that Rache had something inimical in mind. He'd rarely seen Kim flummoxed, but she didn't seem to know how to react to this man. That made two of them.

Why did Rache want a DNA test on him? What did this criminal know about Casmir that *he* didn't? Something about the mother and father he'd never met? Would it turn out he had royal blood? That he was some relative of the king's?

Despite all the old fairy tales about bastard heirs of thrones appearing to claim their birthrights, Casmir was positive he wasn't Jager's son, even by another woman. He had seen plenty of pictures of the king and the queen, who looked a lot more like Kim than Casmir, and their sons and daughter. The family was full of tall, beautiful people. Even if he was some distant relative, why would it matter to a mercenary who, by his every action for the last ten years, hated the king more than *anything* in the universe?

"There's a vid player hooked to the wall next to the bunk," Rache said, pulling himself down to the clip that held Kim's cuff. "Inside of it, you will find a short recording on a chip that was in a capsule that my doctor withdrew from a dead man's colon."

"Ew." Casmir loosened his fists as Rache released Kim without his hands straying anywhere personal. "You mercenaries lead interesting lives."

"Yes." Rache pushed Kim toward the door in the back of the room. "Play the recording. I want your opinion."

"On a... medical research matter?" Kim reached the door and gripped the jamb when it slid open, pausing to look back at them.

"On an archeological matter."

"You've got the wrong Sato then. You want my mother."

"She's busy. As you'll see." Rache extended a hand toward the door.

Kim's eyebrows flew up. Casmir was just as puzzled. How could her mother be involved in something way out here? Something that would interest mercenaries?

Kim pushed herself through the doorway. Casmir glimpsed a bunk and a case of books on the wall, as Rache had promised, before the door closed.

The captain turned his attention, that featureless black mask, back on Casmir, and Casmir abruptly wondered if he should have been more worried about himself than Kim.

"Alone at last, eh?" Casmir managed to crack. "Will there be wine? A nice dinner? I'm not an easy man to woo, I should warn you."

"That sounds incestuous."

"Uhm, what?"

Rache stared at him for another long moment, then soft clicks sounded from each of the doors. Had he locked them? Casmir's heartbeat thudded in his ears, far too fast for a resting state.

Rache reached up and tugged off his hood.

His face wasn't metal. Casmir's own eyes looked back at him.

CHAPTER 20

HOW DO WE GET CASMIR AND KIM OFF their ship before this thing blows up, Viggo?" Bonita knelt on the deck in the cargo hold, the magnetic sole of one boot pressed flat to keep her in place as she worked on the case. She'd ratcheted it down so it couldn't go anywhere, and now she carefully affixed some of the Tac-75 from the ship's armory to the insulating molding, right under the rocket. She was doing her best not to let her hands shake. Casmir's code-hacking device dangled in the air next to her. The same code had worked to open the case a second time, so she probably hadn't needed it.

"We?" Viggo asked. "I have no legs, Captain. I can't go anywhere."

"Getting it over there should be easy enough."

Qin had reported finding the crusher and was luring it back to the *Stellar Dragon*, promising she would aid it in defending Kim Sato and Casmir Dabrowski, as it insisted it needed to return to doing. Bonita hoped she could convince it to carry the case to the mercenary ship, so she and Qin wouldn't have to risk exposure to the vials.

Would Rache allow that? Or would he suspect a trick?

She could only assume he was intelligent, since the entire Kingdom army had been trying to kill him for years and hadn't managed it yet. Even if he did allow the crusher to deliver the case, how would they then get Casmir and Kim out of danger before it blew?

Bonita knew she'd wronged those two and felt a fierce determination to get them back, to make up for her mistake of allowing money to tempt her.

"Do you think Rache will know Kim's background and make her open the case?" Bonita wondered. "Or will he have bothered to look her up? Casmir is the only one he listed on the bounty. They could simply have taken her because she's female and still young enough to sell into the sex trade somewhere."

"Rache is not known for trading in slaves."

"Maybe he wanted her for himself."

Not that Kim was the voluptuous beauty men usually went for. And she was about as warm as a comet's trail. Still, maybe an ice woman would be perfect for the ice mercenary captain. Though Bonita hoped that wasn't Rache's intent. No woman deserved a man like that pawing her over.

"I would assume he knows the identities and occupations of his prisoners," Viggo said.

"Then it would make sense for Rache to have Kim open the case, to check its contents. He may have a doctor, but I doubt it'll be anyone as experienced with such things as she must be. And if we assume she'll be asked to open it, then Casmir might be asked to help. Especially if I hand it over locked." She tapped the code-hacking device. "Wait, what if I *changed* the combination? Do you think that would warn Casmir to be careful? That something was up? Because if I simply meant to cooperate, why would I change the combination?"

"I believe he will be careful, regardless."

"Still… Let me see if I can figure it out." Bonita grabbed the device and closed the lid, hoping she couldn't hurt anything by tinkering with the lock. Casmir's random prodding of a button the first time hadn't resulted in an inferno.

The airlock chimed and a few thunks sounded as the chamber filled with air. Qin was returning.

"Hello, Captain," came her call as soon as the hatch opened.

She looked much better than she had a couple of hours earlier. Bonita wished she could say the same for herself.

"Look what I found," Qin added.

She walked in waving a portable gas tank and leading the crusher. The hulking construct looked remarkably fresh, with all of its limbs attached. But, having seen the other ones in action, Bonita assumed the mercenaries had blown it to pieces and it had simply reassembled itself over time.

"You will assist me in retrieving Kim Sato and Casmir Dabrowski," the crusher announced.

"Yes. Yes, I will." Bonita found it relatively easy to change the combination with Casmir's device. She turned it into all letters: GET OUT. "I better attach his doohickey to the case. He may not have the parts or tools to build another one, especially with mercs breathing down his neck."

She hoped he would think to open the case in such a way that Rache and his buddies wouldn't be able to see the display over his shoulder. She also hoped she was right in assuming that Rache would make Casmir do it. What if he had some hacker extraordinaire in his crew that he would use instead?

"No more second-guessing," she grumbled to herself.

When she finished, she stood and pulled the remote for the Tac-75 off her utility belt. She worried that the case, which had proven impossible to scan through, would block the wireless signal of the transmitter. When she checked the remote, the signal *was* weak, but it came through. She hoped that wouldn't change with a little distance and a couple of spaceship hulls.

"Are you sure you want to do this?" Qin asked. "If Rache survives, he'll hunt you down, torture you, and kill you."

"I'm hoping that he won't survive. And that Kim and Casmir will. They'll have to get that message and find a way to get out of there before I blow up the case. That's why we're arranging a distraction." Bonita waved at Qin and the crusher.

"Oh?" Qin asked.

"The crusher is going to deliver the case to the merc ship. While that's going on, I want you to take this—" Bonita handed another patch of Tac-75 to Qin, "—and plant it on one of the tanks in the refinery, ideally one filled with flammable gas. There's a timer. Don't stick around. Get back here as quickly as possible."

"Yes, Captain."

Bonita pushed one of her floating braids away from her face. "I think that's all the help we can give them. Casmir and Kim will have to take advantage and get out of there. Once you plant that and the crusher delivers the case, get back to the ship. I'm pulling out and crossing my fingers the mercs will have far too many problems to worry about us."

"It's a good plan, Captain." Qin lifted the Tac-75 and nodded. "I'm glad we're helping."

Bonita didn't point out that they wouldn't *need* to help if she hadn't tried to sacrifice Casmir in the first place. She nodded back and hoped this would work out and that she could redeem herself, at least in her own eyes.

She turned toward the looming crusher. "Robot, once you deliver the case—"

"I am a Z-6000, programmed to protect Kim Sato and Casmir Dabrowski."

"Uh, right. Once you deliver the case, you can help Kim and Casmir get out, all right? But wait for an opportune moment." Bonita had no idea how much free thinking the crusher was capable of, but two of them had tracked Casmir halfway across the system, so they had to have decent brains—or the robot equivalent. "Then do your best to bring them back here, and I'll fly them someplace safe."

Wherever that was. Bonita was mildly reassured that Rache only commanded one ship, but if he kept his bounty listed, Casmir would find it difficult to travel freely in any system.

"Understood." The crusher lifted the case. "I am prepared to deliver it."

"Viggo," Bonita said. "Comm the mercenaries and tell them we're delivering the case to their ship."

"Yes, Captain."

"Go now, Qin." Bonita waved at the airlock. "Be careful. If you can help Casmir and Kim, do it, but don't get yourself killed."

"I understand. I'll do my best."

"You've got plenty of oxygen in that tank, right?"

Qin reached over her shoulder to check while giving a puzzled nod. "Yes."

"Good, because as soon as you two are on the refinery, I'm going to move the *Dragon*. Not far, but I don't want to be linked in any way to that other ship when that bacteria gets unleashed, and right now, we're both tubed to the refinery. When you escape, push off and angle for the airlock. I'll run the decontamination cycle and hope that's enough, that this doesn't backfire on us."

Qin's expression grew bleak behind her faceplate. The crusher's vaguely human face held no expression at all. Deadly bacteria wouldn't affect *it*.

Bonita groped for something encouraging to say, but she couldn't manage it. She waved Qin toward the airlock. "Better get out into the refinery now and plant that before the mercs think to look for people over there."

"Yes, Captain," Qin said.

"We have a small problem, Captain," Viggo said, and Qin paused in the airlock hatchway.

"What?" Bonita asked.

"Rache's people demand that you meet them on the refinery with the case. They'll inspect it there and decide if it's safe to take aboard their ship."

Bonita bit her lip. If the mercs didn't take it aboard, the explosion wouldn't damage their ship, and the bacteria wouldn't infect their people. Without pandemonium breaking out on the *Fedallah*, the *Stellar Dragon* would never escape Rache's wrath.

"Tell them that's fine. The case will be there in ten minutes." Bonita looked at Qin and the crusher. "Slight adjustment to the plan. We might need someone who can think on their feet to do the handoff. Qin, plant the explosive quickly, hide the crusher somewhere where he can ambush the mercs, and then you show up with the case. Wait for them right outside their hatch. Don't be too eager to get them to take it on board their ship, but if it's possible to nudge them that way, do it. If Kim and Casmir are there, don't try to speak with them. We sold them out, so they're nothing to us now. At least as far as Rache's people know. Got it?"

Qin took a deep breath, looking intimidated by everything on the list, but she nodded firmly. "Yes, Captain."

She and the crusher lifted the case and disappeared into the airlock chamber.

Soon, Bonita was all alone on the ship. Alone with her thoughts. She wondered if she would survive the day. Or the hour.

Rache's face wasn't *identical* to Casmir's, but it was damn close. Rache had a scar on his jaw and over one eyebrow, his hair was buzzed short, and his features were much leaner. Casmir couldn't stop staring and trying to decide if they would have been identical if they'd led the same lives.

And then his eye blinked. He grimaced. Rache's didn't do that, at least not while Casmir was watching. He also didn't have strabismus. Casmir had no idea yet what was happening, but the words *That's not fair* distinctly floated through his mind.

"What's wrong with your eye?" Rache asked bluntly.

He was regarding Casmir with just as much scrutiny.

"Nothing." Casmir's eye blinked again. He sighed. "A tic. And I have monocular vision. Both eyes are awful without correction. Yours?"

"Perfect."

"Because you had them enhanced with cyborg bits?"

"No. Other things, yes. Not my eyes." Rache tilted his head. "You've had seizures since birth?"

"More or less. You?"

"Never."

"I guess we're not twinsies then." Casmir smiled, though he was bewildered. The resemblance was *so* close that it was hard to imagine them being anything else. Even brothers would never look so similar.

"We'll see what the doctor says." Rache reached for his hood and mask.

Casmir thought the reason the bridge crew had stared at him so curiously might have been because he looked like the captain, but… "Does your crew know what you look like?"

"No. Nobody does."

"Your doctor must."

"No. In fact, he didn't have a sample of my blood until today. I don't use sickbay."

"Ever?" Casmir glanced at Rache's forearm, the scars still visible.

"Not here. When I first started in this career, I had every enhancement to my immune system and cell-repair system that money could buy, so I heal quickly."

"I'm guessing you don't have allergies then either," Casmir said dryly, but with genuine envy. "Every spring, I get hives walking under the pollinating oak and ciern trees along the street leading to my house."

"Your house in the capital on Odin." Rache pulled the mask and hood back over his head. "Right?"

"Yeah." There was little point in lying since Rache seemed to know all about Casmir. "I suppose you looked up the address when you sent the crushers to kill me."

"That wasn't me."

"No?"

"No. I had no idea you existed at all until I saw you on the Odin news feed. It sounded like someone was trying to kill you, and when I learned you were at Forseti Station..." Rache twitched a shoulder. "Perhaps I'm getting ahead of myself. Let's see what the doctor says."

"Wait, if you're not trying to kill me, why did you put a bounty on my head?"

"To bring you here before someone else got to you. Mostly out of curiosity." Rache shrugged again.

Had the bounty been for Casmir to be delivered *alive*? He'd never seen it, so he didn't know. But maybe that was why Lopez had been willing to hand him over so readily. She'd claimed she hadn't thought he would be killed. Neither she nor Qin had known who ran Pequod Holding Company.

"So on a whim, you decided to drop two hundred thousand crowns?" Casmir asked.

"I have plenty of money."

"Terrorizing Kingdom troops pays well, does it?" Casmir couldn't keep the bitterness out of his words. He couldn't forget that this man, this man who looked exactly like him, had killed thousands and destroyed countless ships, bases, and refineries.

"A lot of people don't want to see the Kingdom rise again." Rache's voice iced over. "You don't support Jager, do you?"

"I don't know him at all, other than what the media reports. I don't have a lot of opportunities to interact with royalty."

"No? Who raised you?"

Who had raised him? Who had raised *Rache*? Did he know his biological parents?

"My adoptive parents were—"

The doors slid open, and Rache raised a finger.

The doctor floated back in, coming to a stop against the table. Casmir's neck throbbed in memory of the needle.

The doctor waited for the doors to automatically shut before speaking. "I can say with a high degree of probability that your DNA started out as identical."

"Started out?" Casmir glanced at the other doors, wishing Kim had returned, but maybe Rache was making sure she couldn't until they were done talking.

Rache merely watched the doctor, waiting.

"This isn't my field, so I had to consult the computer, but here's what I've got." The doctor looked nervously at Rache before continuing on.

Casmir hoped this wasn't some awful secret that Rache would kill him over once he'd revealed it. Something about the doctor's face made Casmir think he was worrying about that very thing. But why? Did it truly matter to anyone else if he and Rache—as bizarre and mind boggling as it was—ended up being twins who had, thirty-two years ago, been sent off to different homes to be raised?

"Yours—" the doctor pointed at Casmir, "—has a lot more mutations, mutations that could have been fixed at birth if you'd been born in another system."

Casmir nodded, hardly surprised by that.

"Yours—" the doctor pointed at Rache, "—and I wouldn't know this if I wasn't comparing it to his, had mutations that *were* fixed at birth, which is odd, considering your Kingdom accent."

"Don't think too hard about my origins, Doctor," Rache said softly. "You've been useful these past few months, and I'd like to see you survive your five-year enlistment."

The doctor's bronze face paled a few shades. Casmir scowled, not appreciating the threat, or the idea that Rache might kill someone simply for knowing about him. Did that warning go for him as well? If Casmir figured out what Rache's real name was, would the mercenary shoot him, DNA match or not?

"Enlistment, right," the doctor muttered, the words barely audible.

"Anything else?" Rache asked.

"Just that you've received more radiation over your life than he has and have more damaged mitochondria. You might want to make friends with your female prisoner." The doctor looked around. "Uh, where *is* your female prisoner?"

"My quarters."

A hint of indignation flashed in the doctor's eyes, but he squelched it. "Then I see you're taking my advice preemptively. She's been studying—crafting, I gather from the article I read—radiation-eating bacteria that will happily live inside a human host and protect him from even cosmic rays. Apparently, they simply increase in numbers if there's more radiation available to consume."

"Interesting. She does that work on Odin? Where genetic engineering is strictly forbidden?" Rache looked at Casmir.

"From what I read, her corporation reports that they're not tinkering with the DNA of the bacteria," the doctor said. "They *say* they are simply creating new strains in much the same way that farmers create new varieties of plants by cross-pollinating existing ones. And the government agrees with this because they want radiation-eating bacteria for their space-faring troops. I understand cancer rates plummeted among the crews that initially volunteered for inoculation a few years ago."

"Interesting," Rache repeated and looked toward the door to his quarters.

Casmir preferred it when the men hadn't been discussing Kim. Just because Rache hadn't done anything untoward to her yet didn't meant he wouldn't. The idea of someone who shared Casmir's genes being some psychopathic killer and molester of prisoners floored him. How was that even possible? Casmir didn't even like damaging robots.

"You find anything else remarkable, Doctor?" Rache faced him again, and there was an odd intentness to the question.

"Just what you'd expect, that you've led different lives and triggered different epigenetic changes to your genome."

Rache kept looking at the man, the mask hiding his thoughts, but his scrutiny had to be uncomfortable. Casmir *knew* it was. The doctor prodded the edge of the table with his fingers.

"I didn't find anything else," the doctor said into the silence.

"Good," Rache said softly. "Good. Dismissed."

"Yes, sir." The doctor turned and pushed toward the double doors, his momentum almost crashing him into them.

"Say nothing of this," Rache called after him. "And delete the files."

"Yes, sir. Understood."

The doors closed.

Casmir scratched his jaw. "What else did you expect him to find? Or would you have to kill me if you told me?" He smiled, but it wasn't much of a joke. He was almost positive that had been Rache's underlying threat to the doctor.

"I am skeptical that I can trust you, loyal Kingdom subject," Rache said. "I'm guessing someone has already figured out your unique ancestry and that's why you're being targeted. I have enough trouble dealing with Jager's assassins. I don't need anyone sending your crushers after me. Though if my guess is correct, they're more likely to recruit me than try to kill me. Time will tell."

If Casmir hadn't been chained to the deck, he would have flung himself over to grab Rache by the neck and shake him. It sounded like the man knew who was after him and why.

"Time's not telling *me* anything. If you have answers…" Casmir flexed a pleading hand in the air. He wouldn't have begged a criminal for his own life, but to satiate his burning curiosity? That was another matter. He *had* to know what was going on.

Rache held up a finger and cocked his head. "Understood," he muttered in response to some subvocal communication. "Don't let her on the ship. We'll meet in the refinery and check the case there."

The case. The case full of horrific bacteria and a rocket to launch them? Lopez was giving them to *this* man? This Kingdom-hating man? No, no, *no*.

Casmir jerked at his shackled ankle. He couldn't let mercenaries that hated the Kingdom have a weapon that could end countless human lives on Odin.

Rache pushed himself to the rear doors and knocked. Kim must have been standing right there, waiting to be released, because she pulled herself out of the room, her expression closed, hard to read.

"Kim?" Casmir asked. "Are you all right?"

Before she could answer, Rache gripped her arm. "You've seen the bioweapon before? I assume you're the one who identified it."

Kim blinked a few times and didn't seem to follow him, but then she nodded.

Casmir squinted at her. Whatever she'd seen on that recording, it must not have related to this.

"You're going to come look at it again," Rache said. "Make sure Lopez hasn't tampered with it."

Kim took a breath and recovered some of her normal equanimity. She glanced down at the hand gripping her arm.

"Let go of me," she said steadily, looking him in the face—in the mask—without fear.

He stared back at her, seconds tumbling past, without moving or releasing his grip.

"If you want my help," Kim said, "let go of me. I'm not handling those vials with some asshole pirate looming behind me with a hand around my throat."

Casmir had always admired her willingness to stand up for herself, but he winced, afraid this was a better time to go along with the flow and wait for an opportunity to escape. Unless she'd found some weapon in his quarters that she could use against him? He hadn't put his torso armor back on yet. How much did the thin fabric he wore underneath it protect him?

"I am not a pirate, Ms. Sato," Rache said coolly, "and if my hand were around your throat, you would be significantly more uncomfortable."

He released her, propelling her across the room toward the other door. It wasn't a violent move but a calculating one that sent her over the table and precisely to the target. Casmir had a feeling all of the man's moves were calculating. Because most of *his* were. And they were apparently the same, or had started out that way. Somewhere in the back of his mind, Casmir was screaming. Not because he had a twin but because this man's reputation proved he was the epitome of evil. How could someone with *his* genes be like that?

"Wait," Casmir blurted when Rache pushed himself across the room after Kim. "Are you leaving me here?"

The double doors had slid open when Kim reached them, but she hadn't gone out. She looked at Casmir and then at Rache.

"He's the one who knows how to unlock the case," she said. "If you don't want to force it."

"That's true," Casmir said, "but I'd need my toolkit."

Rache looked back and forth between them. Wondering if they were plotting something sneaky?

Not yet, but Casmir certainly hoped to do so. He needed to get away from Rache and his ship full of Kingdom-loathing mercenaries and think. And figure out… he didn't even know what. But he doubted this was a safe place for him. Curiosity might have prompted Rache to bring him here, but he might soon decide that Casmir knew too much about him.

"Very well," Rache said. "You'll both come."

As he came over to unlock Casmir's shackle, Casmir said, "We'll need our oxygen tanks back if we're going out to the refinery."

"No, I think you'll go as you are. To keep you from being tempted to run off."

"I have to breathe to open locks."

"You'll have about twenty minutes' worth of air stored in the niches of your suit, and there are CO_2 absorbers in the helmet."

"Twenty minutes. Gee."

"Better hope your friends don't screw around."

Rache gripped Casmir by the back of the neck and pushed him toward the door where Kim waited. He didn't squeeze hard, but Casmir couldn't help but think how easily someone with cybernetic enhancements could snap his spine.

"They're not my friends," Casmir said. "Lopez sold me to *you.*"

"We'll see."

As Rache pushed Kim and Casmir into the hands of armored mercenaries who led them back toward the airlock, Casmir was reminded that if everything was true, if he and Rache shared the same DNA, Rache was every bit as smart as he was.

All he could hope was that Rache was also every bit as fallible as he was.

CHAPTER 21

ASMIR TOOK SEVERAL DEEP BREATHS IN THE AIRLOCK chamber before sliding his helmet over his head. He struggled not to panic at the idea of leaving the ship when he only had twenty minutes of air. An *estimated* twenty minutes of air.

What if he hyperventilated and sucked it up faster? What if he had another seizure? He had no idea where his medication was. Would Rache drag him back to his ship and save him if he passed out? Or had his curiosity about Casmir been satisfied now? No need to keep him around?

A big mercenary accidentally kicked him in the ankle bone. His suit, so much thinner than their combat armor, didn't do much to protect him, but at least the lack of gravity kept his foot from being stomped on. He was packed into the airlock chamber with Kim, Rache—back in full armor now—and three men and a woman who had orders to "Keep an eye on Dabrowski." He didn't know if that was because she was an assassin or someone who would know if he was fiddling with electronics in an inappropriate way. Another batch of mercenaries waited in the corridor to follow them out. The doctor hadn't been among them. Too bad. He'd been the only one Casmir had spotted who'd seemed sympathetic and might have been talked into helping.

The ship's outer hatch opened, and his helmet display reported a lack of oxygen in the atmosphere. Casmir had the urge to shove the mercenaries out of the way—or try—in an attempt to get out there for the exchange as quickly as possible. He resisted it. Exerting himself would use up his limited air faster.

The men strode down their airlock tube and fanned out in the refinery, their magnetic boots keeping them attached to the floor. They didn't have to look far for their new cargo. A tall broad-shouldered figure in a galaxy suit faced the airlock tube, the case floating in the air before her. It was either Qin or Lopez, there being no other options. Casmir thought Qin. She was taller and broader of shoulder. But the suit and helmet made it hard to tell. The dim lighting of the pipe- and tank-filled bay, along with the reflection of her helmet light on the faceplate, obscured her features.

A rifle was slung over Qin's shoulder on a strap, but her hands were up in the air and empty. She gestured for the mercenaries to take the case into their ship, but Rache stepped past Casmir and pointed deeper into the refinery. Qin looked but didn't move. She gestured toward their ship again and stepped back, lifting her hands. The case floated without a guardian.

Rache must have spoken to her on a comm link, because she returned to the case, steered it around, and strode in the direction he'd pointed.

What's he doing? Kim texted Casmir, the message popping up on his contact.

Either because Rache hadn't thought of it or there hadn't been time, he hadn't ordered their contacts removed or their chips torn out. That would have been devastating, but Casmir knew from the news that it was a typical torture tactic among criminals and vigilantes. It kept the subject from accessing networks and calling for help, and ripping a chip out instead of having a surgeon remove it tended to have some nasty neural side effects.

I don't know, Casmir replied. *He didn't tell me.*

What did you talk about for so long?

I'll tell you later. Casmir wouldn't be surprised if the mercenaries could monitor their communications. *What was in his room that he wanted you to see?*

A mercenary shoved Casmir from behind. Apparently, he was to follow Qin and the case. Rache was already heading in that direction.

Long story, she replied. *I'll tell you later.*

I hope for both our sakes that there is a later.

Me too.

Every time Qin glanced back, Rache waved for her to continue. Casmir didn't like that they were traveling deeper into the refinery while his and Kim's air wound down.

They left the bay and the airlocks and passed through more cavernous rooms made claustrophobic by huge holding tanks and pipes. Here and there, robots flitted past on tracks that ran high over their heads.

Rache finally stopped Qin. They were in another big bay with tanks and more computer equipment than had been in the others. A processing room? It was likely where the different types of gases were separated from each other.

"You two," Rache's voice sounded over Casmir's helmet speaker. "Come check this. Make sure Lopez didn't take anything out and isn't trying to screw us."

Normally, Casmir might have said something flippant, but he hurried to the case, aware that he was already almost halfway through his twenty minutes of air.

Rache thrust something toward Casmir—his tool satchel.

"Thank you," Casmir said, startled.

For a moment, he was grateful to have all his belongings back, but then he realized Rache simply wanted him to have what he needed to open the case. Logical, but Casmir was afraid to open the satchel here. Everything was piled inside, not neatly secured for use in zero gravity.

"Go back to your ship," Rache said. "Don't get lost."

At first, Casmir thought the message for him, but Rache was speaking on a broad channel.

Qin hesitated, then turned around and walked away.

Casmir felt a fresh twinge of betrayal, stung that Lopez and Qin would truly leave him and Kim here with these people, these hardened and remorseless killers.

"Make sure she doesn't get distracted along the way," Rache told one of his mercs, pointing after Qin.

Aware of time ticking, Casmir focused on the case. He remembered the code from before and tried tapping it in, but it had either changed on its own, or Lopez had changed it. If the latter, that seemed odd. Especially since Lopez had attached the device he'd created to thwart the lock. It floated, tied to an eyelet on the case with a piece of wire. She must have intended for him to get inside. Eventually.

"What's that?" the mercenary woman asked, attractive brown-skinned features behind her faceplate.

Somehow, Casmir had expected all mercenaries to look like brutes. The batch on the bridge had more closely fit his imagination.

"Lock pick?" He picked up the device, secured it to the code pad on the case, and turned it on, hoping Lopez hadn't done something awful, like breaking some of the vials. He doubted a lack of air or gravity would save them all from contamination.

"Are you asking me or telling me?" the woman asked.

"I'd rather not talk at all, if you don't mind. Your boss didn't give me an oxygen tank."

"No? I guess he decided he didn't like you. Or that you're working for Jager."

"I've never even met King Jager."

"He's an ass."

Casmir couldn't identify her accent, but he was positive she wasn't from a Kingdom population center. Not that he cared. He waited impatiently for the device to run. Had it taken this long to crack the code last time?

Less than eight minutes of air left. He tried to stay calm, but his heartbeat hammered against his eardrums. It had taken almost that long to walk over here. Why had Rache brought everyone to the backside of the refinery?

Casmir couldn't hear the beeps as his electronic lock picker tried to crack the new code, but it flashed, warning him it was close. Again, he wondered why Lopez had changed the combination. If she hadn't wanted the mercenaries to be able to open it, why send the lock-picking device along? Was it possible there was a message for him? Could she have guessed that he would be the one to open it?

He looked at Kim, subtly shifting his body to hide the display from the woman looming behind them. She was paying far too much attention to what he was doing. Casmir wagered she was Rache's engineer or maybe a systems administrator.

The new code scrolled across the display. GET OUT.

Shit. Casmir opened the case promptly so the code would disappear. Kim stirred. She'd seen it. Had the female engineer? And how were they supposed to obey the command with all those guns pointed at them? What happened if they *didn't* obey it?

"Your turn, Kim." Casmir strove to make his voice calm, waving her in to look at the contents as he backed away slightly, looking around for inspiration.

Rache watched him intently from a few paces away, but several of his troops had moved off. Some remained, pointing weapons at Kim and Casmir, but the others floated from spot to spot in the room, planting compact black boxes on the tanks. What? Explosives? Were they going to blow up the refinery? Because it was a Kingdom asset?

Casmir gritted his teeth as he stared at Rache's faceplate. The fuel that was generated here supplied all the ships and stations in the belt, everyone mining and living out there. To lose the Saga refineries would be a huge blow to the system.

"Everything is still here," Kim announced. "Several deadly concoctions designed to survive in the harsh conditions of space, eat through your spacesuit, and kill you and everyone on your ship in the most horrible way you can imagine."

Rache walked toward her to look inside.

Casmir pushed off a pipe and eased farther back. Six minutes left. An orange alert was flashing inside his helmet, warning him of the need to attach an oxygen tank. As if he didn't know.

To his surprise, the helmet display also showed some oxygen in the outside environment that hadn't been there before. It wasn't enough to breathe, but why was it there at all? A leak in one of the refinery's tanks? No, there wasn't any oxygen in Saga's atmosphere to be mined.

His gaze strayed to the mercenaries flitting around setting charges, and his stomach sank. Of course. Each of their bombs would have an oxidizer built in, but if they wanted a humongous explosion, sufficient to utterly destroy the refinery, it would be helpful to cause a chain reaction that could ignite the fuel in all the tanks in the place.

As Casmir peered around the bay again, his brain spinning uselessly instead of coming up with the brilliance he needed, he spotted a black shape arrowing toward Rache like a hawk diving for its target. Startled, Casmir almost shouted a warning. But he clamped his mouth shut.

"The woman from the smuggler ship is coming back," someone barked over the comm. "There's no sign of Jackson."

Rache turned as the black shape smashed into his torso, knocking him over the case in a crazy somersault. It was the crusher. *Casmir's* crusher.

"Zee!" he blurted before realizing it wouldn't hear him.

But he couldn't smother his delight. The crusher had recovered. Since it didn't give off much heat, the mercenaries must not have detected it with their scanners.

Weapons fire filled the room, red energy bolts streaking through the dim light. The men weren't afraid to fire toward Rache, maybe believing his armor would protect him. They shot at the crusher even as it gripped Rache, wrestling with him and trying to find the leverage to hurl him into a tank.

Kim looked over at Casmir, and he waved furiously and pointed toward the exit. This was their chance to escape.

He spotted someone in the doorway. Qin. She'd come back for them.

A mercenary lunged for Casmir, but Qin fired her rifle, a bolt slamming into the merc's shoulder. The force was enough to knock his magnetic soles loose, and he floated away, struggling to twist himself back around.

Casmir pushed off another pipe, knowing it wouldn't take the mercenary long to fire his boot jets and get back into the fight. They would all be in the fight soon. Several men returned fire at Qin. She backed out of the doorway and took cover behind the wall. Someone's bolt struck a tank right beside the doorway. A hole ripped open, and a gaseous cloud spewed out.

Casmir dove under it, scrambling for the doorway. A crimson beam streaked through the gas, and fiery orange light flared all around him.

Qin snatched his hand and pulled him out of the room, hurling him into the next bay. He flailed, tumbling through the air with nothing to grab to slow him down, nothing to push off to alter his course.

He started to shout that he wouldn't leave without Kim—his rear helmet camera showed the gas burning, an orange cloud spreading from the tank and blazing like a solar flare. Qin returned to the doorway, firing into the bay to keep the mercenaries from charging through after them.

Casmir imagined a stray bolt hitting the open case, vials exploding and spewing their deadly contents everywhere, spraying everyone's suits…

He finally ran into something that stopped his tumble. A pipe near the ceiling. He tugged himself down it and back to the floor until his boots could attach themselves.

Kim appeared in the burning gas, her suit charred around the edges. A mercenary grabbed her shoulder, trying to pull her back into the bay. With nothing but his tool satchel, Casmir didn't know how to help, but he strode toward the doorway as quickly as possible.

Qin shot the hand that gripped Kim. The mercenary let go but lunged toward them. Qin pulled Kim through the doorway even as she launched herself at the armored man, pummeling his chest and knocking him back into the burning gas.

Kim scrambled toward Casmir. The lack of sound was surreal and made it hard to tell what was going on in the battle beyond the burning gas. The mercenaries had to be talking to each other over the comms, but they'd switched away from Casmir's channel.

A warning flashed red in his helmet. He had less than a minute of air left. He was already lightheaded, his fingertips numb.

Waving for Kim to follow, he pushed off the floor and dove toward the airlock bay. It was faster to fling himself around in zero-g than to run when he had to keep one foot attached to the deck.

When he reached the airlock for the *Stellar Dragon*, the only vessel he could imagine returning to, he almost ran straight out into space before realizing the ship was gone. He gaped out the nearest porthole. The ship wasn't gone yet, but it was leaving. It hovered a hundred meters from the refinery. Did Lopez know about the explosives Rache had set? What was the crazy mercenary thinking when the case sat right in the middle of all that?

Kim caught up and slapped him on the back. Casmir pointed. She looked from their empty airlock to the one where the *Fedallah* was still docked. With seconds of air left, Casmir realized he had to go back that way, had to hope the mercenaries would take him in and wouldn't kill him.

Then Qin caught up with them.

"I blew the charges I set," she said on the *Dragon's* comm channel. "And the crusher is blocking the way. Hurry, the captain is waiting for us."

"Out *there*?" Casmir flung his arm toward the ship, cracking his hand on the airlock hatch.

"Out there. How's your aim?"

"Horrible," Casmir said.

"Hold on to me. Both of you."

"What about Zee?"

"With luck, he's buying us time."

Casmir gripped the back of Qin's suit, careful not to disturb her tank. Kim hadn't spoken, and when she grabbed Qin's other shoulder, her grip was clumsy and she missed twice. Were her oxygen reserves even more depleted than his? Casmir grabbed her with his other hand, making sure she wouldn't lose consciousness and let go.

"Ready," he told Qin, his chest hurting, his lungs trying to gulp in what wasn't there.

Qin pushed open the outer hatch and sprang off, angling for the *Stellar Dragon*, the luminous blue orb of Saga filling the backdrop. The ship floated free, half-tilted, as if she were damaged and adrift. Maybe Lopez wanted the mercenaries to believe that, not that she was trying to escape but that some mechanical problem had resulted in her releasing her docking clamps.

Qin cursed.

"What?" Casmir blinked, trying to focus. His vision was dim, his body lethargic.

"Captain told me the merc ship is getting ready to fire on the *Dragon*. We're almost there." Qin stretched a hand toward the ship.

Casmir felt cold. He didn't know if it was his suit struggling to compensate for the frigid temperature of space, or if his body was shutting down.

A jolt ran through him as they landed on the side of the *Dragon*. Qin had alighted right on the airlock hatch. She hit the controls to swing it open and pulled them inside. As soon as it swung shut and air rushed into the chamber, Kim tore her helmet off and gasped in huge breaths. Casmir hurried to do the same, sucking in pure, delicious air as they floated in the dim chamber.

A pale blue light came on, and the inner hatch unlocked. Qin raced across the deck as quickly as her magnetic boots would allow, charging up the corridor toward navigation.

Casmir didn't know what help he could offer, but as soon as Kim waved that she was all right, he pushed off the bulkhead to follow Qin. The ship rumbled, engines flaring to life. It started accelerating, and Casmir smashed against a wall, then pitched to the deck. Growling, he scrambled and clawed the rest of the way to navigation.

"What's happening?" Qin asked, gripping the back of the co-pilot's pod.

Lopez was cocooned in hers, little of her visible from behind. "The refinery is blowing up. A *lot*. You tell me, Qin. I only gave you one charge."

Qin glanced at Casmir.

"The mercenaries were setting explosives in a processing room as we were opening the case," he said.

"Their ship is still attached to the airlock," Lopez said. "Why would they detonate them now?"

"It's possible that burning gas leak—or you said Qin set a charge?—triggered theirs earlier than they intended."

"I set mine in the first bay, close to their ship, but I hit one of their explosives intentionally once we started shooting at each other." Qin patted her rifle. "It may have set off a chain reaction."

"I don't know why they were setting explosives to start with," Casmir said, alarmed that they might have wiped out Rache and all his men, but relieved to have made it off the refinery.

"While you were gone, I realized there's nothing but wreckage where Saga's other refinery used to be," Lopez said. "Maybe they got paid to blow both of them up. Though I don't know why he would have wanted the case delivered in the middle of all that."

"Is it possible he intended to destroy it along with the refinery?" Qin asked.

Lopez shook her head vigorously. "I'm *sure* he wanted it for nefarious purposes. Either to resell it to someone who would use it against the Kingdom or to use it himself." She tilted the ship, trying to avoid shards flying from the refinery as she backed them away from the dock, but one struck a glancing blow. "The *Fedallah* isn't leaving dock yet. They're going to take a lot of damage if they don't depart soon. They may already have. Not that this is a bad thing for us, mind you."

"They may be waiting for their captain," Qin said. "The last I saw, he was fighting Casmir's crusher right next to the case."

"Maybe he's dead then. I blew up the case." Lopez held up a detonator. "But not until you three jumped out the airlock. Here comes someone else out the airlock." She pointed at a display from one of the rear cameras.

"Zee," Casmir blurted. "He made it. Can you wait for him?"

"I'm maneuvering us around to get out of here now," Lopez said. "That'll take a few more seconds, but I'm not waiting for anyone."

The crusher sprang from the airlock platform with powerful legs, its speed far greater than Qin's had been.

"He's coming straight toward us," Casmir said. "Just give him a few more seconds, please. If we could keep him, he could help tremendously with... wherever we're going next."

"Probably to Hell. The mercenaries still have their weapons locked on us." Lopez squinted at a display. "I'm surprised they haven't... Oh, they've got a problem. Their reactor must have taken a hit. Something is overheating in their engineering compartment. Maybe Qin's charge went off close enough to hurt them."

Even as they stared at the ship, the refinery lit up the night sky, flashing white and hurling pieces of the massive structure in all directions. Dozens of house-sized pieces slammed into the mercenary ship. It pitched, breaking free from the airlock, but not on purpose. Its airlock tube tore in half, one end still attached to the refinery.

"We may have time, after all," Lopez said. "Qin, go open the hatch and let Casmir's toy in."

Kim shambled into navigation as Qin rushed past her. The crusher reached the ship, landing like a tick on its hull.

"Do you think Rache will survive that?" Lopez mused, looking at the destruction on the display. "I think some of the tanks must have blown too."

Casmir shrugged. He had no idea what had happened after he'd fled.

"If he *doesn't*, I'm going to seriously regret sending that money back," Lopez added.

"He actually paid you? For me?" Casmir touched his chest.

"Two hundred for you, fifty for the case."

"And you sent the money back?" He stared at her in surprise.

"When I decided we were going to try to get you back, yes. And I never wanted to give him the case. He just assumed he could buy that from us." She lifted her chin, gaze still locked on the display as the ship flew farther away. "He assumed wrong."

"Thank you, Captain. I know you could have used that money."

"You're welcome."

"The crusher is aboard," Qin said over the comm.

"Good," Lopez said. "I'm getting us out of here."

"Fine with me." Casmir slumped against the wall and closed his eyes, exhausted. "Fine with me."

CHAPTER 22

"**T**HERE ARE THREE KINGDOM WARSHIPS HEADING THIS WAY, Captain," Viggo announced.

Bonita opened her eyes. She'd only closed them for a moment, savoring their victory. Or at least their survival. She was still out the money she'd paid for the case of evil, but the *Dragon* had fuel, and they could keep flying a little while longer. If the Kingdom didn't chase them down. She prayed these warships were after Rache, not her, but she didn't know if she would get that lucky after her disastrous departure from Forseti Station.

"How far away?" Bonita asked.

The largest remains of the refinery were specks in the rear camera now. The slydar-coated *Fedallah* had disappeared from their scanners as soon as they'd moved more than a thousand meters from it. She doubted it had been damaged beyond repair, but she hoped it would take days before it could go anywhere. And she hoped Rache had died on the refinery.

"Two days away," Viggo said. "If we want to head for the gate now, we should have time to reach it before they catch up."

Assuming they could bribe the Kingdom ship that guarded the gate to look the other way.

"Or we could hunker down in Saga's atmosphere for a while and hope the Kingdom forgets about us. Those ships *have* to be coming to investigate the destroyed refineries, not us."

One of the cleaning robots rolled into navigation.

"Being forgotten does sound appealing," Viggo said.

"Captain Lopez?" Casmir asked, stepping into the hatchway.

He'd removed his helmet, and his hair stuck out in mussy tufts, despite the return of gravity.

"You might as well call me Bonita now that we've been through life and death together. Laser is also an option." She arched her eyebrows, though it had been easier to get people to call her that when her hair had been black instead of gray, and she'd had more opportunities to show off her marksmanship abilities.

She also didn't know how Casmir felt about her after she'd tried to trick him and turn him over to Rache. Would he forgive her? Normally, she wouldn't care if someone she barely knew did or not, but he'd helped her, and she'd wronged him. Maybe she'd feel she truly had redeemed herself if he forgave her. At the least, she owed him an apology.

"Laser?" Casmir asked. "The traditional spelling or is a z involved?"

"Always an s. Though in the language of my home system, there's an accent mark over the a. Láser Lopez."

"Oh yes, I can see how that makes a big difference." He flashed his goofy grin.

Kim stepped up behind him, lifting her eyebrows, and his grin faded.

"Ah, can we show you something, Captain Laser?" Casmir asked.

Bonita wasn't sure why, but it delighted her that he used the name. Maybe because he said it matter-of-factly rather than mockingly, like it was fine by him if she still thought she deserved it.

"Is it trouble?" she asked.

Casmir gave Kim a considering look. She twitched a shoulder.

"Never mind," Bonita said. "It's you two. It must be trouble."

She waved them in.

Casmir plopped down in the empty co-pilot's pod and waved an interface cable he'd found who knew where. Kim stepped up and held up a tiny chip.

"We thought you might like to see this," Casmir said and attached one end of the cable to the chip and one to Viggo's universal port. "Kim stole it from Rache."

"I didn't steal it," Kim said. "I had it in my pocket when he opened the door and shoved me across his briefing room."

"How did it get into your pocket?" Casmir asked.

Kim hesitated. "It fell in."

"Yes, I can't tell you how often that happens to me. I'm walking around someone's quarters, and deodorant, hairbrushes, and priceless data chips spring off dressers and into my trousers."

"Funny." She swatted him.

"This is *definitely* trouble." Bonita leaned back in her chair, wondering if this would affect her plan to set course for the gate.

"Honestly," Kim said, "I thought he would search me and take it, but he got distracted."

"To death, if we're lucky," Bonita murmured.

A conflicted expression crossed Casmir's face. That surprised Bonita. Even though he wasn't bleeding from his eyeballs or awash in contusions, she assumed his stay on the *Fedallah* had been less than pleasant. Surely, as a Kingdom subject, he had to want to see Rache dead. Or at least in prison for life.

"There's not much on the chip," Viggo said. "Beginning playback."

Casmir turned and watched the display intently as video footage of some party's walk through a deserted ship started up. A *crashed* deserted ship, Bonita amended, when the team reached a gaping hole in the ceiling with six feet of snow piled below it. They continued to an engineering section where a monkey ran up with a piece of metal.

Neither Casmir nor Kim appeared surprised, but Bonita couldn't keep from sharing a bewildered look with them. "What is *that*?"

Casmir paused the playback. "That is Kim's archaeologist mother." He pointed at the monkey. "And we believe *that* is from a gate."

"Mother? I fail to see the resemblance."

"Thank you," Kim murmured without humor.

"She had her brain transferred to the monkey droid before her original body died," Casmir said. "She's eccentric but not as inexplicable as what they found. If that truly is a piece of a gate, that's not only incredible, it's unprecedented."

Bonita scratched her jaw. "There aren't any spare gates—or spare gate parts—in any of the systems, right? Did someone take that from one of the existing ones? That's strictly forbidden. That's why the gates are all guarded. Nobody wants someone to tinker and inadvertently cut one system off from the network—and the rest of humanity."

"I searched the news," Casmir said, touching his temple, "and there's nothing about a gate with a missing part out there." He glanced at Kim.

"We think an archaeology team may have discovered some spare parts or maybe even an entire disassembled gate. Which, if true, would be the find of the millennium. It might be what we need to finally understand who built the gates and create one on our own, one to return to Earth and find out what happened to our ancestral home. And if we knew how to replicate them, we could expand and colonize more of the galaxy. This could be the biggest news story of our lives."

"Huh," Bonita said.

"I told you she'd be excited," Casmir told Kim.

"I see." Kim's expression remained grave.

Maybe *she* was the one Rache had tortured.

Casmir let the rest of the footage play, but there wasn't much more. "We're not sure how Rache got this, since he didn't tell Kim anything before we left, but he knew that was her mother, and he implied…" He bit his lip, glancing at his friend again. "We're concerned that she's in danger and also that he's after the gate artifacts himself. To sell to the highest bidder, presumably the highest bidder that isn't King Jager."

"Sell?" Bonita raised her eyebrows. She didn't want to get caught up in doing something stupid for money—again—but she was in a worse situation than she'd been in at the beginning of this. If there was a chance to make a few pesos to tide her over until she could get another legitimate gig…

"We believe this footage may have been taken on Skadi Moon," Casmir said. "Before we knew you'd come back to get us, we were planning to take one of the mining ships to try to reach it. There's an archaeology ship in orbit there right now."

"You're planning on going on an archaeological dig? Aren't there still people trying to kill you?"

Casmir grimaced. "I haven't forgotten, but I can't just leave the system and hide forever. I need to stay here and figure out who's after me and how to make them go away. And Kim needs…" He extended a hand toward her.

"If my mother is on that ship or on that moon," Kim said, "I need to warn her that Rache may be coming for her and her team." *If it's not already too late,* her solemn eyes seemed to add.

"And I need to help Kim, because she's been helping me all month, and it's my turn." Casmir smiled, though it had a worried edge.

"What do you want me to do?" Bonita asked.

"Will you give us a ride over there and comm the ship and see if we can transfer over to join them?" Casmir asked. "If Kim's mother is there, they should take us. And if they say yes, you can finally get rid of us."

"Well, *that* would be a relief."

"I thought so," Casmir said. "Will you do it?"

"Yes, but you should know that some military ships are on their way. Two days out. I'm *hoping* they're coming because of Rache and the refineries, but… they may see us and veer off."

"Well, two days is a long time, right?" Casmir asked.

"Oh, ages," Bonita said.

"If they prove to be overly interested in us, we'll come up with something. Or hide down on Skadi Moon."

"Hide? Where?"

Casmir waved to the display. "Wherever that derelict ship has been hiding for centuries."

Bonita snorted but said, "I'll try to contact the archaeology ship."

"Thank you, Captain." Casmir bowed, and they walked out.

Bonita stroked her chin and wondered if there could be any money to be made from the *news story of their lives*. If there were numerous chunks of a gate, could she slip away with a piece and sell it? Would someone pay for footage of the wreck site? Since it looked like she was going to live a little longer, she had to get back to thinking about how to keep her ship flying and fund her retirement.

It was some time later that Bonita realized she hadn't apologized to Casmir.

Casmir tensed when Bonita walked into the lounge, worried she had bad news about the archaeology ship or that she would report that the *Fedallah* had repaired itself and was shooting after them at top speed.

"We're en route to that research ship and the moon." Bonita glanced at Kim, who was jogging on the treadmill, but walked up to Casmir.

He was standing at the porthole, looking toward Skadi Moon. Zee, who stood guard from a few feet away, shifted slightly, prepared to defend him if needed. Casmir smiled slightly, pleased Zee had escaped the refinery.

"I commed them, but they haven't answered," Bonita added. "Not even an automatic message."

"Oh." Casmir glanced at Kim. "Maybe their whole crew is down on the moon checking out their find."

"Maybe." Bonita shrugged easily, but they all knew it was unlikely an entire ship's crew would leave the ship for any reason. "We'll be there in about ten hours. Do you have time to help with some repairs?"

"Does Viggo have more vacuums in need of service?" Casmir smiled.

"We took damage as we flew away from the refinery."

"To… the vacuums?"

"To the *ship*. Some of the shrapnel was large and hit us hard, and I want the *Dragon* to be in good shape in case—" She shrugged again. "Just in case. I know you can do more than tinker with robots."

"Yes." Casmir turned from the porthole. "Do you want me to start now? What's most urgent?" He suspected she was worried about the military ships en route, and he didn't blame her. Since that knight on Forseti had seemed certain he was involved with the bioweapon, he was potentially in as much trouble as Bonita until he figured out how to clear suspicion from his name.

"Not yet." Bonita held up a hand. "I also came to say something I forgot to say earlier."

She took a deep breath—a bracing breath?—and Casmir wondered if she had truly come to talk about repairs.

"All right," he said warily.

"This is hard." Her gaze shifted to the porthole. "I don't know why. Maybe because you're half my age. It's hard to admit you're wrong to a kid. And it's frustrating to realize that life can deal you a set of cards that leaves you desperate enough to set your morals aside. I always figured I'd have it all worked out by the time I was this age, but I've got a history of making bad choices. My mother was like that too. Maybe it's in my genes, and it's too late to change that. Maybe it was always my fate."

Casmir realized she was apologizing to him—or getting to that—and he clasped his hands behind his back and did his best to appear nonjudgmental.

"In light of recent revelations," he said, "I'm inclined to think, now more than ever, that there's no such thing as a genetic fate or predestination. A person's upbringing and life experiences do a lot to shape them. A *lot*."

Bonita waved a dismissive hand, but Kim squinted at Casmir from the treadmill, paying attention even if she remained silent.

"Whatever," Bonita said. "I just want to say I'm sorry. I told myself that whoever put that bounty out for you had to want your brain, or some top-secret information you might have in it. Not that they wanted to kill you. Not that it was devil-spawn Captain Rache. If I'd known that, I never would have... Well, I did, and I'm sorry."

"I forgive you," Casmir said, thinking she wanted to hear that. And he'd never truly blamed her, not when he'd brought trouble onto her ship from the beginning and hadn't thought to warn her beforehand.

"You do?" Bonita sounded surprised.

"Yes."

"Well, good. Thank you. Now if Rache will just turn up dead, my month will be looking up."

Casmir nodded, even though he didn't know if he wished that fate for Rache or not. He deserved it, no doubt, but Rache had the answers to some of the questions burning in Casmir's mind. He might be the only one who did. Casmir wished their conversation had not been interrupted.

"I'll keep trying to comm the ship." Bonita lifted a hand and left the lounge.

"What was that about?" Kim asked when she was gone. "Your eyes got haunted when you talked about genes and predestination."

Casmir held up a finger, realized Rache had held up a finger in the same way, then jerked it down.

He removed a second treadmill from a cabinet, placing it beside Kim's and setting it up with the straps. If he was going to keep roaming the system at a fraction of Odin's gravity, he had better start exercising. He remembered Rache's arm muscles, and his mind boggled at the thought that his own could be anything but scrawny. Of course, he didn't know what kind of cocktail of drugs and growth hormones Rache took to go along with his cybernetic implants.

"Casmir?" Kim prompted.

"While you were in Rache's quarters, he and I had a chat." He strapped the treadmill belt to his waist.

"About why he put a bounty on your head?"

"That was curiosity, I believe."

Casmir nibbled on his lip and walked, his muscles promptly protesting the extra force exerted by the straps. He couldn't imagine *not* telling Kim everything, but he remembered the subtle threats Rache had given to his doctor. For whatever reason, the man didn't want anyone knowing about his DNA. Which made Casmir want to go back to Odin, take a sample of his own blood, and compare *his* DNA to every record in the public and university databases. Maybe Kim could compare it to all the medical records on file with the hospitals.

"He had my blood taken," Casmir said. "And he had *his* blood taken."

Kim missed a step on the treadmill and grabbed the bar.

"We are either twin brothers or I am a clone of him. Or he is a clone of me. If either of those, it would have to have been done at a very young age. I saw him with his hood off, and we looked the same age."

We looked the *same*, his mind corrected silently. Somehow, that notion bothered him a lot more than the possibility that he could be a clone. That was a little unsettling—and how would Sir Friedrich have spoken to his *mother* if he was a clone?—but it was a thing that people did occasionally on Odin and even more than occasionally in the rest of the systems.

Kim stared at him, her legs moving, but her brain appearing stuck.

"Yes, I found the revelation rather alarming myself," Casmir said. "I'm trying to figure out what it means for me, if it changes anything."

"You're sure?" she finally asked. "You saw the DNA test results?"

"No, but I saw Rache's face. I think I may be the only one who has in a long time. The doctor acted like he'd never had access to Rache's blood before and didn't know anything about him."

Kim walked in silence for a while. "Why would anyone clone a baby?"

"I don't know."

"You clone a person or animal after they've proven their value."

"Right. Like my colleague Professor Althaus, who's had the same dog all of his life. Except they're *not* all the same dog. He's admitted that. They look the same and have similar personality traits, but…"

His throat tightened, as if he were having an allergic reaction. No, a *distressed* reaction. He didn't want to be similar in any way to Rache. It horrified him to think that any situation, any upbringing, could have prompted him to turn into a cold-hearted killer. A *murderer*.

"They're *not* the same," Casmir whispered, aware of Kim looking over. "And neither are we. Genes aren't all that make a man, right? Just because *he's* a psychopath…"

"I see why you're disturbed, but whatever Rache has become, it's not a disease. You're not in danger of catching it."

"If it's genetic… Psychopathy is, isn't it?"

"You've chosen that label for him. That doesn't make it accurate."

"Actually, the media is fond of it."

"That *definitely* doesn't make it accurate."

Casmir squinted at her. "You were in his quarters."

"For far longer than it took to watch that video, yes. The door was locked. I was beginning to fear he'd show up later in a negligee and expect sex."

"Usually, the *woman* wears the negligee."

"Oh, is that how it works? You know this isn't my area of expertise."

"What were his quarters like?" Casmir didn't want to be curious or to care at all about Rache, but he couldn't help it.

"Not what I would have expected. Normal. No weapons collections on display. No notches in the wall of people he's killed. He had books. A sketch pad in a drawer. Art on the walls."

"Weird art of grotesquely mutilated bodies?"

"No. Landscapes mostly. From different worlds. There was one that I thought might be the coast outside of the capital, but I wasn't sure. They were all empty of life. Lonely. Except there was a framed photograph of a beautiful woman."

"Huh." That wasn't what Casmir would have expected either. A sketch pad? What kind of villain drew? And *what* did he draw?

"A sociopath might be a more accurate label if you truly do share identical genes with him." Kim sounded skeptical. "I'd want to see the results of that DNA test myself before making assumptions. If your genes *are* identical, a twin brother seems more plausible than a clone, especially since you don't know who your parents are. Does he?"

"It didn't come up."

"Who raised him?"

"That also didn't come up. Our chat wasn't *that* long, despite you having time for negligee fantasies."

"Regardless, I can't believe you have it in your genes to have turned out as a psychopath under any circumstances. You empathize with people, animals, robots, inanimate objects, and even red-headed step lizards."

"It was a red-headed *rock* agama. And I don't empathize with inanimate objects." He couldn't argue about the rest.

"I've seen you apologize to the couch, Casmir."

"Only when I'm absent-mindedly thinking about work and don't realize *what* I bumped into."

"Also the coat rack. And the ottoman. You bump into a lot of things around the house."

"I'm absent-minded a lot."

"I won't argue with that." She grinned and swatted him on the shoulder.

"Thanks. I'd swat you back, but it would be a lot of effort, and I'm already panting here." Casmir waved to the treadmill.

"That's because you haven't been exercising all along. You'll probably wither up like a salted slug when we step foot back on Odin."

"Have I mentioned how delightful it is to have such a supportive friend?"

"Not as often as you should."

"Well… it is." Casmir managed to return her grin, even if his mood was somber. Concerned.

He was glad she was here with him, that he wasn't facing all of this alone. He'd once described Kim to his adoptive mother as *mishpokhe*—family. At the time, he'd been explaining her as not-a-girlfriend-but-a-very-good-friend. It still seemed apt. He had always been aware of the sense of family that transcended blood ties—for him, how not?—and it seemed to be more important than ever for him.

"Pardon the interruption," came Viggo's voice from the nearest speaker, "but the captain wishes to inform you that a combat shuttle has departed from the vicinity of the destroyed refinery. It appears to have originated at the mercenary ship."

"Which way is it heading?" Casmir asked, afraid he didn't want to know, afraid Rache was alive and aboard it.

"The same direction as we are."

Casmir slowed the treadmill and gripped the railings for support.

"If we see him again," Kim said, "you should ask him about his parents and who raised him."

"If we see him again, I think he's going to kill us."

THE END

~

The adventure continues in Book 2: *Ship of Ruin*.

58165369R00172

Made in the USA
Middletown, DE
05 August 2019